About the Author

Richard Gadsby was born in Kent but spent most of his childhood and working life in East Anglia. Frequent visits back to the rolling landscape and country houses of his home county acted as an inspiration for this novel. Family visits to Lincolnshire provided further ideas for locations that have been imagined into the story. He now lives in the province of Cadiz in southern Spain, where the traditional hilltop towns and villages inspired the scenes that are set in a typical Andalusian white-washed town.

The Lords of Belvedere

Richard Gadsby

The Lords of Belvedere

Olympia Publishers
London

www.olympiapublishers.com
OLYMPIA PAPERBACK EDITION

A CIP catalogue record for this title is
available from the British Library.

ISBN: 978-1-80074-973-3

This is a work of fiction.
Names, characters, places and incidents originate from the writer's imagination. Any re-
semblance to actual persons, living or dead, is purely coincidental.

First Published in 2023

Olympia Publishers
Tallis House
2 Tallis Street
London
EC4Y 0AB

Printed in Great Britain

Dedication

This book is dedicated to my mother, who shared my love of daydreaming, and to my brother, who is with me every day.

Acknowledgements

The plot for this novel was fully developed by about 2015, but I didn't start writing it until 2019.

I've edited the text on numerous occasions since completion of the first draft. But I also owe a debt to a number of other people whose encouragement, comments and wisdom have helped me along the way. I'd like to thank all the team at Olympia Publishers for believing that the story had a market from the start. They enabled this novel to become a reality, and make a dream come true. My gratitude is also due to my proofreading team of Francisco Velasco, Charlotte Tedder and Penelope Street who worked their way through many of the chapters, and gave me hope I was on the right track as well as suggestions to improve what I was trying to say. Special thanks to Francisco for his help with the Spanish dialogue scenes.

I would also like to thank all of the members of the Cadiz Write Stuff Group who have listened to and offered their comments on the text, and also helped with the proofreading.

After all of the writing and editing, the final responsibility for the accuracy and quality of the text, of course, remains with me.

Finally, I am thankful to Susan for her constant interest, and for road-testing the final version of the novel. Your support has been unwavering.

Chapter 1

Family Troubles

As the afternoon sun poured in through the window, John, the sixth Viscount Belvedere, sat just to the side of the glare in his study at Hillingstone Hall, gazing out at the rolling grounds of the family estate in the Kent countryside. The estate had been in the family since 1826, and had fourteen acres of formal gardens and private parkland, and two thousand three hundred acres devoted to farming which provided the estate's main income. Lord Belvedere sighed and furrowed his brow as he had many times in the past three years. At the age of seventy-three, he should be looking forward to taking a back-seat role in the running of the estate, but things were not heading in the right direction at all and he was in a permanent state of worry.

The door to the study opened softly and Caroline, Viscountess Belvedere, walked elegantly over to the man with whom she had shared the last forty-five years. He turned to look at her as she approached and her eyes briefly met his before momentarily taking in the view from the window, and then returning to his sad eyes. Her hands went to his shoulders and she smiled reproachingly at him before softening her look. 'Now John darling, you aren't dwelling on things you can't mend again, are you? I hope it's just the beauty of the view that is leaving you transfixed?'

'Oh my dear,' he replied, 'you've caught me again. I know we have discussed it so many times, but I'm afraid this place is running away from us and that I am failing in my duty to future generations. I feel hopeless sometimes. We have a son who has no interest in the family or the estate, two other children who are caught up in their own lives, other family that just don't care as much as we do and wouldn't mind if I fell over some time, and a future that seems to be more and more under the control of someone outside the family. I know you have counselled me many times before, but there is something about Robert Pritchard that makes me uneasy. I had complete trust in his father as our estate manager, but Robert causes me disquiet.'

Caroline sighed and moved her hands to cradle his face as she looked down at him. 'You know you should trust him, if only because of what his father was to this estate. As for the children, they have separate lives to us and the estate, and our best hope should be that they are happy. As for your brother, you know full-well what he would do with the land if he got his hands on it, so I much prefer the idea of you staying fighting fit so he remains firmly on the sidelines. I still believe in you, you know. With you as its custodian, the estate has nothing to worry about.'

'You've always been the better part of me,' John replied. 'You stay positive when all I can see is trouble ahead. I wish Henry was different and I could give my trust to him, it would be such a weight removed. No news from Anna, I suppose?'

Caroline frowned. 'Now come on, we have been over this so many times. You have to accept that it wasn't our fault. We raised him the same as Anna and George and we can't make him behave differently. I wish as much as you do that he had a different personality, but after all this time I just hope he is happy, whether it's in Spain or somewhere else. He was always a very complicated child and it stayed that way as he grew up. You will never understand him, so just accept we can't control him. Anna said she got a text message from him a couple of weeks ago and he said he was OK, and working on something important. Let's hope his mind is occupied productively.'

John shook his head at his wife's reply, and his shoulders sagged as he slipped into silence for several seconds. 'Thank you, darling, I know you're right. It's been such a tough few years, it's not just about Henry. I guess I have to accept Robert's position, as you say. Much of my mistrust goes back to him and Anna's involvement. He was so calm about dating her as if he was born to it, and then suddenly it's all off and he goes and marries Lauren, the girl responsible for tearing George's heart to pieces! What a pair!'

Caroline smiled at him. 'Not revisiting old ground again are you? Honestly, you must accept that young people do relationships differently to our generation. It isn't as tidy as it was when we were younger, but Anna has done well for herself with Alex. Look at her lifestyle! Do you think she would swap that for a life with Robert? And George was always a bit soft with girls – he always fell head-over-heels, and Lauren was just too much for him to handle. Too much for many men, I would say. She and Robert were a good match, both full of themselves. But sometimes now I wonder if she regrets it. There are times when I think they've had words, and if one of them has come off worse I'd say it's generally her. She was so used to winding men around her finger, and now she has a man who is maybe one step ahead of even her, most of the time.'

'Humph,' replied John. 'Of the two of them, I reluctantly see her as the better one. I know she performs well in front of crowds and she always represents the estate well. Also, I can't deny her artistic abilities. She has a way of making this house come alive for the Autumn Fair and at Christmas.'

'You're right about that and doesn't that give you something to think about? It's only ten weeks to the fair,' Caroline responded.

'Good point. I really must think about my speech again this year. Thank you for reminding me.' With that Caroline gave a final smile, and left the room.

John turned back to the window and his mind briefly turned to the subject of the fair, before drifting back to his memories. He and Caroline had three children, Henry, Anna and George. Henry was thirty-five and heir to the title and the estate. As a child his mind had been prone to distraction and there had always been something to tempt him, whether it was climbing trees, bunking off school, smoking pot, alcohol-fuelled teenage parties or that ridiculous business with the Spanish maid. He never had the concentration and discipline to learn about the estate, and once he became part of the 'artistic studio' as Henry had called it, he had spent less and less time at the hall and more and more with his bunch of like-minded friends. They passed their days drinking, taking drugs and occasionally protesting that nobody would ever give them an exhibition platform for their work, although John had never seen any evidence that there was any work to show.

Henry had left the estate permanently when he was twenty-three and moved to London. He had become increasingly alienated from the family. For a while, he had argued that his allowance should be increased due to his status as heir, but on this point, John and Caroline had stood firm as a matter of principle. It didn't take much to realise that he was spending his income on the group's living expenses and that much of it was going to waste. They had tried to entice him with a wage for returning to the family home and helping in the running of the estate, but he just complained he wasn't cut out for that sort of thing and they were somehow being mercenary in expecting him to work for an increased income. His visits home had become increasingly rare and the state of his health and mind on some occasions had been distressing for all involved. Eventually, Caroline had told him to go and be happy somewhere else if he couldn't manage it at Hillingstone.

The only family member that was in contact with him was Anna, his junior by three years at thirty-two. Anna was headstrong and a high achiever. She had found the constraints of a rural estate limiting, and from an early age had taken to boarding school with ease. She had excelled at most subjects, only showing a distaste for more hands-on lessons like art. She had become a first-team pick in most senior school sports and had taken to the horses at Hillingstone like a duck to water from the age of seven. She spent a lot of time with Robert Pritchard, the son of the old estate manager, who was a similar age to her and together they learnt stable work. They both developed into self-assured teenagers and would often push each other to dares. At the age of seventeen, they became lovers, and while their relationship became more casual after two years, they enjoyed baiting each other when Anna returned to the estate from either university or work trips abroad. Into their early twenties, they were still taking advantage of each other's lustful nature.

Anna gained a first-class honours degree in law at university and was taken on by a London-based international business law firm. On being called to the bar, she had assumed a caseload that dealt with mergers and acquisitions worldwide and had travelled extensively. She met her husband on one of these trips when he was representing the other side in a merger of two global businesses. Alexander Berryfield was just as driven as her and the two of them had married four years ago and now lived in Buckinghamshire, although they had a second home in Singapore, where both their businesses had offices.

Anna had a less judgemental relationship with Henry than the rest of the family, and found it easier to accept his behaviour when he was only a minor part of her life. She was clinical towards his life choices but was quietly satisfied at being the one who kept in irregular contact with him and was the provider of news to the family concerning Henry.

John and Caroline's third child was George, who was now twenty-nine. George was lacking in breadth of character and his efforts as a child had often seemed to show a misunderstanding of what was required. He would follow instructions to the letter without thinking any further and was never especially good at anything. Although he felt he should be different to his peers as the son of a viscount, in fact he was just an average ability boy, mid-table academically and sports-wise. But he did show enthusiasm to learn the ways of running a large estate, especially when he saw, at the age of eleven, that Henry's ability to get distracted meant the elder son's place in going on to run the estate was far from certain. He had gone to agricultural college at the age of eighteen and had done well in both arable and livestock aspects, and John and Caroline began to relax into seeing him as the natural heir to running the estate if Henry didn't change his ways, even though the title would of course pass to Henry.

Lord Belvedere sighed again, as he moved his wayward look out of the window towards the pond which marked the end of the formal hall gardens. Why, oh why, had George fallen into the spider's web spun by Lauren Radley? He'd been doing so well, until he'd fallen in love with her at the age of twenty. She was the local beauty according to Caroline, but John had a less charitable view of her. She was fifteen and the flirt of the village and attended the local school. George had been captivated by her since meeting her in a pub. Lauren had proved to be fully capable of handling the interest she stirred in boys and men from that early age. She found it hilarious that the younger son of the lord of the manor doted on her, and flirted and teased him as she did with anyone presentable who showed her any interest. Whether she had initially realised just how besotted he was remained unclear, but after a few months of his attention she knew very well. He spent the next eighteen months trying to impress her and she even attended parties at the estate as his date, but sensitive George hadn't realised she was spending plenty of time with others too.

It all came to a head when George found her making love with an estate labourer in one of the fields one spring day. His father hadn't wanted to know the intimate details, but apparently George had chastised them both before becoming overcome with a mixture of rage, jealousy and passion and had run back to the house in a state of anger. Caroline had tried to calm him down, but it had been Anna whose down to earth lecture on 'what a woman does with her body is a woman's business' that had shocked him into silence.

From then on, he completely blanked Lauren and his humiliation was much laughed about behind his back. He threw himself into estate duties to shift the burden and was getting back on track, when after about a year he saw Lauren at Home Farm one day. She was flirting with Robert Pritchard at the stables, and that caused him an agony of pain. Pritchard thoroughly enjoyed his discomfort and pulled Lauren towards him for a passionate kiss.

Although Lauren had tried to push him back, not wanting to cause George any more anguish, the closeness of their half-embrace did the trick, and George's spirits were crushed again. It became obvious over the next few weeks that Robert and Lauren were an item, and George suddenly announced that his education wasn't complete and he was taking a role as trainee manager of an arable farm in Lincolnshire. He left the estate four weeks later.

While in Lincolnshire, George had met Mary at a Young Farmers' social event. They hit it off and after a few months together left their secure jobs and took on a smallholding, which they planned to run organically, which was Mary's particular interest. He borrowed some money from his parents to help with the set-up costs, but after visiting them six months into their tenure, Caroline told John they shouldn't expect to have the loan repaid, as the smallholding was a major financial challenge to George and Mary and money was tight.

Since then, George only returned to the estate on family occasions and kept well away from any dealings that might involve contact with either Robert or Lauren, who were now a permanent feature of Hillingstone life as husband and wife. Lauren was now still only twenty-four but had a way with people that immediately disarmed them, especially if they were men. She helped Robert in some of his duties, especially farm budget management, but also showed a talent for decorating the hall for special events and interacting with visitors on open days and at private events.

'Oh God,' was all John could say out loud as he ran through these thoughts. The weight of wanting to retain the estate in its current form was a heavy burden, but what worried him more was the succession issue. His brother, Andrew, was a successful land agent and kept bringing up the subject of selling off part of the estate for housing development. That would release substantial funding to the family and lower its costs at the same time. But this grated with John and his discomfort wasn't helped by Andrew's comment that Robert Pritchard could see the attraction of the proposal as well.

'If only…' muttered John under his breath. Despite his worries, there was a small part of him that still believed one of his children would, and could, step up and take their place as head of the estate. Anna had the brains and drive, George had the farming knowledge and Henry, well he was the eldest son and heir. Surely, he would see where his position truly lay at some point?

Chapter 2

Something Important

The Honourable Henry Belvedere sat in the corner of his favourite bar. He liked this place best because it always remained darkly lit, despite the warm glow of the red and orange wall lights set at intervals around the place. The one brighter area was over the bar, giving the serving staff the appearance of performers in an intimate Shakespearian drama in a small theatre.

There was always noise in this bar with loud conversation, story-telling and laughter. Henry melted into the surroundings, sitting in a corner either on his own or with the locals. The only feeling of his visibility came from an occasional glance from the manager, who seemed to narrow her eyes as she gave him a piercing look. Then the moment was gone as she turned away like a camera shutter had clicked and captured the required image, and she returned to cleaning, talking or serving. She wasn't very mobile and couldn't move with much speed, but there was a sense of purpose to each movement combined with an economy of action. Whenever she looked his way, Henry felt her eyes were boring right through him.

He loved this part of Spain. The town was small but busy enough to have some bustle and a strong sense of community. With some of the local families, it felt like they hadn't left the town for generations. He imagined the small, terraced stone houses being passed down from grandparents to parents to children with no one ever thinking there was a world beyond the town limits. The town stood high up on the hill, a beacon across the plains, its ancient churches and the remains of the castle signifying a splendour of old which didn't seem relevant in the modern world. But this place still stood after thirteen hundred years and gave the impression that its rock-solid base would guarantee its existence through the next thirteen hundred years.

The town was full of winding narrow cobbled lanes, built for horses and carts but now required to cope with cars and vans. The streets went up and down like a rollercoaster, and around each corner was an adventure into a new scene that might be houses, shops, a church, a bar or café or a mixture of them, until one final corner led to an abrupt end to life, the edge of the town suddenly falling away down the steep rocky hill. It was a dramatic, vibrant place filled with endless chatter, especially in the evenings, bizarrely interrupted each day by the silence of the siesta when the whole world seemed to stop.

It had taken Henry some time to get used to siestas. The whole town closed and suddenly silence prevailed as if the streets were in lockdown. At first, he found it disconcerting, then he tried to use it as painting time, a natural opportunity to concentrate on his canvas with no other distractions. But he craved company and a feeling of being alive, so in the end, he did what the locals did and rested. In his case, this was made easier by the quantities of alcohol he consumed in the evenings, plus a more-than-fair-share of weed.

Like his siblings, Henry had received an allowance from his mother and father, payable while they were all single. Anna and George were already married and so no longer received theirs and it had caused a lot of tension that Henry still took his £2,000 a month at the age of thirty-five. They had both pleaded with Lord Belvedere to stop his allowance many times, pointing to Henry's wild tastes, which consisted of alcohol, soft drugs and carnal pleasures. Had Henry been inclined to help his father in the running of the estate, he would have been paid a substantial salary, but hard work seemed a concept that he was happy to remain detached from.

Instead, he had pretty much wasted most of his time and money since leaving university at the age of twenty-two, having had to stay for a further year to re-sit his final year and still only ending up with a third-class degree. He had left for Spain three years ago, fed up with the constant battles and arguments with both his parents and the wider family. His 'plan' was to rent a small house in Spain and indulge what he claimed was his passion for water-colour painting. He argued that in a country of such diverse landscapes and strong use of bright colours, his mind would open and soon he would have a gallery of his own work that would provide him with an income. As the eldest son, he was expected to take on the running of the estate as his parents moved into their seventies, but he said he could find no joy in this prospect and would happily pass up the opportunity to either his brother or sister, knowing full well that his brother wanted to stay away

18

from the family home as much as possible, and his sister travelled internationally in her work as a business law specialist.

His allowance was more than enough to cover his two-bedroom town-house rent. The second bedroom was his studio, filled with lots of interpretive pieces, which looked like random strokes of a brush in different colours, as if he was trying to create an image from his mind, rather than reflect a scene that actually existed. In addition, his allowance covered enough for materials, food, drink and cannabis (which he had procured early on from a contact on the edge of town), but he had an expensive habit in the form of the intimate company that he liked to keep, being young Spanish men of the same persuasion. This was his most costly activity but he was completely incapable of going without it. He'd known he was attracted to both men and women since an early age, but after initially being sexually active with girls in his teens, he'd only been with men since he was nineteen. There was something so beautiful about Spanish boys – their soft brown eyes, thick dark hair and that gorgeous smooth olive skin. They looked athletic by nature and he couldn't get enough.

Sometimes, old school or university friends would visit him, some leaping into his lifestyle as if freed from their conventional lives, others appalled by his lack of direction, morals and state of health. Initially, he would be able to obtain money from them, either by treating them as paying guests or by straightforward begging. This helped his line of credit, which was stretched most of the time at local shops and bars. He'd settled into an understanding with the manager at the bar, an uneasy agreement that he would clear or at least reduce his tab from time to time, in exchange for the customers he brought in. She never offered him any sign of approval but didn't throw him out either.

So here he was again, sitting in the corner on a sultry night surrounded by his creature comforts – sweat, laughter, noisy chat and the voices from the television football commentators, heard occasionally over the conversation in the bar when the live match suddenly got more interesting. His companions tonight were an odd pair. One a drunken old man with whom Henry sometimes played 'who's gonna buy the next drink', and the other a late-twenties prostitute he'd been with a couple of times but had lost interest in. He lacked the seductive, fresh charm that Henry found irresistible, only offering a few minutes of rough pleasure based on how quickly he could earn his fee before disappearing to spend the proceeds on his own drug habit. Henry had quickly tired of him and tonight the conversations between the three of them had been to a pattern and were now drying up, the would-be lover slowly realising his punter wasn't up for it, and the old boy more-or-less rambling to himself. A haze had descended over Henry's mind and he felt able to relax into the cushions and let his mind wander into pleasant thoughts about the manager's son who worked with his mother in the bar. He looked about eighteen, with a gorgeous complexion, big brown eyes, and a stunning slender-but-toned physique. There was a purity about him that attracted Henry. He didn't get any sense that the boy was gay, but felt sure that with the right introduction and chat-up lines he could persuade him to open his mind to the pleasures of male-on-male company.

They'd only had one brief conversation a few months ago. Henry had tried smoking a joint in the bar without thinking and the manager had given him the evil eye. She looked as if she was coming over to lecture him and then at the last second, had asked her son to go over instead. Henry felt a shiver down his spine when the boy asked him to stub the joint out. He did so instantly as if he was in a trance, trying to hold the young lad's eyes for as long as he could. He treasured the simple manners, cleanliness and silkiness of the request for weeks after. It captivated him and from that moment the boy, Juan Marco, had been his number one fantasy.

The time reached midnight, and as Henry's previous lover moved away from the table with a look of rejection and annoyance, he realised the drunken old man had slipped away into sleep and his own evening was over. As usual, he waited for the attention of the manager to be called to another customer before he slid out of the bar as inconspicuously as he could.

But as he left, her eyes bored into the back of his skull, and she stuck a note on the bar with the latest additions to his tab.

Chapter 3

A New Course

The annual Hillingstone Autumn Fair was held every bank holiday weekend in August, and opened up the grounds of the estate and Home Farm to the public. There were displays on the history of the estate, changes to farming methods over the centuries, have-a-go opportunities for children sowing seeds and other activities, and horse rides. A full range of retail outlets booked marquees and gazebos to sell their goods, alongside charitable organisations trying to raise funds and awareness. This was also the only time of the year when the Belvedere family opened up limited parts of the hall for public viewing, which always attracted good crowds.

Robert Pritchard was entrusted with much of the work for the event as estate manager, assisted by his wife Lauren. They organised parking, publicity, the booking of catering trucks and all of the retailers and exhibitors, plus livestock events. There was always one part that remained with the family to organise – a classic car show outside the hall. Lord Belvedere chaired the working party for this, assisted by local and national classic car club officials, with Anna's husband, Alexander, also involved. The involvement of the family was always a proud tradition for Lord Belvedere and he particularly appreciated his son-in-law's assistance, although with Alexander being a car enthusiast and owning several vehicles himself, he saw it as having fun rather than as a responsibility. At the close of the fair, Lord Belvedere would announce the winners in the car show and give a short summary of the estate's major achievements in the year so far, before rounding off with a thanks for everyone's attendance and a hint of the challenges coming in the next year.

Lord Belvedere had arranged to meet with Robert and Lauren in his study five weeks before this year's fair to run through the arrangements. After exchanging pleasantries, he asked for an overview of the planning.

'Everything's going according to schedule, sir,' replied Robert. 'All the marquee and gazebo spaces are booked. There are some changes to exhibitors this year, but there will be a similar feel to the event as in previous years. I've made a change to the way we contract with the commercial outlets for their space. Instead of charging them a flat fee, the agreement now reads they pay ten per cent of their turnover. I think that will be to the estate's advantage, based on my estimates of previous years' takings.'

Lauren looked at him quizzically for a moment, before recovering her composure.

'How was that received by the businesses? Is it normal to take a percentage of their revenue?' asked Lord Belvedere.

'It's done by many other venues, sir, and I thought it best to look at maximising the estate's income, notwithstanding that the event is really about the estate reaching out to the community. The proof of the pudding will be in the eating. There will always be some companies that drop out each year and some new ones who fancy giving it a try. The main thing is that we are fully booked again, and of course, we make no charge to charities that take a stand.'

'Quite right,' replied Lord Belvedere.

Robert decided to change the subject. 'How is the classic car show planning going, sir? Any increase in the number of cars on display this year?'

Lord Belvedere noticed the change in topic, but his enthusiasm for the car display won through, just as Robert had guessed it would. 'Yes, all fine too, we expect a hundred cars this year, with marshalling provided by two of the owners clubs. They will be instructed on the entrance and exit routes for display vehicles and the passes needed to gain entry. We'll have them parked up at the side and partly to the front of the hall, and they'll need to park on part of the lawns too.'

This gave Robert an angle to continue the conversation. 'Oh dear, that is something to be avoided if at all possible, but you've thought about it in great detail, I suppose? Of course, the grounds staff will do all they can to restore the grass afterwards.'

Lord Belvedere rose to the bait and replied a little testily: 'We have considered other alternatives but really this is the only option for the space required, and I have given my approval.'

Robert smiled and nodded. 'Right oh, sir. I'm sure it will all be fine.'

Mission accomplished he thought; subject changed, diversion put in place, alternative route taken. He decided to continue along this path.

'Lauren has discussed the open areas for the hall this year and agreed the visitor route with the housekeeper and Lady Belvedere has given her approval. Lauren, you have some new plans for decorating the hall this year, don't you?'

Lauren was glad of her opportunity to take on the conversation in view of the tension that had been creeping in.

'Yes sir, I've agreed a colour theme with Lady Belvedere, so we make it look as if the hall is adjusting to a different season. We'll make good use of what light there is by opening blinds that face west, changing some of the furnishings for green and tan as a colour theme and we're going to use a lot of cardboard this year for creating features that theme with autumn. There's one particular idea that we're working on which is to create a cardboard play area for children in the former nursery. My guess is that a lot of the little ones will love going through a cardboard maze and through a snaking tunnel painted with lots of animals on the outside. It's low cost to create, but I think children will love going through again and again, and we have so much cardboard at this time of year because of harvest.'

Lord Belvedere mused for a second or two. 'I'm sure that will all be perfectly fine.' His thoughts were turning back to the days when his own children were making full use of the nursery. 'Well, I must wrap up as I have Andrew coming in to see me in a few minutes. He has a few thoughts about...'

He stopped as he realised Robert was looking directly into his eyes with a presumptuous expression. He remembered that Andrew's thoughts of raising funds from the sale of estate land for housing development were already shared with Robert, reflecting their close relationship due to Andrew acting as a second pair of eyes over the estate budget managed by Robert. The last thing Lord Belvedere wanted to do now was to give any satisfaction to his estate manager that somehow the latter was already ahead of him.

'... our priorities for next year,' he finished, as blandly as he could.

Robert gave him a casual smile that couldn't be interpreted one way or another, but behind his eyes, he felt his pulse quicken and hoped his smile hadn't appeared too smug.

Robert and Lauren said their goodbyes and left the study. As they walked across the driveway away from the house she asked him: 'What's the reason for changing the commercial arrangements for exhibitors this year? You kept that quiet.'

Robert gave her a brief glance and smirked. 'Well, I think we've been over-generous in the past and it's time to move with the times for our benefit.'

'You mean the estate's benefit.'

'I mean our benefit in the widest sense. I'm sure the estate will get more revenue, especially from the catering outlets, but as I have pretty much total control over the billing arrangements, I don't think there'll be any challenge to the figures I present and I'll make sure the estate sees a positive result anyhow. But I think there should be some kind of bonus for us for all this creativity!'

Lauren faced him as they walked, a chill running down her spine. 'You're not going to fiddle the books, are you? Why would you do that? Your family have been here for over forty years and we have a good life. Why would you gamble with that?'

Robert stopped and faced her and their eyes met. He checked quickly that there was no one behind them and his eyes narrowed and his voice hardened. 'My father was treated as a general dogsbody by these people, so don't tell me how long he was here for. They worked him senselessly, there was no appreciation of the extra hours that he put in, just a few "kind" words of appreciation which cost them nothing. If you look at what they paid him and compared that to his hours, he was paid less than what is now the minimum wage. I know. I worked with him sometimes, getting up at silly o'clock to complete works in the fields, or going out at night to meet a vet when there was a problem with some of the livestock. Everything, and I mean everything, got routed through him. He was this family's gofer!'

Lauren looked wide-eyed at his anger. 'So what, you're planning on lining your own pockets to make up for what you see as his shortfall? And if you get caught, what then? You'll lose your job, you might have a criminal record, you'll lose the house, you might even go to prison!'

Robert snarled. 'Do you think I have no brains at all? I'm clever enough and won't be getting caught! This lot are light years behind me. I'm not fucking stupid enough to leave an audit trail behind me. I always make sure that the budget adds up, and whatever I take out goes back in, but what I do with "borrowed" funds is my business. I've done currency exchange

24

deals, crypto currency purchases, share purchases; I even won some money on the Cheltenham Gold Cup using funds from the estate! Oh and by the way, you're a beneficiary too. How else do you think I paid for the Majorca private yacht cruise? That bracelet that cost eight hundred pounds? The money came from my extra-curricular activities too, so don't knock it.'

'Why the hell did you tell me that? I knew nothing about it! I saw some bank transfers going in and out of the estate account but I assumed they were legit. What about Andrew? Isn't he supposed to have oversight of the accounts?' Lauren's voice was rising to fever pitch.

'Start walking in case someone sees us!' snapped Robert. 'You need to know only what you need to know. Andrew and I have a very civilised arrangement; he turns a blind eye as long as the numbers add up at the end of each quarter, and he and I have a little side deal worked out anyway. You'll get to hear about that at some point. I was going to tell you soon anyway but after that little outburst maybe I won't!'

Controlling her voice now and trying to look business-like as they walked on, Lauren said: 'I don't want any part of it. Leave me out, the stench stays well away from me.'

Robert looked at her once more. 'Seeing the bigger picture was never your strong point, was it? The way I have things planned, in less than two years we'll be out of here with a substantial cut of a deal that doesn't involve lying, cheating or stealing anything, just taking what is rightfully ours. How does circa £1.4m sound to you from a partial sale of land on the estate? Legitimately paid for information provided and assistance rendered. I can offer Andrew a lot of information about the quality of the land, likely access routes for housing, etc. Plus, I have friends in the construction industry and can work on plans in the background without anyone noticing, something that Andrew can't do. Anything he says formally will get back to John. But his role is to work on John and try to get his buy-in. I can work on establishing the site value and development costs with no one knowing.'

'Andrew would never hurt his brother or the estate,' retorted Lauren.

They reached the gate to the stables and came to a halt and Robert looked at her. In a matter of fact way he said: 'Look, it's quite simple. We get £1.4m and then we bugger off and buy our own small estate. Lincolnshire appeals because arable is more profitable than livestock. I'll run it as efficiently as I can, make it work. And we'll have plenty of cash left over to live the life that we deserve. You'd look good in a convertible, think about it. As for Andrew, he knows this estate is going to rot. After

John, who is there? That drug-infested weed of an eldest son? Miss high-and-mighty legal expert who cares fuck all about the family estate? Mister loser, whom I expect will end up running a hippie commune? Come on, this place is finished and Andrew knows it. John would have the option of leaving the running of the estate to Andrew you know, assuming John goes before him. But he won't break the line of inheritance and fears that Andrew would sell off large parts of the estate. But wouldn't that be doing him a favour? There's no one coming up behind him so whether he likes it or not, he's going to be working this place until the day he drops. A smaller estate would give the family coffers a big boost and reduce the load on him. Think about it. You see, I have a soft side as well as being ambitious for my lifestyle.'

Lauren looked at him seriously before sucking her cheeks in and walking into the estate office, her anger subdued.

Andrew Belvedere walked into Lord Belvedere's study, and they chatted briefly about Andrew's children, all of whom were doing well in their careers away from the family estate. David was in commercial banking, Leila was an accountant and Jasmine was a part-time interior designer. Then John moved on to the purpose of their meeting.

'So, I assume you asked to see me to talk about this land proposal?'

'Well, I think calling it a proposal is a bit strong,' replied Andrew with a smile. 'It's an idea and I think it has positive merits, and like all good ideas, I think you should think about it.'

John frowned, but Andrew smiled warmly and continued: 'The estate has about two thousand three hundred acres devoted mainly to agriculture. Some parts perform well, for example the yield on crops has always held up, mainly because Robert is smart with planning his crop rotation. As market prices for, let's say, traditional winter vegetables fall, perhaps because of declining popularity among younger consumers, you can switch to others that are more immediately saleable, for example asparagus or spinach. But within a few months, you can switch back again if wholesale prices go up. In the summer, you have a huge choice of fruit and vegetables being helped by generally warmer weather, plus rapeseed oil is easy to switch to with a guaranteed market always available. Robert has been canny with his decisions and has served the estate well. You have two growing seasons so you have a year-round income. Of course, you know all this already.

'Then you come to the livestock side. That isn't so financially rewarding. While the estate trades on a reputation of locally-farmed quality meat, the price for lamb and pork is always under pressure and beef isn't always a reliable option and there's pressure on margins there too. Dairy is a cut-throat business...' His voice trailed off and John gave a slight wince.

'On top of that, you have a proportion of the land that has to be given over to fallow, preferably every two years, thus taking an amount of income out of the estate for those areas. It's a necessary act to enrich soil quality but the land remains idle for that period. Then you come to the real challenge, in my opinion.' Andrew lowered his head in exaggerated deference to John. 'Climate change is not a short-term issue. For many of my farming clients, they see this as their biggest challenge. The weather is increasingly unpredictable, drought heat-wave conditions being followed by storms almost of biblical proportions.' He smiled and reminded himself inwardly not to wear the salesman's hat too obviously, and John's slightly vacant gaze back confirmed he needed to come to the point.

'So, by diversifying into something rock-solid, that pays a premium for land purchase, injects capital into the estate, lowers the cost base and most importantly reduces the financial risk to the estate' – his voice emphasised these last words – 'selling off a small proportion of the less productive land for housing seems a move that is at least worthy of serious consideration. Do you see my point?'

John leant back in his chair and his face became sombre. Despite the feeling that Andrew was always a little too smooth for his liking, he knew there was a serious side to their discussion. He thought for a few seconds allowing his mind to start throwing up objections, but Andrew had anticipated this reaction and jumped in: 'As I say, I think there is merit to the idea of at least exploring the opportunities, and of course the amount of land to be allocated' – he thought this sounded better than "sold" – 'would be very modest compared to the entire estate. Then there would be other factors to consider once an outline plan was being considered – the size of any development, the number of dwellings, the style and construction materials, the type of buyer who would be considered as a good match for the estate, etc. These are all details that would have to be worked through in some depth way before any planning application was made. It would be absolutely vital that these were considered in absolute confidence. '

He could see the concern in John's face and added for good measure: 'Rest assured this would be treated as "top secret" while preliminary discussions were underway.'

John still had a frown on his face, but there was a sadness in his eyes that made Andrew feel he was making progress with his argument. John replied: 'There is a lot to think about. I... I will have to take counsel from others in the family and possible professional advice. You mustn't think that I don't trust you but I have to make sure that any move in this direction has the heart of the estate as its primary interest.'

Andrew gave a slight smile, but felt a prick of his conscience when he heard the words 'You mustn't think...' He was well aware that acting as a land agent would earn him a sizeable commission if he was the broker in a deal to sell off part of the estate, even a small part. But he had decided on a defence to this issue already.

'For my part, John, I recognise that you, and perhaps others both inside and outside the family, might feel I could have a conflict of interest if I was a party to any agreement of the type we are talking about. For that reason, I would work for just half of my normal fee, should matters proceed to a confirmed proposition. I wouldn't want you to feel that my motivation was anywhere other than on securing the future of the estate.' He considered now was a good time to casually mention some numbers as John was showing signs of regretting his earlier attack. 'What matters is the long-term management of the estate when you are no longer able to give it the time it deserves, and a few million pounds into the coffers would certainly help in giving *you* the chance to plan confidently for the future.'

This broadside had a noticeable effect on John, whose position in his chair seemed temporarily frozen. Andrew took the opportunity to rise from his own chair and say with business-like control: 'I've hopefully given you lots to think about but there's no immediate time pressure of course. In fact, why don't you think about it for a few days and then give me a call and we'll arrange to meet up for lunch in a couple of weeks. It will give you some space to think about things without anyone else chirping in your ear. You need some time I imagine to contemplate your vision for the future,' he said with a knowing smile. He knew full well that John wouldn't mention this to anyone else except Caroline at this stage. Any talk of 'other professional advice' was just bluster on his brother's behalf. On decisions concerning the estate, John would never allow others to have significant influence.

John rose from his chair and shook Andrew's hand. He tried to give the impression of a man in full control of his destiny, but felt like he'd just lost two inches in height.

Chapter 4

Going Down in Flames

Henry sat in his usual spot at the Café de Luz. The irony of its name always made him smile. The café-bar was named after the nearest coast, but there was little enough light in here at the best of times.

His companions tonight were Philip Cottle and his wife Clare. Philip was an old boarding school friend whom Henry had kept in contact with, tied by their shared memories of a love of alcohol, tobacco and women. They had shared the best of times together as teenagers, getting drunk together for the first time, and experiencing the first passions of sex on the same evening with two girls picked up in a pub in Maidstone when the boys were sixteen. Philip had always been better at balancing academic requirements with a free-spirited youth, whereas Henry had found it increasingly difficult to function once he discovered the pleasures of intoxication in all its forms.

When they were sixth formers, Philip had been the first to know about Henry's experimentation with boys. Henry had explained that he was unsure of whether this was just a phase he was going through or a journey to becoming bisexual, but that he couldn't get enough of trying anything new of the drug that was sex. Philip had certainly treated it as a phase in Henry's sexual development, but as Henry became more and more attracted to men, the two boys still felt able to open up to one another and accept each other on equal terms, and their friendship had continued well after they left school.

Philip had been over to Spain twice before and the two of them had enjoyed riotous nights in several bars and smoked weed, and on one occasion visited a local brothel, where Henry had engaged in certain acts with one of the women, much to his surprise.

But this evening in Café de Luz was a little different. Philip had married Clare fourteen months previously and this was his first visit back

29

to Spain since then. They had stayed in Henry's house the first night, but they booked themselves into a local hotel the following morning at Clare's insistence. She said this was because she didn't want to invade Henry's space; the truth was she had taken an instant dislike to him. Henry could understand why – the house was dirty, messy and cluttered. Moreover, Henry appeared to be a complete wastrel, a man who was as much a mess as his home. This didn't matter of course when Philip had visited him on his own as they spent most of their time drunk. Now it was very different.

The conversation was stilted on this last night of their visit. Philip had been a good friend and given two hundred pounds to Henry which was much appreciated, meaning Henry had been able to buy food and drink. But on this night Henry didn't want to get massively wasted, although keeping the drinks topped up would have helped with the atmosphere between the three of them. Philip and Clare were leaving first thing in the morning and Clare had made it clear she didn't want to be up late, despite gentle pressure from Philip to make an effort with his old friend this last night. But in truth, Henry didn't care if they retired early as he had his eyes on an intimate adventure tonight with young Juan Marco behind the bar.

'So how long before the first picture is selling then?' asked Philip. 'You have a natural flair with the brush, especially with landscapes. What are your relationships like with the galleries here?'

Clare's eyes widened as Henry replied half-heartedly: 'There are irons in the fire, but these people trust their own and it takes time to encourage them to embrace an outsider. But I'm active in that regard, very active.'

The conversation continued for another forty-five minutes with staccato questions and answers. Henry bought them more drinks but missed himself out on the last round. Clare spotted it and slyly asked: 'You not drinking this round, Henry? Are you saving yourself for something?'

Henry turned his head and looked vaguely in her direction. 'There are nights when one feels alive and the senses are peaked. This is one of them, it's an artist thing.'

Clare felt uncomfortable with his answer and gently probed Philip's thigh under the table. She looked up at her husband. 'Well, it sounds like Henry is in a creative mood tonight Philip. Why don't we say our farewells and leave him to it?'

Philip looked at her defensively. 'I don't think we need to turn in just yet. We haven't got to be up that early.'

Against her normal values, Clare slid her hand round to his crotch and replied quietly: 'Who said anything about turning in?' She disliked being too public but this was a performance with a means to an end.

Henry picked up on her script and smiled at Philip. 'It's OK, old friend. You get off, it's not a problem. You have a pretty wife who no longer wants to share you.' They shook hands warmly and exchanged a few pleasantries about meeting up again, maybe in England this time. Henry and Clare locked eyes and touched hands. There was indifference in one gaze and ice in the other.

Once they had gone, Henry signalled to the bar for another drink. He hoped the young boy would come across for his order, but instead it was one of the older male bar-hands. That wasn't a good start, he thought. He sipped his port so that the effect of the alcohol would be gradual. He needed to pace himself. Another one after this and then it would be maybe half past eleven, by which time the bar would be thinning out just a little. Perhaps one last drink then and he could attract Juan Marco's attention. He'd give him a signal to come over to the table, a warm look in his eyes, perhaps a gentle compliment, and then a casual movement of his hand to the inside thigh and a longer, lingering smile... then perhaps a night of sweet pleasures to look forward to! Henry smiled to himself as he settled back into the cushioned high-bench seat, immersing himself in his dreams for a few moments.

By 11.40, only a few regulars were left in the bar, but too many for Henry's liking and he was starting to get nervous. The woman who ran the bar usually let Juan Marco go off duty first at midnight in view of his youth, and that didn't give him enough time. Then, to his relief, a family of locals decided to leave and were followed out of the door by two older men. That just left Henry and two other older men, both of whom were drinking alone and had their eyes glued on the TV that was showing the post-match analysis of a La Liga game. This was his chance.

The young boy was cleaning glasses behind the bar and tidying up. Henry stared hard at him, hoping to generate subliminal powers that would make him look upwards. To his surprise, the boy complied and Henry raised his empty glass and offered a warm smile. With the merest flick of his head to acknowledge the request, the boy reached up to the bottle of port behind him on the shelf and headed around the bar and towards Henry. It was all going to plan.

'*Gracias. Esa camiseta te queda bien,*' Henry said, as he looked warmly into the boy's eyes. He quickly searched for a shy smile in the boy's eyes in response to his compliment about the T-shirt, but there was nothing there. Henry's juices were flowing now and his passions were aroused, assisted by the alcohol.

'*La vida tiene mucho que ofrecer cuando eres joven. Quizás te gustaría que te ayudase a descubrir alguno de esos placeres.*' he continued, moving his left hand to the inside of the boy's thigh, as he hoped to entice him into a youthful exploration of some of life's pleasures. He held his gaze.

Juan Marco froze. His eyes were transfixed. Slowly, he turned his head towards the bar, looking for someone to help him, but there was no one. Then to his right and out of view of Henry in his seat came a shriek in English that startled both of them: 'Leave him alone you filthy pig! Get away from him!' The woman who ran the bar came into view and glared at Henry. Then she turned to the two old men who had been watching the TV and whose necks were now turned towards the unexpected loud voice and foreign tongue: '*Iros a casa ahora*!'

The two old men looked at each other and then slowly rose, draining the last of their drinks as they did so. They edged slowly towards the door, one man leaning heavily on his stick. He turned back to the woman with a look of concern that he shouldn't be leaving a woman on her own to deal with the strange young Englishman, but the fire in her eyes was bright and when she saw his apparent reluctance to leave, she screamed '*ahora*!' again, leaving him in no doubt that a return home immediately was the right choice.

The woman waited until the door closed softly behind the two old men, before whipping around to Henry, whose hand was poised like a karate chop in mid-air, having taken it off the boy's thigh.

'Don't you ever touch him again!' she screamed in accented English. 'You're a foul-smelling, wasted human being who isn't fit to kiss his feet! He's worth a hundred of you, you drunken piece of shit!'

Henry sat rigid in his seat, his jaw open in disbelief. He felt like he should run for the door, but was paralysed by the words that lashed him in his native tongue. They came out of nowhere; he had no sense that this woman had any knowledge of the English language, and here she was chastising him for touching her son which in his mind wasn't the worst thing in the world, even if it was a mistake, but she was doing it in English!

Who the hell was she? The best he could do was stammer:

'I'm sorry! I didn't mean anything by it, honestly, it was just a bit of fun!' That inflamed her eyes again so he added: 'No it wasn't a bit of a fun, it was a mistake, I'm sorry, I'll leave!'

He started to rise from his seat, thinking that perhaps he should revert to Spanish as a rather late attempt at respect while planning a swift dash for the door, but she lunged to her left pushing Juan Marco to one side as she blocked his escape route. She stood there as wild as an enraged ape, before screaming at him still in English: 'You stay there you piece of shit! Juan Marco, get out of here now! I'll be home when I've finished with this turd!'

Juan Marco turned to his mother and started to protest about leaving, but she threw her hand towards him and screeched '*ahora!*' leaving him reluctantly to obey her instruction.

The woman and Henry stared at each other, his face filled with confusion and hers with rage. She started up again: 'I've tolerated you in this bar for months, even though you turned my stomach the first moment I set eyes on you. God knows why! Your filthy clothes and hair, your smell of drugs and sweat! I just hoped that one day you would leave this place and crawl back to that big house of yours in England and never come back! But I should have known only a man would have the strength to go back and that's not you! You disgust me! You are weak and always were! And now this! You reach out and touch my son as if he is your possession, so you can play your disgusting games with him!'

Henry sat stunned. The same question came back to him – who was this woman? What did she mean when she said he had always been weak? He decided that bravado was the best response, attempting to summon up his most bullish Englishness mixed with the Dutch courage provided by the port. After all, attack is the best form of defence surely?

'Now look here, I've said sorry for this misunderstanding but I can't go back and change things now. I think there's a lot of heat in this room and we both need to calm down. I am sorry again for what you saw, but it wasn't as bad as you're making out. He is a really nice boy and a great credit to you! I think I should leave now and we'll both benefit from some calm reflection on what has happened, and I'll be more than happy to wait a few days to let the dust settle before returning.'

For a woman of limited mobility, she moved quickly. She reached the table where one of the elderly customers had left his glass and spun, releasing the beer glass directly towards Henry's head. Too late he saw it, and as he tried to lean back to miss the missile it caught him on the side of the temple, his momentum carrying him back awkwardly onto the long seat and then taking him down on the ground, causing the table to fall over and his own glass to shatter onto the floor. As he staggered to his feet, now more determined than ever to get to the exit, she screamed: 'You filthy piece of shit! You will never understand how disgusting what you've done is! What do you mean about returning to this bar? If you ever set foot in here again I will kill you!'

She lunged towards the other table recently vacated and Henry guessed she was going for the glass on there too. He ran for the door and as he opened it, the glass shattered against the open edge above his head. He jumped straight through the opening onto the cobbles and ran towards his house, getting away from this mad woman being the only thing on his mind.

The following morning, Henry awoke from a desperate night's attempt at sleep. He'd slept for a couple of hours before the scenes being replayed in his head forced him awake again. He'd gone to the kitchen to see if he could dull his mind back to rest with some wine, but all he'd found were empty bottles and filthy glasses. He settled for a glass of cold water instead, thinking sobering up might be a better option if he wanted to think clearly about what had happened. As he went back to his mattress the same questions kept coming back to him. How could she know he came from a big house in England? How could she accuse him of always being weak? Who was she? Why would she threaten to kill him if he went back?

By the morning his mind was no clearer. To approach her again to apologise might be the right thing to do, but could provoke another attack. Her insults implied she knew things about him which was creepy. It made him think of home. Perhaps a short escape from here wasn't a bad idea for a few days; he could beg for more funds at the same time. Sure, he'd have to put up with snide remarks and feigned concern for his welfare and he couldn't put up with it for long, but that was nothing unusual. After rising at about ten a.m. and showering, he felt hungry, and had to make do with the dry crusts of bread he found as there was nothing else in the kitchen. He had money left from Philip's kind gesture which would buy him a cheap flight back to England. He'd text Anna and let her know he was coming back and she would let the family know, even if she wasn't going to be in England herself, which was often the case. He would just give her the bare details – he was coming back for a few days, catch up with the family, no big issues, no need for fuss.

He booked his ticket using his phone and then dressed as smartly as the dishevelled mess in the bedroom would allow. As he chose the cleanest things to pack, he picked up some of the discarded clothes from the floor and tried to squeeze them into the overflowing linen basket. 'Note to self: need to do some washing,' he said out loud. As he left the house, he had a spring in his step and felt a clarity of mind for the first time in months. Going back to England was never a preferred option, but this time it exactly felt like the right bolt-hole. He strode up the hill towards the Plaza de Espana where there was a taxi rank. As he reached the edge of the plaza, he turned right and then froze.

Just six paces away was Juan Marco coming athletically towards him, his hands full with shopping bags. The boy froze too. Henry's eyes darted to either side of him to check that the boy's mother wasn't there. Then he spoke quickly, instinctively: 'Look, I'm sorry about last night. It was a mistake and I hope you don't feel too bad about it. I'm going back to England for a while... just like your mother... umm... please could you just tell her I'm sorry, just tell her.'

Juan Marco still stood frozen to the spot as Henry spoke. He turned his head from side to side with a frightened look in his eyes. Henry was confused, then suddenly realised that perhaps the boy was trying to say he didn't understand. Perhaps his English wasn't as good as his mother's. Henry started again, in Spanish, anxious to get the words out as quickly as they would come. '*Lo siento. Voy...*' Juan Marco's expression hadn't changed, if anything his eyes had become more scared-looking and he was looking over Henry's shoulder. Henry's voice trailed off, and he turned round to see the boy's mother giving him the evil eye from the other side of the narrow road. As Henry started to put his hands up to show he meant nothing and that he was leaving immediately, she stood still but raised her walking stick at him, jabbing it, then lowering it and edging over the road towards them both, her eyes never leaving Henry's.

She muttered to Juan Marco to take the shopping home and then levelled her stick in Henry's stomach, hissing at him: 'Did you not get the message? You wait until you think I'm not here and you try again? If I see you again you are a dead man!'

'No you don't understand!' he cried. 'Look, I'm sorry about what happened, it won't happen again! I was just telling him the same and that I'm leaving the country for a few days. It's no problem, everything's going to be fine!'

Her eyes flared again. 'Things will only be fine if I never set eyes on you again! Go back to England and stay there! You could never have enough sorrys for what you did, you disgusting animal!'

'I've said sorry, what more do you want me to say? It wasn't that bad, just a simple mistake. I live here, this is my home. You'll have some space for a few days!' he said in exasperation, but that seemed to provoke her further.

'You really don't remember me, do you? All those years ago at Hillingstone. The quiet, shy, Spanish maid. You, the boy struggling with your poor teenage emotions! And you couldn't help yourself, could you? You saw an older woman out of her home environment and desired her, you begged me to make a man of you and when I resisted you tried flattery and then bullying! If I wouldn't help you then you would make up stories and get your parents to dismiss me! When they found out, did you stand by me? Did you speak up? Did you take any of the blame? No! You hung me out to dry, blamed it all on the cheap Spanish woman who seduced you! They fired me and gave me no reference after two and a half years! Do you know how difficult it was to get another job with no history to show for the past two and a half years? I had to take anything offered, and then that ran out because…'

She stopped dead in her tracks and froze. Henry was still rigid, struggling to take her words in. Maria from Spain had long ago been forgotten in his mind, but he took a step backwards as he recoiled from the idea that this woman, this old, sick, woman could have anything to do with that Maria, a sensual, feminine woman of thirty-three who had entirely captivated a young, confused boy of seventeen. He stared back at her waiting for her to resume her attack, but she seemed dumb-struck as if she'd said something she shouldn't have and could now neither go forwards nor backwards. Henry's mouth closed and, unbelievably, he realised that he had the upper hand, but no words to take advantage of it.

Then he saw Juan Marco coming up behind his mother, obviously having decided that this time he wouldn't leave his mother with this strange Englishman. '*Madre, esta todo bien*?' he said in a concerned voice.

Her jaw dropped and she turned towards him, her face collapsing as she replied: '*No ahora hijo mio!*' with a gasp.

Henry felt a dim light go on in his mind, quickly growing in intensity as the penny dropped. 'Juan Marco...' he stuttered. 'He's mine... you, you... you can't be her, you can't!'

Maria turned to face him, her face deathly white, her eyes like daggers. 'See what you have done,' she said, raising her walking stick again and pushing it into Henry's stomach.

Chapter 5

The Prodigal Son

Preparations were nearing completion for the Autumn Fair at Hillingstone. More than five thousand visitors were expected and would be greeted with a full range of country pursuits and attractions, plus retail outlets and catering. Detailed planning had been carried out for the preparation of the rooms in the hall that would be open to the public for a small donation. Lauren Pritchard had organised the cardboard box trail for the children, with painting completed by some children from the local school, plus a couple of budding artists from the families of estate workers. Lord and Lady Belvedere were enjoying a post-dinner drink in the drawing room, together with their guests, who had all played a part in the planning of the fair. It was tradition that they thanked everyone for their efforts with a formal dinner in advance of the event. The guests included Andrew and Kate Belvedere and their children, some charity representatives, Anna and her husband Alexander, and Robert and Lauren Pritchard. Suddenly Anna's mobile phone buzzed.

'Really darling, don't you think you should have turned that off?' asked Alexander. 'It's probably only a work call and they should know you are otherwise engaged for at least the next couple of days! I don't think any of us here will allow you to fly off to Singapore for an "urgent" meeting now!'

The group politely laughed. 'Sorry,' replied Anna. 'It's just a text. I'll be quick, I promise.' She rose from her seat and walked out of the room, softly closing the giant wooden door behind her.

'Now, I'm sure Alexander that nothing will drag you away from the car show next week,' chuckled Lord Belvedere.

'No absolutely not!' laughed Alexander.

The door opened after a few more seconds and Anna came back into the room, her face looking slightly flushed. 'Well, that is a surprise,' she said with emphasis. Then she hesitated. This wasn't the right place for family news, particularly not of this nature.

'Is everything all right, Anna? 'asked her mother.

Recovering, Anna looked at her mother and said in as offhand a way as she could: 'Yes fine, it's just a bit unexpected, that's all. A deal I had been advising on and was due to complete tomorrow night has just broken down. My client was messaging to say don't do any more work and that they'll let me have further information tomorrow. Very strange. I thought this was one of the easier corporate transactions I'd been involved in recently, but it's hit the buffers for some reason.'

Her mother smiled and Lord Belvedere announced proudly for the benefit of the guests from the charities that his daughter was an expert in international wheeling-and-dealing.

When all the guests had gone and just Anna and her husband were alone with her parents, she spoke up: 'Earlier on, when I left the room for that text message, I made up a bit of a story because of the assembled company. In fact, the message was from Henry. He's on his way home, or will be shortly. He had a flight booked for this afternoon but he's cancelled it, but he says he'll be back in a couple of days. He plans to stay for two or three weeks, but can't commit to anything after that. So he'll be here for the fair, although I can't see that as the reason for him coming now.'

Her parents exchanged glances. 'Oh my,' said her father. 'Can we fit him in, I mean can we prepare his bedroom for him? Do we know what sort of state he's in? Where can we put him that will keep him out of the way? I mean, obviously, not out of the way, but not appearing at the fair or at least not being a major part of it, or—'

Caroline cut him off. 'Of course we can have his room ready and I'm sure Anna's right, he's not coming back for the fair. There's no need to think he's planning to come back to muck things up,' she said reprovingly to her husband. 'Anna, how does he sound in his message? Did you get any sense of how he is?'

'Not really, Mother, although his text is more lucid than most, and he seems focused on coming back in an optimistic sort of way. He said he had a couple of things to sort out in Spain, but felt positive that this was a good time to come back to the UK. Who knows, but he seems more upbeat than he's often been in the past.'

'Good, well, let's hope that he's feeling bright and happy and that perhaps coming home will be a pleasant experience for him. I'm sure that's possible, isn't it, darling?' she said, looking directly at John. 'I mean he could just enjoy being around us and the fair might be a pleasant little distraction, and might even make it easier for him just to relax?'

John looked suitably reprimanded and nodded: 'Of course, of course, that might work well.'

'You've not heard from him for a while, have you, Anna?' asked her husband.

'No,' she replied, 'he seemed a bit messed up last time I messaged him, but he seems a lot brighter now. I'll ask him to clarify when he'll be arriving and then maybe a small group of us can welcome him. Maybe we can pick him up from the station – you'll have one of your fancy cars here won't you?'

'Yes,' replied Alexander, grinning like a schoolboy at the prospect of running the Volvo P1800 on an errand.

***

In Spain, Henry had decided to cancel his initial flight back. His mind had been a whirr since this morning's unexpected meeting with Maria and Juan Marco. So many questions running around inside his head – why had he not been able to recognise her at any time in the past few months? If that was down to the way she looked now, why did she look so ill? She looked like she was in her sixties instead of around fifty, walking with a stick and lacking co-ordination. Was Juan Marco really his son – could he have been somebody else's? Why hadn't she told him that she was carrying his child? When did she find out? What would he have done if she had told him? He shuddered at that question, knowing the answer already.

His mind was still made up about returning to England, but he always feared the possible consequences. Half of him wanted to escape as fast as he could, the other half was his conscience reminding him of all those obligations his parents had tried to drill into him, falling on deaf ears most of the time – responsibility, maturity, duty, gratitude, family, morals, values – the list was endless and Henry had felt they were words of torture, designed to trap him or make his free spirit conform. Now, at the moment of his biggest shock, he could hear the words of his parents inside his head like a rhythmic beat, repeating over and over again. They still sounded like instruments of torture, but the worst one was "obligation". That one wouldn't leave him alone, and the only way he could remove it from his head was by drinking himself to sleep that night.

The following day he woke with numbed senses, but he re-booked his flight for the afternoon of the next day. He stared around at the mess and dirt and, for the first time in months, felt a whiff of shame that he could live in this squalor and think it was normal. He resolved to start cleaning up at least before he departed, but five minutes effort was depressing enough and he decided to hire someone to do a better job. The house next to his and a couple of others in the terraced row had a cleaning service, and he'd seen the vans and cleaners going in and out. He decided to step out into the warm sun and see if he could speak to one of them.

The first two houses were locked and there was no sign of anyone there, but a few doors down he saw a girl come out of one of the properties carrying some linen in a basket. He approached her and asked if they had someone they could send to his place today. The young girl eyed him suspiciously and Henry lowered his face to avoid her stern look. He was well aware that some of the locals didn't like him. He offered her ten euros to call her boss, but she was still reluctant. After increasing to twenty she made the call and told him someone would be there before noon to see how much work there was. Henry gave her an apologetic face and said there was a lot to clean up and some washing needed doing as well. He would leave a key if needed so they could finish and return his washing while he was away.

After walking into the town for a coffee he returned to the house and, a few minutes later, a girl of about eighteen and her boss turned up to inspect the place. The looks on their faces said it all and only when Henry took out eighty euros did the older woman nod and agree to a few hours work, on the condition that they would do a decent, but not perfect, job. He left them at the house for a while and when he returned at half past six, the young girl was just returning with some freshly laundered clothes. Henry tried to make polite conversation, but she had little interest with all the mess to clean up.

Then he had a thought – she was about Juan Marco's age, perhaps he could do a bit of digging? He started by asking her if she was still at school, and she replied she was in the final year at the local high school. Then he said he knew a young lad about her age who worked in Café de Luz, a boy called Juan Marco – did she know him? She frowned but nodded so Henry tried a few enquiries. What was the matter with his mother? Was his English any good as he had heard that the mother spoke good English? Did she know where they lived and who owned the bar? The girl was impatient and brief with her answers, making it clear she wanted this cleaning job done as quickly as possible. But he gleaned from her that the mother had multiple sclerosis, Juan Marco spoke decent English but wasn't overly proud of it, and the two of them lived in a small apartment about five minutes' walk from the bar, which was owned by the couple who also owned the bar. Maria was just the manager, but the girl knew that her movement and mobility were getting worse and Juan Marco was desperate to stay close to her. He sacrificed his continuing education to work in the bar, partly to help financially, but also to keep an eye on her.

Henry stayed sober that night and ate at a different venta. His thoughts weren't clear, but that damn word 'obligation' kept coming back to him. Now that he knew Juan Marco was probably his son, he felt some disgust at how his erotic thoughts had led to such a profoundly regrettable incident. He wondered if he should do something to make it up to him, not just an apology. If this was his son, what an awful imprint to leave on the boy's mind! Perhaps he could do something for the boy, try to make amends by making his life easier, even if only in the short term. Maria was another matter. He felt shocked by her appearance but powerless to even contemplate how he could help. In fact, the idea felt alien to him. He'd never been much good at thinking about other people, let alone caring for them, and there was no point in pretending otherwise on this occasion. So if there was anything to be done it would have to be for Juan Marco, but what to do was just a field of fog at the moment.

His one clear thought was to return to England for a while. Complete distraction and re-exposure to a different world would probably clear his head, and something might come up then.

He messaged Anna to tell her of his revised travel plan. She replied that Alexander would pick him up from the train station to cover the four miles back to Hillingstone. Alexander and Anna were such a good match, he thought to himself. Both clever, determined and decisive. Henry had never warmed to Alexander much but that was partly because he had never made any effort to know him. But there wouldn't be any tension on the journey back, he was more non-judgemental than any of the family, and his connection with Anna was worthy of his respect, for if anyone could give him straight-talking advice it was Anna, even if he hadn't always listened.

***

Alexander was there to pick him up as agreed, looking like a countrified version of Roger Moore, as he got out of the gleaming Volvo P1800 estate to shake Henry's hand. Even Henry had to smirk; it felt like they were filming a scene from *The Saint* as they loaded his luggage and pulled out of the car park. Alexander made most of the conversation, talking about the car, the fair and his and Anna's busy lifestyles. By the time they reached the hall, Henry hadn't said many words and it felt comfortable that way. He wanted his return to be low-key and the timing coinciding with the fair was really rather comforting. He wouldn't be the centre of attention.

As he climbed out of the car, he felt nervous. This was the place of so many arguments, so many tears and hurtful comments, mostly from him. But this time, at least he was coming back for his own reasons and had thoughts on his mind that would keep him detached from the other family members. Anna was the first to step out of the side door of the hall to greet him: 'Well hello you, you look... OK, I guess!' She smiled at him and he could see in her eyes she was examining him for signs of improvement, and wasn't really seeing any.

'I'm fine. Probably don't eat enough and probably drink too much, but they're just two of my many vices,' he said with a wry smile.

His mother stood at the door giving him the once over, and he could see the effort in her eyes not to be judgemental. 'Henry, it's good to see you home. I hope your flight was OK and you weren't too uncomfortable in that car of Alexander's.'

Henry walked towards her and took both of her wrists in his hands, raising his eyes to hers. 'Trust me, I've been in worse,' he replied. He felt his mother's repressed warmth in her gaze as she tried to figure out how to react to him, and felt an awkward tenderness towards her, like a young boy realising for the first time that he's disappointed his parents. 'I'm here for a while and I appreciate you putting me up at short notice. Now you don't need to say anything. I know you will say this will always be home, but you know what I mean. I'm happy in Spain, but everyone needs a change now and again, and with the fair being on this is a good time to see the place come alive and catch up with things, while remaining a wallflower. I'm trying to say that I don't need any extra attention that distracts you all from the fair. Just let me blend in.' He smiled apologetically as his mother betrayed a slightly hurt look. He knew how she would react, but he'd spent most of the past fifteen years being awkward, and felt it necessary to remind her that wasn't likely to change now.

Her face gave way to the act she was good at. 'Of course, Henry. You have your own life and we won't hassle you. But you're always missed, as I'm sure you know.'

Chapter 6

Seeking Calm

Henry knew dinner with the family that night was a given, but it was going to be a small group, just his parents as well as Anna and her husband, so he figured he could handle it. He wouldn't see his father until dinner, and knew there would be some delicate dancing around, as his father was always on the lookout for a sign that he was going to return to the family "firm". At least his mother had learnt not to ask questions that might lead to disappointment. Henry's younger brother, George, and his wife Mary weren't arriving until tomorrow.

As dinner was served, Lord Belvedere tried his usual approach of asking Henry about the 'news' from Spain, and so the dance commenced.

'Well, Father, all is well. I find the Spanish air meets with my approval and invigorates my senses. Paintings are started and some finished, others are put away for inspiration to return later. You can't rush these things – you have to *feel* right to finish a work. There are various places I try to exhibit work for free in the hope of making a sale – cafes, restaurants, etc. Some are more successful than others.'

'Oh good, it sounds like you're making a living, that's a step forward,' replied his father. Henry raised his eyebrows in response. 'I don't suppose our Kent countryside will inspire you so much, but who knows. The fair brings a cascade of life and colour to our world and you may find something in that.'

Henry could sense the awkward dance steps and changed the conversation to the fair. Enthusiastically, his father took up the gauntlet, and the rest of the dinner passed pleasantly, with Henry restricting himself to words of encouragement and support. His mind was distracted by recent events in Spain, but that gave him an outward air of calmness that the others seemed pleased with. At the end of the meal, he was alone with Anna, Alexander having gone off for a late evening tour of the marquee area with

Lord and Lady Belvedere.

'I couldn't help noticing you handled Father better tonight than some others I remember,' she said.

'Yes, he seemed easy to distract tonight, it's the fair.'

'So why now for your visit? You probably didn't even realise the fair was on did you?'

'No,' said Henry, 'although the timing is good. I reached a bit of an impasse in Spain and needed a change of scenery. Just some things I need to work through, and here is as good a place as any to take a break.'

Anna stared at him for a few seconds. 'Money problems?' she ventured.

'No more than usual,' replied Henry. 'Something came up and perhaps I need a short-term break to sort that little matter out. Once I've made a decision then things can go back to normal. I may need to ask your advice about something actually while I'm here, if that's OK? Your absolute discretion would be required.'

'Intriguing,' smiled Anna. 'Of course, come and find me when you… have got your story straight!' she teased.

'Hold on just a moment—' jabbed Henry, but Anna cut him off.

'Don't worry. I'm just teasing. Whatever it is, you know you can speak to me about it. I shan't tell a soul, including Alex. Now, I'm off to bed, so no doubt we'll see each other in the morning. That is, if you're still in touch with mornings…'

As Henry's face broke into a sarcastic smile, she politely kissed his cheek and left the room.

Henry got out of bed at ten the next day and, unusually for him, had a clear head. He struck the breakfast table a glancing blow as the maids were clearing the last of the food and dishes away, and decided to go for a walk into the private gardens at the back of the hall. From there, he could exit through the gate and go into the parkland, which wasn't affected much by the fair preparations, which were mainly visible from the front of the house. After an hour-and-a-half walk, he headed back to the house and decided to go around the other side of the hall to see the layout for the fair, sticking to the outside of the marquees and stands where possible. It was a hive of activity with the event starting in two days. Tents and marquees were in various stages of erection; portable toilet buildings had arrived and were being put into position; a wooden platform was being constructed for the presentation of prizes; signs were being erected for visitor guidance; the grass where some of the classic cars would be parked was being given a final cut; and temporary fencing was being erected for the livestock paddocks. Henry cast his eyes towards the stables and was about to head off in that direction, when he changed his mind. They had no special appeal for him – unlike George and Anna, he had never taken to horse riding. So instead, he headed back towards the house to grab some lunch, but as he approached the side entrance he caught sight of an old Land Rover pulling up at the front. He slowed his pace and watched George and Mary climb out and head towards the main entrance. He paused as he reflected on their appearance – less the son and daughter-in-law of a viscount and more a pair of sheep farmers, he thought. George really had decided to do things his way.

George and Mary were surprised by his appearance at lunch. George in particular seemed shocked, but settled once Henry advised his was just a passing visit and he had no part to play in the fair. Then Henry started asking questions about how their own farm was progressing and, as George and Mary slowly started to elaborate, a kernel of thought developed in his mind. Could they use a little help on their smallholding in exchange for some sharing of knowledge? Free labour, or maybe a small allowance and board in exchange for a strong, willing pair of young hands? Was it an idea to see if he could offer Juan Marco an opportunity to broaden his life experience, as a one-off – maybe a few weeks in England working on a farm, seeing how things are done, giving him skills and the opportunity to travel? Of course, he had no idea whether Juan Marco had any interest in working the land or animals, but could he dress it up as some sort of work experience opportunity, mixed with developing his English language skills?

After lunch, Henry retired to his room with the remains of a bottle of wine from the lunch table. He had missed this companion over the last couple of days, and it would be a good accompaniment to developing his thoughts.

From the stables estate office, Robert Pritchard had caught sight of Henry working his way around the marquees. His eyes locked onto the lanky, unmistakeable figure for a few seconds. 'Well, well, well, if it isn't the druggie boy back on terra firma,' he said, partly to himself.

Lauren was in the smaller office next door, 'What was that you said? Something about drugs?'

Robert got up and walked to her open door. 'The Honourable Henry is back in town, or should I say the Dishonourable Henry, back to tap up daddy for some more cash to buy dope, hashish, smack, coke, whatever!' He was enjoying himself now.

'You're so down with the kids, aren't you?' replied Lauren sarcastically.

'I couldn't give a toss for the names they call it, but if he needs a hand sourcing some "shit" then I'm pretty sure Tom or Matt could help him out. And I'd be happy to oblige with a suggestive introduction if needed, in return for them giving me a cut.'

'Honestly,' replied Lauren, 'you've no proof they smoke dope out in the fields.'

'You believe what you want,' responded Robert, 'but I know what I smelt that day and it was sure-as-hell weed. Oh, and by the way, I expect George "the loser" will be back today with his jumper-and-wellies wife. Now you're not going to flirt with him again, are you, honey? You know what sort of trouble that caused before,' he said, grinning.

'Are you determined to cling to the past?' replied Lauren. 'Sometimes you're such a child. Haven't you got enough work to do with the livestock events?'

Robert shrugged his shoulders. 'Just enjoying the natural order of things, that's all.'

***

The next day, Henry hung around George and Mary more than he would normally do, but as they were taking in the final preparations for the fair it didn't seem unnatural that they would walk together. Henry tried to find out how things were going at the Lincolnshire farm. It seemed like they were putting a brave face on the workload, and he was feeling surer that they would be receptive to a short-term work experience student, which is how he would sell it to them. He resolved to run it past Anna first in a loose way, but it would have to wait until after the two-day fair was over.

The fair was a success, blessed with two days of warm sunshine and throngs of people enjoying the entertainment. The smell of livestock pervaded the outer areas away from the hall, replaced by the smells produced by the catering outlets in the areas closer. Everyone was in a good mood, especially Lord Belvedere who, despite the pressures leading up to the fair, always found respite in the event itself, when he could breathe a sigh of relief that success was now out of the planning team's hands.

Henry kept a low profile and mingled mainly with the public, knowing that hardly any of them were likely to recognise him. On the second day, he risked heading indoors after lunch to see the cardboard box trail that had been set up in the old nursery room. It was a riot of children crawling through the snaking tunnel, pointing at all the painted animals on the outside when there was a queue, and then rejoining the queue quickly to go through again. The room was full of happy noise and smiling faces, and Henry looked hard at Lauren Pritchard supervising and taking the plaudits from the parents. She looked at home, he thought. He'd never seen her as maternal, but she seemed in her element, mixing genuine pleasure at the children's sense of fun with self-confidence at the popularity of the activity. She might be a lightweight in his mind, but he had to give her credit for her impact on today.

While he was looking at Lauren, a soft voice next to him suddenly said: 'Well, hello stranger. It's good to see you in this room again.' Henry knew the voice instantly, but was still surprised that he hadn't spotted Mrs Tanner, the retired housekeeper, before now.

'It's been a long time,' he said timidly. Mrs Tanner had always been kind to him as a child and remained good-humoured throughout his destructive outbursts. She had maintained a calm way with him, and would often invite him into the kitchen when he seemed about to go off the rails again. As he reached his mid-teens she had less influence with him, but had always remained civil and polite.

'How is Spain going for you? You're not as tanned as I expected.'

'No, I don't get out as much as I should,' replied Henry. 'Artist's mentality, trying to work you know.'

'Uh-huh,' said Mrs Tanner, as non-judgemental as ever. 'Lauren has done well with the children's entertainment, don't you think? Quite a success and she wears it well.'

Henry looked at her with a wry smile. 'Yes, she does. Not on the same level as George, is she?' he said knowingly as Mrs Tanner smiled back.

Henry noticed Anna was just coming into the room and wondered about speaking to her now about his idea. He kissed Mrs Tanner on the cheek as he made his move away, and nodded his head towards the next room as he approached Anna. Anna took the hint and they entered the library. Henry closed the door behind them.

Anna spoke first. 'Ah, is this the point where you corner me for advice?

It's rather busy out there and I want to get outside for the last of the event judging, and Alexander will expect me to be by his side when he takes the glory for handing over the trophies in the classic car competition!'

'Yes, I'm sure,' Henry answered. 'Just a quick starter for ten. Do you think George needs a hand on his farm? I can't help but feel he and Mary are over-stretched.'

Anna looked at him incredulously. 'What? You're thinking of taking a sabbatical as a farmhand on an eco-friendly passion project? Next you'll be telling me you've found God!'

'No,' laughed Henry. 'It's not for me, more for a friend. Well, an acquaintance I suppose.' As he started to flounder he added, 'It's someone in Spain, a young man who might benefit from some practical experience. I'd be sort of doing him a favour, and maybe George could benefit from his labour in return for showing him the ropes, that sort of thing.'

Anna raised her eyebrows suspiciously. 'Young man, you say—'

Henry cut her straight off. 'Don't start thinking like that, it's nothing like that. It's just doing someone a favour, trying to give them a leg-up.'

Anna looked at him coyly. Should she give him the benefit of the doubt? Something told her there was more to this as Henry wasn't given to putting others first. But she was short of time and needed to get outside again. 'It sounds OK, in principle. Let's talk later.'

On the final day of the fair, the classic car show judging took place, and Lord Belvedere gave his customary closing speech afterwards, before the fair officially closed. He'd thought long and hard about his words. Should he say anything about the future of the estate, drop any clues or give any hint of changes to come in the estate management? But after consideration, he decided to stick with something fairly bland, ending with: 'The estate continues to rely on hard-working staff to keep it running, and we don't ever know what may be just around the corner, but I know we all work for the best future possible. My thanks, and those of my family, are due to the many hundreds of people who have contributed to this year's Autumn Fair, and I can honestly say I think this been the best yet. Thank you all for coming.'

Chapter 7

Plans Afoot

The day after the fair ended, George and Mary were planning a swift return to Lincolnshire as they were the main source of labour on their smallholding. With Anna having given her basic approval of his idea, Henry thought he would speak to them directly to get the ball rolling. If he waited until he'd spoken to Anna again, he knew there would be in-depth questioning and lots of prodding and prying. He wanted to retain control of who knew what.

Henry knocked on their door in the morning as they were packing. 'Sorry to disturb and I won't keep you long, I can see you're anxious to get back.'

'Yes,' said George. 'Intensive management is required when you're organic, so I wish you well when you return to Spain,' he finished hurriedly.

'Look, I might be able to do you a turn on that front.' As George frowned, Henry continued: 'Not me, you understand, but I know of a young man in Spain who could do with some practical work experience, developing his learning of how to make a living from the land. He's young, strong, hard-working and has a decent grasp of English, I think. In return for his free labour, could you offer him instruction and knowledge together with board and lodging? If you're concerned about costs I would try and help out on that front from my allowance… or possibly from selling one of my paintings' – he regretted the stumble – 'you're clearly heavily reliant on labour and I can assure you the young man would put his back into it.'

George had an inbuilt sense of distrust in Henry, based on his past fifteen years of debauchery and wastefulness. Something smelt fishy. 'I really think we can manage as long as we can get back home swiftly. Trust is crucial for anyone we employ and interviews, references, etc. all take time and I'm not really sure it's for us.'

Henry's face tightened. Perhaps he should have spoken further to Anna

51

first. Mary was looking at George seriously. He felt the heat and turned to her saying: 'Don't you agree, Mary? We really have to be very careful and you never know how things may turn out.' His words were spoken progressively more quietly, as his wife's gaze didn't leave his face.

Mary spoke quietly: 'If he's young and hard-working then it may be an advantage to us to consider it, George.' She turned to Henry: 'Does he have any interest in agriculture, Henry?'

Henry's talent for waffling returned with ease. 'I know him to be a diligent student and keen to learn. He's involved in food and drink production and consumption, but I think he would benefit from exposure to the wider world of industry' – he had chosen the wrong word, he knew instantly – 'and the horticultural process. I think he needs his mind broadening and this would be a great opportunity for him to learn about the value of the earth. I can vouch for his commitment to learning. Maybe you could offer him a trial to see how it goes, with no commitment from your end. Two or three weeks maybe? No cost to you, except a bit of time.'

Mary looked back at George, who was still hesitant, and decided not to wait for him to find another way of saying no. 'I think this is something we can consider. Can you arrange for him to visit us so we can have a chat? If he's what you say he is, then a strong back and arms might be appreciated.'

George looked sheepish but lacked the earthiness of his wife, and stayed silent. Henry nodded: 'Let me work on it and see if I make some arrangements. I won't keep you any longer. Have a safe journey home.'

***

Three days after the fair, and when most of the clearing up had been done, Lord Belvedere called for the usual de-brief with all the team, to review what had worked and any problems or issues that had come up. He asked Henry to sit-in, in the hope it would encourage his engagement in the future of the estate. Henry felt obliged to join the gathering, and hoped he could find the right balance between indifference and politeness to put on a decent show.

Consideration was given to visitor numbers (up); public feedback (generally positive); access and exit arrangements (well managed); quality of on-site catering (mixed reviews); volume of litter (always a cause of some angst and a feeling that more effort needed to be put into recyclables);

the car show (glowing praise); and biggest success (undoubtedly the painted cardboard box trail in the nursery, also noted for its use of recycled materials). Lauren Pritchard sat at the table basking in the glory and trying to combine serenity with modesty. Robert Pritchard looked smug as he felt both the reflected glory from his wife, and the satisfaction in knowing that they both provided the backbone for this event.

On finances, Lord Belvedere commented: 'I expect, Robert, that it's too early to say what the effect of the change in revenue arrangements will be, you needing to find out turnover from the various franchises and stallholders?'

'Yes, that's right sir, although I believe from initial conversations we have every reason to hope for a meaty increase in estate income.' Robert had conducted snapshot polls from especially the catering and retail outlets during the two days, and suspected the ten per cent coming to the estate would triple last year's income. 'Of course, the fine weather also helped the cause,' he added.

Henry studied Robert and Lauren from time to time. He saw they were enjoying themselves more than he expected and were acting like they knew something that nobody else did. It interested him more than expected, and he rather enjoyed the slightly different atmosphere, which made it easier for him to make the odd comment. At the end, his father spoke to him after the others had filed out.

'Henry, thank you for your involvement. I really do appreciate your time. The estate has evolved over the years as you will have seen. I hope you've seen progress; we can't stand still and there are always challenges to look forward to.'

Henry knew this conversation was coming at some point in his stay, and gritted his teeth now, preparing to disappoint, again. 'Yes, Father, you deserve great credit for how things have come along. Your team, including the Pritchards, looks strong.'

Lord Belvedere winced at their name and Henry picked up on it. 'We are doing our best, but sometimes I think we are becoming a little reliant on those two and I'm not awfully comfortable with that.' He left the sentence dangling, like a twig blowing in the wind.

'I'm sorry, Father, but my passions haven't changed and I think you would find me a poor addition round here. I know I'm the eldest son and you have every right to have expectations of me, but this isn't the life I'm cut out for. You know I will always wish the best for you and the estate, but you will need to use your judgement wisely as you plan the future management of it. I can't give you any assistance. I'm sorry.'

The words were cutting but necessary. Lord Belvedere looked crestfallen and bit his lip. 'I see, things haven't changed,' he said disappointedly. 'How long will you be staying here?' Henry looked surprised at what he thought was a request that he leave. Lord Belvedere swiftly added: 'I'm sorry, I'm not trying to imply you're not welcome. Of course, you must stay as long as you like. I merely wondered if you had a specific purpose in being here.'

Henry felt embarrassed and pressured. 'I... I... need some thinking time really. There's a local issue in Spain that needs a fresh approach. I thought that different scenery would help my thought processes and I think it will, I mean it has. Look, it may be that this issue in Spain might help here, I don't know. I'll think on it and see if I can work something out.'

Lord Belvedere raised his eyebrows and looked at Henry with a slightly puzzled expression. But he didn't press the point and said he would see Henry at dinner.

Shit, thought Henry, as soon as his father had left. How could he have blundered into saying that? He hadn't given much away but even to raise the subject in an obtuse way... stupid, stupid thing to do. He must speak to Anna before things got out of hand, and with her and Alexander leaving soon he needed to get on with it.

Henry made his way back to the house feeling slightly desperate. He went to Anna and Alexander's room but she wasn't there. He tried the library with no luck. Then he saw one of the house assistants and asked him if he had seen Anna, and was told she was in the kitchen talking to the cook. He headed straight there.

When he walked in, Anna was mixing a large bowl of ingredients for tonight's soup. 'Hello, do you have time for a quick catch-up? When are you leaving?' he asked.

'We go tomorrow. We're both in London for a few days to start with. Then back overseas – different places,' Anna replied. Henry frowned and added: 'Would now be a good time?'

'Well, I've sort of got my hands full at the moment!' Henry just stood there, and Mrs Bassett, the cook, felt the awkward silence, before saving the moment.

'It's OK, Anna, you go if you need to. I can manage this.'

Anna gave a look of annoyance towards Henry but came away from the table. She continued with the intense look as she walked past him and out into the corridor. He was going to get a grilling if he asked her anything that aroused suspicion.

Henry followed her out. 'Shall we walk into the gardens?'

She gave him a questioning look – so privacy was important? She waved her arm to indicate he should lead on through the back door into the gardens.

Henry began. 'It's about that idea I floated the other day.'

Anna quickly retorted. 'I guessed that much.' Henry knew he had to get on with it.

'I've already broached it with George and Mary. Umm... George seemed a bit offhand, but I think Mary's more practical and could see the upside of a young, strong, pair of hands.'

'Right,' responded Anna. 'So why do you need to talk to me again? There's something you're not telling me, Henry. Look, you're my older brother and at thirty-five, I don't feel the need to kid-glove you. What's the story with this boy? How old is he? Are you getting into something that's going to cause a shit-storm, because if you are I want no part of it?'

Henry felt his temperature rising. Christ, he wasn't intending to spill the beans. 'He's eighteen, I think. Yes, he must be. He's the son of a friend... well, sort of a friend. I mean, look, he's a good lad and I just want to help, that's all!'

Anna crossed her arms and fixed her gaze on Henry, tapping her foot impatiently. She looked as if she was about to move away.

'OK, OK, for fuck's sake!' blurted Henry. 'Do you remember that Spanish maid we had at the estate years ago?'

Anna's gaze became more intense. 'What, the one that you shagged, oh no, sorry, the one that seduced you and took your innocence?' she said in a sarcastic voice.

Henry ignored her tone: 'Well, she has a son and he seems a good sort of a boy and they're struggling, and she isn't well and—'

Anna cut him off. 'He's yours, isn't he? For fuck's sake, Henry! What sort of a plan is this? So your leg-up is to bring him here to work on your brother's farm, and you think nobody will think there's anything funny going on? Don't you remember, charity isn't your thing, everybody will smell a rat! Why the hell don't you just give him some money and tell him to go away. And his mother as well! Be realistic – responsibility isn't your best feature, is it?'

'I can't do that,' stuttered Henry. 'I never have any money. Besides, this is more of a gesture. This is my way of paying him off by doing something for him. It amounts to the same thing.'

Anna stood scowling at him. 'No, it isn't the same thing! By bringing him over here you're just creating a situation that could horribly wrong! You're a gay man who, in his teenage years, experimented with both sides, and this boy is the result. It happens. Get over it! You don't owe him anything. Have you thought that maybe he's better off without you? Even if his mother's sick, it's her and him and it's probably better that way. Have you lost control of your senses? Are you struggling to find some purpose in your life, and suddenly you think you have a son and that changes everything?'

The comment hurt Henry and resentment welled up inside him. He spoke with dark, stabbing words: 'Don't use this as an opportunity to criticise me! You and everybody else always criticised me! I could never do anything right growing up. Nobody ever accepted that I was different, emotional. Everything was about how I ought to be, not how I was! I wasn't like you and George and none of you cared, none of you! Oh and before you run off, I might have just mentioned something about it to Father, just dropped a hint that I'm working on something in Spain that might have an impact here.'

Anna's jaw dropped. 'What, you told father... what? You wouldn't...'

'I just hinted, that's all! But you know what? This is my life and I make my own decisions. Don't forget who's the eldest, and who gets everything if it all changes round here!' he snapped.

Anna was half-turned to stomp away, but her cold eyes fixed on Henry. 'You mixed-up bastard! You poor, mixed-up bastard. Only you could be so self-obsessed. Things might change around here faster than you think, but what would you care!' Anna walked furiously away towards the hall.

It took a few minutes of Henry wandering around the garden on his own for his resentment to subside, and for her comment on things changing to register in his mind. He hadn't a clue what she meant by that. He had no knowledge of anything changing at the estate, and his father seemed to be perfectly in control at the Autumn Fair wash-up meeting. The only thing that had struck him was the 'Ready Brek' glow that had been on the Pritchard's faces. Were they on a rise to greater power? Were they part of some sort of takeover plot? He couldn't believe that were true. His father would never allow the estate, Henry's inheritance, to go to an outsider. After a few seconds, the significance of those words came back to him – when in the past four years had he ever had those thoughts about the estate?

He returned to his room and decided against going down for dinner. Anna and Alexander would undoubtedly be there if they were leaving tomorrow, so he asked the cook to send some food up to his room with a bottle of port, which would mellow his mind for the evening and night.

He rose late the next day, and decided that his time at the hall was coming to an end. This visit had been one of the calmer ones but it was going downhill fast. To keep his mind busy, he decided to do an afternoon recce to the estate offices where the Pritchards were based. Maybe he could pick up some clues after Anna's comment yesterday.

As he got close to the stables, he could see Robert exercising Anna's mare in the paddock. It reminded him that this had never been his place of play and his confidence fell. As Robert turned at the end of the paddock, suddenly the connection between Anna and Robert came into Henry's mind. Was that what Anna was hinting at? Did she know what was going on with the Pritchards and was in on it? Henry needed to tread carefully. He had never paid them any attention, but that was partly because he found their self-confidence sickening. Maybe he had under-estimated their ambitions.

As Henry reached the paddock rails and looked up, Robert stopped the horse and raised his head high to look as imposing as possible. Then he walked slowly and deliberately across to the rails, intending to take full advantage of his position on horseback, over the man standing on the ground.

'Good afternoon, sir. We haven't seen much of you since your arrival, other than at the meeting yesterday. I hope you find the estate in good hands,' he said with one hundred per cent civility and nought per cent respect.

Henry needed his own display of bravado, even if he was less than comfortable facing the man towering over him. 'You appear to have everything under control, I'm sure my father is grateful.'

Robert looked directly into his eyes like he was locked on with heat-seeking missiles. 'Just doing our jobs, sir, as best we can.' Time for the charade to end, he thought. Can't play reversal of fortunes for long, so let's find out what he wants and get rid of him. Robert dismounted saying: 'Anything particular I can help with, sir?'

'No, I don't think so,' replied Henry casually. 'Just looking for a heads-up on anything happening on the estate really. Any new plans, projects for next year, feedback on this year's performance against budget, etc.?'

Robert eyed him suspiciously and decided to get Henry into the office on his own turf, also knowing Lauren was inside, and that Henry had never been able to stand her company – her charm and self-confidence always intimidated him. When George had been trying to win Lauren, she'd noticed how Henry always flushed when she walked into the room, and became instantly tongue-tied. At first, she thought it was because he fancied her, but Robert and some of the boys in the village had soon burst that bubble, and told her the nicknames they'd already made up for him.

'Why don't you come into the office, sir? I can show you some of the plans on the walls for what crops we intend to grow where next year, which fields will be left to fallow, which fields will require drainage improvements, etc. Plus, we can talk livestock numbers.'

As they walked in, Robert called to Lauren to join them from her office. With her tight jeans and top, skinny waist belt, knee-length boots and hair in a ponytail, she had the desired instant effect. She broke into a surprised but warm smile, enquired after Henry's health, chatted easily and looked like the perfect hostess. Robert turned his face away, unable to suppress a smirk.

Robert let Lauren talk for as long as he could get away with and, having had his fun, briefly pointed out the various diagrams and maps on the walls and their points to note for Henry's benefit. When he was almost at the end of his summary, he noticed Henry seemed to be distracted by something on the desk next to his. 'Is everything OK, sir?'

'Erm... yes, I think so,' replied Henry. 'What are they?' he said, pointing to some finger-length wrappings on the desk.

Robert looked directly at him, knowing that Henry knew exactly what they were. 'Oh those, they're marijuana joints,' he said slowly. He smiled before adding: 'I hope you don't think they're mine, sir. I confiscated them from two of the farm hands earlier. I can't control them smoking dope in their own time if it doesn't affect their work, but I think ploughing with a tractor and inhaling is way beyond acceptable, particularly as I thought there was a bit of race going on,' he said dryly. 'I hadn't got round to chucking them in the bin... but I'd be a bit worried if Andrew Belvedere spotted them in there when he and I are going through the accounts later. Erm... I couldn't trouble you to dispose of them in one of the kitchen bins could I, sir?' Robert was sticking his neck out hugely, but Henry's history made this a gamble with good odds. Robert's mind was alive and his mouth dry, what a stroke of luck, a heaven-given opportunity to find out if the weakness was still present. He waited for the reply, not moving a muscle.

Henry's mouth was dry and his eyes became misty. He wanted to speak but no words came out. He swallowed, then swallowed again, then felt a shiver down his spine. God, he was tempted! The correct answer was so obvious – decline and tell him to bury them, put something on top of them in the bin, grind them into the ground, the options were endless, but... he felt the weakness... it had been six days since his last joint. His mouth wouldn't work but he was in danger of dry-gargling. The seconds ticked by, no rescue came. 'Well, I suppose I could do that for you, just this once.' He stepped forward smartly and rushed them into his jacket pocket, beads of sweat breaking out onto his flustered face.

'Thank you, sir,' said Robert smoothly, 'I won't let it happen again. Now, is there anything else I can help you with, sir?' The atmosphere was electric.

'No, no that is fine, thank you,' replied Henry still flushed. 'I must be off.' With that, he headed out of the door.

Robert stood frozen to the spot, waiting to make sure of his success. He turned his head slowly, and watched for thirty seconds through the window as Henry walked away, the hand never leaving the jacket pocket. As he turned towards Lauren's office, he found her already leaning against the door frame, studying him. His eyes shone like a predator who'd just made a kill.

She said quietly: 'You just had to, didn't you? He isn't the enemy, he doesn't pose any threat to you.'

'I didn't create the opportunity, but as for playing it out, yes, I had to. When you get a chance like that, take it, be ruthless,' he replied, before turning back to the window.

Henry made his way swiftly back to the house, by now twitching to light one of the joints. He knew there wouldn't be any lighters in the house, but the kitchen would have matches. He popped his head in and asked the cook for a box of matches, giving her a suitably guilty look when admitting that he still needed a crafty cigarette from time to time. Then he headed straight out to the formal gardens and through the gate into the park. After a few paces, he lit the joint, and laughed out an 'ahh,' as he took his first drag. Ten minutes later, he was in another world.

He decided to leave the other as a treat for later, but didn't need the hassle of dinner tonight, especially as there would only be him and his parents. After walking for half an hour, he headed back to his room, but as he climbed the side staircase leading up to the first floor, he heard Lady Belvedere's voice talking to one of the cleaning staff in the corridor. 'Claire, you haven't seen Henry, have you?'

'No, my lady, but I believe he went out for a walk. I saw him about five minutes ago coming back into the private garden.'

'Ah, good, he must be on his way in. He normally comes in through the side door, I'll just check here.'

As she open the door to the side staircase, Henry had already turned around and was creeping downwards, but it was too late.

'Henry, good I'm glad I've caught you. Are you going out again?'

Henry turned, still light-headed from the joint. He gave her a wide smile, which he instantly regretted. 'Umm... I think I dropped something in the garden, I'll just be a minute.'

'Wait, please, just a moment. Could we have dinner tonight, just the two of us? You don't have any other plans do you? The house has gone quiet again with Anna and George having gone. It would be nice to catch up and your father isn't feeling well.'

Shit, thought Henry. Guilt trip time. He could hardly refuse if his mother would otherwise be on her own. 'OK, Mother, that will be fine. About seven?' She nodded. He smiled again, this time a little less enthusiastically, and then slowly descended the stairs on his way to a false errand. Bugger, the second joint might have to wait until another day.

By dinner, Henry's head had cleared and dinner with just his mother didn't seem so much of a threat. She was personable and pleasant company, and they wouldn't be both tensely waiting for his father to say something that made both of them squirm. Henry had just told his mother that he was planning a return to Spain in the next day or two. Her face fell.

'Oh, Henry, I was hoping you would stay a little longer. It's been nice having you back. We've all noticed that you seem calmer and happier. I'm delighted things in Spain are giving you a sense of purpose, but couldn't you stay another week?'

Henry slowly shook his head. 'I'm sorry, Mother, but there are things that I need to attend to. A new project. Just needs a gentle push in the right direction and then I can rest easy.' His mother's face showed concern and Henry felt a pang of conscience, but then an annoyance, that yet again, he was being expected to dance to somebody else's tune. 'I'm sorry, Mother, but I must go, probably the day after tomorrow,' he said decisively.

Lady Belvedere looked at him earnestly. 'Henry, I want you to know how much you're still needed; I still need you. This house still needs you. Your father, he still needs you. I'm concerned about him. He's not well. We don't know what it is but he isn't as well as he looks. It would be lovely if you could be around more, just more frequent visits if you can manage it, or longer stays?'

Henry's resolve was dented, but that sense of annoyance wouldn't go away, a sense of entrapment. He knew what he should say, and did so with as much civility as he could muster. 'What's the matter with him? He seems well.'

'Yes he looks OK, but he's losing weight and struggling with his appetite. He's been to the doctor and they've booked him in for blood tests. They'll be done tomorrow and then we'll see. The doctor is coming here.'

Henry nodded. 'Good. It's best to get these things checked out. Hopefully nothing to worry about,' he said solidly and with eyes down, to avoid his mother's look. Feeling the need to conclude the subject, he added: 'Let's see how things turn out and if I can help with coming back for longer visits or weekends, then I'll do my best.'

His mother gave a half-smile and said: 'Thank you, of course I'll help with the flights you know...' She didn't finish her sentence as Henry's head shot up and fire blazed in his eyes.

'You don't need to—'

This time it was Lady Belvedere who cut him short: 'I'm sorry, Henry, I didn't mean to imply that you couldn't...'

Henry thrust his seat back, wiped his mouth with his napkin and said starchly as he rose: 'Yes you did. Goodnight, Mother,' as he stalked out of the dining room, leaving his mother in tears.

Chapter 8

Fighting Fire

The following day Henry booked his return flight to Spain. His patience with Hillingstone had run out, and he felt the old frustrations of being trapped, even with all this open space around him. Things hadn't gone well with his mother the previous evening and he resolved to at least be civil today, especially as she hadn't said when the doctor was calling.

He found his mother in the drawing room at eleven a.m. He decided to be business-like in his tone. 'Good morning, Mother. I wanted to tell you I'll be leaving tomorrow for Spain. Is there anyone on the estate who could run me to the station at about nine thirty? When is the doctor arriving today to see Father?'

Lady Belvedere looked at him sadly. 'The doctor will be here at noon-ish. I'm sure one of the groundsmen can take you tomorrow, or you can ask Robert Pritchard?'

Henry shuddered, before replying: 'I think I might ring Mrs Tanner and see if she can drive me. I probably owe her a decent conversation anyway, as I haven't seen much of her since I came back. Mind you, with her being retired now perhaps I was never going to. Have you told Father that I know about his health investigations?'

'No I haven't. I think he would prefer it that way, no fuss, you know. But could you come and speak to him later today before you go off tomorrow. Just spend a little time with him, maybe give him some comfort over you returning sooner next time?'

Henry pursed his lips and told himself to breathe in and out a couple of times. 'Of course I can do that,' he replied dutifully, promising himself the second marijuana joint as his reward.

Later in the afternoon, Henry went to his father's study. They were both over-optimistic with each other about the next few months, Lord Belvedere about his energy for tackling the challenges on the estate into next spring, and Henry about his intentions that he would return more regularly in future. What Henry really promised himself was he would do things on his own terms with the family now; being looked down on by his siblings, especially, had worn thin.

His lift to the station with Mrs Tanner was arranged, and gave him a few minutes alone with her on the journey. He presumed she wouldn't be aware of his father's health issues, but casually asked if she saw much of his parents and, in a light tone of voice, whether she thought they were both in good health. Mrs Tanner seemed relaxed in her response, confirming Henry's suspicion. He then asked her about Maria, the old Spanish maid, again in a casual tone.

'You know, I thought the other day of Maria. Do you remember her, the Spanish housemaid?' Mrs Tanner looked surprised and replied cautiously that she did. 'I know I was very young at the time,' he continued. 'Probably not my best moment, I panicked and wasn't as honest as I could have been. But sometimes I wonder what happened to her.'

Mrs Tanner wasn't sure where these questions had come from, and decided that plain and simple answers were the best response. 'Yes, you were very young and found yourself in a difficult position. You had to be guided by your parents, and of course they wanted the best for the estate and the family. You shouldn't worry, I'm sure she ended up OK,' she said cautiously.

'Yes, I hope so,' said Henry. 'She was a good worker, wasn't she? She would have been able to find another position?'

Mrs Tanner hesitated for a moment, knowing full well that she had been instructed by Lady Belvedere not to provide a reference. Notwithstanding that, as housekeeper, she had provided an unofficial letter to help Maria find a job, as she had held her in high regard as a hard-working, honest girl, who had just fallen into a situation that was never going to end well for her.

'Yes,' came her reply, 'I know that she did find another job, but after that, I lost touch with her.'

What she didn't say was that she found out about Maria's pregnancy several weeks later, when Maria had called her in tears, begging for help, after being dismissed from her new job for persistent morning sickness. It had upset her greatly to tell Maria that she couldn't do anything more for her and to cut off any further ties. She didn't know if Maria had had or kept the baby, but these questions from Henry now were strange timing, and made her feel that someone was poking an old sore. Fortunately, Henry said nothing further on the subject and they soon reached the train station.

Henry had a plan of action upon returning to Spain. He would speak to Maria as bullishly as he dare, and attempt to persuade her that he should be allowed to do something for Juan Marco. He would make it clear that this wasn't a bribe or an attempt to make up for previous events, but a one-off gift of an opportunity to help him make his way in the world, and there wasn't anything else on offer. He wondered if Maria's health would be an objection, but hadn't been able to think of a solution, other than a vague notion that maybe he could find somewhere local to his brother's farm where she could stay, out of sight.

He decided to strike while the iron was hot. This would be dealt with on his terms and he hoped that a week away would have calmed Maria's temper. The following morning, he strode through the cobbled lanes towards the Café de Luz, his heartbeat increasing with every turn of a corner. When he reached the last turn, he looked cautiously around the edge of the final building, and saw Juan Marco setting out tables and chairs. She wouldn't be used to seeing him at this time of day, and he hoped the surprise would give him a temporary advantage. He waited until Juan Marco had his back to him lifting a table into position, and slipped quietly inside the door, moving swiftly to the bar.

'Good morning,' he said brusquely, as her eyes frowned in surprise. 'Now I haven't come in for a fight or argument again, all I want is to make a proposal to you.' The words horrified him as soon as they came out. 'That is… I mean I want to suggest something to you as a peace offering between us.' Maria raised her hand to slap it down on the bar, but Henry wouldn't be put off. 'Now please, hear me out – if you still want rid of me afterwards then I will go and never come back, and that will be an end to our dealings. Please, hear me out.'

Maria was silent and still, and Henry had his chance. 'You previously outlined the harm your dealings with me and my family had done to you and your family. It was a long time ago, but I recognise the outcome for you was far worse than had ever been intended, and I regret my part in it. Now, listen, please!' Maria's eyes were flaring up again. 'You have a son, and… well I played a part in that, too. I see you here in difficult health but with a son who appears loyal, hard-working and supportive of you.' Maria's face softened a little. 'I'm sure he wants to look after you, and in return I'm sure you want to offer him the best future too. It might be possible that I could offer Juan Marco a little time in England, studying and furthering his education.'

Maria reacted sharply with a look of horror and Henry felt his chance was in danger of running away. Instinctively, he grabbed a glass ashtray on the side of the bar and brought it down on the surface with a loud crack. He glared brightly at her. 'Madam, I have only asked for one chance to speak to you, and if my offer isn't accepted then I have promised never to come through that door again. All I am asking is for an opportunity to put my case. For the last time, will you please hear me out!'

The loud clatter on the bar brought Juan Marco inside and he instantly recognised the visitor. As he started to speak to his mother in Spanish, Henry turned to her and in a flash of inspiration said quietly: 'Does he know who I am?'

Maria stopped her words to her son abruptly and mouthed 'No' at Henry.

As she started to speak to Juan Marco again, Henry continued: 'Perhaps he should be told then, unless...' His words hung there. Maria glared at him and then gestured to her son to go outside.

Henry gave a half-smile and said: 'Thank you. I will be brief and then I will go. Now, my brother has a small farm in England, you remember him? Well, his is an intensive farm and he is short of labour. In return for Juan Marco providing some much-needed labour, George and his wife will help him develop his English further, teach him about the principles of arable farming, you know, crops, vegetables that sort of thing, and they will provide him with a warm and comfortable room and all his food. This would be for possibly a three-week period, maybe extending to six. This isn't to persuade him that he has a future in England, but to offer him knowledge and education that he could put to good use in Spain. The climate out here is, of course, very different and so are some of the crops, but I'm offering to help broaden Juan Marco's experience and knowledge of the world, and the principles of what can grow in different soil types, and how the land can be managed, will be just the same. I'm over-simplifying of course' – Henry realised this was the understatement of the decade – 'but I think he will pick up transferable skills. I realise that agriculture may not be his choice of career, but you know better than anyone that local produce is the basis for your business and many others in Spain.' His sales pitch was coming to an end.

'I realise that leaving you might be a problem for him, and so, I will commit, if you can bear to set foot in England again, to provide you with a flight too and somewhere to stay for the duration.'

Maria's patience was running out, and Henry held his hand up. 'OK, I've said what I came to say and I hope you will think on it. When you have made your mind up, perhaps you can send a note to me – I'm at number seven, Calle de Juan.'

He turned and made for the door, as Maria replied: 'I don't think England ever did me any good at all.'

Unbelievably, and with incredible cruelty, Henry stopped and turned. 'Mrs Tanner sends you her best wishes. She really does.' As he walked away he knew that was a low blow, even by his standards.

Maria slumped on the bar as soon as Henry stepped into the street, stunned to hear Mrs Tanner's name after all these years. She had been the only one from the estate who had tried to help her eighteen years ago, and Maria had been deeply distressed by the severing of their relations. What hurt most was it reminded her that she'd had some happy times in England, some very happy times. The work at Hillingstone had been comfortable and the housekeeping team were good company. Her language skills improved, she developed a reasonable social life and it felt like a family home, albeit on a large scale. She also loved the horses, having been a rider herself from a young age. Her time in England had been such an adventure, and even though she always planned to return to Spain to live after a few years of travel, she hadn't reached the tipping point by the time she was forced out.

In her heart, she wanted nothing from Henry or England. Henry was about as unsuitable as a father could be, and it still made her feel nauseous when she thought of his actions in the bar that night. But she also worried about her son. His life revolved around working with and supporting her, and he had finished his education early because of her health. He wasn't earning much at the bar, was reluctant to consider anything that would take him away from her, such as going to university, and wasn't socialising as much with his friends as he should be.

Maria moaned as she raised herself up from the bar. Juan Marco came in and asked why she had even spoken to the Englishman again, and she told him he had come to apologise, again. Her son asked if this was now the end of it and Maria looked at him feeling helpless. She knew that he deserved to know the truth, but wasn't ready to tell him about his father now. She needed more time and perhaps that made Henry's offer easy to reject. She smiled at Juan Marco and told him that the Englishman was now gone and he needn't worry any more, they had spoken their last words.

Over the next few days, Maria thought on and off about Henry's offer. She didn't want it personally, but her conscience about Juan Marco's limited life in Spain bothered her. What should a good mother do? What was in his best interests, not hers? She had tried persuading him that he needed to make a career for himself, but as an only child in a single-parent family, he was extremely protective of her, especially since her multiple sclerosis diagnosis five years ago. She was on medication, but there were times when her body was slow to respond to her mind's instructions, and she had become more unsteady on her feet over time. There were days when she could walk with support from her son, and others when she needed her sticks. Long term, her movement would reduce and her eyesight had already deteriorated a little, which meant she couldn't always see the imperfections in the cobbled streets, and had fallen over a couple of times already this year.

Both Maria's parents were dead and she'd been an only child. She had cousins in Spain about fifty kilometres away, but didn't see much of them, and her four-year absence from Spain more than twenty years ago had put a gap between her and her distant family. None of this seemed to matter when she came back with her infant. He became her world; spending time with him when she wasn't working became her joy. Juan Marco had a happy childhood, enjoyed school, was shy but polite with others and had one special friend at school whose parents owned a cattle farm. They kept horses and Juan Marco had taken to riding like a duck to water. He still went to his friend's farm to ride once a week, at his mother's insistence.

But Maria knew their closeness, and more particularly her illness, was holding him back now, and she would become more dependent on him in the future. She knew he wouldn't take up any opportunity away from her, so anything he did would need to leave him assured that her needs weren't being compromised. He had brains, manners and a warm nature and she was immensely proud of him, but he was capable of much more.

She thought of how lonely she might feel returning to England, but if she could see her son at work or be close to him at the end of the day and could see him enjoying himself and growing, was that enough reward? She was still upset about Henry mentioning Mrs Tanner, who had been a good friend to her, and the possibility of seeing her again, if that was real, made her feel emotional.

She considered her options for another two days and then came to a decision. She wanted Juan Marco to have the opportunity to decide for himself, so she would need to talk with him about the offer which would need careful presentation. But if he wanted to accept then she was clear on one point – Henry's involvement must be completely hidden, and that included his identity as Juan Marco's father.

She found time to talk to Juan Marco first thing the following morning, before they headed to the bar to open up. She explained that, as he knew, she had worked in England a long time ago and had loved the experience, and learnt to speak the language well. Through a conversation with a guest house owner in the town who had an English family to stay, she had been told about a work exchange programme that offered foreign young people the chance to live and work in England for a few weeks, with board and lodgings provided, in exchange for labour around the small farm they ran. As well as working, the package included education from the owners in arable farming practices, and also the opportunity to develop their language skills through daily life there. This sounded believable as there were similar schemes provided by others in Spain.

Juan Marco's first question was what about her, predictably. Maria told him she could find local serviced accommodation so she could see him daily. Then he asked how they could afford this trip, and she replied that their landlord felt Juan Marco deserved this opportunity, and had offered to reduce the rent on their apartment by fifty per cent for up to six weeks while they were away. For spending money, Maria would dip into the fund she had put aside for Juan Marco's university education, as he wasn't likely to go, but this was exactly the type of opportunity that the money should be spent on. He wanted to see the website and the application forms for the programme, but Maria told him he needed to make a decision in principle straight away as there were other applicants, and that meant a yes or no today. She had spoken to the owner of the bar the previous day and he had agreed to their leave, as long as they gave him two weeks' notice of their departure.

Juan Marco's final question was about England. Her time there was long ago, and with all of this trouble with this Englishman recently, why should he go there? Was he involved? Maria shook her head, and said as convincingly as she could that it was just a coincidence. That man was now gone and nothing to do with this offer. His behaviour towards Juan Marco had even disgusted himself, and he didn't represent what English people were like. In fact, he was as far removed as it was possible to be.

As the bar was closing that night and they were clearing up, Maria asked him for his decision. Juan Marco was reluctant to commit without seeing further details and she could see he was looking for a way out. She smiled and told him she was disappointed but understood, and she would ring the farm in England first thing tomorrow and tell them to give the opportunity to someone else. But she could see in his eyes that he wasn't one hundred per cent sure of his decision. She said nothing further and after they headed for home, she had an inkling that maybe a good night's sleep would provoke a change of heart. She was right.

The following day, Juan Marco said he had changed his mind and left it to his mother to make the phone call. She now composed a letter to Henry.

On behalf of my son, I accept the offer of up to six weeks in England working and learning on your brother's farm. I think this is no less than he deserves, but if it wasn't for the fact that I couldn't provide him with this opportunity I would otherwise reject it, and have nothing further to do with you or your family. You must understand that this acceptance comes with some rules. If you cannot comply with any of these, I absolutely reject your offer, and you are to have nothing to do with me or my son again.

Firstly, he must never know that you were involved in this plan or that he is working on a farm connected to you.

Secondly, he must never know that you are personally connected to him. He is my son and has no father that he knows of.

Thirdly, you must guarantee that your brother will treat him well and provide for him, and will have no knowledge of his connection to you.

Fourthly, you must provide his flight and pay for his transport from the airport.

Fifthly, I want nothing from you for myself. No flight, no transport, no accommodation, no money. You are only to provide what is agreed for my son.

If anything happens to my son while he is in England as a result of your actions, I will hold you personally responsible and will do everything I can to ruin you.

We will be able to travel any time from the middle of October, but must be back in Spain before Christmas.

If you accept these terms please reply by note. Do not come to the bar ever again. I do not want to see you again here or when we are in England.

Maria Ruiz Garcia

Chapter 9
Digging up the Past

Henry read Maria's letter with dulled emotions. Her delivery was cold – take it or leave it. He shrugged his shoulders; there was nothing to do but accept her terms. Once the visit was over he'd have done something for the boy and his debt was paid. The one thing that peeved him was having to give up on going to the bar, but there would be others. Maybe it was time to find somewhere new where there were no ghosts from England.

He wrote a short note to Maria – terms accepted, arrangements to follow – and put it through the door of the bar before it opened. Then he went for a coffee and texted George to say Juan Marco was available from next month, on a two-week trial basis. Did he want to make the arrangements or let Mary take it over? George ducked as Henry thought he would, and gave him Mary's number. He rang her and assured Mary of the boy's enthusiasm and willing nature. He'd cleared it all with his mother who would be staying locally in England, but there would be no interference from her or Henry. Juan Marco was keen to learn and it should go fine. If they had any problems they should call his mother, or Henry as a last resort, but they should understand the boy believed his mother had arranged the visit through an acquaintance in Spain, and was too modest to accept this as a gift from a third party. Henry's name should, therefore, be left out of it and in any case, he wasn't planning on being in England during their visit.

Mary thought it odd that Henry was distancing himself, but he emphasised the free labour and put up sufficient bluster to silence her, guessing that financial pressures were weighing on her and she couldn't afford to turn down an extra pair of hands, for such little outlay as food and a room. They agreed a date in October and Henry communicated it back to Maria. She responded by asking him to draft something that looked like an official invitation from the farm to satisfy Juan Marco's need for detail, which Henry wrote out and got a local printer to produce. The following day he panicked about whether they had passports, and enclosed a note to

Maria with the invitation, but she confirmed they both had them and told him not to concern himself with flights and transport from the airport, as she wanted to make the arrangements herself. However, she would send copies of the invoices to him and, to his surprise, she also enclosed an invoice from the bar for his outstanding debt, which she invited him to settle beforehand, otherwise the deal was off!

Henry settled grumpily two days later. The sooner this woman was out of his hair the better.

On the 16th October, Juan Marco and Maria set off in a taxi for the airport, both nervous for different reasons. He fretted about meeting strangers in a different country, and she was nervous of meeting anyone from her past, even if they were unlikely to recognise her. She would avoid spending any time with Henry's brother just to be sure, and while she had never met Mary, it was best to minimise contact anyway. At some point she would like to contact Mrs Tanner, but that wasn't as important as making Juan Marco comfortable.

On arriving at Doncaster-Sheffield airport, the pre-arranged taxi took them to the farm outside Lincoln. Maria was relieved that George was out in the fields and Mary received them cautiously, but politely. She warmed quickly to Juan Marco, aided by his good looks, and Maria noticed how her eyes stayed on Juan Marco's face, with occasional glances down at his athletic physique. Maria left, thinking her son's charm would lead him to a comfortable stay, and the taxi took her to her local guesthouse accommodation.

George met Juan Marco at dinner and was as stuffy as Mary was enthusiastic. He still didn't trust Henry's act of apparent generosity, and asked lots of questions about Juan Marco's parents, upbringing, education and what he hoped to get out of his stay. But he couldn't fault the boy's civility and apparent work ethic. Juan Marco spoke with really quite decent English. He had never met his father as his mother had been abandoned when she got pregnant, he had a little knowledge of crop-growing in Spain, and was comfortable with horses. Most of all, he was keen to help them, work hard and improve his education which had been cut short by his mother's ill health. He didn't know much about his mother's time in England many years before, but he knew she had earned a living doing casual bar work in the south of England, and had learnt to speak the language well. There was nothing that George could question, and he had no choice but to give Juan Marco the benefit of the doubt.

Work started the next day. George and Mary decided to split their time so that both parts of the farm could benefit from Juan Marco's help. George was focused on ploughing and seeding the winter crops, while Mary looked after the livestock and the cottage garden that made them almost self-sufficient. There were two carthorses that did most of the ploughing for the three acres of fields, and George explained they better fitted the ethos of the farm than a tractor, and required less capital investment. Once Juan Marco had mastered harnessing them, he took to the ploughing with ease, and George could only shake his head at the calmness and control Juan Marco displayed with the animals. He put his back into everything over the first few days and George began to relax in his company, enjoying talking about crop rotation, soil management, the effects of weather, etc., with such a willing pupil. Mary too felt his easy temperament, his willingness to get his hands dirty and to ask questions, whether about his duties or speaking English. He looked no older than his eighteen years, but his calmness and thoughtful mind appealed to her, along with his physical presence which she admitted to herself was pleasant. While she didn't normally take much care of her appearance around the farm, there were days when she put a little make-up on, much to her amusement, and even George commented on it once. She laughed it off, saying she thought she had a dentist appointment in Lincoln that day but had got the wrong date.

George would drop Juan Marco off at Maria's guesthouse most evenings, or he would take them to a pub or a more built-up area so they could explore, leaving them to make their own way back home. Juan Marco insisted on helping on the farm on Saturday mornings, but he and his mother had the rest of the weekend to themselves and explored the local area, often with George or Mary dropping them somewhere. Maria stayed polite but quiet on purpose whenever they were together. After two weeks, George and Mary invited her to dinner on the Saturday night. She was alarmed and tried to make excuses, but when Juan Marco joined in on their side she had no choice but to accept, but knew she would have to be on guard if they questioned her about her time in England.

Mary went to pick her up and chatted light-heartedly about how pleased they were with Juan Marco's efforts. Mary wished they could keep him longer, but joked that slave labour died out in England long ago! Maria was genuinely proud of her son but couldn't allow herself to relax, either now or over dinner. One slip and her link with the family would be known. Mary wondered why the mother couldn't be at ease like her son, but thought perhaps her English wasn't as good as she had first thought, or maybe being away from home didn't suit her as well. Hopefully a good dinner would bring her out of her shell.

When they sat down at the dinner table, Maria refused wine, giving her medication as the excuse, which was partially true. Mary's conversation was animated, and the number of times Maria noticed her eyes sparkling at her son, made her think she was a little excited by him. Juan Marco was polite and exuded a reserved natural modesty, but if he felt any attraction towards Mary, he didn't show it. As for George, he couldn't shift a formality in his manner, which reminded Maria of what he was like growing up during her time at Hillingstone.

Their conversation varied between life in Spain, the climate, organic farming, Maria's background and Mary's upbringing. When George started talking about his childhood and family, Maria felt her pulse quicken and knew she had to remain subdued, and was relieved that Juan Marco enthusiastically asked lots of questions. He was amazed by the family history and the size of the estate, but was a little surprised that George didn't have closer links until he remarked that estate life didn't entirely agree with him. Fortunately, George didn't mention his brother and Maria was relieved that Henry had kept the privacy part of their agreement. What she knew was coming at some point in the evening, were questions about her time in England and she wasn't looking forward to it. It would require vigilance on her part to be vague where necessary, while also remaining civil.

She spoke at some length about her illness when asked, and was able to explain when she first noticed something wrong, the diagnosis and subsequent medication, and how the condition was likely to progress. Both George and Mary listened attentively and showed genuine interest and concern, which softened her mind a little. As they came to the end of the subject, George asked: 'Your English is really so good. Both you and Juan Marco speak so well, the language teaching in Spain must be first-rate. What age do they start in schools?' Maria was alarmed but knew she had to react quickly as Juan Marco was smiling.

'Yes, it's true that they start as early as five in Spain and English is a big focus. Juan Marco also benefited a lot from me being able to help him with homework, and of course practice a little.' Juan Marco was waiting for her to say something about her time in England, but it looked like it wasn't going to come. She looked at him seriously and hoped he got the message.

'And what about the work experience programme that Juan Marco is hopefully enjoying here,' smiled George. 'Was that sort of thing a little too early for you? I understand you worked over here some years ago? You really seem to understand our language, sentence structures, etc. as if you'd lived here.'

Maria hesitated fatefully, and Juan Marco jumped in: 'I think my mother is being a little modest, Mr Belvedere. She did work in England for some time before I was born, as I told you before.'

Both George and Mary nodded and Maria was forced to say defensively: 'It wasn't for long, and it was a long time ago. Honestly, it isn't important. I just did some casual work as a lot of young people do, and it helped a lot with my English.'

'How old were you?' asked Mary.

Maria hesitated again before replying: 'It was before Juan Marco was born.'

'So you had just left school, or were you a little older?' persisted Mary.

Again there was a delay in Maria's reply noticed by all. 'Er... I was older... I could do similar work in England to what I was doing in Spain, so I decided to travel a bit and explore before I was too settled.'

Juan Marco cut in: 'I always remember you telling me you saw the film *Notting Hill* in England when it first came out. That's her favourite film!' he beamed.

'Oh I love that film,' said Mary, laughing. 'I know it's corny but it's such a feel-good story! Came out in 1999 didn't it?' George muttered that he couldn't remember and Juan Marco looked at his mother.

'It can't have been then surely,' said Maria hurriedly. 'I know I'm getting old but my memory can't be that bad.'

'Oh don't worry, I'll look it up on my phone,' said Mary, getting up to walk towards the sideboard where her phone was.

'No, it's OK it doesn't matter,' said Maria quickly. 'As you get older you forget things. Anyhow it was a long time ago and I did bar work, some cleaning jobs, anything to pay for my accommodation in London, although I moved around a bit.'

Juan Marco listened to his mother and was confused at what he was now hearing. He said matter-of-factly: 'I thought you only visited London;

you said you lived outside it, in Kent.'

Maria felt her blood pressure rising again and countered: 'Kent, London, it's all very close together. Some parts of London are in Kent, Juan Marco. The borders are blurred.'

'Quite right,' said George, inadvertently rescuing her. 'Did you ever get as far as Maidstone? The family estate is not far from there.'

'No, not that I remember,' said Maria coolly, looking at her watch. 'Oh look at the time, I must be getting back to the guesthouse, I don't have a key. Could you call me a taxi please?'

Maria's heart missed a beat when George replied: 'Oh there's no need for that. I'll drive you back.'

She inwardly breathed a sigh of relief when Mary answered: 'No don't be silly George, you've been drinking and so have I,' holding up her wine glass. 'Of course we'll call you a taxi Maria and it will be on us. It's been a pleasure to have you here tonight, a family, the two of you,' she said, raising her glass in turn to Maria and then Juan Marco, with extra sparkle in her eyes as she looked at him.

Juan Marco hugged his mother goodbye when they heard the taxi pulling up outside, and as George and Mary said their farewells at the door, he edged slowly back down the hallway pulling out his phone from his pocket. He searched "Notting Hill release date". 1999 was the answer. His mother told him it was her favourite film every time it came on the TV, and she never stopped adding that she saw it in England when it was first released. He'd never bothered to check when it was released – 1999, the year before he was born in June 2000.

Juan Marco went to bed in a thoughtful mood and couldn't switch off. He'd always assumed his father was Spanish, and all his mother had told him was his father had left her when he found out she was expecting. The number of times she kept going on about being in England the year *Notting Hill* was released. There was no way she could have the got the year wrong, which meant she must have been pregnant with him that year, and returned to Spain to give birth. So he was conceived in England, perhaps to an English father? That seemed likely, although it wasn't impossible that he could have been Spanish or indeed any other nationality, as many people travelled abroad and London was full of people from other countries.

Maybe he was overthinking it, but his mother had never told him anything about his father and it hadn't really mattered before. But he was eighteen now, and whatever had happened it was a long time ago and there couldn't be any harm in knowing the truth. He was old enough and grown-up enough to be treated like an adult, and if his mother didn't tell him now, then when would she? When he was twenty-one, twenty-five, thirty? What was the justification for waiting? He wouldn't make judgements if it had been a casual relationship that suddenly became a bit precarious with the pregnancy, or perhaps his mother had been serious about a man and been dumped when he found out she was expecting. Or perhaps she had a relationship with a married man and it had blown up, and he refused to leave his wife. There were lots of possibilities, but it seemed slightly hurtful to him that for the first time he had doubts about her story, not helped by his mother's behaviour at dinner. She'd been reluctant to admit her previous presence in England, and was cagey about where she lived and worked. She'd always told him she'd worked mainly outside of large towns and had only visited London as a tourist; now she was loose about the past and seemed to have moved around a lot more. He put his head on the pillow and decided that he would talk to his mother the following night. He wouldn't probe or hurt her feelings, but she needed to recognise he was a man now and had the right to ask things about his father.

The following day on the farm was normal, although Juan Marco was quieter. It didn't matter because it was wet outside and he spent most of the day seeding winter crops, and talking to George two rows away in steady rain was almost impossible. He arranged to meet his mother in the local pub for dinner, which was only a short walk for him and a short taxi ride for her. He answered her questions over dinner about the farm easily and matter-of-factly, because he was saving his mental energy for the right moment. Over coffee they became quiet and he took his chance.

'Mother, I hoped you enjoyed dinner last night with George and Mary. They're really nice, aren't they?'

Maria looked at him with eyes that were silent and dull. 'Yes, they seem to like having you around and I am glad you are enjoying it. Mary in particular has taken a shine to you, no?' A sharpness returned to her eyes.

Juan Marco gave a thin smile in acknowledgement and replied: 'I think she likes having different company, that's all. They spend a lot of time together on the farm with only part-time help.' Maria raised her eyebrows and tilted her head forwards slightly, but said nothing more. 'I realised when you were talking about your time in England that I didn't know much about it really. You travelled around more than I thought and were more adventurous. Did you have good fun?'

Maria's expression changed again and her eyes and face firmed up. 'We all have a past, my son, but it was a long time ago. Some bits I enjoyed, others were more difficult. But I knew when the time was right to go home.'

Juan Marco sat tight-lipped. She wasn't going to make this easy. 'Erm… you told me that my father split with you when you were pregnant. Did you meet him in England? I always thought he was Spanish,' he ventured. Her look was serious and uncompromising.

'All that you need to know is that you are my son and I love you very much. If I felt you needed to know more then I would have told you,' she replied coolly.

'But was he Spanish or English or… well if you met him in London he could have been from anywhere.' Maria's eyes narrowed and he realised this could be misinterpreted. 'I mean London is an international city, people come from all over the world to visit and work there. Spanish, Portuguese, American, Mexican, French. I just mean you could have been close to someone here from any country.'

'Don't fish, Juan Marco,' replied his mother. 'There are times when it's not polite to ask things. I said I had good times here and some not so good, and maybe there are some things that I don't want to talk about or remember.'

Juan Marco sat frustratedly. He was eighteen and it sounded like his mother was pulling up the drawbridge entirely on her terms. Maybe he should risk being more direct, lay down a marker.

'OK, I understand. But as you say, it was a long time ago and wounds heal? Perhaps when we get back home you will tell me what happened? I'm eighteen now and would like to know who my father was, even though I trust your judgement completely and have no interest in meeting him. If you don't want to talk about anything else to do with him, like your relationship, then I won't pry. Just who he was, how you met him, where he came from, that's all.'

Maria fixed him with a stare. 'That's enough,' she said coolly.

Juan Marco returned to the farm in a darker mood than when he left. He slept better, only because his desire for knowledge had been replaced by mistrust and resentment, which let in no light for dreaming.

The next day, he was winter crop seeding again, but when the rain slackened off and George was talking to him about the balance between dry and wet conditions, he had to apologise for asking him to repeat some points. George asked him if everything was OK, and he told a white lie that his mother hadn't been so well the previous night, and he was just anxious about her. George offered to run him over to the guesthouse before dinner if he wanted, but Juan Marco replied that it was OK, she just appeared more tired than usual. He would ring her later but let her rest tonight.

It was just Mary and Juan Marco for dinner that night, as George had a Young Farmers social event to go to. Before he left, George mentioned to Mary that Juan Marco seemed a bit distracted and that his mother wasn't well. Mary said she would check with him over dinner.

Juan Marco wasn't very talkative through the main course and before serving up the dessert, Mary asked him if his mother was OK. He raised his head, gave her a glum look and said she needed some time on her own.

'Is she well? I mean is her MS playing up?' she asked. 'I can't imagine what it must be like for her living with a chronic condition like that, especially one she knows will get worse over time.'

He looked up again sullenly. 'She's fine. I meant what I said, she needs to spend some time on her own.'

'Have you had words, Juan Marco? I mean have you and your mother had a disagreement or something? It's OK, people have disagreements sometimes. Are you feeling unsettled here, that maybe it's time to go back to Spain? Or is your mother wanting to go home?'

'No!' he said, looking up slightly distressed. 'It's nothing like that. I'm enjoying being here and learning, it's great. It's just…' He stopped and his head dropped again.

Mary gave a half-smile. 'I tell you what, why don't I grab a couple of glasses and a bottle of wine and we can talk for a bit before dessert. Would that help?' she said rising from her chair. He looked sullenly at her again but she was already on her way to the wine rack. She opened the bottle and started to walk towards the table with both glasses filled, then stopped halfway, and giving him an impish smile said: 'Now, shall I leave the bottle over there, or…' He smiled at her and she said, 'That's better. Now, why don't you tell me what's on your mind? It can often help to share a problem, especially with someone who isn't part of the family and doesn't take sides.'

He half-smiled. They both took a sip of wine and he began. 'You know as a child you always trust your parents totally. They look after you, they clothe you, feed you, take you places where you need to be. They are your world and you believe in them one hundred per cent.' She nodded. 'Then you get older, start to think about your own life away from them a bit more, start to form your own opinions instead of always accepting theirs.' Mary nodded again and took another sip of wine. 'Then you reach an age when the questions you ask or things you talk about are more grown-up. It doesn't happen overnight, it's gradual, but if there's anything you feel they've held back on, you want to know more?'

Mary nodded again and as he took a drink, she thought of the other night at dinner with them both, when Maria had appeared slightly evasive. The thing that had stuck in her mind was the *Notting Hill* year. Anybody who was that much of a fan would have known when the film came out, and afterwards she had noticed what Maria was saying about her time in England didn't seem to quite match up with what she had previously told Juan Marco. They had drunk a fair amount of wine, so she figured maybe her mind had got fuzzy so hadn't dwelt on it. But she had made the connection herself straight away about the film. If Juan Marco was eighteen, and *Notting Hill* had come out in 1999 and Maria had been in England then, he was probably conceived in England. 'Go on,' she said to Juan Marco, taking another sip.

'Well, I've never known anything about my father,' he said, 'and to be honest, I never wanted to know. My mother said he abandoned her when she became pregnant and that's it. I always assumed they were together in Spain and then he ran off when he found out she was expecting, like some men do, and… well, then I came along. But the other night, you know when you were talking about the *Notting Hill* film—'

'The date, I know,' said Mary nodding as she cut him off. 'I picked up on that too. The year before you were born. You hadn't realised.'

'No,' he replied. 'I hadn't even thought to check when the film came out. All I remember is every time it comes on the TV she gets all excited, says it's her favourite film and that she was in England when it came out. I never even thought about it.' He took another sip.

'So you asked your mum about it yesterday?' guessed Mary, taking another drink.

'Yes and she clammed up on me. Won't tell me anything. Just told me to mind my own business. I mean, I don't want to hurt her and I respect her so much, and if the relationship with my father was hurtful or painful or the circumstances were… I don't know… even worse, then I would understand that.' Mary looked at him, impressed with his emotional maturity and compassion. 'But I just want to know who he was, where he came from, how they met, that's all. If any of it is, you know, really bad then she can leave that part out, but I'm eighteen now and I want to know who he was.'

Mary smiled at him sympathetically. 'Yes, as we grow up we have a different relationship with our parents, don't we? Maybe it's different when they get really old and they look less than themselves, but it takes a long time to reach that point. But I understand how you feel and, in your position, I'd feel the same. The time when you start asking questions is generally the time when you should be told the truth I'd say. That is if the questions are asked in the right way, and the parent feels like you're old enough to understand the information. Of course, you're right as well about the circumstances. I hope there is nothing to fear there because it would make it a lot more difficult for your mother to talk about; you would have to tread very carefully and be gentle and patient with her.' He nodded back at her. 'Do you have any concerns about that?'

'No, I only know what I told you, but she has never got angry when saying she was abandoned, maybe just a feeling that she was better off without him,' he answered.

'Let's hope so,' said Mary. 'And now for dessert if you're ready? Tarta de manzana I think you call it – apple pie?'

He smiled back. 'Yes. I mean *si. Gracias.*'

Mary cut the slices of pie and he chose ice cream to go with it. She pointed to the wine bottle with a questioning look before bringing the dishes over and, as he laughed, she went back for it.

'So what's your plan now?' she asked.

'I don't know. I asked her if we could talk again when we got home, but she told me it was enough. Being shut out isn't good, it's making me resent her and I don't like that feeling. She's my mother and I love her, but she has to recognise that I'm a man now.'

Mary smiled. 'Yes, you are, and a very sensitive one too.' She slid her hand across the table to lay on top of his and squeezed gently. Their eyes locked, a little too long for both of them. She looked down, blushing, and removed it. 'You've made a real impact on the farm. We're very grateful to you and if we could afford to pay you then we would. You've more than covered the costs of having you here, far and away, and I'd like you to stay for the full six weeks, if you want to.' She looked up at him again tenderly. His eyes were warm and bright, and she felt his mood lifting.

'Of course, I'd like that too.'

'OK, then how about I try and have a little word with your mother? I'll be gentle and try not to upset her, just have a woman-to-woman chat with her, tell her I've noticed you've started looking unhappy, and ask if there's anything I can do to help. If she doesn't react badly, I'll say you and I have had a little talk and maybe she needs to realise that you're older now, and your questions are natural, and she needs to trust you. If I get any bad reactions then I'll back off, but I'll be as subtle as I can. What do you think?'

Juan Marco smiled warmly. 'That would make me feel so much better, thank you. I don't know what more I can do and I don't want this eating away at me.' He stood up smiling, and she took that as a sign that he wanted to thank her. She leant over as she rose, their arms closing around each other's necks, their faces touching. She held the embrace longer than she might have, his smooth cheek against hers, enjoying his scent – half-man, half-aftershave, as she felt her breathing shorten and pulse quicken. As they released from each other she felt slightly giddy and put her hand on the table.

'I'll go and ring my mother now, if that's all right,' Juan Marco said brightly. She nodded.

'Do. I'll clean up the dishes.' When she reached the worktop, she put the dishes down and turned to make sure he'd left the dining area. Then she ran her fingers through her hair and said quietly: 'Pull yourself together, Mary!'

Chapter 10

Missile Launch

Mary decided not to talk to Maria for a day or two, and advised Juan Marco not to bring the subject up with his mother again. When George commented that he'd noticed Juan Marco's mood had brightened and asked whether it was a result of Maria's health improving, she replied she thought that she was better, and he had appreciated her interest when she spoke with him about it. 'Better left to women,' was George's casual response.

The next day, she checked with Juan Marco if it was still OK to talk to his mother, and he confirmed he'd stayed away from the subject and she was back to normal with him. So Mary decided to call her and check if it was OK to visit.

'Hello Maria, it's Mary. Are you OK?' There was a short silence, then Maria replied she was fine and was there anything wrong at the farm?

'No, everything's fine. I just thought I'd come over and see you for a chat this afternoon, just to give you a bit of company? Maybe we could go out for tea or coffee?'

Again there was a moment's delay before Maria replied. 'No you don't need to do that. I'm well and enjoying the peacefulness looking at the gardens from the lounge and doing some reading.'

'It's OK, it's no trouble at all. I can give you an update on Juan Marco's progress, and it would be nice to see you again after dinner the other night,' continued Mary. 'Is four o'clock OK?'

'No please, you don't need to,' resisted Maria.

Mary took the bull by the horns and said confidently: 'It'll be my pleasure. I'll see you around four.' She hoped Maria's reticence wasn't an omen.

That afternoon she went into the lounge at the guesthouse and found Maria, who initially rose as if she was about to tell her to go away, but her manners intervened and she sat down again, still unsettled to Mary's eyes.

Mary tried to make polite conversation but it wasn't easy, and she began to see Juan Marco's problem. If Maria did open up, she seemed to be the type of person who only did it on her terms. She would have to tread carefully.

'He really is a pleasure to have around,' continued Mary. 'He was a bit quiet a couple of days ago and seemed a bit down, although his mood has brightened now. I wondered if perhaps he was getting homesick.'

Maria said nothing initially, but to remove the awkward silence replied: 'No, I think he's fine and enjoying it here.'

'He's at a difficult age, isn't he? Half boy, half man, lots of questions no doubt, some of which are different to when he was younger. But it's obvious how close you two are,' said Mary with a smile.

Again there was a look of distrust from Maria, eyes staring back that said: 'Keep Out – No Trespassers!' Mary inwardly frowned, the risk of offence getting higher.

'Is he still in contact with his father?' she asked.

Maria's eyes hardened as she replied: 'I don't think that is any of your concern. My relationship with my son is very close and we don't need anyone else.'

'No that's fine, I'm sorry I didn't mean to pry. It's just that Henry didn't say anything about a father when he made the arrangements, so I just thought I'd ask,' said Mary, feigning innocence.

Maria's reaction was immediate, as her eyes widened and the colour of her cheeks deepened as she stared harshly back. 'It's none of your business and Henry doesn't know anything about his father. Why would he? Thank you for coming to see me but I'm sure you must be busy at your farm, and I want to go back to my room.' With that she rose from her chair and stalked stiffly to the door.

Mary stayed seated for a few seconds and then called out: 'Goodbye, sorry if I intruded!' as the door closed firmly.

As she drove back to the farm, she thought about how she was going to tell Juan Marco she couldn't help with his hopes. He'd be crushed and she didn't want to hurt him. Perhaps it would have been better if she hadn't interfered, Maria was a stubborn woman! It was time to confide in George before deciding how to proceed.

They were in bed when she brought the subject up.

'What's the matter?' said George, giving up trying to read his book due to Mary's long face.

'Oh it's just Juan Marco, or rather, his mother. You know he was a bit down for a couple of days? Well I spoke to him and it turns out he doesn't know who his father was. He says it never bothered him before, but the things Maria was saying over dinner the other night were inconsistent with some of the stuff she'd told him before, and it got him thinking about his father. But when he spoke to her and started asking questions, she basically clammed up and told him to mind his own business. That's what was bothering him. He figures if she won't tell him now then she's not likely to.'

'Humph. That seems a little far-fetched. Maybe she's not ready to tell him yet, but he shouldn't just think that it's always going to be that way. He's still only eighteen,' replied George. 'There's plenty of time.'

'Maybe... but I think he may have a point. I offered to have a little woman-to-woman chat with her, nothing heavy, you know, just it might help with another female gently feeling around the subject. I kept it roundabout and tried to suggest he's growing up now and maybe his questions were legitimate... well not that explicit, just natural for a young man of that age to start showing more interest.'

George looked at her. 'Didn't you think you were best off keeping out of it? I bet that went down like a lead balloon.'

'Well yes, possibly, but I saw how unhappy he was. You know he and his mother are really close, and the way he described it this is the first time they've ever had a fight... so I thought offering to speak to his mother in a sort of woman-to-woman way might help lighten his load. That's why he perked up – he thought that me offering to help might work.'

'And it didn't I guess by your long face?' replied George.

'No. I had good intentions but boy was she frosty! I mean I was as gentle as I could be, and she really closed the shutters and told me to butt out. And then when I mentioned Henry's name, well her face was like thunder!'

'What did you mention his name for?' asked George, confused. 'I thought we were supposed to leave his name out of it.'

'Well, yes, with Juan Marco for sure. But I just had a random thought that when Henry made the arrangements, he never mentioned a father. So I thought that I could use that angle as a backdoor route into her telling me a bit more, you know, assuming Henry would know about Juan Marco's domestic arrangements in Spain, but hadn't passed anything on to us. I was just playing the innocent.'

'I see,' replied George. 'That didn't work then. I think I would have left his name out of it. She's never brought his name up, although maybe she wouldn't with all the cloak and dagger stuff about Henry's involvement. So, what are you going to do now?'

'Hmm, that's the dilemma. We both like him and I see his position and owe him a response, if only to warn him that his mother might be a bit short with him, especially if she thinks he put me up to it. But obviously he's going to be disappointed, and neither of us wants him to go back to being sulky and unhappy, do we? The way he spoke it was like this is the first time his mother hasn't been honest with him.'

'All you can do is tell him you tried,' replied George. 'Maybe you shouldn't have got involved, even if it was for the right reasons. It's his problem ultimately, and it's between him and her. If it's the first time that he's argued with his mother then he'd better get used to it, because it won't be the last.'

'No, suppose not. I'll tell him I tried tomorrow and try to keep it light. But she's a frosty one, you know, that mother of his,' she said turning to look at George. 'He thinks she's keeping stuff from him about her time in England. Don't you think it's odd that she never mentioned to us over dinner she'd spent some time here when she was younger, until pushed? And then did you see the look on her face when he jumped in a couple of times to pick her up on what she said? And then there's *Notting Hill* you know, the film. She was awkward about the date of it and any real fan would know the year. I think that's the problem. If she was here in 1999 and Juan Marco was born in 2000, then she probably met his father here, so he could be English. Whatever Juan Marco knew, I think he assumed his father was Spanish and that he was conceived over there.'

'Bloody hell, you've got an imagination haven't you!' responded George. 'She's entitled to have had a past and not to go around telling everyone, even her own son! People get confused over dates and stuff, I didn't spot anything wrong. Maybe she did meet his father over here and had a one-night-stand. Perhaps she doesn't feel like owning up to it.'

Mary grinned. 'Woman's intuition… she's hiding something!'

George snorted. 'Well, you had better say what you've got to say to him and then stay out of it. Latin women can be fiery. I remember a Spanish maid we had at Hillingstone years ago, she was serious and broody, very quiet, and I wasn't keen on her at all. I was only young and kept my distance. Apparently, there was some fuss with Henry and she was made to leave quickly and there were tears. She was called Maria I think,' he said offhandedly.

Mary felt a chill had turned her to stone. 'What?' she said, stunned, looking straight at George's face.

'Oh for God's sake, not this Maria,' he blurted. 'Honestly, what planet are you on? This was years ago, I was just a child, maybe ten or eleven. I don't think I was ever told the full story, I just remember Anna telling me that Henry had caught her being naughty or something, or she'd caught him being naughty. Anyway, I think she tried to blame it on Henry and my parents weren't having any of that, and she got the sack. It's not this Maria – crikey, this girl was only young, maybe mid-twenties? Henry would have been... sixteen-ish, I guess. I mean he could be pretty wild, but that would make her about forty-five now, and this Maria, I mean Juan Marco's mother, must be about fifty-five or maybe sixty? Even if life's been unkind to her and with her illness, it's a bit of a leap to put two and two together and make four! Besides, I don't recognise anything about her. Surely there'd be something that I'd recognise after all this time, her eyes or something?'

Mary stared back at him. 'Oh for God's sake, your imagination!' he gasped. 'I think it's time to go to sleep. Please, please, don't dream about this and tell me all over breakfast!' he said, turning onto his side facing away from her. Mary continued staring at his back.

She calmed her breathing and gently touched his back. 'All right, I'm sorry,' she said quietly. 'Goodnight then.'

As Mary turned away from George, her eyes were wide-open as her face hit the pillow. She knew that at some point tonight sleep would come, but there was no fear of dreams – all her thoughts would be while she was conscious. Her mind was racing – Henry, Maria, Juan Marco... something happened at Hillingstone... Maria's hardness... keep Henry's name out of Juan Marco's trip... his father might be English... The dots were being joined at lightning speed.

The following morning Mary awoke suddenly, and her mind kicked straight back to last night's conversation. She fizzed with energy to find the truth as quickly as possible. Her options were either to tackle Henry head-on or speak to Anna, to see what she knew. Of the two, the second seemed more sensible. More homework was needed before plunging into anything with Henry, who she didn't have much of a relationship with. Mary texted Anna after George had gone out into the fields.

Mary: *Hi Anna, how's things?*

Anna: *All good thanks. In Singapore doing due diligence on another possible takeover! All good with you?*

Mary: *Yes, we're fine. I just wanted to ask if you remembered anything about a Spanish maid that worked at Hillingstone about twenty years ago. George started telling me a story last night, and just as it was getting interesting he ran out of detail! You know what he's like. Do you know the rest of the story?*

Anna: *Not sure I do. It was a long time ago. Why did he mention it?*

Mary: *Oh just pillow talk. He said something about the girl being sacked because she was up to something or other and Henry caught her, or the other way around. He said he was very young and wasn't told much, but you told him what there was to tell? I think he thought there might have been something going on between them, but said he was too young to understand. How sweet! I just wondered if you had the juicy bits to tell! She was called Maria apparently.*

Anna: *I don't recall the circumstances. I wasn't that old myself.*

Mary realised she wasn't getting anywhere and that she'd have to be more direct.

Mary: *Did you know we've got a Spanish boy doing work experience with us for a few weeks, arranged by Henry?*

There was no response from Anna for ten minutes, who was now becoming alarmed at Mary's questions. Did she lie and say she knew nothing about it, or admit that Henry had discussed it with her? How much did George and Mary know about the boy's background? She decided to tread carefully, but not lie to Mary over a situation that was of Henry's making.

Anna: *I think Henry mentioned it in passing, but I didn't get the impression that it would be this soon.*

Mary: *Well, he's here, and a very nice young man he is! Polite, charming and hard-working too. The mother I'm not so sure about! She's here chaperoning him and can be a bit caustic! He had a bit of an argument with her and was down for a couple of days – I think she's hiding something and he had got wind of it.*

Anna: *OK. Glad he's being useful to you.*

Mary's sense of frustration was growing, but the next message she received from Anna was to say she was busy and had a conference call, so had to go. Her instinct was Anna knew more, and it was suspicious that Henry had spoken to her about Juan Marco's work experience. She'd text Anna later and just have to be blunter, and in the meantime she'd avoid Juan Marco.

In the afternoon, she told George she was going shopping and having picked up a few bits, went to a café next to the supermarket. She texted Anna to ask when she would be free, but waited for twenty minutes with no reply. It was night-time in Singapore but she expected Anna would still be up, so rang her. It went to voicemail so she left a message: *'Hi Anna, it's me again. Look, I don't want to put you in a spot, but I need to settle a burning question. I just need a yes, no or don't know. I'm not bothered about the boy, but you know George and Henry don't get on and I just want to be able to manage the situation if it goes off with a bang. Call me please.'*

In Singapore it was half past ten at night, and Anna was still up but they had been entertaining friends, hence her phone went to voicemail. She listened to Mary's message and thought through her options. She didn't see why she needed to get involved in this situation; Henry was the culprit and if he had chosen to leave out certain details when making the arrangements for the trip, then that was between him and George. If the boy suspected that something was up and was pushing for an answer, then let him take it out on his mother. Yet again, when it came to her brothers making and sorting out problems, it seemed to Anna she was always expected to do the heavy lifting, even though she had very little to do with their day-to-day lives. Her decision was clear – she wasn't going to get involved and Mary needed to back off. The truth would probably never come out anyway. So, she deleted the voicemail message and went to bed.

The lack of response left Mary annoyed and frustrated, but her conclusion was the same as Anna's – drop the subject and hope it would go away. Her plan was blown out of the water later that evening.

After dinner, George had driven Juan Marco to his mother's guesthouse, but within an hour Juan Marco was back, his presence announced by a slamming of the back door. They heard him stomp into his bedroom and slam that door too, followed by draws opening and shutting loudly, and what sounded like swearing in Spanish. George and Mary were watching television and looked at each other.

'What on earth is he up to?' asked George rising from the sofa.

'I'll go,' said Mary. 'Sounds like he's mad about something. If it's to do with him and his mother, I'd better deal with it. If it's something else, I'll call you.'

'I told you to stay out of it,' responded George. 'I really hope you haven't created a rumpus!' Mary pulled a face as she left the room. When she got to Juan Marco's door she could hear him crying and talking angrily to himself. She knocked gently and asked if he was all right.

'Go away, just go away! You've made it worse!' came the response.

'Can I come in?' asked Mary tentatively.

'Go away, I said. I'm not leaving until she tells me the truth!' he shouted.

'What do you mean leaving? Juan Marco, please let me come in and tell me what's happened.' The door flew open and he stood there, his face red with misery and bloodshot eyes.

'She says we've got to leave tomorrow! She's sick of this place and wishes we'd never come! She blamed me for speaking to you about who my father is, and says I've been disloyal to her by going behind her back! Well I'm not leaving and I'm fed up with being lied to! I asked who my father is and she screamed at me to get back here and pack my bags! Well, I'm not going, I like it here and I'm not done, she can go back alone if she wants, but I'm not going anywhere until she tells me!'

George's face appeared at the door but before he could speak, Mary said firmly: 'Leave it to me. I'm dealing with it. Right now he needs understanding and support; I mean it, go back to the lounge.' She spoke so sternly that George turned around and stalked off. Mary sat on the bed next to Juan Marco and put her hand on his knee: 'Listen, Juan Marco. Nobody can force you to do anything you don't want to, do you understand? We're happy for you to stay but it's not doing you any good to get worked up like this, OK? You need to calm down and try and get a good night's sleep, and then we'll talk first thing in the morning when your head is clearer. It's late now and nothing is going to get resolved tonight. I promise you things like this are better resolved on a new day when everyone has calmed down a bit. Now, I suggest you shower and I'll leave a glass of brandy by your bed for when you come back in. Sip it slowly and it will help you sleep. Do you understand?'

He listened, raised his puffy face and slowly nodded. 'Right, OK, try not to dwell on it tonight, just focus on tomorrow being a new day with a new start. OK?' she added. He nodded and Mary left the room. As she walked back to the lounge she knew that a storm was brewing, but George had to be kept out of it. If her suspicions were right he would go through the roof.

She gave George a brief summary but said she would take charge of it in the morning, and he should focus on the farm.

At half past eleven the phone rang and George answered, fearing bad news at this time of night. A lady from Maria's guesthouse asked to speak to Juan Marco. He asked Mary if it was OK to disturb him and she went to check, but as he was asleep, suggested that he phone them back in the morning, unless it was urgent. Mary waited next to George as he took the message from the caller and then put the phone down. He looked seriously at her: 'I think you'd better wake him. His mother's fallen down the stairs at the guesthouse, she's in a lot of pain. They've called an ambulance.'

Mary's mouth dropped open and she muttered: 'Oh God!' before turning and heading to Juan Marco's bedroom. She gently woke him and told him about the call, and that George would take him to the guesthouse straight away to meet the ambulance. He was shocked but dressed hurriedly, and with an ashen face ran out to George's waiting Land Rover. When they arrived at the guesthouse, the paramedics were lifting Maria onto a stretcher and she was crying in pain. Juan Marco went to her side as they carried her into the ambulance, and told them who he was. The first paramedic told him they suspected she had broken her hip, and did he want to accompany her in the ambulance? After a quick discussion with George, he climbed into the ambulance and George returned to the farm to pick up Mary, so they could follow in the car.

The hospital confirmed her broken hip after an X-ray, and as Juan Marco wanted to stay overnight, George and Mary drove back home. They were shocked by the amount of pain she'd been in, and any thoughts about their family argument were pushed to the back of their minds.

The following morning Juan Marco called and told them Maria needed a hip replacement, and that surgery would be carried out the following day. They planned to keep her in for ten to fourteen days afterwards, but they would also need to run tests on the state of her MS which, if it had deteriorated, might lead to a change to her medication. He was concerned about being able to visit her and stay on' at the farm, but longer-term prospects for recuperation and her future ability to work, together with his own need to earn money while Maria was out of action, all clouded his mind. Maria's funds for the trip had reduced by more than expected, which was another worry.

George and Mary discussed the options and agreed that he could stay on at the farm, but they couldn't and didn't want to pay him wages. Henry had stated that Juan Marco's stay wouldn't cost them anything other than board and lodging, so anything further would have to come from him. George was clear: 'I don't see that we have any option. He can't stay here on any other basis, and while his mother recovers until she is fit to fly, he will either have to find employment in this area, rely on his mother or on Henry. We can't pay for any accommodation elsewhere, and I don't know how her funds are as they were only here for another two weeks anyway. Perhaps she's running low. Maybe he could find supported temporary accommodation – there are probably charities linked to the hospital that help with that sort of thing. We can research that for him, but as for doing anything more, I think that's it. At the end of the day, Henry organised the trip and we should contact him and let him take this over. It's his responsibility.'

Mary knew he was right, although she doubted that Henry would feel responsible, but she agreed to contact him anyway to avoid George speaking to him directly. She called Spain that afternoon, hoping that Henry would be somewhere between the previous day's hangover and the next drink, and might therefore be semi-sober. There was no reply so she left a voicemail message, then thought better of expecting a call back, and rang him again thirty minutes later.

He answered in a laconic tone, clearly feeling the effects of the previous night's intake. 'Helloo, Henry speaking.'

'Hello Henry, it's Mary, George's wife.'

'Really? You don't normally phone me. What can I do you for?'

'There's a problem with Juan Marco, well more specifically his mother. She's had a fall and been taken to hospital. It's quite bad unfortunately and she'll need a new hip, plus further investigations into her MS. It's a shame because he was doing really well here, but he's going to be short of money. As you know, our funds are limited, and you made the arrangements for him to stay on the basis that it wouldn't cost us anything. We have no complaints, because he has worked his socks off and shown real interest in the farm, but he needs supporting now and we can't help with that, other than helping him to actually find somewhere. We think his mother is running out of funds, so financially he's in a difficult place. We need to ask for your help in looking after him.'

'Hold on a moment,' said Henry. 'I'm in Spain and you're in England, so why is it my problem? I helped with setting up his work experience sure, but what happens in England is really not my problem, is it?'

'Henry, the circumstances are exceptional and you made it clear that his visit wasn't going to cost us anything, and I'm sure at one point you said you might give him an allowance as well. You also said that if there was a real problem we could contact you, and that's what we're doing. We have real affection for him and want to help him, but this is way out of our league. I'm just asking you to pick it up, as you said you would, if there was a real problem. We're happy to help him find some local accommodation close to where his mother is, but we can't pay for it, you know that.'

'Look, Mary, I'm sorry for the situation and all that, but I'm in Spain and there's nothing I can do. I don't have huge wedges of cash just lying about. My gift to him was to arrange the trip and you can't hold me to anything else. He can't have long to go anyway!'

'Oh, Henry let me make this clear! Maria is in a bad way and he needs to be close to her, and have something to live on, and she may need somewhere to go to recover temporarily before she goes back to Spain. We're not asking you to cover her medical bills, that's all through the NHS, but she may take weeks to recover from this operation and then travel back to Spain. For that period, Juan Marco needs to live close to her and you're his... you know, sponsor, so we need you to step in and manage the situation.'

'Mary, this situation needs to be handled on the ground, not from here. I'm sure George can deal with it. Just get him to phone Mother and I'm sure she'll stump up some cash. It's no good talking to me about money, all I know is I'm always short of the stuff. Now look, I really must go and there's no need to keep me in the loop on this, there really isn't... bye then.'

The line went dead and Mary's pulse quickened, infuriated by Henry trying to wash his hands of the situation. She thought about getting George to ring him. It would end up in an argument, though, and Henry wouldn't change his approach, especially for George. There was only one option, it was high risk but it was her only card. She rang Henry's number again.

'Now look here Mary, I've said—'

She cut him off. 'No, you look here, Henry. You haven't satisfied your responsibilities. Juan Marco is your responsibility and he needs *your* help.

You don't get to make one gesture and then walk away.'

'What the hell are you going on about? He's in England under your care so, actually, he's your responsibility, so sort it. I'm—'

She jumped in again. 'Listen, Henry, the next call will be from George, and I'm much easier to deal with, trust me. If he has to deal with you then I'll make sure he knows the *full* story beforehand, do you understand? The full story!'

'What are you going on about you funny woman... your mind is playing tricks on you. What full story? You're mad, quite mad!'

'Oh, Henry, don't be naïve.' Mary hesitated, her finger poised on the trigger. It was now or never. 'Don't you think I've worked out what's going on? Your supposed act of generosity to an almost stranger. No contact to be made with you while he's here. Don't let Juan Marco find out that you're behind his trip. You staying in Spain while he's here, instead of taking an interest in his progress and visiting him. Maria, the woman you had a fling with at Hillingstone eighteen years ago, who then got sacked, and hey presto, guess who's just turned eighteen...' Mary was breathless now, and fell into silence as she heard herself blurting out her suspicions.

The phone was silent for a few seconds, confirmation of what she suspected, surely.

'What?' shouted Henry back. 'I had a fling with someone with the same name as his mother and, according to you, that makes you Sherlock Holmes? You're mad! Where did George dig you up from, your mind's gone!'

Mary jumped straight back at him, fearing he'd end the call again. 'Your act's pathetic! I can see right through you, he's your son and you don't want to face it! If I'm wrong, then deny it, go on, deny it! But you'd be surprised what Maria let slip when she was here!'

This was another bluff, but Mary was riled and determined to keep pushing the knife in.

'She wouldn't admit anything of the sort,' snorted Henry. 'She wouldn't own to knowing me if she could help it, not ever! You're guessing, sweetheart, and making a right royal hash of it! Stop wasting my time!' The line went dead again.

Mary knew she would have to tell George now and hope that he could persuade or threaten Henry with exposure, if necessary. He'd be livid when he found out they had been used to wet-nurse Henry's own son.

She waited until dinner was on the table, and as they ate she started

93

edgily to draw the picture: she'd been suspicious of Henry ever since George had told her of the Spanish maid at Hillingstone; Anna hadn't wanted to tell her anything although she could tell she was holding back, and had admitted she'd known of Henry's plan to arrange Juan Marco's trip before they did; finally she recounted the conversations with Henry when he didn't deny her suspicions. As expected, George was furious.

'Why the hell didn't you tell me as soon as you knew?' he raged.

'Because I needed to check whether it was just my suspicious mind, or whether there was really something to it! I knew what this would do to you if I was right, so I tried to be sure by checking with Anna and then confronting Henry! I was trying to protect you!' pleaded Mary.

'That bastard's going to get what's coming to him,' shouted George. 'I'm not babysitting his illegitimate child, I want him out of here! If he doesn't take responsibility I'll tell our parents what he's been up to, and insist they cut him off without a penny! And, Anna, she bloody knew and decided not to tell us! Whose effing side is she on? She'll get a bloody rocket, but not until I've dealt with that bastard!'

George flew off his chair and went for his mobile on the sideboard, leaving Mary frozen at the table. He dialled Henry but got no reply and threw his phone on the floor. Mary looked up at him. 'Please sit down and finish your dinner! You know what he's like in the evenings, he probably won't even pick up. Please, at least get the rest of this in your stomach.'

George strode up and down and round the table, unable to curb his temper, but after several tours he came to a stop and grabbed the back of his chair, paralysed at his inability to do anything. Then he picked his phone up and took it back to his chair. He sat and gulped down his food as fast as he could. As soon as he finished he stomped off with his phone and tried Henry again, with no success. Mary knew she was powerless and just had to let him get on with it, but part of her thoughts were reserved for Juan Marco, the innocent victim in all this.

George came into the lounge after Mary had cleared up the kitchen. He slumped down on the sofa, less angry but frustrated. He said he would keep ringing Henry until he went to bed, and left the room frequently to try again. At about 10.45 p.m., Mary suddenly heard his raised voice in the kitchen: 'Henry you absolute devious bastard! How dare you foist your illegitimate child on to us so we can provide him with an education which is your responsibility! He's not staying here any more and I'm throwing him out! Even by your selfish standards you're scraping the barrel. He's your problem so sort it. Find him somewhere!'

Henry was drunk as normal, but always ready to deliver a performance. 'Hallo, George, how are you? Very nice to hear your voice. What was that? How am I? Oh, I'm very well, thank you very much for asking.'

'This isn't some sort of joke, you cretin! This is typical of you, you don't change! Deal with it, or I'm telling Mother and Father what a little shit you've been! I'm sure they'll be delighted to hear about your bastard child from the Spanish maid. "Oh, you know Mother, that one that you fired because you took Henry's side against her's. Yes, the one that he humped and got pregnant and you believed him, again."'

'Oh please, George, don't be such a drama queen! The little tart got what she deserved, and you really think our parents are going to give two hoots about her, or the fact that I have an unofficial offshoot of the family? Grow up, it's a storm in a teacup. Who knows, maybe they'd even like to meet him!'

'You don't live in the real world Henry, you're a disgrace and—'

Henry cut him short. 'Don't think that I don't know what this is really about, George,' he teased. 'You're intimidated that I've extended the family bloodline. What, are you bothered that he might take your place in the family tree, eh? You've always expected that I'll roll over and die sometime and guess who inherits the title then? That's right, isn't it Georgie boy? You think he stands a chance of knocking you out of line to be the next Viscount Belvedere? Well keep that thought in your mind, because you know what, I might just marry her and make him legit. Now do me a favour and fuck off!'

The line went dead and George exploded into the lounge, screaming at Mary how he couldn't believe Henry's jibe that all he cared about was who came next after him in the family tree. He ranted for a couple of minutes, before Mary reminded him that Juan Marco needed help and what was going to happen to him now?

'I don't give a shit. But what I am going to do is phone Mother tomorrow, and tell her that there are two bastards in this family, not one!'

Chapter 11

Deeper and Deeper

Mary didn't get much sleep that night, worrying about how she was going to break the news to Juan Marco that he had to leave the farm. She had to give him a reason to leave immediately without George being involved, otherwise he'd learn the full ugly story which would crush him just when he needed to be at his strongest. It might be that Maria had already paid for her accommodation at the guesthouse for the full period, and Juan Marco could move into her room, but after that, there were so many potential problems – where he went next; the state of Maria's finances; how long she would be in hospital; the time she needed to recuperate before returning home; where she would go for the recuperation. Longer term, would she still be able to work when she returned to Spain and how would they manage then? Her mind was flooded with worries but the first priority was to deal with the here and now.

She expected Juan Marco would call with an update after surgery and must need to come back for a shower and change of clothes. She waited for him to ring and packed up his things to take them to the hospital, from where she could drive him to the guesthouse, assuming it was all paid-up. She double-checked with the guesthouse, who confirmed Maria had pre-paid the room, so this was the safest option. Juan Marco called at half past three and told her the surgery was complete, and could she collect him so he could freshen up, before returning to the hospital for when Maria came out of the anaesthetic. Mary agreed and as she had already packed his things, set off with the intention of telling him the new plan on the journey home.

As they headed out of Lincoln she began: 'Look, I've been doing some thinking and I think the easiest option for you is to stay at the guesthouse, at least until the end of the booking your mother made. While there's no problem with you staying at the farm, we have to be practical and you know how much time we have to devote to it, which means taking time out every day to get you to and from the hospital isn't really an option. The guesthouse is on a bus route to the hospital and you can come and go as you please that way. While we'll be sorry to lose you from the farm, your mind is going to be elsewhere for a while. I hope you don't mind but to save time, I've packed your things into your case and it's in the back.'

Juan Marco looked surprised. 'But I thought I could stay with you, that way I could still help on the farm when I wasn't at the hospital? I could walk to the guesthouse to catch the bus, that would work, wouldn't it? Besides, I'll miss the farm and the teaching and the help with my English.'

Mary gave a brief smile. 'I think it's better this way. We'd love to do more but you've seen the pressure we're under, and we need to focus on that, and you'll still get to practice your English at the guesthouse anyway. It'll be fine, and I'll come and see you in the evening sometimes to make sure you're getting on all right. Right now, your priority should be your mother. There'll be other decisions for you and her to make once she comes out of hospital, so there'll be a lot of change to manage going forward.'

Juan Marco sank into silence as they drove out of the city, but spoke quietly again a few minutes later: 'I'm worried about what will happen to her when the hospital says it's time for her to leave. I don't know whether she will be fit enough to fly back home straightaway, or whether she will have to go somewhere else to recover. I understand you have some smaller hospitals where they have recovery beds, but what if there are no beds available? I also have only limited savings and while my mother hasn't run out of money yet, she won't be able to afford a private care home at the figures they gave me at the hospital.'

Mary turned and gave him an uncommitted smile. 'Don't worry about those things right now, just focus on your mother feeling better. There are a few days to go to see how she feels and check her progress before anything like that needs to be considered. Just try and relax and deal with problems one at a time, OK?' Juan Marco nodded and said nothing more until he was taking his case out of the car.

'Maybe I can come to dinner with you one night?'

Mary gave him another indifferent smile and said, 'Maybe' as she closed the window and drove off, feeling embarrassed about her tone which must have seemed cool to him, but knowing that protecting him from George and his anger was more important.

Mary left it three more days, before stealing a moment while collecting logs for the fire to call Juan Marco for a progress report. 'She's still in a lot of pain,' he said, 'and moving her leg is difficult because of it. The doctors say they're worried about infection, as the wound is raw and weeping and it's not healing as it should. They don't want to think about moving her out of the ward until she is improving.'

Mary said she was busy for the next two nights but would take him for a meal the following night, which she knew she had no intention of honouring, but for which an excuse could easily be found nearer the time. Over the past few days, George had been threatening to phone his mother and tell all, but Mary had managed to keep a lid on his temper for the time being as Juan Marco was out of their hair and, temporarily at least, he and his mother were being taken care of. She also persuaded George to let the dust lie with Anna, until there was a clearer picture of where Maria and Juan Marco were going to go.

In the meantime, Henry had been waiting in Spain for someone in the family to give him a rollicking. He knew his father wouldn't call. George had already vented his spleen and his mother was a possibility, but the most likely candidate was Anna. Something along the lines of: 'Well, your secret's out now isn't it, well done! Stew in it!' But there had been no phone call, which left him feeling George probably hadn't said anything yet. Henry's mind went back to the decision he'd made when last in England – deal with the family on his terms in future – and he began to wonder if this was an opportunity to take the lead on managing the situation. As well as earning some Brownie points from his parents if he appeared to be showing some responsibility, it would also be a way to rub George and Anna's noses into the dirt. Another appearance in England could also be linked to a show of concern over his father's health, which would be a good PR move, and if the Maria and Juan Marco situation needed steering it might be better if he could recce the ground beforehand. He began to see a chance opening up to take centre stage.

Mary called on Juan Marco at the guesthouse at the end of Maria's first week in hospital. She apologised for not ringing earlier but said she didn't have time for dinner after all. He told her that his mother was still in pain and would be in hospital for another week, at which point they were planning on moving her to a convalescent hospital, although there weren't any beds forecast to be available. Otherwise, they would need him to consider whether she could find a place to stay privately with home care, or they could look at a nursing home, the cost of which might be recovered from the Spanish government, but there could be gaps that would need to be met by the family. The doctors were not willing to issue a fitness to fly certificate for at least another three weeks. Other than empathising with him Mary felt trapped, and obliged to offer to go with him when he met the discharge team.

On her way back to the farm her phone pinged with a new message. As she parked she looked at it and was surprised to see it was from Henry, asking how things were. She replied cautiously that Maria was slowly recovering, but would need a place to stay for recuperation in a few days, to which Henry responded with: *Hmm. I'm back in the UK later this week.* When Mary asked if that was an offer of help there was silence, and when she tried to ring him it went straight to voicemail. Infuriating man!

Henry felt a shiver of delight at the prospect of being at the centre of things again. He booked his flight back to the UK for Thursday, managing to find one credit card that hadn't reached its limit. The following day, he phoned his mother and told her he was coming back to stay for a few days, and smoothly enquired after his father's health.

'There's news,' was all she would say, and they'd tell him more when they saw him. In his mind, a vague plan was starting to come together. The only bit he wasn't entirely sure of was when would be the right time to shock the family with his own news that he had a son!

The day before his flight to England he texted Mary again, asking where Juan Marco was staying. When she asked him why, he told her she had asked him to step in and manage the situation and that was what he was doing. She asked him what his plans were and again got the same response. Suddenly she felt out of the loop and worried for Juan Marco. She tried texting again with no reply, and Henry's phone went straight to voicemail. Then, at ten p.m. her phone rang, and seeing Henry's name come up she quickly took the phone into what had been Juan Marco's bedroom.

'What's going on Henry?' she demanded.

'I'm managing the situation,' said Henry in a smug voice.

'What's that supposed to mean? Stop talking in riddles and tell me what you're up to!'

'Answer me one question,' replied Henry. 'Can you pick me up from Robin Hood Airport tomorrow afternoon at four thirty?'

'What... what are you flying into there for? What's going on Henry?'

'Yes or no?' came back the blunt answer.

'Not until I know what's going on!'

'All will be revealed then, that is, if you're picking me up. Otherwise I'll handle things on my own.'

'For fuck's sake! You're playing games! Don't you realise how difficult this situation is for everyone?' Mary shouted.

'Well let me arrive and make everyone's life easier then; I can either do it with your help or without. It's your choice.'

'Oh God!' moaned Mary, knowing that he had her over a barrel. 'This better be good, whatever it is! I've spent enough time away from the farm trying to help Juan Marco, and I'm running out of excuses!'

'The flight's coming in from Malaga tomorrow. See you... oh, and thanks, Mary,' ended Henry in a velvet voice.

Mary had a meeting in Lincoln with a potential customer for organic root vegetables the next morning, and knew she'd have to lie to George about its length, and then make up an excuse about meeting up with an old college friend for dinner. At least George had two part-time labourers on Thursdays, so her absence wouldn't be felt so much. The following afternoon she met Henry at the airport. He was all cool detachment and civility, asking after George and the farm. Once they cleared the airport approach road, Mary turned to him and asked what he was up to. Henry smiled, told her to calm down and checked that Juan Marco would be at the guesthouse in the evening. When she confirmed he would, Henry said slowly: 'Now, why don't you tell me all that's gone on, right from the beginning. Don't leave anything out. I want to know the full story from the day they arrived here, and then I can think while you talk.'

'Never mind that!' cried Mary. 'What are you planning to do?'

'Well, that all depends on what you tell me. We've got less than an hour, so I suggest you start.'

Mary gave a loud huff, and then started to recount the details of Juan Marco's time at the farm, jumping about to start with but flowing better as she went on. There was so much ground to cover: his help at the farm; what he had learnt; polishing up his English over dinner; their dealings with Maria; the eventful dinner when Mary's suspicions had first been aroused; Juan Marco's frustration at his mother's refusal to tell him about his father; Mary's involvement in trying to help... on and on. Henry broke in occasionally with 'I see', or 'go on' or 'that's interesting', very rarely deviating from greasing Mary's wheels, even when she started laying into him about his phone response when she asked for help, and especially the difficulties he'd caused between her and George. The best response she got from him was a 'sorry about that'.

By the time they reached the guesthouse, Mary realised she'd done all the talking and was no wiser about what Henry planned. 'Don't worry, leave it to me,' said Henry. 'From what you've said, he needs practical help and I've an idea I can assist. There's no need to wait, I'll see if I can get a room here tonight, or I'll get them to refer me to another place if need be. You go off and thank you, Mary, for all your time on this. And I'm sorry for causing trouble between you and George. Bye now!'

Mary watched as Henry strode into the guesthouse, uncomfortable at his apparent confidence and worried that he was up to something. There was no way she was driving away, so turned the car around as if she was leaving and then parked up.

Inside the outer entrance hall, Henry rang the bell and waited for someone to meet him. He asked first if they had a room for the night and found they had one, so took it, planning to ask Mary to pay the bill the next day as he had no money, and didn't want to make contact with his parents, which would lead to all sorts of questions as to why he was in Lincolnshire, and why he wasn't staying with George and Mary. He asked which room number was Juan Marco's, explaining that he was a family member making an unexpected visit, and then went up the stairs hovering outside the door to take in some air, knowing he needed all his bravado and bluff for what was to come. Juan Marco answered his knock and gaped open-mouthed at Henry.

'Hello Juan Marco, I hope you're well. May I come in?'

Juan Marco was frozen to the spot, then noticed Henry looking beyond him into the bedroom. In his mind, the image of the bed, combined with Henry's presence, created a horrific scene. Henry realised his thought process and took one step back. 'Oh, I'm sorry, of course you might prefer we talk elsewhere. Is there a quiet lounge area or a snug where we can go?' He instantly felt foolish using a word like 'snug', which would probably mean absolutely nothing to Juan Marco and, moreover, sounded like a cosy, intimate place, no better an option than a bedroom.

'What are you doing here, what do you want? I want nothing to do with you, I thought my mother made that clear! How did you even know where

I was?'

'There's much to talk about Juan Marco, I believe I have a lot of explaining to do. At this stage, I only ask for your trust that it's in your interest that you listen to me. I can answer a lot of your questions I'm sure, and I hope offer some help with your current problem, your mother's health I mean.'

Juan Marco glared back at him. 'Go away, I don't trust you and my mother hates you. I don't know how you found us but we don't need anything from you.' He stepped backwards and started to close the door, so Henry moved his hand towards the door and took a small step, which Juan Marco met with an angry look.

'Just to start you off,' said Henry, 'I arranged your trip over here with your mother, as a way to apologise for my behaviour towards you in Spain. There's plenty more I think you should be told, but you need to be adult-enough to listen, not just react.'

The words had the desired effect on Juan Marco who protested: 'I am an adult, don't speak to me like that!'

'Then I'm asking you to make a big decision now,' Henry said smoothly, happy that he now had a strategy. 'There's more I will tell you and I think you deserve to know. There are things that I believe a man of your age has the right to know, but we need to be able to discuss those things as men. I will be truthful with you and I can only ask you to listen to me, but if you send me away then I will leave with that knowledge hidden from you.'

'What can you know that I need to hear?' demanded Juan Marco, still holding the door.

Henry gave him his most reassuring smile. 'Wouldn't it be best if we sat down somewhere to discuss that?' He waited for a few seconds and then continued: 'You'll have lots of questions as we go on I'm sure…'

Juan Marco scowled at him. 'Not here, the lounge might be free or we can go in the breakfast room maybe, if I ask.'

Henry took two steps back and gestured for Juan Marco to lead the way. The lounge was occupied by a couple of guests and members of the owner's family, but when Juan Marco asked if they could use the breakfast room he was given the OK, and he led the way down the hallway towards the front door and into the room.

'OK, let's begin,' said Henry, after they both sat. 'I've told you I arranged your visit here with your mother. George is my brother. I knew that he would appreciate your help and that you could learn from the experience, and Mary has given me a full account of your progress and they are both delighted with your positive attitude, desire to learn, manners, and your all-round helpfulness. They've been keeping me updated occasionally, but you'll understand that I needed to keep out of sight, which was one of the terms your mother set me. It was really important that you benefited as much as possible from this experience, I owed you that.'

Juan Marco grimaced. 'So if that is all, then why are you here now? You've done your bit and that's it.'

'Well, Mary has informed me about your mother's injury, and what happens from here must seem complicated to understand and a little daunting. The reason for me coming here is to make a proposal to you that would give your mother a comfortable environment in which to make a recovery, but would also offer you the chance to continue your education here, building on what you have already learnt about farming. George and I come from a farming family, but on a much larger scale than what he runs in Lincolnshire. It might be possible for your mother and you to stay at that much larger farm together, while she recovers. What do you think about that possibility? I know it's a shock and I'm happy for you to take a couple of days to think about it and, of course, I'll answer as many questions as you like.'

'Why would we want anything more from you, and why would you make this offer when you know my mother doesn't like you?' asked Juan Marco. 'You arranged a work experience trip and that's it, you don't need to offer anything more. We don't want to owe you anything. All we want is for my mother to get well soon, and then we will return to Spain and never see you again.'

Henry sat silently for a few seconds then said: 'You know it may be a while before your mother recovers, and she may have more time to spend in hospital or in a nursing home. There's a limit to what you can expect your government to pay for. I don't know all the rules, but you need to think of your own resources and how long they will last.'

'This isn't about money!' Juan Marco said, fiercely throwing his chair back. 'We don't need you or want anything more from you. I would never have accepted the trip if I'd known it came from you!'

'I arranged it, that's all Juan Marco. What you have achieved here, the relationship that you've developed with George and Mary, is all down to you. You have learnt some life-long skills, things that you can build on. Don't let your feelings towards me colour that.'

'Don't tell me how to feel! George and Mary are your family, not my friends. Now I know who they are I don't want anything from them either! You can all stay away from us!'

Henry looked earnestly at Juan Marco, knowing he was losing this battle and it was time to bring in the big guns, even though he hoped that he could have introduced them in a calmer atmosphere. He sighed as he started.

'Juan Marco, I'm sad at what you're saying and I hope that you will think differently in time. But there is something else I have to tell you and I think you need to know; it's about your mother.'

Juan Marco coloured again and pounded his fist on the table. 'No, I won't listen to you any more, just go! You don't know anything about my mother!' he said as he lurched towards the door.

'It's about your father too,' came the cool reply. Juan Marco froze and glared back at him. 'I know from Mary that your mother has kept things from you and it's upset you.'

'What's it got to do with you?' snapped Juan Marco.

'Maybe you should sit down again,' Henry said as he gestured to the chair. Juan Marco remained rooted to the spot so he continued: 'I think you've guessed that you were conceived while your mother was here in England eighteen years ago, and that your father may be English? Well, I can tell you you're right, he is English. I know that because in fact... in fact... I'm your father.'

With a roar Juan Marco hurled himself at Henry, hitting his head and raised arm with a right-hand punch, then slamming punches into him using both fists. As Henry tried to swing his head away, his momentum caused his chair to topple over backwards. As Juan Marco went in to resume the attack, the door flew open and four members of the guesthouse owner's family burst in. 'What on earth is going on here! Stop this at once!'

Juan Marco glared at the woman and turned his attention back to the prostrate Henry, only for the woman's husband to shout out: 'Now that's enough of that!' He and his son wrestled Juan Marco back and pinned his arms behind him, dragging him back to the doorway. 'Calm down!' the man shouted. 'Or we'll call the police!'

His wife and daughter went to help Henry up, who was bruised and bleeding from his face. 'It's OK!' he gasped. 'The boy's just had some upsetting news.'

Juan Marco strained at the grip of his captors and shouted back: 'It's not true, it's not true, you're a liar!' flailing his legs in Henry's direction.

'It's OK, Juan Marco, it's OK, I know you're upset but it's true. You only know the end of the story. Let me tell you the rest!'

With that, Juan Marco renewed his attempt to escape his captors and get to Henry, cursing and shouting. The guesthouse owner shouted 'call the police!' to his wife and she ran to the lounge for the phone, and any further attempts to calm Juan Marco were hopeless. After thirty seconds more of struggle, they were joined at the door by two men who were also staying at the guesthouse, and stood bemused by what they saw. 'Help us here with him, face on the table!' shouted the guesthouse owner, and the four men used their combined strength to force Juan Marco over the table, and slap his face into the surface where Henry's fallen chair had left a gap. After a few cries and shortened breaths from Juan Marco, his resistance gradually gave way and he started to sob as his muscles relaxed.

'If these gentlemen release you, Juan Marco, are you going to behave?' Henry asked after a few seconds in a schoolteacher's voice. 'The police are on their way now and perhaps if you are calm no further action will be taken, but if you start again then you'll be introduced to a British police cell. Do you understand?'

Juan Marco gave a muffled 'yes', and the four men gradually relaxed their grip on him, with a warning from the owner about trying any funny business again. Henry picked up the fallen chair and gestured for Juan Marco to take it, then asked the owner if there was any chance of some water, which he sent his daughter to fetch in a jug, the glasses already being on the table for the morning's breakfast. A minute later she returned with the water, and as Juan Marco was now slouched forward on the chair with his head in his hands, her father thanked the two guests for their help and let them return to their rooms. Once Henry had taken a drink, he looked at the owner and his wife who had re-entered the room.

'Would it be possible for me to have two minutes alone with him? I realise that his actions aren't acceptable, and the fact that he's had a shock is no excuse, but he needs to hear from me what's going to happen unless he very quickly apologises and behaves in a more grown-up way.' Juan

Marco raised his head at this, but the fight had gone out of him. The husband and wife reluctantly agreed on condition they remained outside the door, and if there was any further violence then that would be reported to the police as well. When they left the room Henry said quietly: 'Now, you're not going to attack me again, are you? I know you don't like me and what I've said is upsetting, but I'm prepared to tell you the truth about how you came into this world. Before flying off the handle again, I suggest you consider whether there's anybody else who is prepared to tell you that truth.'

Juan Marco raised his head and sneered at this insult to his mother, but Henry continued, feeling more sure of himself.

'I'm not afraid to be blunt with you and, like it or not, there's only two people on this planet who know where you came from, and I'm one of them.' As Juan Marco stared back, the realisation of Henry's words hit home, and his facial expression became more sullen and less angry. 'Now then, I don't think tonight is a good time to continue this conversation, do you? Do you want me to leave you to the police, or do you want me to have a word with them and see if we can let this thing be. I don't think it's a good idea for me to stay here tonight any more!'

Juan Marco slowly nodded at him, so Henry walked to the door and quietly asked the owners if they would agree to him briefing the police, and seeing if they would agree to a verbal warning. Henry would then find somewhere else to stay the night. The man wasn't happy with this last suggestion and more-or-less insisted that either they both stay or they both go, as he wasn't having Juan Marco run around like a loose cannon. Henry thanked them for their patience and understanding and added, as he pulled the room door closed so Juan Marco couldn't hear: 'Juan Marco discovered tonight I'm his father and he had no idea, that's why he's so upset. He's been kept in the dark by his mother who's now ill, as you know, and suddenly this news has come his way. He needed to know, but I hope you can understand his emotions are all at sea.'

The police arrived shortly after and, having spoken to the owners and Juan Marco, accepted his word that he wouldn't misbehave again. After he apologised to the owners, he and Henry went to their rooms for the night.

All this time, Mary had been sitting outside the guesthouse in her car, unaware of what was going on inside, but expecting Henry to leave at some point. Instead, she saw the police car arrive, and followed them into the guesthouse in a panic, unsure of who she should be asking after. The woman who ran the guesthouse told her what had happened and, at the request of the police, Mary waited outside, and then left with them when they told her the matter had been a domestic quarrel now resolved, and the people involved had retired to their rooms. So much for Henry handling things in his own way.

She texted Henry from outside demanding to know what had happened, and got a reply saying: *All settled now. I'll talk to him in the morning again but he had to know. He got fired up! I'll keep you posted, but you need to let me deal as the family connection has him riled too.*

Henry avoided breakfast the following morning and just had coffee, which he could make in his room. Afterwards, he sat in the entrance hall reading a magazine, hoping to catch Juan Marco before he had a chance to visit his mother. When Juan Marco appeared, he stopped as he saw Henry and scowled.

'I hope you slept OK last night. I know you probably want to see your mother, so I just wanted to agree when we can speak next. I would rather you knew everything as soon as, really. Like I said last night, I will tell you the truth, how your mother and I met, etc., and I won't leave anything out, but you need to consider what help I… I mean my family, can offer you and your mother in the weeks ahead. It's her recovery that's the most pressing thing,' he said, hoping this would touch a nerve.

Juan Marco thought of swearing at him and leaving, but the truth was he wasn't in the mood to visit his mother, and had planned to walk the country footpaths until lunchtime. He decided he might as well get the rest of the story now, to allow him to figure out his emotions for when he next saw her. He told Henry he was going for a walk and saw that Henry's footwear wouldn't be adequate for muddy paths. Good. Henry could tell him what he had to say in the car park, and then he could be alone with his thoughts for a while. They moved outside and Henry began.

'I met your mother on the family farm where she was working as a housemaid, domestic servant, do you understand?' Juan Marco nodded. 'Well, she regularly cleaned my bedroom and, being a lazy teenager, sometimes I was still in bed when she knocked on the door. I let her into the room most of the time, despite my appearance. At first, she would often try to leave and say she would come back later. But I wouldn't be any further ahead later anyway, so gradually she got more comfortable with

107

coming in and cleaning and tidying around me. I talked to her after the first couple of times and, while she was shy, your mother's English was not bad and I found her amusing. Well, amusing is the wrong word, more charming, I think. She dressed nicely off duty and neatly when on it, and gradually we built up our conversations and she became a bit of a challenge to me.' Juan Marco glared back at him and Henry knew he'd better be careful with his language. 'So, OK, I was young, a little younger than you and was full of testosterone and interest in... well, you know, I found her attractive. Over a few months that increased and she was reluctant at first, but well, eventually we became lovers. I know this is maybe hard for you to understand, but I'm asking if you can relate to a young man, not dissimilar to you, finding an older woman attractive. Can you relate to that?'

Juan Marco understood exactly what he was being told, but wasn't going to give Henry any kind of approval. All he said was: 'Go on.'

'OK, it went on for a while, but then the family discovered the affair, and you have to understand that your mother was employed by my mother and father. Once they found out, she had to leave, but I never knew your mother was pregnant at any time, I promise that. She left the house quickly and I never heard of her again, until we met again in Spain under different circumstances. I was young, naïve and foolish and didn't really know what I was doing. I don't know whether you can understand that? I was just a mixed-up boy, trying to make sense of the world and his own feelings and emotions.'

'You think I should feel sympathy for you?' said Juan Marco with sarcasm. 'My mother has had all the difficult times since then, not you. No wonder she feels the way she does towards you. You and your family left her in the cold.'

'They didn't know she was pregnant either, Juan Marco. No one did.' As Henry said these words he knew they were probably a lie, because he was sure Maria would have asked Mrs Tanner for help.

'And now, you are planning to put it all right?' Juan Marco said in the same sarcastic tone. 'You're going to offer me and my mother a place to stay, and introduce me to your family as your long-lost...' He couldn't bring himself to say the word, but the look of fright on Henry's face painted a bright enough picture. 'No, I didn't think so.'

'You're racing away there, Juan Marco,' Henry said quickly, 'but let's see how things develop. I mean that, don't judge everything now. I think I can help you and your mother right now, let's see how things go from there.' As he said these words, Henry felt Juan Marco's bluntness had knocked him back, but he hadn't forgotten those words he had spoken many months ago – 'from now on, everything on my terms.' He wasn't going to be bullied or chastised any more.

'Not really a great story then,' said Juan Marco. 'I'm going for my walk.'

'Juan Marco, I said I'd tell you the truth and I have. It's not glorious but you had a right to know, and whatever you feel about your mother, she wouldn't have told you and I think you know that. All I suggest is you take some time to think about it. I can arrange for your mother to have a comfortable place to recover, and for you to be in the same place and continue your learning as she does so. That's all.'

Juan Marco turned his back and walked purposefully off towards the footpath sign, his mind disgusted by this crazy plan that involved him and his mother presumably being hidden on a farm somewhere, like stowaways on a ship. He didn't trust Henry or that he'd been told the full truth, and they were better off without him. There must be a reason for Henry to want to help them now, and it was likely to be something that was to his advantage, not theirs. He couldn't see any reason for them not to cut off all ties with this family, and to think that Henry thought it was OK for his mother to return to a place that had treated her so badly!

Henry now had to return to Hillingstone, as his purpose in coming to Lincolnshire had been fulfilled, aside from the fact that he had very little money and no place to stay. He needed a train ticket down to Kent, and as Mary was the only likely source of practical help, he rang her on the pretence of her running him to the station. She agreed to take him to the closest station and on the way there he hoped to soften her up for the train fare, by filling her in on the previous night's events. As Mary listened, two things were clear to her: firstly, she didn't trust his motives in offering sanctuary at Hillingstone for either of them, and had no idea of how he could arrange it without arousing suspicion, and secondly, Juan Marco's exposure to his English family had been disastrous.

'Why are you doing this Henry, offering them a place to stay? Have you any idea how you are even going to manage it and how many lies will have to be told?'

'It seems like the right thing to do,' he responded. 'I mean, I understand I'm hardly a father figure, but I have a sense that I should offer help, a duty if you like. Before you say it I know I'm not hot on duty.'

'Things haven't turned out well so far, so do you really think if it happens this will make things any better?' she asked.

'Don't know. But is there a case for managing the message?' he responded. 'I mean, if George is still planning on spilling his guts to Mother and Father, don't I need to be ahead of the game? What's the score between you two anyway?'

Mary cast him a harsh look. 'We can take care of ourselves, thank you very much. And despite you dropping us in it by planting your illegitimate son on us, we'll get over this little bump in the road! Is that why you're planning this Hillingstone offer then, your primary concern is to stop George spilling the beans? Shameful!'

'It's not a primary concern, Mary, but as you brought it up, I'm fed up with being treated as a waste of space by this family. Fine, I'm not perfect and have different needs to the rest of you, but I'm still part of this family, a significant part.'

'When it suits you,' snapped Mary. 'And if that's a reference to being the eldest son and the future family line, then that's pathetic even by your standards. George told me how you dangled that in front of him on the phone. Honestly, is this all a game to you?'

Henry shrugged his shoulders. 'I'm not the one who's playing games, threatening to tell mummy and daddy what naughty Henry has been up to.'

Mary flashed him another look of daggers, and Henry realised he wouldn't be getting his train fare paid. Mary dropped him off in silence, and Henry phoned his friend, Philip, to blag the ticket cost down to Kent on the pretext of meeting up in London in the next few days.

Mary drove back to the farm full of private thoughts which she couldn't, or in some cases didn't want to share. But after all Juan Marco had been through and was yet to face, she wanted to see him to find out what his thoughts were about everything that had happened, how his mother was and what his plans were. She also wanted him to know that whatever he thought of the Belvedere family, she and George had no idea when he came to them that he was Henry's son, and they wouldn't have allowed themselves to be used in this way if they had known, even though they could at least take some credit for what they had been able to offer him. She

110

thought about how to contact him, but concluded he wouldn't respond to messaging or a call, so took a chance that evening by driving to the guesthouse after dinner with George, on the pretext of visiting a friend in the next village.

The guesthouse owners were apprehensive about another visitor for Juan Marco, but Mary assured them that Henry wouldn't be returning and that she just wanted to check he was all right. They were still reluctant but Mary's previous visit counted in her favour. They did say that Juan Marco's room was only available for two more nights and then he would have to find somewhere else to stay. There was also the question of Henry's unpaid room bill. She paid the bill and, at her suggestion, waited for Juan Marco in the hallway. When he appeared, his face wore a cool expression and he stared for a couple of moments, before saying 'go away, please,' and starting back up the stairs.

'Juan Marco, I just want to check you're OK. Henry's gone and won't be back, but you've been through a tough time and I just want to know you're OK. How's your mother?'

He turned on the stairs and glared at her, not fooled by her approach. 'She doesn't need your concern and neither do I. We'll do fine without your family.'

'It must have been a terrible shock to you about Henry. Please believe me, we didn't know, if we had then we'd never have been part of the charade he created. We would never have been part of any game, Juan Marco, we're not like that. We took Henry at his word that he was offering a willing, deserving young man the chance to learn some practical skills, and who would really help us at the farm in return. That's all it was and we kept to our side of the bargain, and so did you! You were really helpful and enthusiastic, we really enjoyed having you around! All this other stuff about your family and your parents… God, we never wanted it to happen, or for it to end up like this. Please believe me!'

Juan Marco stared at her harshly and then his expression softened. 'I don't know what to believe, but I felt we had good times on the farm and for that I am grateful. The circumstances, well… I prefer not to think of that, and the sooner my mother and I are back in Spain the better. And now I'm hungry.' He started to climb the stairs again.

'If you haven't eaten, let me buy you something! They won't serve food here at night, unless you have a burger or something in your room?'

Juan Marco froze and then realised he'd given the game away, as he'd only had a snack at the hospital after his walk, and hadn't thought about an evening meal and was now genuinely hungry. Mary realised she'd found a soft spot.

'Let's go to a pub and let me buy you something. Henry told me you'd gone off on a bit of a hike to think things over, and maybe you forgot to eat something after. Come on, let's have a last meal together. We'll go to the next village, not this pub here.'

Juan Marco stood on the stair looking at her, and then quietly said: 'I'll go and get my jacket.'

When they got to the pub, Mary could see he was famished and insisted he ordered a steak. She wasn't going to admit to already having eaten, so just ordered a light starter, saying she didn't feel hungry. He had a couple of beers and she drank a glass of wine, and gradually he let her in to his thoughts, finally admitting that Henry had tried it on with him in Spain, which partially explained his dislike of him. Mary was incredulous, and responded by telling what she knew of Henry's past from George, and their tone of conversation became lighter as things went on. Juan Marco asked about the family farm, and Mary coyly told him that the family farm and Hillingstone were one and the same.

By the end of the meal they'd both relaxed a lot, and drove back to the guesthouse in good spirits and looked at each other warmly when she parked up, trying to find the right words for the goodbye.

'Message me if you're ever unsure of something,' she said warmly. 'You've been caught up in something that isn't your fault and I'll always help if I can, even though the farm is out of the question for obvious reasons.'

Juan Marco smiled back at her. 'Yes, now that you've told me about Henry and George's relationship I can understand that. Look, I really am very grateful for everything you've done for me, and for trying to help with my issue with my mother. I think the issue was bigger than both of us though,' he smiled.

Mary laughed and looked into his eyes, holding her expression until he blushed and lowered his head. In a moment of madness, she took his face in her hands, slowly moving in to kiss him gently on the lips. She kissed him once, then her hand slipped around his neck and she went in a second time; he resisted for a couple of seconds and then relaxed, even when she

112

kept the contact a little longer this time. She broke off and looked into his dark, warm eyes, before turning her body towards him and releasing the seat belt, this time leaning in to him and opening her mouth to kiss him more fully.

She felt her skin sizzle when he didn't push her away, her body pleading to be touched and her lips becoming more forceful. If he touched her now then her urges would overwhelm her. But he kept his hands lightly against her sides, and she felt the frustration welling up inside her that she wasn't going to be satisfied. Desperate, she stroked her hand up inside his thigh, and as she almost reached the top he groaned while his mouth was still engaged with hers, giving her the encouragement to squeeze his penis. He gasped while still kissing her and tried to push his pelvis up, giving Mary all the encouragement she needed to climb on top of him. Then his hands lunged for her buttocks, then slid up her back in a sweeping motion, before moving swiftly around to her breasts. As Mary ground herself into his lap and his hands roamed freely, he broke off the ongoing passionate kiss.

'Are you sure you want this?' he gasped.

Mary glared into his eyes, but said nothing as she locked her mouth onto his again.

PART TWO

Chapter 12

Never Say Never

Henry Belvedere waited at the station for his lift to Hillingstone, and was dismayed when Robert Pritchard pulled up beside him in a 4x4 pick-up truck, giving him a smug grin and a cheery wave as he stopped. Henry's mind went back to the incident with the cannabis joints and he shuddered, but as he grabbed the door handle, told himself to think of his evolving plans and focus on the immediate future. He needed to act like he was in control.

'Welcome back, sir,' said Robert smoothly. 'We weren't expecting you back so soon, but it's a pleasure of course.'

'My parents were aware though,' replied Henry and then added, in case that sounded condescending, 'it's been planned for a while. I'm aiming to be back more frequently.' The look of surprise in Robert's eyes felt like round one to Henry, so he decided to press home his temporary advantage as Robert pulled away.

'How're things on the estate? Is the ploughing up to date or has it been too wet?'

'We've got everything under control,' replied Robert in a cool tone. 'It's been wet rather than cold and that's created a few challenges, but I'm experienced at managing things, as you know.' The slight hint of sarcasm wasn't lost on Henry. Round two to Robert.

'And what about Christmas? The place always looks a treat, and Lauren does a fantastic job with decorating the hall and the party for staff and the village children.'

'Both under control and going according to plan. This year will be the best, I'm sure,' came the reply, as Robert continued the dance. Henry decided to cut the small talk and move things forwards.

'I wanted to raise an issue with you actually. I was going to come and ask you for a favour at some point, and as we're here now I may as well bring it up. There's a young man I've come across in Spain' – he winced as he realised how Robert would digest these words – 'and he's keen to do some work experience on a farm in England. He's fit and strong and has recently been on a work placement here, which has come to an early end. He's done well, but would benefit from continuing for a few extra weeks, and I thought maybe a change of scale would add a new dimension as his previous farm was much smaller. I know you're coming to the end of the growing season at Hillingstone, but there are always jobs to be done, aren't there? Maybe you could use his extra labour as well as teaching him some things?'

Robert turned towards him and gave a semi-interested look, wondering what Henry's real agenda was. 'Is this boy a personal friend of yours, sir, or more a friend of the family?'

Henry flushed at the direct nature of the question and felt his temperature rise, but resisted the desire to blurt out the first thing that came into his mind. 'He's umm… he's not really a friend… more of a young man that I've taken an interest in. I mean, someone whose mother I know, and through her, I've got to know of his circumstances. I found out his work placement has come to an end early and if I can help… I mean, if the estate can help him… to continue his short-term education programme then I'd be… grateful… I mean, happy to offer him help.'

Robert turned his face towards the side window and smirked at Henry's discomfort, before regaining his composure. 'So what would be the arrangements, sir? Would he live at the hall or do you require him to stay with me and Lauren, or will he live off-site? What sort of hours do you have in mind, how will he get to and from work? How long do you expect his stay to be? I think I'd need to interview him to assess what he already knows and how his time might be managed.'

'Erm… quite. I haven't got all the details sorted yet, but I wanted to check in principle whether you could make use of him for a few weeks. One thing I can guarantee is that if he comes, he'll work hard and be willing to turn his hand to anything, and he's a good student from what I hear.'

Robert turned his face away again and smirked. Just exactly what some of the teaching had involved didn't need much imagining. 'Well, sir, if you give me a broader picture of what you're looking for when you've got all the details, then I'd be happy to give it some thought.'

'Thank you, Robert. I've only just been made aware of the change in his circumstances, so I'll make further enquiries and speak to you again.' Robert smiled in acknowledgement, and that was the end of the conversation for the rest of the journey.

Henry didn't want to be on his own when he arrived at the hall, as he wasn't ready to be alone with his thoughts just yet, so he sought out his mother after taking his case to his room. Lady Belvedere asked for tea to be brought to the sitting room so they could talk privately.

'I'm glad you've returned so quickly, although you look a little thin to me. Have you been eating all right, Henry?'

'I'm a little absent-minded about eating sometimes,' he replied, 'but I've never been one for big meals, you know that. Eating a regular dinner just doesn't fit in with how I like to use my time.'

'Well, let's hope we can feed you up a bit while you're here. You're looking a little gaunt, you know, and I want to feel you're well, I need to feel it. Your father has his diagnosis now and it's important that we present a healthy image when we see him, so he has lots of encouragement to get better.'

Henry opened his mouth to ask the obvious question, but Caroline pre-empted him. 'He has prostate cancer, not badly but enough to explain his need to pee more regularly, especially at night, his weak flow and the small amount of blood he sometimes gets. There is an option to have the gland removed but it comes with some risks. Instead, they're likely to suggest hormone therapy to manage the symptoms. If it doesn't get any worse than it needn't affect his life expectancy, and of course his overall general health is good.'

Henry nodded slowly. 'How does he feel about it, I mean the diagnosis?'

'He's OK, I think, slightly relieved that he went to the doctor as it had been on his mind a while before he mentioned it to me. Sometimes, asking for help reduces the worry that something might be wrong, because you're actually doing something about it. He knows it's not terminal, but inevitably it's making him think about his mortality and before you say anything or protest loudly, the future of the estate too. I know exactly how you feel about your destiny and that it doesn't involve running the estate, but I'm asking you for some sensitivity here, do you understand, can you understand? I want to present your father with a family that loves and supports him and wants the best for him, so I don't want any disagreements or negative conversations while you're here. We all have different views but this isn't the time to air those, am I clear? I want us to put him at the centre of our thoughts, not where we'd rather be instead.'

Henry stared back at his mother before slowly nodding his head.

'And that also applies to Anna and George, too. It's not just you who's being singled out. They'll be coming soon and they both know what's expected of them.'

Henry nodded again and said 'OK.'

At dinner that night, John, Caroline and Henry talked easily and comfortably for a time over John's diagnosis, treatment and recovery, and the only moment of slight tension was when John started to ponder on the future of the estate. However, Caroline swiftly reminded him this was a time for positive energy, and there was to be no talk of any other issues.

When Henry returned to his room, his mind was full of thoughts colliding with each other, then exploding. Nothing could stop them. Names kept appearing, and as he downed the rest of his port, he fell into a deep sleep with the names shooting across the black sky, streaming like banners in a continuous breeze – Juan Marco... Maria... George... Mary... Father... Mother... Robert... Lauren... Anna...

The next morning, he awoke with a start and his mind was immediately active, but some of the clouds had gone. The idea of Juan Marco coming to Hillingstone needed further thought, and he knew he couldn't influence some factors that could ultimately defeat the idea, but there were other things he could do that might help smooth the way. One of these involved organising somewhere for Juan Marco and Maria to stay, and so, after dressing, he set off to visit Mrs Tanner, the retired former housekeeper at the hall.

Mrs Tanner had retired five years ago and lived in an estate cottage, which had been part of her employment contract and gave her life tenancy. The cottage was close to the edge of the estate and in a secluded spot, with trees to both sides and a garden to the rear, also tree-lined. In her working days, she had mostly walked to the hall which was twenty minutes away, but to leave the estate required the use of her car so she was less visible nowadays, although she still attended events and gatherings at the hall on a regular basis, and kept in close contact with some of her former colleagues. Henry was relieved to find she was in, when he knocked at the door at about quarter past ten.

'Henry, this is a surprise! Lady Belvedere told me you might be visiting the estate more regularly but I didn't expect a personal visit, although you're not unwelcome. When did you arrive? I thought you'd be spending quite a bit of time with your fa... your parents.'

Henry noted the slip of tongue and smiled. 'It's OK, my parents and I had a good chat over dinner last night, after I arrived yesterday afternoon. It was a pleasant evening, considering the circumstances. I'm glad my mother has shared her confidence with you,' he said warmly.

Mrs Tanner gave the briefest of smiles and said: 'Yes, it's not good news, but she is such a positive person and your father will only benefit from having her calm optimism around him. He is a healthy man and the prognosis isn't really that bad.'

'No, quite,' replied Henry. 'Umm... I was wondering if we could have a chat about another matter, actually, if it's convenient. I hope I haven't caught you at a bad time?'

'Oh my lord, where are my manners?' replied Mrs Tanner. 'Of course, do come in. I have a lunch appointment in town at half past twelve and some clearing up to do, but nothing that can't wait.' She showed Henry into the kitchen where there was very little mess that *he* could see, and asked him what he would like with his coffee – cereals, bread or egg on toast. When Henry told her she didn't need to go to that trouble, Mrs Tanner reminded him that she knew his lack of routine very well, and that he wouldn't have had breakfast, so he'd better speak up. Abashed, Henry thanked her and asked for some toast.

After some polite conversation, Henry came to his point. There was no point in beating about the bush with Mrs Tanner. If you weren't straight with her she would always send you packing.

'The thing is, do you remember the last time we spoke we talked about Maria, the former housemaid here?'

Mrs Tanner frowned before replying: 'Well, we didn't really talk about her; I think you asked a couple of questions, that's all.'

'That's right, I'm sure. Well, I had the most almighty shock recently. I discovered she lives in the same town as me in Spain and, even more shocking, I frequent the bar that she runs without even realising it was her!'

Mrs Tanner neither moved nor spoke, just kept her eyes on Henry's, so he continued. 'After she revealed who she was, we talked and... eventually came up with a plan to do something for her son...' His voice trailed off.

121

'Oh, Henry,' sighed Mrs Tanner as she lowered her face. 'Nothing good will come of this.'

Henry sat in silence for a few seconds, thinking time was his friend, then spoke quietly. 'I know what you're thinking and you're right, of course, and I've had to face up to it. Even with my lack of responsibility over the years and the haphazardness of my mind, I couldn't escape the reality of what is a fact. Through many difficult conversations I've had with her, even I've been able to realise that she went through the mill all those years ago, and I was the cause of it and did nothing to support her, for any number of reasons. I hope you can understand that I felt I had to offer some help, even after all this time. I'm not going to claim that I've changed my ways or that I can be his actual father, but I had to do or give him something, can you appreciate that?'

'What did you do?' Mrs Tanner replied quietly.

'I arranged for him to do some work experience in England to broaden his education and life experience, hoping that he could take what he learnt back to Spain, and maybe build a solid career for himself that would support both him and his mother. I arranged it a long way away from here, a farming placement that I thought might be of use to him back home.'

'And?' was all Mrs Tanner said.

'Things went well and may still turn out OK, but Maria's had an accident while she's been here, and it's meant his work placement has had to end prematurely. The boy is called Juan Marco. She's in hospital in Lincoln at the moment, but it's possible she may need somewhere to stay after discharge while she continues her recovery. Once she's fit and well, they'll return to Spain and I don't intend to interfere in their lives any more, as I don't think either of them wants that.'

Mrs Tanner's face became gaunt and sullen as she looked at Henry, shocked at what she thought he was hinting at. 'I see. And you've got a plan have you, Henry?' she said coolly.

'No I haven't, and I'm just trying to check some practicalities at the moment as to what might be possible, if needed,' he stressed. 'I may not need to offer them anything, her health may improve quickly, they may prefer to make their own care arrangements, etc. Do you see? I'm just scouting for possibilities at my end, that's all, in case they become dependent on my short-term help.'

Mrs Tanner's expression didn't change and Henry realised she would make him do all the talking.

'OK, well the sort of practicalities I was thinking about were finding Juan Marco somewhere to stay, and maybe continuing his education while Maria recovers, and finding a place for her to stay that will enable her to access local medical services in a comfortable environment, perhaps more welcoming than a care home, bearing in mind she's from a foreign country. It's possible that none of this may be needed or they reject any offer of help from me, but I would just like to work out what might be possible.'

Mrs Tanner thought about asking Henry if he'd spoken to his parents about this, but dismissed the idea as pointless. Of course he hadn't and wouldn't. But was he really considering asking her if she could help behind his parents' backs, her former employers, people to whom she owed loyalty and thanks? Henry had always had an unconventional mind, and what seemed plausible to him was way off the normal scale of most people, but if he was asking her for some assistance in such an underhand scheme then she required him to spell it out, loud and clear, so she could hear him say the words.

'So why have you come to me, Henry? What possible ideas could I have that would not compromise my position on the estate, or the relationship I have with Lord and Lady Belvedere?'

Henry hesitated and swallowed, then took a last bite of toast and gulp of coffee, playing for time to set his poker face. 'Please don't feel I'm putting any of this on your shoulders, Mrs Tanner. I have the utmost respect for you, and the tenderness you showed me when I was younger has never been forgotten and never will. I trust your judgement but more than that, I trust your instincts towards people and evenness of hand towards anyone you meet, no matter what their position is. You always treated everyone the same – with fairness, respect, politeness and courtesy. You offered help where it was due and a firm hand where it was not, but nobody ever felt harshly treated by you.'

He detected a softening in Mrs Tanner's expression, the appreciation of her values being taken as a fair compliment, rather than an appeal to her vanity, and felt encouraged to go on.

'There are a number of priorities here, not least of which is my father's health. I wouldn't contemplate doing anything that jeopardised that and – this might shock you – at some point I will tell my parents about Juan Marco's existence, irrespective of whether I can assist him now. I feel I owe

123

that to Maria and this family owes her something too, although I can't work out what yet. It was me that let her take the bullet and the debt is mainly personal, but I feel at least my parents should know he exists. But I also wouldn't expose you to any conflict of interest. I know how much you have given this family, and the idea of breaking the trust between you and them isn't acceptable.'

Mrs Tanner looked incredulously at Henry. 'You wouldn't actually tell your parents, surely, Henry! It can only cause them confusion and hurt and they don't need that, especially now!'

'I didn't say that I would do it now, Mrs Tanner, but at some point, I have to admit my part in her departure and take some responsibility. I know that's not like me, but you don't know how much difficulty she has been through since then. Her health is poor and yet her main concern is her son's future, and he's loyal to her.'

Mrs Tanner knew more than Henry thought about the difficulties Maria had initially faced, but her interest was piqued by his reference to her health. 'You said she's had an accident, what sort of accident?'

'A fall and her hip is broken, but she has an underlying chronic condition that will only get worse – multiple sclerosis.'

'Oh, the poor woman! That must be dreadful, how advanced is she?'

'She has mobility issues already and her coordination will continue to deteriorate,' replied Henry.

Mrs Tanner's expression was now one of concern, and she had to remind herself to stay firm against what she thought Henry was leading up to. 'So what are your thoughts Henry?' she prompted.

Henry sighed. Part of his performance was an act, part of it was genuine, but he felt he'd got close enough to the edge for now. A sly retreat was the right course of action.

'I think I've taken up enough of your time,' he said. 'I had this outline idea that maybe Maria and Juan Marco could stay somewhere privately on the estate, she to recuperate and he to continue his farming work experience, but perhaps I'm not thinking straight. There'd be a lot of cloak and dagger stuff and maybe I'm just too muddled in my thinking. I do want to help them if needed, but I think your instincts are right as always Mrs Tanner, and I should leave well alone. They, and particularly her, are not my problem. Thank you for your courtesy as always and I'm sorry to have troubled you. Do enjoy your lunch.' With that, he rose and left the cottage.

After he'd gone Mrs Tanner sat for a while, stunned by the disclosures, and to think he had thought of asking her for help behind his parents' backs! And yet, she felt something for Maria's position. By the sounds of it she hadn't had an easy life, and now a broken hip too. But there was no point in dwelling on it, there were chores to be done and then into the village for lunch.

When Henry returned to the hall, his mother came out onto the gravel drive to greet him. She chastised him for missing breakfast, but cheered up when he told her he'd been to visit Mrs Tanner who had looked after him well. She informed him that George was coming down for a flying visit in two days' time to see their father, but could only stay one night and would be on his own. The following weekend, Anna would be back from overseas, so she was arranging a family party for the Saturday night. Henry nodded and confirmed he'd still be here, but as his mother turned to walk back to the hall, he said: 'Oh, Mother, there is one issue I need to speak to you about, actually.'

Caroline turned and smiled: 'Yes, what is it?'

'Erm… I'm afraid it's a bit of an old story but I'm terribly short of money again. I know you wonder where it all goes and sometimes I do too, but the credit cards are all maxed-out again. And what's worse is I had to borrow some from George and Mary, and I don't want that hanging about if he's coming down here at the weekend. It might get awkward.'

Caroline looked back at him and sighed. 'What are we talking about Henry? How much?'

'What to ease my general position, or just what I owe him?'

Caroline huffed again, before saying: 'Both.'

'Well, five thousand would make things simpler on both fronts. That would include George's cash.'

'Dare I ask how much you owe him and what for?'

'Well, I had a sort-of idea about some travel in Spain to look for some new views to paint, but the trip took a bit longer than expected and the cash ran out.'

'Oh, Henry, I do wish you would think before you do things like that! You know that George's finances aren't great and they struggle with turning a profit on that farm of theirs. I don't know why he lent you the money, but why on earth didn't you come to us instead? Oh, on second thoughts, don't answer that question! Really!' she finished as she huffed again.

'Thanks, Mother,' said Henry with an attempt at an apologetic face. 'Please don't say anything to George because, the thing is, I went via Mary, and I'm pretty sure he probably doesn't know about it, but she's giving me grief about repaying her.'

'I expect she is!' exclaimed his mother. 'Henry! Going behind your brother's back, for heaven's sake! I'll transfer the money to your account today!' With that, Caroline walked smartly back to the front door.

Henry puffed out his cheeks and exhaled. He'd dodged a bullet and the five thousand would help with his debts. He could ensure he minimised his contact with George while he was here, and he could also pay Mary back for the guesthouse in Lincolnshire, which she probably paid for. That would also give him an excuse to contact her again and see what was going on with Maria's discharge.

Chapter 13
Another Skirmish

Two days after Henry returned to Hillingstone, the hospital told Juan Marco they were keeping Maria in until the start of the following week, as her infected scar hadn't properly healed. If she was better by then, they had reserved a bed in a convalescent unit, but she would need to take it up immediately. Maria had given him money to move into a guesthouse in Lincoln that was within walking distance of the hospital.

Since his night in the car park with Mary, he'd had no contact with her, and figured it would be difficult to ask her for help again. Mary's own state of mind since that night was a mixture of nervousness and excitement. The former was from the shocking reality that she'd committed adultery with a partial member of her husband's family. This sense was gradually taking over from the remaining tingle from having seduced her handsome young lover. She realised that any future contact between them would have to be one hundred per cent on the straight and narrow, but her concern over what Henry was up to meant she knew that further contact was probable.

Things did not go well for Juan Marco when the hospital told him, the following Monday, that Maria's wound infection was still too acute to move her into a lower dependency bed. She was still weak, sore, and struggling with the basic exercises from a standing position. Their preferred option was to discharge her to a nursing home later in the week. They gave him a list of local places with rooms available, and directed him to the finance team to talk about charges for her care. He left the hospital feeling deflated and exhausted.

Phoning Mary for advice was the obvious but uncomfortable option, maybe texting her in advance to make sure they could speak privately. But within a few hours of leaving the hospital, there was a bitterness welling up inside him towards the Belvedere family, particularly Henry. He could barely contemplate the use of the word 'father', but the injustice of that bastard coming from a privileged background, taking advantage of people as he grew up, then transitioning into a supposed adult but living the decadent life of a wastrel, feeding off other people's generosity, sickened him. The contrast between his mother's own hard life and Henry's life of ease and idleness, was cruelly stark. Part of him wanted to scream at Henry: 'This is your problem, sort it out! Give my mother the care she needs because you owe it to her!'

But the idea of contacting Henry turned his stomach and, even if he could overcome his own objections, how could he ever overcome his mother's?

He thought again about texting Mary, but was there any point? She couldn't offer any alternative place to stay, staying on the farm was now impossible, and he knew she didn't have money to help pay for care. George and Mary had their own lives, and it seemed to him they were far removed from the grandeur of Hillingstone that Mary had described.

Another two days passed before he received a text message from Mary asking if he was OK, and if there was any news about Maria's discharge. She finished by saying George was away for a couple of days, so he could call her any time before Saturday night, before rapidly sending him another message, because the first one looked like she was inviting him to renew their passionate evening! Juan Marco snorted mildly at the last message and gave a wry smile. Things had got overheated that night, but he couldn't blame Mary for anything; it was just a heat of the moment thing and he'd given in, and it was enjoyable at the time, but not part of reality now. He decided to call her, and they exchanged small talk, both skirting around the elephant in the room before moving on to his mother's situation.

'You don't really have much choice do you?' said Mary. 'It's going to have to be one of the care homes. I'm happy to research them for you today and tomorrow, and give you a list of questions to ask if you like? I could come with you if you're visiting any before six p.m. tomorrow.'

Juan Marco sighed before replying: 'It's all very complicated, I don't know what to expect and the funding is so strict. There will be forms and claims against the Spanish government, and all I want is to get my mother back to Spain as soon as possible. We don't belong here.'

'Are you OK? You've got somewhere to stay?'

'Yes,' came the one-word reply.

'Is there anything else…?' Mary stopped mid-flow, suddenly realising that he might be bothered about the other night after all.

'Don't worry, it's not that,' he said quickly, realising why she had stopped suddenly. 'I just… think sometimes about the offer he… Henry made about staying at Hillingstone instead. I don't want anything from him for me, but after all the pain and difficulty he's caused my mother, while he's living well off his family in some grand house and drinking away his money in our town, it's so unfair. Maybe he owes her some help, no, he does owe her for all that he put her through!' he said with emotion in his voice.

'Oh Juan Marco, you shouldn't think about that as being remotely likely! Henry can't ever be relied on to stick to his word, and he's never been any different. I'm sorry but you should dismiss those thoughts totally. He's a waste of space and just says whatever comes into his mind, with no understanding of how he would actually manage it. The idea that he would find a place for your mother somewhere on the estate, I mean it's just… madness, just madness. He wouldn't do it because his instinct for self-preservation would take over! I'm sorry, I know how you must feel, but don't think about him doing anything to help. It's just words to him, you'll do a much better job of sorting something out yourself.'

Juan Marco went silent and then said through gritted teeth: 'What, you mean he was just bullshitting me, just saying something to make himself look good? He even talked about me continuing my training at Hillingstone!'

'It's just words, Juan Marco, just words. Don't ever pin your hopes on him.'

'Uhh' was all Mary heard down the line, then: 'I've got to go now,' and the line went dead. She exhaled and shivered, maybe she'd been too frank with him and should have held back. After all, he was under a lot of pressure at the moment. She felt a knot in her stomach.

Mary didn't have long to dwell on it, and had only just taken a sip from her freshly-poured glass of wine when her mobile rang again, and she felt a slight relief that it was Juan Marco wanting to talk again. She looked at the screen but it was Henry's name showing.

'Hello Mary, how's it all going? I've got some good news for you – I've got the money for you for the guesthouse, if you give me your account details I'll send it over.'

'Henry, err, hi, I was just… err… has George turned up yet, that is if you're ringing from the hall?'

'No, he's not here yet. Mother says he'll be here about six. I was planning on giving him a wide berth other than when we're with Father. Is everything still OK between you two? What's his mood like?'

'It's fine, fine. He's calmed down a bit and I don't think he'll say anything to your mother about Jua... you know...'

'OK that's good,' replied Henry, 'because I'm still working on a plan down here for them both. It might take a couple more days, but there'll be an option I think. Do you know what's happening with Maria?'

'I think she's staying in hospital for a couple more days, and then it looks like she'll have to go into a care home temporarily. The wound isn't healing as they'd like and she's still in pain. Juan Marco's looking into nursing homes now.'

'OK, well if you give me his number I'll let him know that I'm trying to sort out an alternative, like I said I would. He's proud and maybe he won't accept it but it's the principle of the thing. I told him I would look into it and I don't want him to think that I'll say something and then just bail out. I mean, obviously I've got a track record, but I'm trying to put something right here or make amends or... you know what I'm saying.'

Mary's jaw was tight and her throat dry. 'Erm... I think he's doing a pretty good job handling it on his own. I mean I'm not sure an intervention from you is the right thing, that he'd take it in the right way.'

'Yeah, I know that,' Henry replied, 'that's what I'm saying. I'm trying to offer an alternative. The only thing worse than failing, is dropping him like a stone and disappearing off the face of the earth. I said I'd work on something and just want him to know that, you know, I'm trying. No guarantees, but I said I might be able to help and I want him to know he's not on his own, just give a positive message, that's all. Can you give me his number?'

Mary froze, her hand gripping the phone so hard her skin was turning white. She couldn't let Henry call Juan Marco after the conversation she'd just finished. It would end in fireworks and she'd get shit from both sides.

'Mary?'

'Umm... I don't think it's a good idea at all to call him. He really doesn't trust you and I think you should just leave him be. I'll update you when I hear what he's managed to sort out.'

'Is that what he said when he rang you?' said Henry, slightly hurt. 'I know he doesn't have a lot of time for me but I thought I gave him something to think about, last time I spoke to him in Lincolnshire. Do you think it would be better if I saw him face to face?'

'No, I don't think it makes any difference either way. He doesn't want anything from you.'

'I understand that, but he also needs to consider his mother's needs. His anger wouldn't prevent him from doing the right thing for her, surely?' Then he blew out his cheeks loudly before continuing. 'Mind you, if he doesn't care for me that's nothing to what she thinks. Christ, maybe I should back off. OK, look, you've obviously had the conversation with him, just give me his mobile and I'll send him a text. I'll keep it short, and just tell him to stay in contact with me if he feels he wants anything. I don't want world war three starting, but I'm not leaving it as it is now after the talk we had. I know I'm not Mr Reliable, but I think I got some Brownie points for telling him stuff about the past. Something tells me that I need to keep reinforcing the message that he can trust me to be straight with him, at least right now. This may be the only chance he'll ever get for direct contact with me, so it's important I follow up, even if he throws it back in my face. What's his number?'

'This isn't a good idea Henry.'

'What's his number please, Mary?'

'No, please, this won't work.'

'Mary, is there something you're not telling me? If not, then give me his number please.'

'No. Oh God, look I didn't mean to put the boot in but he was angry anyway so—'

'So what, you've been sticking the knife into me, have you? Well, thanks for that! I'm a total shit I know but this isn't about me, Mary, for once! I've contributed zero to his life so far and I don't suppose that I'll contribute much over his lifetime, but right now I might just temporarily be able to make him feel just a little bit calmer, but you've decided to piss on my party anyway! You didn't even give me a chance after I'd actually talked to him, which I foolishly told you about, only for you to use it against me! This is just typical of this family – ignore, denigrate, demean the useless tosser Henry! You're a weasel Mary, now give me the fucking number!' he shouted.

'I'm not going to—' Mary started.

'I said give me the fucking number, or I'm coming up to see you tonight while your husband's not there, and you'll find my methods of persuasion are fucking debased!'

There was a sharp intake of breath from Mary, and then she rattled off Juan Marco's number and pressed the red button on her phone.

With his adrenalin pumping, Henry repeated the number three times as he walked over to the writing desk in his bedroom, and wrote it on the notepad that the housekeeping staff always left. His mind was focused and he wasted no time in texting Juan Marco, reminding him that he was willing to work on the idea he'd spoken about when they last met, and to let him know as soon as possible if he wanted him to make progress. He was going to say he'd spoken to Mary, but as he couldn't rely on her any more he decided to take his chances and leave her out of it.

When Juan Marco read the message, he angrily threw his phone across his room and cursed. How could Henry have the gall to send him a message like that, when his own sister-in-law had just made it perfectly clear that his words were worthless? This family! They couldn't even support each other, let alone do anything for anybody else! He left his guesthouse room and went for a walk to find some food and drink, aiming to drink himself into a happier mood and try to chat up a girl. After his encounter with Mary his lust had been reawakened, and he felt like another night of satisfaction to ease his tension.

With no reply to his text message, Henry was even more determined to find an option for Maria that would be hard to refuse. If he could find the right place for her to stay, then it would put pressure on Juan Marco to do the right thing for her, and he might have to fall in line without Henry having to do anything specifically for him. It was Friday evening now and he'd heard a car pull up, which presumably meant George had arrived. That meant there'd be dinner tonight which he couldn't really get out of, but he knew George would have to keep it civil in front of their parents. Tomorrow morning he'd go back and visit Mrs Tanner, and see if her sympathies had been impacted by their previous conversation.

He knocked on Mrs Tanner's door the next morning but there was no reply. Her car was parked in the drive, so she may have gone for a walk or to the hall. He thought she was likely to be somewhere on the estate, so he headed back to the hall and went to the staff office to see if they knew where she was. Mrs Carter, the housekeeper, told him Mrs Tanner had gone away for a few days to see an old friend, and wouldn't be back until the following week. Henry couldn't hide his frustration at this news and spoke sharply to Mrs Carter, who embarrassed him by apologising for being the bearer of bad news, but asking him not to speak to her like that in future. Henry stammered an apology and left. His mindset had gone from feeling in control to suddenly feeling powerless and angry. He stalked around the hall for two minutes looking for George or his mother, determined to create an explosion with the news that he had a son, and was bringing him to the estate!

Not finding either of them, he decided to return to the kitchen and demand a bottle of wine from Mrs Carter, but the thought of having to see her again so soon and put on a show of politeness enraged him. The red mist had descended as it had many times before, and he was in no mood to see anyone now. Desperate, he remembered the decanter of brandy in the drawing room and marched in without even thinking of checking if anyone was in there. He poured himself a huge glass, downed it in one, then a smaller one and finally stomped up the service stairs to his room with the decanter, slamming the door and locking it behind him, intending to drink until sleep cooled his boiling temper.

Chapter 14

A Friend in Need

Mrs Tanner arrived at Lincoln railway station with one plan and no other options. She hoped that Maria was in the main city hospital, but if she wasn't then she'd have to try the others until she found her. No hospital was going to give her patient details over the phone.

She took a taxi to the hospital and asked at the main reception where Maria Ruiz was being treated, assuming it would be an orthopaedic ward, which it was. Maria was in a side room, and Mrs Tanner was relying on luck that Juan Marco wouldn't be there in the middle of the afternoon. She peered through the small window in the door and saw that Maria was alone and asleep, or at least drowsy and resting, and slowly entered the room. She stopped a few paces from the bed to stare at the patient, her eyes and brain working in tandem to connect facial recognition with memories. Mrs Tanner's face froze with doubt as she looked at the still face on the pillow, filling her with dread that she'd come to the wrong room. The top half of her body wanted to turn and exit, but her legs seemed buried in concrete, forcing her to remain rooted to the spot. The only thing to do was allow her eyes to complete their minute examination of the face and hair in front of her.

If this was the same woman Mrs Tanner remembered, then Henry hadn't exaggerated the effects of Maria's ill health. The skin had lost its smooth olive complexion, the hair was greying, and the overall appearance was of a woman much older than Mrs Tanner had expected. She forced herself to breathe normally to relieve her tension, which enabled her legs to unlock and carry her to the chair next to the bed, which she quietly sat down on. She spent the next five minutes looking at Maria or around at the contents of the room, beginning to consider whether she'd made the right decision coming here, and anxious not to disturb the resting patient. Then

134

Maria's eyes opened slightly and she murmured in Spanish: 'Juan Marco, is that you?' Then her eyes flickered urgently like a camera shutter taking multiple pictures of an object, the lens gaining focus of a face that she recognised more with each millisecond.

Her mouth opened and she inhaled, but seeing the shock in her eyes gave Mrs Tanner the courage to speak: 'Hello, Maria, I'm sorry to shock you but please don't be worried. I heard about your accident from…' she hesitated and stopped herself from saying Henry's name, '… and wanted to come see for myself that you were all right. I hope you don't mind me coming?' she said with an edgy smile.

Maria's eyes were fully open and bright now, and Mrs Tanner felt some relief that the beautiful brown eyes confirmed the identity of their owner.

'How did you… I mean… Why…?' Maria's mind was trying to process Mrs Tanner's presence, caught between some warm memories and an image of Henry's face as the person who must have initiated this visit, in one way or another.

'Don't worry,' replied Mrs Tanner, 'nobody else knows I'm here. I've come for my own reasons and not been put up to it by anyone. Is your son due to visit any time soon?'

Maria stared back at her, wondering how much of the story she knew. Words wouldn't come, so she rolled her head from side to side at Mrs Tanner's question.

'So you had a fall and broke your hip? How is your recovery going?'

'I'm not sure. I still have a lot of pain and the wound from where they opened up my hip isn't healing as it should; they think it might be infected. I should be out of bed moving around, but it's so painful to try to walk.'

'I'm so sorry,' replied Mrs Tanner. 'I spoke to the nurses about your other health condition,' she lied. 'Does that complicate things?'

Maria nodded. 'My movement isn't as good as it should be anyway, and my vision gets blurred sometimes, but I don't know if that's because of the painkillers. I'm desperate to be out of here and back in Spain, because I know Juan Marco will do a wonderful job of looking after me, but I'm having to go to a nursing home as soon as the infection looks like it's going, and they'll organise physio for me from there. We should have been back in Spain now, I wish we'd never come,' she said, tears starting to flow.

Mrs Tanner comforted her for a while and then to cheer her up, she asked about Juan Marco.

'Oh he's a lovely boy!' enthused Maria. 'He's kind, gentle, hard-working, sensitive and so loyal. He has a natural warmth to him and people like him wherever he goes! He's so diff...' She stopped and Mrs Tanner nodded slowly as she briefly smiled down at her.

'It's OK, I know, I've known ever since you first rang me and asked for my help. It had to be, and I thought that I tried my best to help you get another job and provide you with an unofficial reference, but I wasn't under any illusions about how difficult it was going to be for you. I always thought you'd end up back in Spain fairly soon. But there isn't a month that goes by that I don't think of you and how things ended up. I always liked and trusted you, and while I didn't know how long the estate would be enough for you, I hoped that when you left it would be on good terms and we could stay in touch. As it turned out, I'm left feeling that I didn't do enough – getting older does that to you, you know – you look back on things and think you justified to yourself at the time that you couldn't do any more, but the harsh reality stares back at you, making you feel that your own position was more important in your mind than anything else.'

'I don't blame you, please,' said Maria. 'You were the best friend that I had there and you taught me so much about English culture and values, and you helped with my language skills. I always thought it was circumstances that ruined our friendship, not anything that you or I did.'

Mrs Tanner frowned back at her and sighed. 'I'm sure I would have tried harder if I'd known how things would turn out, but there you go, we don't get the benefit of foresight. So, what about now? How much have you thought about recovering enough to get back to Spain?'

'I want nothing more than that,' said Maria. 'But it's so complicated, the health system here, I don't know how it all falls together. Juan Marco is trying to understand it all, but I think it's going to be expensive to stay in a nursing home. I'm hoping they will keep me here as long as they can, and then maybe I can leave and go straight back to Spain with him.'

Mrs Tanner looked at her seriously. 'I know that things must seem very strange, but our health care system is very stretched and hospitals want to move patients on as quickly as possible, as there's always someone waiting for a bed. Why don't I go and have a word with one of the nurses and see if I can get an update from them?' Maria nodded her head slightly and Mrs Tanner left the room and headed for the nurses' station. After waiting for a nurse to come off the phone, she asked to speak to someone who was dealing with Maria, and was told that her nurse was on her break but would be back in ten minutes, so Mrs Tanner waited for her. When she was introduced, the nurse beckoned to Mrs Tanner to come into the office.

'What's your connection to Maria?' asked the nurse. When Mrs Tanner replied that she was a friend and former employer, the nurse pursed her lips and seemed uncomfortable, before saying: 'Look there's only a limited amount of information I can give you. You're not family and her son is supposed to be looking into nursing homes, and really he's the one that needs to take some action.'

Mrs Tanner looked mildly displeased. 'She seems to be in a lot of pain and says movement exacerbates it, plus her condition is complicated by her MS.'

The nurse fixed her eyes directly onto Mrs Tanner's, before saying cagily: 'Look, there are some patients who don't cope well in hospital for whatever reason. Some of them don't give out positive messages about the future. We think she could be doing more to aid her recovery and… well, let's just say that the financial side of things may be on her mind.'

Mrs Tanner was horrified. 'Are you suggesting that she's putting it on somehow? That's a cruel suggestion, surely!'

'No I'm not suggesting she's putting it on, but I think she feels if she leaves here she gets stuck in the system somehow and forgotten about, and there will be weeks of nursing home care and fees, and that getting back to Spain becomes unnecessarily delayed. As far as we're concerned, we think that antibiotics and painkillers can manage her infection and general pain, and there's no reason for her to have more than a few days in a nursing home, and then she can go ahead and book her flight, if the airline will take her. Her MS doesn't help her balance, of course, but it isn't yet so advanced. She should be beyond the point of post-op recovery and we need that bed for other patients. We just think that maybe the cost of nursing home care is an issue, or perhaps she's worried about the burden that will be placed on her son in Spain. But either way, she should be ready to move towards a faster rate of recovery, and the best place for that is in a different environment, if she's not ready to return to Spain now.'

Mrs Tanner thought for a moment. 'So does it have to be a nursing home? Could she go somewhere else where her care could be managed, with visits from a doctor, physio and district nurse visits maybe?'

'Yes, of course it could. She needs to see that future track to recovery

137

and that staying here isn't an option.'

'I see,' replied Mrs Tanner, before thanking the nurse and returning to Maria's room.

'How did you get on?' asked Maria, pain showing on her face.

'OK, I think. How's Juan Marco getting on with the nursing home visits?'

Maria looked concerned before replying: 'He's only just got the list of available places; it's a lot of work for him you know and in a strange country.'

'Well, how about if there was another option? What if I could... arrange somewhere to go that was more comfortable, more independent, more... homely?'

Maria looked back at her confused. 'I don't understand.'

'Well, if I was able to offer you... somewhere to stay. Somewhere where you could have access to a GP service and receive any home visits for wound care or physio. Perhaps where I could assist with those things? I'm talking about staying with me Maria, just for a few days, weeks, whatever...'

'But where do you live? You can't work at Hillingstone any more so where are you?'

'I'm still at Hillingstone, at least I live on the estate. The house is mine for life but it's private, nobody disturbs me, just the occasional visitor. I could care for you without being interrupted or bothered by anyone else, and help to get you better. Nobody else needs to know, especially anybody on the estate. That includes Henry. This would be between me and you and, of course, Juan Marco. Would he be prepared to go back to Spain if he knew you were being looked after? You say he's very loyal to you but is that partly out of concern? If I could persuade him that you would be well looked after, would that be enough comfort for him?'

Maria was lost for words and said nothing for several seconds, then she closed her mouth and looked away, thinking about Juan Marco. Their relationship had been strained over the last couple of weeks and she wasn't sure why. She assumed it was because he was concerned about her health and possibly money, and perhaps the stress of it all, but he'd become distant from her and their conversations were getting shorter and more disjointed. Perhaps he was just homesick, in which case returning to Spain might give him a lift. The alternative was that he stayed in England, but where could he go? It didn't sound like Mrs Tanner was offering him a place to stay too, so maybe it was best all-round if he returned to Spain. Maria turned her head back to Mrs Tanner: 'Are you sure you can do this without causing yourself any problems? I don't want to be a burden and I'd hate for you to get into any trouble over me.'

'Yes, I can do this Maria and I'd like to help you. You've not had an easy life I imagine, and maybe helping you now is my way of trying to right a previous wrong. I know you don't blame me but it would ease my conscience if I could help you get better now,' Mrs Tanner said smiling.

After a few more minutes of talking about how things had changed at Hillingstone, Mrs Tanner left for her guesthouse, leaving Maria to talk over her news with Juan Marco that evening.

When he arrived he noticed she seemed brighter. 'Yes, I am feeling a bit better and I have some news about leaving hospital,' she said brightly. 'It might make your life easier too without having to check all those nursing homes.' Juan Marco's face was a mixture of confusion, questioning and relief. 'I managed to find out the number of an old friend in England and decided to ring her for a chat. She lives alone in a nice house and I think she's a bit lonely, and as we talked and I told her about my situation, she offered me a room in her home when I leave here, to help me recover. She says she doesn't mind looking after me and she'll help with all the medical appointments and things. Isn't that good? I offered her money for food and utilities and she just laughed, and said we'd talk about it in a couple of weeks!'

Juan Marco frowned and said: 'Who is this old friend, you never told me about her before?'

'Well I knew lots of people, I mean a few people, when I worked in England before, and it was a long time ago, and I just thought about her and rang her for something to do. But isn't this good, Juan Marco? I can be looked after by her and get fitter and stronger, and you can return to Spain and get back to your normal life! Then in a couple of weeks, maybe I can book the flight to come back home too!'

'But I don't want to leave you,' he protested. 'How could I? I don't even know this woman, this person? It is a woman?'

'Yes, she is someone I used to work with many years ago, near London. That will be good for flights back home as well, won't it? At last, we can make plans for the future and it will be good for you to return to the bar and get back to work. Don't forget, when I come back I will have to rely on you more, so this will give you a chance to get ahead a little bit.'

Juan Marco was still taken aback by the suddenness of this and the abrupt ending to his UK trip. 'Are the hospital OK with this, have you discussed it with a doctor? What about your infection?'

'Yes, I spoke to the nurse and a doctor this afternoon and they are happy, so I can make the arrangements right away. It will save us a lot of money, Juan Marco, and I can catch up with my friend. We used to laugh a lot together!'

Juan Marco fell into silence and his thoughts turned to his apparent imminent departure from the UK. This journey had been one of so many ups and downs, and yet in the blink of an eye, it was over. 'I want to make sure you get off OK,' he said finally. 'I'd like to meet your friend and make sure you can travel comfortably.'

Over the next two days, Mrs Tanner visited Maria at the hospital and talked more with the staff about discharge arrangements and future medical care, but always in the afternoons, when Juan Marco didn't visit. The rail tickets having been purchased, discharge was arranged for Monday morning, and Maria introduced her son to Mrs Tanner. Try as he might, he couldn't find a reason to distrust or dislike her. When he asked for her address, Maria butted in and said she'd call him with it later, but they must get off, otherwise they'd miss the train. The taxi stopped at his guesthouse on the way to the station to collect her suitcase, where Juan Marco said his final farewell to his mother, promising he would book his flight back home immediately, and reminding her to ring him with the address and let him know as soon as they arrived. As they prepared to drive away, he took two steps back from the taxi, and before the rear window was closed he heard his mother say: 'I'm looking forward to seeing Hillingstone again,' and then the taxi was gone.

Chapter 15

Deceit and Other Emotions – Part One

During the train journey down to London, Mrs Tanner and Maria talked about all that had happened to Maria since leaving Hillingstone, starting with her problems finding work, especially when her morning sickness started, and later, when the pregnancy was obvious to all. Then her return to Spain and her parents, and the tensions that created. They talked about Juan Marco growing up and her diagnosis with multiple sclerosis. Mrs Tanner asked when she had realised that it was Henry that was visiting her bar in Spain, and Maria told her she knew straight away, but it had taken her a few times to be convinced that he didn't recognise her. She took small comfort that her condition, plus a busy life as a working mother and her age, had at least spared her that. Mrs Tanner asked why she hadn't refused him entry, but she replied that she didn't want to draw any attention that might stoke his memory. Plus, in the early days, he paid his bills and often brought others into the bar. Now she was able to admit that perhaps she could have avoided all that had happened by barring him earlier, due to his out-of-control tab.

Mrs Tanner also asked about the planning for Juan Marco's work experience, and the reason for it. Maria gave her all the details but said she'd finally agreed because she couldn't offer Juan Marco anything like it herself, and she thought he'd lost too many opportunities to further his education because of her condition, one way or another. She wanted nothing more from Henry and had had no contact with him after they flew to Spain. Mrs Tanner nodded her head slowly, calculating whether Henry had had any contact with Juan Marco that Maria didn't know about.

She plucked up the courage to ask whether Juan Marco knew Henry was his father. Maria replied that he didn't, although he had guessed that his father was probably English because he'd worked out the dates, but she'd sworn Henry to secrecy as a precaution anyway. Mrs Tanner was feeling uneasy by now and knew she'd have to tread carefully, not just now, but for the whole time Maria would be staying with her. She anticipated the next question before Maria opened her mouth.

'How did you find out about us being here? Was it George or Mary – you must still be in touch with them?' Mrs Tanner inwardly breathed a huge sigh of relief that her own plan of action was going to be credible.

'Yes, it was Mary,' she lied. 'She telephoned me one night as she occasionally does, not often, but when there's some news, you know. I didn't know you were here before, but she rang to ask for my advice about your care options after your fall. She said Henry had arranged for a Spanish boy to come over for some farm work experience together with his mother, and that the mother had had an accident and was in hospital. She said your name and I almost fell off my chair, because I knew it of course straightaway. I didn't let on to Mary, of course, but guessed that if Henry was involved, well…'

'You didn't have any conversations with her about us, I mean who he is?' Maria asked in an alarmed voice.

Mrs Tanner wasn't enjoying this twisting underhand conversation, but knew that, for now, falsity was the only course. 'No, I didn't want to go down that route. I thought it highly likely that they wouldn't have known about Henry and kept silent about it, so I said nothing.'

Maria breathed out loudly. 'Thank God! I don't want Juan Marco to know about him, ever! When we get home, I've told Henry that he's never to come anywhere near us or the bar again. I wanted this opportunity for Juan Marco to make something for himself, after that we're finished with him!'

Mrs Tanner nodded.

'I'm glad you didn't talk to Mary for another reason too. I don't like her interfering ways. You know, I think she persuaded Juan Marco to push me to tell him about his father, because she said he'd become unhappy at their farm, but I don't believe he opened up to her – I'm certain that she put doubts into his mind and got him worked up. Our relationship was so close and then she started interfering and we had rows, and since then, well… I think it's forgotten now, but he had all that pressure on him after my fall and all the visits, and they told him he couldn't have all the time off to visit me, and left him to deal with the hospital… I think they just wanted rid of him. I don't like her.'

Mrs Tanner was feeling more and more like she'd stepped into a snake pit. When Henry had slyly set the hare running, she ought to have stayed well clear. After all, she knew his history of manipulation for his own purposes, and now she was paying the price for her own sense of misplaced historic guilt. She was unsure whether Henry had had any direct contact with Juan Marco. She'd refused help to Henry and then gone behind his back, and now had lied about having spoken to Mary. This was going to need her utmost concentration to avoid a disaster. The only plus was at least she'd avoided offering any help to Juan Marco, and it was a huge relief to know that he would soon be back in Spain, out of the way.

Chapter 16

Deceit and Other Emotions – Part Two

Juan Marco stood rooted to the spot as the taxi drove off, only his head moving as the car turned the corner and went out of sight. He felt numb. He knew exactly what he'd heard – his mother was on her way to Hillingstone, and this woman, Mrs Tanner, was not just any old work colleague, but someone tied up with the estate. So at the very least, part of what Henry had told him was true. His mother must have worked there, so what chance was there that the rest of his story was true? And this information had all come from Henry, none of it from his mother, absolutely nothing! And now she was brushing him away, going back to a previous part of her life where he didn't matter and didn't feature, removing him from the picture like an artist overpainting an object on an old canvas.

He turned and walked up the steps back into the guesthouse, his mind consumed with anger and resentment. Henry was the last person he could call trustworthy, and yet it seemed he was one rung higher up the ladder than his own mother! He sat on his bed and his rigid face gave way to tears, running down his cheeks and soaking his trousers. After two minutes he convinced himself to stop, for fear that the river wouldn't otherwise end, and in the hope that his mind would clear and tell him what to do. One thing was for sure – he wasn't booking a flight back to Spain until he felt one hundred per cent better than he did now. He decided to text the girl, Emma, that he'd met the other night, and see if she was free for a drink. When she replied she was, his spirits were lifted from thinking he'd have someone to talk to tonight and get drunk with.

Over breakfast the following morning Juan Marco stared at the flight-booker app on his phone – just a few clicks and he'd be away from here and his bitter emotions. But he was still upset and angry about his mother's willingness to return to a place that had apparently caused her so much pain, and at the same time, it reminded him of how she had isolated him from

144

this part of her life, and his entry into the world. His mind turned to contacting Henry to find out if he meant what he'd said about helping out, especially as it was just him now, and there'd be no battle to persuade his mother. He was angry towards his mother – two could play this game. He sent Henry a quick message, but his heart sank when he'd heard nothing back after two hours, so he decided to cut his losses and have one more day in Lincoln, before booking his flight home the following evening.

At Hillingstone Henry awoke at eleven, after the usual heavy drinking during and after the previous night's dinner. Conversations with his father were easier at the moment after his diagnosis and, for once, he felt his just being there was enough. He didn't look at his phone until midday, and was surprised by Juan Marco's message, especially as it was a much simpler proposition without Maria. He wondered when Mrs Tanner would be back to see if she had softened, but began to doubt whether this was now the right course of action, as the emotional leverage he hoped he had with Maria didn't apply to Juan Marco. So perhaps a new solution was needed. The obvious one was to try and accommodate him with Robert and Lauren Pritchard, as they had the largest staff house on the estate and had at least two spare bedrooms. But he was intrigued why Juan Marco was asking about coming to Kent when his mother's care must have been arranged in Lincolnshire, so he decided to ring him.

'Juan Marco, hello it's Henry. I read your text message, but you didn't say where your mother is going, so what are you thinking?'

'Does your offer only apply if it's the two of us then?' came the testy reply.

Henry was taken aback a little. 'No, that's not what I'm saying but I thought you'd want to be close-by, and if her care is in Lincolnshire then...' he trailed off.

'Who says it is?' came back the reply in the same tone. 'My mother has made her own arrangements with one of her friends who will look after her. She'll be in London.'

'London? Right, I see, OK. That's not too far away from the family est... farm,' he corrected himself. 'Can you leave it with me and I'll see what I can do? I can't promise anything, like I said before, but I'll try and help.'

Juan Marco smiled sarcastically at Henry's slip, remembering what Mary and George had told him about the family home. He said goodbye to

Henry, and decided to stay another couple of days in Lincoln and put a bit of pressure on him if he could, as he'd nothing to lose, and a flight home was easy to arrange anyway.

Henry's mind went into overdrive trying to think if there was any other place Juan Marco could stay, but it made sense to see if Robert would play ball, as no one would think it odd they were letting a work experience student stay, and it would be low key, away from the family until such time as it suited Henry. The only downside was Robert working out the connections and having Henry over a barrel, so he'd have to be careful how much he disclosed.

After lunch, he walked across to the estate office but found only Lauren there. She told him Robert was at their farmhouse catching up on paperwork, and offered to drive Henry over, which he accepted.

As her car pulled up at the house, Robert stood up and glanced out of the study window, surprised by the sight of Henry stepping out. He'd chosen to stay at the house so he could work on some finances undisturbed, as the less Lauren knew of his creative accounting the better. When Lauren drove away, leaving Henry standing outside, Robert's confidence increased, guessing that Henry must be after something. He moved to the door and opened it, his face sporting a patronising smile.

'Hello, sir, what can I do for you?'

'Hello, Robert, I was wondering if we could have a word about something that we've spoken about before? Perhaps I can come in?'

'Certainly, sir,' said Robert, throwing open the door as he stood aside. 'The lounge is the second door on the right. Can I get you anything to drink?' he asked, as Henry turned around in the room wondering where he should sit. 'A gin and tonic perhaps?'

'No, I'm fine thanks,' replied Henry, not wanting to appear a soft touch.

'Are you sure, sir, I was about to have one myself?'

'Ah well, in that case, erm… thank you very much.'

'So, this matter you wanted to raise with me again…?' said Robert teasingly as he sat down, drink in hand.

'Ah yes… we had a brief talk a few days ago when I mentioned I might have a friend from overseas who was looking for a work placement on a farm, for a limited period of time. Well, things are a little firmer now and he's able to start right away, if I can arrange something. I think I said before he's been on a small farm for a few weeks and done very well, but through no fault of his own, he can't complete the placement. It's something to do with a family illness at the farm, I believe, and they can't offer him the input they were giving before. He's been learning about crop rotation, organic production, seasonal crops, etc., but the important thing is he puts his back into it and is keen to learn. He'll turn his hand to anything that increases his knowledge. I'm wondering if you might be able to make use of him on the estate for maybe a couple of weeks, perhaps a little longer running into the Christmas period? There's normally quite a bit of work involved in dressing the house up, for a start, if other work becomes short?'

Robert's senses were alive as he looked confidently back at Henry. 'Well, sir, we can always use an extra hand at most times of the year, so perhaps something would be possible. Does he know anything about livestock? Are you proposing paying him or is this just free work experience?'

'Erm… I'm not sure on the livestock front. Oh yes, I remember he did mention chickens and pigs. Don't worry on the money side, I'll take care of any expenses, I don't want the estate to pick up any costs, that wouldn't be right. Just your time and instruction would be appreciated.'

Robert nodded slowly, thinking of more uncomfortable questions to ask. 'What's his English like? Can he handle horses, mucking out, will he handle "dirty" jobs if needed? You know, places where tractors can't reach, like drainage ditches.'

Henry flushed at the thought of Robert using Juan Marco as a dogsbody, but realised he had to go along with whatever he said, hoping that this was just some kind of test. 'Yes, as I say, the small farm had no problems with his work ethic from the brief conversations I had with them. I'm not sure about horses but erm… he's Spanish, so possibly yes, I mean they like horses, don't they?' he said weakly, realising immediately how pathetic it sounded. 'But mucking out, absolutely!' he said with exaggerated force.

Robert thought for a few seconds, partly to decide whether to continue the game, and partly for effect, but there was only one way to find out what Henry was up to, and discover whether there were any secrets that he could use to his advantage, now or in the future. 'As I said before, sir, we'd normally interview the individual and take references, but are you suggesting something different here?'

'Ahh… I'm very happy that the young man is of good character and

I'll vouch for him. This is just for a short period only you understand, and I'll see that any costs you incur are reimbursed, so perhaps we could agree something informal? There is just one other thing that I need to mention. We'll need to find him some accommodation, and somewhere on the estate would be the most convenient and lowest cost option… I had a thought that maybe he could stay here, with you and Lauren, as it might make communication easier between you and, after all, you've got the best knowledge of the workings of the estate. How does that sound?'

Robert's poker face concealed a picture in his mind of himself as an executioner, holding the axe high above the head of the kneeling victim. The victim's face wasn't clear – it could be Henry or the young Spanish boy kneeling – but it didn't matter. He sensed Henry was sleepwalking into giving him the axe, and all he had to do was take it.

'I'll have to talk to Lauren, of course, but in principle, I think we might be able to sort something out. Presumably, you'd like this to be between ourselves, sir?' he said slowly.

'Oh, yes please. Do you have my private number? Here, let me give it to you. Perhaps you can message me later when you've spoken to Lauren, and I can confirm his arrival details in the same way. His name's Juan Marco, did I tell you that already?'

'Yes you did, sir, but I had forgotten. I'm sure having a name will help when I speak to her, it makes him sound like a person rather than a complete stranger!' Robert said in a jokey tone, designed to lighten the atmosphere and bring the discussion to a conclusion.

Henry rose to leave and, after an awkward handshake, they parted company, Henry declining a lift back to the hall as he could use the walking time to phone Juan Marco and give him the news.

'Juan Marco, hi, it's Henry. Look I think I've managed to sort something out for you here on the farm. It may only last until Christmas, but I've got a place for you to stay as well I think, in one of the farmhouses. I'll confirm later tonight but it's definitely just you, isn't it? And you'll turn your hand to anything on the farm as part of your training?'

'That was fast, I thought you might need more time,' said a surprised Juan Marco. 'Yes it's just me, I told you my mother is staying near London somewhere.'

'Near London? I thought you said it was in London?'

'Well, I don't know the exact location yet, she's ringing me with the address, but she said it was in London or near it, I don't remember her exact words.'

Henry felt a moment's panic that this wasn't as tied down as he'd thought, but recovered his composure and brushed it off. 'OK, when can you come down? It will be a train to London and then the tube, I mean underground, to London Victoria, and then you have to catch another train to Maidstone. Do you think you can handle that, and do you have money for the ticket?'

'I'll manage,' replied Juan Marco. 'I can come down the day after tomorrow?'

'Excellent, I'll message you later to confirm the accommodation is sorted and make the final arrangements. I really hope this will be a good experience for you, Juan Marco.'

'Oh, I'm sure it will be, in lots of ways,' replied Juan Marco before finishing the call. His mind was already playing out the scene when he came face-to-face with his mother.

When Robert messaged Henry later to confirm that Lauren was happy to provide a room, Henry contacted Juan Marco to go over his travel arrangements. All was set for two days' time, which was just before George and Anna were due to arrive for the family weekend.

Chapter 17

Secrets

Juan Marco arrived on Thursday and Henry went with Robert to collect him from the station. Robert tested the young man on the journey back to Hillingstone, asking him what he'd learnt at his previous farm about crops and animal management, quickly confirming what Henry had told him previously about it being a small-scale operation. He didn't know how much Henry had explained about what to expect at Hillingstone, and was keen to see how comfortable Henry was talking about it.

'Have you ever driven tractors?' he asked Juan Marco finally.

'No, but I'm sure I can learn.'

'Yes, you'll need to. While a lot of the land at Hillingstone is contracted to outside farmers, we still have about five hundred acres under our own management, plus we maintain the formal gardens around the hall. Has Mr Belvedere told you about the grand hall—' he said as he glanced at Henry's face in the rear view mirror.

'Ah no...' interrupted Henry. 'I've not had much time to talk about the size of the farm and house. I thought it would all become clear over the course of a few days,' he said hastily. 'I thought perhaps you could start with a personal tour of the farm areas tomorrow.'

Interesting, thought Robert. Want him kept away from the hall maybe? 'That sounds like a good idea, sir. That was my plan and then we'll put you to work on Saturday Juan Marco, if that's OK?'

'Of course,' replied Juan Marco indifferently, having also picked up on Henry's dodge around the hall question, and confident that Henry had no idea that Mary and George had already filled him in on the history of the family estate.

Robert's suspicions grew when Henry asked to be dropped off at the stables and estate office, rather than the hall. Everything reinforced their previous conversation at the farmhouse about the arrangements being private. Robert had intended to stop by the farmhouse and allow Juan Marco to drop off his luggage and settle in, but it now made sense to introduce him to Lauren at the office first. Henry said his goodbyes and started his walk back to the hall, after promising to call in on Juan Marco after his farm tour the next day.

'So, this is the hub of the farm operation and estate management. Lauren and I work from here, plus we have two part-time colleagues who help with admin, ordering stuff, checking deliveries, that sort of thing. We employ directly nine other people, including a gardener for the hall, two other grounds maintenance people, three labourers and two stockmen – you know, animal livestock handlers? Look, if you don't understand anything just let me know, OK? Are you understanding this – I mean the language? Your English seems OK from what I've heard.'

'It's fine,' replied Juan Marco dismissively.

Robert felt slightly irritated at what felt like an offhand response. Was this kid being a bit arrogant? Did he think he was 'a bit special' because of his still-to-be-discovered link to Henry? He made a note to push him very hard to relay a clear message about who was in charge.

'Right, OK, we'll go inside and I'll show you the offices, not that you'll be spending a lot of time there, and introduce you to Lauren, my wife. She acts as my assistant on a full-time basis so you'll see her around, as well as when you're staying at the farmhouse.' He walked into the offices and over to his desk on which Lauren had stuck a number of post-it note reminders, and then looked at his phone which was flashing with messages. 'Can you just give me a moment to check who's called? It's probably nothing urgent as they'd try the mobile as well, but just to be sure...'

'Yes, fine,' said Juan Marco lightly, glad at having the opportunity to go to a window to look at the two good-looking horses in the paddock that he'd noticed as they parked up.

'I just need to make a quick call, won't take a minute,' said Robert looking up. As he turned away, Juan Marco shrugged and looked back through the window. A few seconds later Robert started speaking, but after a few seconds he broke off. 'Juan Marco, can you give a moment please, there's something I need to discuss which is private. Can you just wait outside? Lauren! Can you come out here and take over?' He waited for a response but there was none. 'Lauren, now please!' he yelled, before muttering: 'Oh for Christ's sake, she's probably on her phone,' and then waving his hand towards Juan Marco indicating he wanted him to leave.

Juan Marco took the hint, and left the office and walked across the gravel track to the fence rail, where he leant, admiring the two large glossy-coated horses, introducing himself to them in a gentle Spanish voice. After a minute he heard light footsteps on the gravel behind him, and then a silky, feminine voice.

'You must be Juan Marco. I'm sorry about that, I was just on the phone. I'm Lauren, I assist Robert in running the farm and I'm also his wife, as I'm sure you already know,' she said smiling.

As she spoke Juan Marco turned to face her, and the interest aroused by her voice was supplemented by a quick appraisal of her eyes, face then figure. He forgot himself for a second and stared into her eyes, feeling a sudden rush of attraction, before composing himself and smiling back: 'Yes, he did tell me. I'm very happy to meet you,' he said with affected modesty.

Lauren held her hand out to shake his and he looked down at it, thinking how much more pleasurable a traditional Spanish greeting of a double-cheek kiss would be.

'Sorry, I'm not used to shaking hands with everyone,' he smiled, still hoping that his instant attraction wasn't obvious. 'In Spain we greet people differently,' he added, as he reached his hand out.

Lauren gave a polite laugh. 'Yes I know you do, and I'm not averse to being friendly with people, but I think it would be a bit forced now, don't you?' Her eyes shone brightly back at Juan Marco, as she enjoyed the pleasure of another man incapable of hiding his obvious attraction. He slowly nodded back at her, realising that his attempt at face-saving was of no use. 'Do you like horses? I heard you attempting to sweet-talk them.'

'Yes, I spent quite a bit of time with them in Spain. I have a friend whose family have a farm and stables and used to ride with him, although it's been a while since the last time, too long.'

'Well, we have just these two here, one is Robert's and the other belongs to Anna, who's the daughter of the owners of the estate. She isn't here much so Robert tends to exercise her mare as well as his own, but perhaps he'll let you ride one of them if you have some spare time, but I warn you, he's a competitive rider, so if I were you I'd stick to saying you're a novice, unless of course you're really good?'

'Thanks for the advice. We'll see how things go. I imagine I'm going to be worked quite hard so probably won't have time.'

Lauren held his eyes for a couple of seconds and tilted her head slightly. Was he dodging the question?

'Well OK then, let's see if Robert is finished on the phone. He'll look after you most of the time but I'm often in the office and sometimes up at the hall, working with the housekeeper. I look after some aspects of the hall at event times, as well as helping with estate administration. Of course, I'll also see you at the farmhouse as you'll be staying with us. The room's already made up for you and I hope you'll be very comfortable, but if there's anything else you need you only have to ask.'

Lauren opened the door and with Robert having finished his call, she walked in. 'OK, I've introduced myself and I'll see you back at the farmhouse later, Juan Marco,' said Lauren, as she twirled around and flashed a smile at him, before walking elegantly into her own office.

Robert watched and smirked as Juan Marco's eyes followed her all the way to her door, already wondering whether her charms could be of use in digging up dirt on his relationship with Henry. 'OK, well you've met my better half but it's back to me now. Why don't we take a little drive around the estate, and then I'll drop you back at the farmhouse and show you your room. You can unpack and freshen up, get something to drink and we'll be back just after five thirty, and Lauren will cook something.'

Juan Marco nodded, and as they headed out to the old Toyota Rav 4, reminded himself he'd need to watch his behaviour around Lauren.

They had dinner that night with a bottle of wine, and Juan Marco carefully answered all the questions about his life in Spain, including how Henry had been a customer in the bar they ran. To change the subject, he asked lots of questions about the estate and hall, feigning ignorance when he already knew most of the answers from his time with Mary and George, but it gave him an easy ride. As they were finishing dinner, Robert's mobile phone went off and he excused himself to the lounge.

'Hello, sir, just checking that Juan Marco's all settled in?'

'Yes absolutely. How's it all going? Does he seem OK? It's a lot for him to take in.'

'He seems fine, he was quiet at first but he's met Lauren now and you know she has a way of relaxing people. He seems to have taken to her.'

'Yes, yes she does, that's good. Erm... I just wanted to say something extra to add to what we talked about before. I'd like this arrangement to be private between us you recall? In addition, you may not know that we've got a family gathering this weekend to show some support for my father, and I'd just like everything to be very neat and focused on him, so I'd appreciate you keeping Juan Marco away from the hall, just to avoid any questions, you know. I really want the weekend to be all about my father. Is that OK?'

'Understood, sir, no problem,' replied Robert grinning.

Juan Marco made his excuses fairly early that night, after checking he'd have to be ready for half past seven the next morning and, in truth, he was tired from the journey down and his mind was busy enough to only need his own company.

Anna and Alexander arrived at the hall late the following afternoon, and took tea in the sitting room with Lord and Lady Belvedere and Henry. Anna ignored Henry as much as she could, which struck him as odd. The last time they'd spoken was before Juan Marco's trip had been arranged and she'd been furious with him, but that was weeks ago and, knowing her personality, he found it hard to believe she was still simmering. Was it possible that she'd spoken to George in the meantime? But that didn't seem likely as it wasn't her style to just talk in the shadows; if she had something to say it would be to your face. Perhaps it wasn't worth tackling her as her coolness might be unrelated; probably she'd received the same warning as he had from their mother that she didn't want any distractions this time. In any case, it would be apparent from her attitude towards George whether words had been said. George was about as subtle as a bull in a china shop when his temperature was raised, and was bound to bring the subject up once he was face to face with Anna. Henry considered the other possibility that Anna was just resentful at his more frequent visits to the hall, and on reflection, he took this as more likely, which just happened to flatter his ego as well.

The gathered family had a light dinner, as a small supper would be served when George and Mary arrived later in the evening. Lord Belvedere showed genuine pleasure at the extended company, and Henry took every opportunity to be attentive to him, knowing how much that would needle Anna. When George and Mary arrived it was already ten o'clock, and the conversation was mainly then over the state of their farm and Lord Belvedere's health, but Henry noticed their cold and suspicious looks towards him. With the flow of wine, port and brandy, Henry began to enjoy himself immensely and took great pleasure in continuing his quips to both his mother and father, which they appeared to accept as pleasing, but caused Anna and George to temporarily sit stony-faced. Henry took half a bottle of port to his room as his treat when they retired for the night, and was alive with excitement at the prospect of being so far ahead of everyone else in the need-to-know stakes.

On Saturday, the family agreed to Lord Belvedere's suggestion of taking a walking tour around part of the estate, which caused Henry's pulse to race. He jumped in and suggested they head to the park at the rear of the hall, and then through the woods towards Mrs Tanner's cottage instead, and was relieved when his parents decided to go with his suggestion. Henry stayed close to his parents, and saw that George and Mary were in a line with Anna and Alexander ahead, and decided to keep a close eye on their body language. After a while, George and Alexander strode ahead in conversation, leaving the women a few metres behind. They walked in silence for a couple of minutes, each waiting for the other to start off. It was Mary that gave way first.

'I think George is still silently fuming about our Spanish guest, but his anger is directed at Henry, although you know what George is like, he probably won't say anything unless provoked. But if Henry keeps laying it on with a trowel, then all hell might break loose.'

'What's the current position? Are he and his mother still up your way, or did her health improve and they return to Spain?' replied Anna quietly. 'Look I'm really sorry that you ended up with such a mess on your hands. I should've told you what Henry was planning, I'm so sorry.'

'They've definitely not gone back to Spain, but the boy's not keeping me in the loop any more. The last time I spoke to him, he was looking at care home options for a few weeks in Lincoln, and was presumably going to find temporary accommodation near to her. But I offered my help in looking through the options and he never got back to me, so I guess he's handled it himself. But Henry…'

'Henry what?' Anna asked, as Mary had trailed off.

'Well he was in a rage and started shouting that he might be able to offer them options here, I mean on or near the estate!'

'You're joking! How could he do that? What for both of them? Yonks ago he more-or-less threatened he would bring the boy to Hillingstone at some point, and I assume enter the gates in some sort of flag-waving procession, like the crowning of a new heir! He even went so far as to drop

155

a hint to father, although I don't think he can have said it in the way he alluded to, it must have been obtuse, otherwise sparks would have flown by now. But you're right, when he's in one of his rages the mud gets flung in all directions.'

It was Mary's turn to say 'you're joking!' now. 'He wouldn't have spoken to your father about it in a direct way, no way, he wouldn't do that. He has these wild ideas but hasn't the foggiest as to how he's going to put them into action. I told him that, and I told Juan Marco not to believe it for a second too! Henry was mad when he found out and said he was going to speak to him directly to "assure" him that he could genuinely help.'

'What, you think he'd already mentioned it to the boy?'

'Oh yes, but I think it was a throw-away comment at the time. After he'd lashed out at me he said he was going to take charge, and make it clear to Juan Marco that he was genuinely trying to offer an alternative option. But it's madness to think anything would come of it. I'm out of the loop now and hopefully that's us done, I mean especially for George's sake, because at one point he was so angry he was threatening to come and see your parents and blow the lid off Henry's secret! He's at least shelved that plan, I mean I think he has. He just left me to deal with Juan Marco in the end, although – and don't say this to him – I kept up contact with him behind George's back. I just wanted to help him because, to be honest, Juan Marco is a really nice young man! He's smart, polite, hard-working, sensitive – he couldn't be more different to Henry!'

Anna turned to her with a frown. 'You sound like you're quite taken with him!'

Mary briefly blushed before trying to rescue herself. 'Well it's not that, it's just he's well… sensitive… I mean maybe it's the fact that they breed men in Spain with a bit better communication skills than our lot! I mean look at your brothers!'

Anna laughed and left the point alone, as she could tell Mary was defensive. 'I'm going to think out loud, just let me do this for my own satisfaction. So if Henry was going to get them both down here, he'd have to find a care home locally which I guess he could do in Maidstone. But would he have the ability to execute that, I mean talk to the staff, explain her condition, would the boy be willing to help him, arrange transport, and what about money? If it meant dipping into his own pocket then he'd be as useful as a chocolate fireguard. OK, now the boy… what's his relationship like with Henry? Probably not great if you say he's as nice as he is, which means he won't trust him. So if Henry brought him to the estate he'd have to squirrel him away somewhere. So where? Nowhere near the hall; I don't think Henry's got strong enough relationships with anyone suitable on the estate who has accommodation and besides, Robert would find out about it, I'm sure. He doesn't have any time for Henry, and if a mouse squeaks on the estate Robert finds out about it. No, thinking it over, it isn't realistic that Henry could have got them down here, I'm fairly certain of it. Does that make sense to you?'

'Yes, I think you're right. He's just too high up in cloud-cuckoo-land to pull it off,' agreed Mary. 'When he and I last spoke he really laid into me, and I wasn't planning on confronting him, but he seems too relaxed to me here… that's my one suspicion. You know how he likes his vanity play, trying to make out that he's one step ahead all the time. Do you think he's just trying to wind us up?'

'Oh yes, he's been doing it ever since we got here. I think that's what his agenda is, just trying to make us feel that he knows something we don't. In reality, I don't think there's anything in it but… it would be nice if we could make him squirm a little, just turn the tables a bit. What do you think about making a song and dance of the way he spoke to you? You know, tell him how hurt you were and that you haven't mentioned it to George, and you'll consider not doing so if he apologises. Try and make him feel a bit guilty, and then skirt around the "what's happened to them?" question.'

'Yes, that sounds believable, I could do that,' answered Mary. 'You know I don't really care about what happened to the mother because to be honest, I didn't really like her. She was the sort to keep secrets and attack anyone who got too close to her. But the boy, Juan Marco, I'd be happy to just find out he's out of Henry's way. If he's back in Spain then so much the better and if not, then I hope he's got enough intelligence to stay well away from him. I'll try and strike while the iron's hot – let's see if I can drop back to their group and get him on his own.'

The two women smiled at each other and both slowed their pace to wait for Lord and Lady Belvedere to catch up and, as they did so, Anna hooked her arm into her father's and displaced Henry, who fell back behind them, where Mary had now taken her place. The manoeuvre wasn't lost on Henry, who grinned.

'Well Henry, we haven't spoken since… now when was it, a few weeks ago when you were up in…' She hesitated and glanced up at him, and he smiled back before replying.

'Yes, that's right,' not wanting to give in so early in the game.

'It was certainly a surprise,' she countered loudly, hoping her attempt to up the stakes would have the desired effect. Henry looked at her for two or three seconds and decided this wasn't the time to fight a battle. 'Yes we had a frank conversation I recall, but I'm not sure we did finish it. Why don't we take this trail here that leads out into the park again? We won't detour for long and we can catch the others up soon.' Mary nodded and they began their diversion back into the late autumn sun.

'You know, the last time we spoke you said some very rude things to me and were quite threatening really. It's not my place to lecture you on manners but you distressed me, and I had to put on a bit of a show for George and tell him it was something else. If I'd told him what you said, I think he'd have it out with you,' began Mary.

'Hmm, you're assuming it would go well for you if you told him you were still helping Juan Marco,' came the slippery reply.

'Oh, I could talk my way out of that easily. I was in contact with him of course but only by phone every few days. I was genuinely concerned about both their futures, and I could make George see that offering Juan Marco my help with his mother's care was the right thing to do,' she said light-heartedly.

'Really? Is that a fact?'

'Oh I'm sure of it. Then, of course, George would be mad and he would come after you, and the influence I have over him not telling your parents your little secret would have been lost. So I think you definitely owe me an apology.'

'Is that what you really want, Mary, because if it is, it's easily delivered. But are you sure there's nothing else that you really want instead?'

'What, like how it went with Juan Marco when you spoke to him like you said you were going to? I think I already know the answer to that – I should imagine if you had the balls to try he probably hung up on you straightaway. After all, he's hardly your biggest fan. And the idea that you could sort something out for his mother's rehab, now that's really funny!'

Henry was holding his own until now, but the last comment irked him. Someone was trying to push a needle of criticism into him, and he bit his lip, reminding himself that he had to keep his cool and focus on getting things on his own terms.

'Yes that was certainly going to be a big challenge. Perhaps one that I couldn't rise to.' He determined to say nothing about Juan Marco. If she really wanted to know about him, then she would have to ask specifically, and he was banking on her not wanting to appear desperate.

Mary noticed he offered nothing more on Juan Marco, and had to calculate whether to try again. 'So do you know where they are at the moment?'

'In transit, I believe,' said Henry noncommittally, congratulating himself on such a vague response.

Mary thought for a few seconds. To where? Here? Spain? Surely Maria wasn't well enough to return home, so had Henry pulled something off? No, he couldn't have sorted anything out for Maria; he would have needed money for private care and that would have to come from his parents, which was inconceivable. And if he hadn't sorted her out then Juan Marco wouldn't have accepted parting from her, so Henry must have admitted defeat, and they must be heading back to Spain after all. Ha! He'd lost the game!

'Probably for the best,' she said wistfully.

'Indeed,' came the final reply.

The conversation thus concluded, they headed back to the main walking party, and Mary nodded and smiled at Anna's enquiring face as they approached.

Dinner that evening was lively and increasingly good-humoured as it went on. Both Anna and Mary showed their relaxed state of mind, and Alexander's easy charm even encouraged George to join in. Lord Belvedere was feeling optimistic about the light-touch treatment for his prostate cancer, which consisted of some changes to his diet and only scheduled scans at this stage. Henry found it very easy to blend into the background with everyone else being so vocal. He managed to slip away to his bedroom earlier than the others, helping himself to a quarter-bottle of brandy on the way out.

He decided to refrain from making any contact with either Juan Marco or Robert on Sunday as it was taking an unnecessary risk, bearing in mind that both his sister and brother were due to leave later that day. So, on Monday, he went to the estate office in the late morning to check on Juan Marco's whereabouts, where Lauren told him Juan Marco and Robert had gone to look at a poorly-draining field at the edge of the estate. She offered Henry the use of one of the quadbikes to go and find them, and Henry's initial intention to refuse was swiftly reversed, when he conjured up an image of the shock he would create in appearing out of nowhere, Steve McQueen-style. He surprised Lauren when he accepted, and after she gave him instructions on the controls he set off. Sure enough, as he skidded to a halt along the track at the edge of the field, Robert's expression was open-mouthed, and he had to stop himself from completing the phrase, 'What the…' Juan Marco looked bemused, standing in the drainage ditch almost up to his thighs in muddy water.

'Hello, both!' grinned Henry like a schoolboy. 'My you're muddy there, Juan Marco. What have you got him doing Robert?'

'Searching for a cracked pipe, sir,' said a still shocked Robert. 'There's a leak from one of the irrigation pipes that we spotted in summer but hadn't had time to fix. He's learning one of the maintenance tasks that we have to perform.'

'Right, I see. All OK, Juan Marco? I knew you'd get stuck in and put your back into it. Robert knows how this place ticks, I mean works.' Juan Marco merely nodded. Henry turned back to Robert: 'How did the tour go on Friday? Sorry I couldn't catch up until now, with the family all being at the hall.' He felt a huge flush when he realised he'd forgotten the presence of his hidden son right in front of him.

'It's fine, sir, you can leave the day-to-day plan to me. If I need to check in with you then I'll phone, but otherwise I can keep him busy, that's what I'm paid for,' replied Robert slightly testily.

'Right OK, that's fine, I just didn't want you, either of you, to think I'd forgotten about you. OK, well I'll be off back to the office on my trusty steed, well er… you know what I mean,' Henry answered, as he fired up the engine of the bike.

Juan Marco had the presence of mind to duck down into the ditch, fearing what was going to happen next, but as Robert shouted a warning to Henry that was drowned in the roar of the engine, Henry turned the bike around using too much throttle, causing the tyres to spin on the mud and shower Robert with a spray, leaving him shouting 'fucking twat!' as Henry roared off.

Chapter 18

A Homecoming

Since her arrival at Mrs Tanner's cottage, Maria had felt comfortable and welcome, despite her slight anxiety at the risk of being discovered. But Mrs Tanner had reassured her that she was largely left in peace and had no reason to be worried. Her cottage had a decent size garden at the rear, which was hidden from view and backed onto the estate wall, so there was no chance of anyone exercising in the garden being visible, other than from within the house. Maria had been registered with a GP and had been referred to a physiotherapist. When she expressed fears about being spotted in the car, Mrs Tanner said: 'Don't worry, I don't expect anyone will recognise you and if anyone questions me, I'll just tell them I have an old friend staying with me for a few weeks who is recuperating from an operation, and isn't very mobile but needs peace and quiet. I'm very certain that they'll leave me alone, and I won't be pressured to introduce you.'

In truth, the only intruder she was concerned about was a flying visit from Henry, and she didn't have a plan to deal with this, other than to hope she could quickly get Maria out of the way. At the moment, she didn't know if Henry was still at the hall.

On her first full day, Maria had texted her address to Juan Marco, but actually given the address of Mrs Tanner's sister in Beckenham, at her suggestion. She asked him if he was now back in Spain, and he'd replied that he was still making his final arrangements. She reminded him to contact their landlord and the bar owner in advance so they would know of his return, which he acknowledged with a 'will do'. In fact, he had already contacted them to advise that Maria had had an accident, and they wouldn't be able to return for a few more weeks while she recovered.

Maria was still sore after the hip surgery, and her lack of mobility wasn't helped by some arthritis, which had started in her mid-forties, and the fact that she was moderately overweight. She started walking slowly around the cottage, but at this time of year, trips out into the garden were few and far between. Mrs Tanner could see that the stubbornness which had been a good quality when Maria worked at the hall, was now perhaps a disadvantage. Nevertheless, the two of them were able to pass many happy hours talking about Maria's life in Spain, Juan Marco growing up, and all the comings and goings at the estate over the past twenty years. Maria longed to risk seeing the hall again, and it wasn't long before she agreed to a late afternoon drive towards the building in the November darkness, to take in the view of the workplace which had given her so many memories. There were even bitter-sweet thoughts of her affair with Henry, which caused her to shudder with a mixture of guilt and revolt. While Henry hadn't been innocent when she first slept with him, and she had no clue that he might be anything other than heterosexual, his wide-eyed passion for her, and lust to explore every sexual act possible, had completely consumed her in a way that she hadn't felt since she was in her early twenties. As a thirty-three-year-old faced with a seventeen-year-old with a non-stop libido, she had become detached from reality, and over-indulged in the opportunities offered to the point of foolishness.

She tried to ring Juan Marco a couple of times in the first week just to check he was OK, but also to ease her conscience about the deterioration in their relationship. He didn't pick up or respond to her messages, and she assumed he was busy or using his free time to resume his social life, which gave her a little comfort. After her third message a couple of days later, he replied saying: 'Sorry for not being around but everything is OK, I'm just really busy!' before enquiring after her health.

When she asked him how things were back home, he said he hadn't noticed anything different and repeated that he was busy. She couldn't help but feel he was taking advantage of their separation to grow away from her, which caused her a tinge of sadness that she was losing the boy he had been.

Juan Marco was indeed being kept busy by Robert, but refused to be beaten by anything. Even Robert was surprised by his stamina and work ethic. It seemed he would follow any instruction, carry out any task and learn anything new without a moment's delay. Whether he was repairing fencing, harvesting winter crops in the tractors, mucking out the stables, learning about health issues with one of the stockmen, or driving produce to a local wholesaler, he just got on with it. At the end of the day, he would go back to the farmhouse and shower, and then sit down to dinner with

Robert and Lauren and be polite, even friendly company. It was obvious to all of them that he found Lauren attractive, but he didn't behave foolishly, and Robert was used to other men trying to charm her and make her laugh anyway. Any thoughts that he had about Henry and Juan Marco's relationship being sexual seemed remote, unless Juan Marco was the world's best actor.

Robert had no intention of backing off with the workload, and just accepted that he would have to be satisfied with a slow and steady approach to finding out what Henry was up to. It was now mid-November and thoughts were turning to Christmas on the estate, so some of the upcoming tasks would blend hall and farm sides, including equipment servicing and replacement, and sourcing and erecting the hall Christmas tree. His assumption was that Juan Marco would be gone before the holiday break, but he would make what use of him he could. The hall decorations were always organised by Lauren and the housekeeper, and if Juan Marco was light on other tasks then he could help with that.

One mild afternoon, when Robert was at an agricultural engineers workshop, Juan Marco was left to muck out the stables and have an early finish. He was on the second one when Lauren came out of the office and loitered, with a smile that said she wanted to chat. They played at boy-meets-girl for a few minutes while he finished the cleaning, and then he went to fetch the horses in from the paddock and give them their final feed. As he walked Robert's mare to the door, Lauren said: 'You should ride her you know, before you put her away. Come on, you said you could ride and the harness is hanging up there and the saddle is next door, so why don't you both have a little workout? Robert won't mind and you can just do it for ten or fifteen minutes. Go on, spoil yourself!'

Juan Marco shook his head. 'No, I'd rather ask permission first. It's not right.'

'I'm giving you permission! In fact, it's an order. I'm giving you an order to show me what you can do, unless of course you're not really up to it?' Lauren said with a flirtatious look.

Juan Marco gritted his teeth and felt the insult to his prowess had to be answered. He kitted the horse out and as he was only slightly shorter than Robert, didn't have to make much of an adjustment to the stirrups. He mounted the mare easily and took her back into the paddock, where he walked her slowly to establish her responsiveness to his reins movements, and then progressed to a trot and then a canter. The horse felt his confidence and settled without alarm, and Juan Marco went through some manoeuvres, stopping, starting and turning, beginning to enjoy himself, as Lauren watched on quietly, finding herself slightly aroused at this display of beast-taming. After five minutes, Juan Marco walked out of the paddock and decided to show off his *pièce de résistance* in the small jumping paddock next door. He walked slowly into the arena, with Lauren open-mouthed at what she couldn't believe was happening, and then got the horse up to trotting speed around the obstacles, before performing a tight left turn, and taking the first of three low-level fences in an easy stride, then clearing the other two. A few more tight turns and two more jumps were done, including the low wall, before he went back to finish calmly over the three original fences. Clean round, no faults, just as he expected. As he walked the horse slowly to the gate and let himself out, Lauren controlled her urges and replaced her look of wonderment with a haughty smirk.

'Well, aren't you the show off! You know modesty isn't that attractive in a man who then performs like that!'

Juan Marco dismounted at the stable door and said calmly: 'I wasn't trying to impress, I was just enjoying myself,' finishing with a half-smile.

Lauren felt this contest had resulted in a minor defeat for her, and as she turned to go back into the office said loudly: 'I can feel a competition coming on, you and Robert. I wonder who will want it more.'

Neither Lauren nor Juan Marco had spotted the dark blue Range Rover, which had crept up the track towards the estate office on its way back to the hall, stopping about one hundred and fifty metres short to watch the impromptu display of horsemanship. Lord Belvedere assumed this was a lesson under Lauren's supervision, but he was fairly sure she didn't ride, or at least wasn't so good that she could teach, but perhaps this very capable rider had just asked for use of the facilities for a fee. As he moved the car forward he drove slowly past the stable, looking at the young man removing the saddle, checking if he knew him. The young man didn't look away from his task so he had to rely on a sideways view, and didn't recognise him, but made a mental note to ask who he was the next time he saw Robert.

Henry was now at a loose end but to his own surprise, was relaxed and quite happy. Juan Marco was out of sight and being kept busy and didn't require any babysitting from him, which was actually a relief and lowered the risk. Anna and George had now both gone and wouldn't return until

Christmas week – and Maria was out of the equation too. There was no good reason for him to return to Spain – his work was here for the time being, in the form of a project which was all his to develop and present, at the moment of his choosing. What fun! Having time on his hands and being in a considerably better mood than when last at Hillingstone, he decided to visit Mrs Tanner again, as she must have returned from her travels by now. He called on her late one morning hoping for a spot of brunch, but was left to wait outside the door even though he could hear movement inside. As his knock grew louder by the third time, Mrs Tanner came to the door and said through the letterbox: 'Who is it please?'

'It's Henry, Mrs Tanner, just come for a chat if that's all right.' He thought it a strange question as he'd seen her in the lounge as he approached the cottage, and thought she must have seen him too.

'Can you give me a minute please, my dear, I'm just moving some furniture and having a tidy up. I won't be long.'

'Do you want a hand with anything?' shouted Henry in reply.

'No it's quite all right, just hold on,' she shouted back, as she edged away from the door.

Henry raised his eyebrows in bemusement, but at least she was in, so unless she was in a hurry or about to go out which seemed unlikely, then he was probably OK for the food.

'Well this is a surprise, Henry, I wasn't expecting you. You can always telephone me you know and check that I'll be here, I wouldn't want you to have a wasted journey,' she said after she'd opened the door.

'Well it's not much of a journey really is it,' he laughed, before adding 'mind you, it's a bit of a walk from the hall I suppose, but sorry, making appointments isn't really my style. I hope you're fine, you seem to have got everything ship-shape again.'

He asked about her trip but she was a bit vague about where she'd been, trying to stick to 'the north of England' in her geographical pinpointing, despite his efforts to tie her down to somewhere specific. In the end, she almost seemed reluctant to admit that she'd been to Yorkshire to stay with a friend, and the only reason he could come up with was perhaps she had a man friend! Well well, perhaps even people in their seventies were game for a laugh he thought, before shuddering inwardly at the thought of his parents making love. Mrs Tanner spoke in general terms about visiting York and Scarborough, but he thought she was hiding behind the purpose of her trip, which appeared to be staying with the friend rather than anything else.

Henry's good humour improved his communication skills, and he asked more than he normally would about the cottage, managing the garden, her plans for Christmas, etc. In the back of his mind was a thought that he should give an update on their last conversation about Maria and Juan Marco, but the problem was Mrs Tanner's interest lay in Maria and on that score, he couldn't really claim any success. He couldn't take credit for providing Juan Marco with a comfortable temporary place, and then shrug his shoulders and say that he didn't know where Maria was, but understood she was safe and well. For that reason, he said nothing. After a small brunch, which Mrs Tanner was more reluctant to provide than normal, Henry went to the kitchen with his crockery and placed it down by the dishwasher, noticing that there already seemed to be two of everything on the worktop – two mugs, two cereal bowls, two small plates, causing him to breathe in sharply, as it occurred to him that Mrs Tanner had company! Perhaps the man from Yorkshire had come back with her and that was the reason for the delay at the door! He must be hiding in one of the bedrooms. Embarrassed by his own thoughts and for her sake, he thanked her and left without delay.

As soon as Mrs Tanner had watched him head up the path and disappear from view towards the hall, she went upstairs and knocked on the door to the second bedroom before entering. Maria sat on her bed with a look of horror on her face.

'What have I done? I should have never come here. He is the last person in the world I want to know I'm here, and I said I never wanted to see him again! I must pack, I'm sorry but I have to go!'

'It's OK, please relax. You're OK. He only drops in from time to time, and as it's usually on foot I can see him coming from the lounge. He definitely didn't see you, your secret's... I mean our secret's safe. You're doing so well and in another couple of weeks perhaps you can go home, but you mustn't take risks now!'

Maria wailed for a couple more minutes, but Mrs Tanner managed to placate her, eventually, with a lie that Henry would telephone if he was planning to visit in future.

As Henry walked away from the cottage, an idea crystallised in his mind that he would like to introduce Juan Marco to Mrs Tanner, almost as a trial run for his eventual plan to tell the family about his secret son. Best to start on a small scale, perhaps. The problem would be dealing with

166

questions about Maria's absence, but as Juan Marco knew where she was and could vouch for her safety and comfort, perhaps this could work. Clearly, Mrs Tanner had backed away from offering any help, but Henry also knew that her manners were impeccable and her judgement first rate. If she could take to Juan Marco, show him a little warmth, be as non-judgemental as she had always been with Henry himself, then maybe it was worth a shot. It was a risk, he could see that and it might backfire, but if he used it as a trial run for the family, he might pick up a few tips on how to tackle the eventual bigger challenge.

Juan Marco was still being kept busy five-and-a-half days a week by Robert, and Henry had stayed away for a few days as per Robert's request. But he sent him a text message to ask if he could call in on Saturday afternoon to check all was OK. Robert was reluctant and said that he thought Juan Marco was heading into Maidstone after work, leaving Henry to think he might be better contacting Juan Marco directly. But a little later he received an unexpected invitation to Sunday lunch from Lauren. As Juan Marco would be there Henry accepted, with some minor feelings of caution.

As they ate that weekend, Robert and Lauren both gave a good account of Juan Marco's conduct around the farm and in the house. Robert was slightly more guarded with his praise, leading Henry to suspect there was something else he wanted to say, but perhaps not in front of his wife. But as lunch wore on, the conversation moved easily between the estate and life at the hall, with Henry dealing uncomfortably with questions about his renewed visits to the estate, until Robert civilly said that he knew Lord Belvedere had been a little under the weather, and understood that might be part of Henry's reason for spending more time there.

As usual, Henry drank too much, and started to itch to drop into the conversation his thoughts about introducing Juan Marco to Mrs Tanner, as a friend of the family. When he could wait no more, Robert raised his eyebrows and gave a non-committal response, before saying he saw no harm in it, and Lauren agreed. Juan Marco's ears pricked up at this point, and rather than being worried about a sense of offence being caused at the likelihood of him being introduced in an underhand way, his mind lit up at this opportunity to make his entrance into his mother's hiding den. He'd often thought of how he was going to achieve this. With Christmas coming up he thought there would be an exchange of calls and messages about whether she was coming home to Spain for Christmas, or whether he was coming to join her, as they had never been apart at this time of the year before. Instead, he would have a direct path to her door, and just hoped Mrs Tanner was a good actor to cover her surprise when she saw his face standing on her doorstep!

Robert's mind was also on Christmas arrangements, which had been his planned attack route to find out more about the length of Juan Marco's stay on the estate.

'As I've said to you before, sir, some of the field-based duties will be coming to an end around the tenth of next month, and if he does have spare time then Juan Marco could assist with decorations in the hall, if required. But on that subject, will he still be here then, I mean for Christmas? Lauren and I normally have a house-full for a couple of days, and while I have to pop out for animal feeding and checks, as do the stockmen – possibly Juan Marco might be able to help with that too – I just assumed he'd have his own Christmas plans?'

Henry hadn't even thought of that, but Juan Marco stepped in: 'It's fine, I expect to be spending Christmas with my mother so I won't be taking up any room here. She's in England at the moment too with a friend, and we might either be together there, or possibly we'll return to Spain. I was planning on sorting it out at the start of December and then I'll let you know, if that's OK? But you don't have to worry about my room being taken for your guests.'

Robert nodded his thanks and acknowledgement before Lauren added: 'Oh, that's a shame you can't be here for Christmas, I'm sure we could have squeezed you in somewhere! But you must at least come to the estate party, mustn't he Robert? The estate and hall teams have a party in the hall each year which is our Christmas do, but it includes suppliers, contractors, members of the parish council and church, wholesalers, plus they get to bring their partners too. It's great fun, and occasionally a family member turns up,' she said giving Henry a coy smile.

Robert threw his head back and replied: 'Oh yes and who can forget the karaoke, Lauren's party piece! Now that's something you have to see, Juan Marco – the voice of the wanna-be for everyone's pleasure! Unmissable, and she treats it as her *X Factor* audition every year!'

As Henry and Juan Marco sat bemused, Lauren said animatedly: 'I could have been a star, should have been a star! I was robbed by this country life!'

168

'That sounds like a date then,' said Juan Marco, trying to ignore the sparkle in Lauren's eyes as she looked at him.

'So what's your plans after Christmas, Juan Marco?' asked Robert, half-wondering if he should be addressing Henry, but hoping that his question would cause some confusion either way.

But Juan Marco rose to the challenge and said as he glanced at Henry: 'We haven't discussed that yet, Henry, have we? While I would like to continue my training, there are other considerations, including whether my mother wants to return to Spain. But hopefully we can talk about it prior to Christmas?'

Henry was impressed at Juan Marco's competence in answering the question, and only nodded and smiled in response. The irritation caused to Robert was further increased when Lauren added: 'We'd love you to stay longer if possible! You're no bother at all.'

When Henry made a move to leave, Juan Marco asked if he could join him for the walk back to the hall, and Henry found himself agreeing far too casually due to the effect of the alcohol. He hoped, as he walked unevenly away from the farmhouse, that his mind would clear before they got too close to the building, and he could suggest a route back to Juan Marco that meant he didn't get too close. Juan Marco could see Henry wasn't in the best state for clear conversation, but was enthusiastic about seeing Mrs Tanner, and said he hoped within the next few days he'd have news as to how his mother's recovery was going. He then fell quiet for the rest of the walk, his eyes hardly leaving the outline of the hall once it came into view.

Henry's head had cleared a little once they were within four hundred metres, and he pointed out two ways that Juan Marco could take to get back to the farmhouse, if he didn't fancy simply reversing his steps. Juan Marco asked if they could take a tour of the exterior of the hall, pushing his luck deliberately.

'All in good time, my boy,' slurred Henry. 'There are ways to do things and ways to avoid. I'm not ruling out anything you understand, we just need to take it step-by-step. Of course, I understand your interest – look let's walk on a little.' As they got to within two hundred metres he stopped. 'Now up there on the right, first floor, *primera planta, a la derecha*, two windows in from the side, is my room. The one next in is spare and then it's my parents' room. Most of the rooms upstairs are bedrooms and bathrooms or dressing rooms. There are some used for storage or office work, my father's study, and then around the back are staff rooms. The ground floor is the main reception area, lounges, sitting rooms, whatever you call them in Spain – I forget the word – *salon* is it? – Then there's the kitchen, dining rooms times two, a ballroom, you know, where they hold parties – that's where the staff Christmas party will be – and so on. We can get closer one day for sure, I told you I won't sell you out. Now if you don't mind I need a piss. I don't think I can make it back to the house, so I'll go in these trees. Take care of yourself and go back now. Bye!'

Back at the farmhouse, Robert and Lauren had finished clearing up, with Robert not having done much before returning to the lounge to put the football on the TV. He wasn't best pleased with discovering nothing further about the link between Henry and Juan Marco, and was still annoyed when Lauren entered the room.

'Well, that's lunch and dinner dealt with,' she said as she patted her tummy from the armchair. 'You didn't really get anywhere with your questions, did you?'

'I'm beginning to get bored!' he snapped back. 'There's definitely something dodgy going on between those two. Of the two of them, I'm not sure who's the man and who's the boy! It's a question of role reversal! That young man is just a little bit too self-assured for my liking. I'm much more certain of tripping up his honourable partner if I can get him on his own. He seemed keen to introduce him to old Mrs Tanner for a spot of approval-seeking. You know, I think I'm reverting to my original thoughts – Juan Marco's his rent boy and it's the older man-younger guy thing going on. Henry's found the love of his life and wants to break him into the family gently.'

'You think? He could be putting on an act, but there's something that tells me he's not.'

'Oh come on!' snorted Robert. 'Your ego just doesn't like the fact that he might not actually be hot for you!'

Lauren raised her eyebrows, and her face betrayed a tiny amount of doubt which was enough to satisfy Robert, but inside she was sure Juan Marco did fancy her.

Three days later, Henry was thinking about how to call on Mrs Tanner and introduce Juan Marco. He didn't want to arrive unannounced after the other day, but the idea of making an 'appointment' irritated him. He would introduce Juan Marco in a low-key way, as she would know who he was from their first conversation. The rest he would leave to her imagination, and he'd have to trust that her manners wouldn't fail her. It occurred to him that she might react badly and think he was taking a step too far, but he'd have to accept the risk. After all, the family's reaction was likely to be far worse.

In the end, he decided to call Mrs Tanner, partly to lower the risk of a bad reaction, but also in the hope she would take this as a sign of his respect. 'Hello, Mrs Tanner. It's Henry. Is everything OK with you?'

'Yes, I'm fine, thank you. I don't know what I've done to deserve all your kind attention! I feel very flattered that you think of me as a good friend since you've been back, but I hope you're not neglecting your family. Your father needs your support right now, I imagine.'

'Thank you for your kind words, Mrs Tanner. My father is bearing up very well and he really appears fine in himself, but I think he's enjoying seeing more of us all at the moment. That's not what I'm ringing up about actually. I have a friend staying here at the moment and I'm gradually getting him out and about on the estate, and I just wondered if I could pop in and see you with him tomorrow, if you're not planning on going anywhere. It would only be for half an hour, just enough time to sink a tea or coffee, and then we'll leave you to get back to your day. You know how it is with guests sometimes – you can show them buildings but they're inanimate, and you can't have a conversation with one!'

Mrs Tanner felt her tension rising. She was determined not to reveal to anyone voluntarily that she had a guest staying, and she could hardly get Maria out of the cottage, unless she took her into the village and then collected her afterwards, which was a bit of a hassle. Her instinct was to decline, perhaps say she wasn't well, but she'd told too many lies recently and wanted to put a stop to it. Who could Henry be visiting with? What did 'friend' mean? Her instinct was he would be male, and perhaps Henry was doing a trial run of someone he wanted to introduce to his parents. She bit her lip. 'Er... I'm not sure about tomorrow, Henry. Perhaps you could find someone else you could introduce him to, the hall has quite a few people there. Oh, possibly I'm not sure, what sort of time were you thinking?' Poor Mrs Tanner – her obliging nature and respect for the family were ingrained.

'About five? Would that be OK, or a little later?'

'No, five would be OK.'

'OK, thank you Mrs Tanner. See you tomorrow.'

After Juan Marco had finished work at four, he showered at the farmhouse, and Henry met him for the walk to the cottage. They were nervous for different reasons, and Henry asked Juan Marco to let him take

171

the lead with Mrs Tanner, knowing that as soon as he said Juan Marco's name she would make the connection as to who he actually was, and might be less than pleased with his use of the term "friend". Juan Marco also expected a reaction as soon as she saw his face, but wanted to ensure her recognition of him wasn't given away to Henry.

When they reached the cottage, Juan Marco hid behind Henry in the doorway, but as soon as Henry and Mrs Tanner exchanged greetings, he edged himself around Henry and stared hard into her eyes with an abrupt shake of his head, followed by a smile.

'Mrs Tanner, it is a pleasure to meet you. Henry has told me a lot about you and your influence on him growing up. I am very grateful that you would give me a few minutes of your time, and we won't keep you long I promise. I have already seen a few parts of the estate but these old cottages have existed since the estate was created, Henry says, and I would be charmed to see inside one.'

Mrs Tanner stood stunned, but the impressive gusto of Juan Marco's introduction led her much more easily into role play than she could have expected, as she stuttered: 'Erm… well, that's fine… do come in and have a seat. I can show you the ground floor but upstairs I like to keep private, if that's OK.'

'Certainly it is, I wouldn't want to disturb you.'

As Mrs Tanner and Juan Marco led the way into the lounge, Henry followed, shocked by Juan Marco's forwardness. Mrs Tanner asked what they wanted to drink and Juan Marco relaxed into an armchair, leaving Henry hovering uncomfortably. He made his excuses and followed her into the kitchen, on the pretext of assisting her with the drinks, but the few seconds head start gave her precious time to compose herself as she heard his shoes on the wooden floor.

'Sorry about that, I didn't expect him to throw himself at you like that. His name is… Juan Marco.'

Mrs Tanner turned slowly around: 'Yes, I guessed Henry. He's young and looks Spanish so it seemed likely.'

'You don't seem surprised! I thought you might react after our conversation before!'

'I've known you a long time, Henry, and maybe there isn't much that you can do to shock me now. What's your purpose in bringing him here? Is it just to share the burden? I imagine you haven't told anyone else.'

'No,' said Henry sheepishly. 'That's about the long and short of it. He's here to gain agricultural work experience but there may be… well, I don't want to compromise you further, Mrs Tanner, so let's leave it at that.'

She nodded her agreement. 'Well he seems pleasant enough, so let's get through these drinks and then you can go after a few minutes chat. I can ask him a few questions and let's see how we do, but Henry, I must ask you not to bring him here again. You need to respect how difficult this is for me with your family.' This time Henry nodded.

They returned to the lounge and Mrs Tanner did her best to ask questions about Juan Marco's home in Spain, and how long he'd been in the UK, what he'd been up to and what he thought of the estate. Their performances were both without a stumble. As they went to leave, Juan Marco made sure he was behind Henry, and managed to turn around to whisper in Mrs Tanner's ear as Henry stepped outside: 'Please tell my mother I'm waiting for my Christmas invitation.'

Once they were gone, Mrs Tanner slowly climbed the stairs, dreading Maria's reaction not just to Henry's visit, but also to what she now had to tell her. Maria sat on her bed almost rigid with shock and incredulity, tears streaking her cheeks.

'What is going on?' she stuttered. 'Why is my son here, I thought he was in Spain? What is he doing, and with him?'

'Oh, Maria, I'm so sorry! Henry has found a way to reach him and bring him here, and I fear he's told Juan Marco who he really is! I… I had to keep all my wits about me to avoid revealing that I already knew him. It hit me like a thunderbolt to see him standing there!'

Chapter 19

Christmas Is Coming

For Mrs Tanner, it felt like game over. She'd gone behind Henry's back by bringing Maria here, and it couldn't be long before he'd find out and be furious with her. But that paled into insignificance with Juan Marco's position in all this. He knew where his mother was and had manipulated or, at best, managed Henry into bringing him here too, in full knowledge of who he was, despite his mother's attempt at secrecy. Juan Marco was one step ahead of everyone, including Henry, who couldn't have known Maria's location. It could only be a matter of time before Juan Marco told him, although how and when Mrs Tanner couldn't imagine.

She racked her brains trying to work out how Juan Marco knew where his mother was staying, but couldn't fathom it. She was at least able to keep Maria from knowing that her situation had originally been revealed by Henry, because she'd already blamed Mary for this, who was now a soft target for future use. The one comfort she could give Maria was about Juan Marco's behaviour on his visit. He'd indicated he didn't want Henry to know Maria was here, which was at least something. And his Christmas comment gave some hope that he wasn't looking for a fight.

Maria was distraught and confused. Juan Marco must surely know that Henry was his father and must have been talking to him behind her back. For how long? Did Mary know all along that Henry was his father and played along, before finally telling her son? Bitch! Or had Henry had direct contact with Juan Marco and told him himself? But surely he wouldn't have had Juan Marco's telephone number. Had Mary given it to him? Bitch! Or had Henry gone direct to Lincolnshire and stirred this all up? She didn't think him capable. Henry had sworn to keep out of their trip to England, and to George and Mary never knowing his connection to Juan Marco – had he broken his promise? Bastard! Maria's mind was half-consumed with anger towards the Belvedere family, and half-shocked by Juan Marco finding out where she was, and not letting on until it suited him. How had he found out? She hadn't told him, she was sure Mrs Tanner hadn't told him, and Henry didn't know, according to Mrs Tanner's description of his behaviour.

She wanted to speak to her son as soon as possible. She was angry with him, but also concerned if he now had the whole story worked out. But whatever he knew, it must have come from Henry, so she had to rely on Henry having only given an edited version. He wouldn't have told the whole truth, and that would provide her with the best approach.

Maria texted Juan Marco that evening to say she had no idea he was at Hillingstone, and could they meet? He kept his reply simple and arranged to come to the cottage after work on Saturday afternoon. When the time came, Mrs Tanner made herself scarce so they could be alone.

'My boy, what are you doing here? I thought you were back in Spain.'

'And I thought you were staying with Mrs Tanner in London. There's no point in fighting over the details, we're both here now. How is your recovery going?'

'But how did you know I was here?'

'It doesn't matter.'

'I want to know. Did Henry or Mary tell you?'

'Mother, I think we're beyond that now. Look, I know who Henry is, so we have to deal with the present.'

'What's he told you?' she exclaimed sharply. 'I bet he's not told you the whole truth!'

'OK, so tell me, I'll listen in the same way as I listened to Henry. You want to tell me the whole truth now? Good, I'm ready for it.'

'What did he tell you first!'

'Are you going to tell me the whole truth now? What does it matter what he said if you're going to tell me the whole truth?'

'Why are you being like this, Juan Marco? I was trying to protect you. Don't you feel any respect for your mother now?'

'Of course I respect you but we have to deal with this moment. Do you respect me enough to tell me the whole truth now? Or perhaps it doesn't matter, I know what I know, I don't need to know any more. So let's talk about your recovery and getting back to Spain. Are we returning before Christmas or after?'

Maria was stunned by the change in her son. The boy with unswerving loyalty and a desire to protect her was now talking like a man, challenging her.

'I could ask you why you didn't tell me you were coming back to stay at the very place that you have been so angry about for so many years,' he continued. 'But I found out, without deceit, and decided I wanted to know why you chose to risk coming back here just to be with your friend, but still wanted to shut me out of this part of your life, even though you knew it directly involved me, and was something I wanted to know more about. But there's no point in arguing or fighting over this, we're both here and I want our love to be restored. Either tell me what you want to tell me, or let's move on and talk about your health.'

'We need to go back to Spain,' Maria said firmly. 'I'm feeling better, still a little sore and walking isn't easy, but I think I'm well enough to fly. You can book the tickets now and we can fly home tomorrow or the next day.'

'What do the doctors say?'

'Just that. I'm making progress but it will take time, but I may as well spend that time at home than here. We can go.'

'Then why didn't you contact me to tell me you were ready to come home? Don't get angry with me, please, just answer. Are you happy here with Mrs Tanner for a little while longer perhaps? You've renewed your friendship and maybe you want a little more time here? That's OK mother, I will understand.'

Maria fixed with him with a stare. 'No, I am ready to go home... now that *he* is knocking on the door and I have to hear his voice. No, we are leaving.'

It didn't escape Juan Marco that his mother still hadn't told him the 'whole truth', which meant that she still wanted to keep things from him. But it didn't matter at this point. Henry's story sounded at least half-believable, and he had to accept that if Maria had unpleasant memories perhaps she would never want to talk about it. But he decided on one final try.

'Did you have a relationship with him, or was it a one-off?' The fire was back again in her eyes.

'He used me! Isn't that good enough for you?'

'Did you and my father have a relationship?' he asked quietly, feeling every ounce of the impact of those words. Maria's face froze and she looked

176

ashen, unable to speak. Juan Marco kept his eyes locked onto hers, giving her no escape. Then she let out a whimper, lowered her head and slowly nodded. He breathed a sigh of relief.

'He doesn't know you're here, so if you want to stay a little longer that's OK, if Mrs Tanner is happy with it. But I've been staying with the estate manager and working, learning some really good things and I'm enjoying it. I'd like to stay a little longer to complete my work and help their preparations for Christmas. We could go back a few days before Christmas if you want.'

'Why do you want to be around him, Henry? Doesn't he disgust you?'

Juan Marco shrugged his shoulders. 'I don't see much of him. He hasn't told anyone who I am, so they just treat me as a temporary farm worker.'

'I still want to go home now. This has been such a shock.'

'I want a couple more weeks, Mother, if Mrs Tanner will let you stay. I've already told the estate manager that I'll be here for about three weeks more and I've enjoyed it, there's stuff I want to finish and I've made some new friends here. Can you speak to Mrs Tanner and see what she says?'

'Juan Marco… no…' she pleaded.

He smiled at her, but his face had a firm expression and he stood up to go. 'Let me know what she says. I'll be able to come and see you more often now.'

After he'd gone, Maria collapsed into tears. She'd not thought about Christmas at all, and suddenly it was creeping up and imposing a deadline. She wanted to be back home for Christmas urgently and to have Juan Marco with her, away from the influence of the estate and its people. Once Mrs Tanner returned from the village, Maria told her what they'd discussed. Her friend sympathised and confirmed staying for longer wasn't a problem. In fact, she'd wondered if Maria would be OK to go home before Christmas and, if not, then she'd planned on inviting her to stay on and celebrate with her, and give her company until the new year. Now that they'd discovered Juan Marco was here, he could stay over Christmas too, if that would make Maria happy. The news didn't give Maria the comfort intended.

Over the next few days, Juan Marco returned to his farm and estate duties, and called on his mother every third or fourth day, messaging in advance to ensure it was safe to visit. That also gave him an opportunity to get to know Mrs Tanner a little more, and they became more comfortable in each other's company, especially as he made it clear he would avoid coming with Henry again. His work routines started to adapt to the season, as he spent more time delivering winter crops to wholesalers and local businesses, which took him away from the estate more and calmed all their nerves. Nevertheless, Maria was firmly focused on returning home as quickly as possible, and started to do short walks around the cottage garden to improve her strength, despite the cold and wet weather in the last week of November. Mrs Tanner extended her invitation for Juan Marco to stay with them over the Christmas period, but he was reluctant to accept for two reasons.

Firstly, he didn't know how he could explain it to Henry in view of what had happened before. Secondly, he was uncomfortable about his time at the estate coming to an end. The more time he spent with Robert and Lauren, the more he had an opportunity to see if there were prospects for staying at the estate beyond Christmas, despite what he'd suggested to his mother about returning to Spain in a couple of weeks' time. He was enjoying the experience of being in a different environment, being more independent and being treated as one of the estate workers. In truth, he was enjoying this adventure much more than he expected, despite his animosity towards the Belvedere family.

In Henry's mind, Juan Marco wasn't about to go home to Spain either. The grand revelation of his existence was still his master plan, and he was pondering how to raise Juan Marco's profile on the estate as a way of introducing his presence. It occurred to him that Christmas might be an opportunity for the big announcement with the whole family gathered, so there would be maximum impact. To that end, he'd been thinking about where Juan Marco would stay over Christmas. He knew that Robert and Lauren were expecting a full house, so he was mulling over trying to get Juan Marco a room in the domestic staff area of the hall. Not only would this further his overall plan, but it would take Robert's influence down a level, as he still worried over his reliance on Robert's discretion. Of course, this would need his parents' approval so he'd have to float the idea to them first, and they'd have to meet Juan Marco in advance.

With the idea of persuading Juan Marco that a move to the hall was the best option, Henry set out on a damp and cold morning to the estate office, to check on Juan Marco's whereabouts. As he approached the timber office building, he could hear a Spanish voice coming from the stables, and guessed that Juan Marco must be mucking out the horses. In fact, as he reached the first stable, he found his son attaching a harness to Anna's mare.

'Hello, Juan Marco, how are you? Are you preparing her for Robert to ride?'

'Er, no, I was going to exercise her myself. Lauren suggested it as Robert is tied up with suppliers,' he replied defensively. 'Lauren said it would be OK.'

'I didn't know you could ride! Are you proficient, I mean you know what you're doing?'

Juan Marco looked at him cautiously, but before he could say anything Lauren popped her head out of the office door. 'Hello Henry, everything OK? Juan Marco's just harnessing up Arabella for a little exercise. He's a very assured horseman as I'm sure you must know.'

'No, I didn't as it happens, but don't let me interrupt. I could never get to grips with it myself, but happy to watch someone who's got the gift.'

Juan Marco felt uncomfortable being looked at by two people who were now expectant.

'Go on, Juan Marco, don't keep her waiting!' exclaimed Lauren, bemused at Juan Marco's sudden reticence. With a shrug, he continued to secure the harness and then went into the bridle room for the saddle. Three minutes later he was up on the mare and walking her into the paddock, where he went through a gentle exercise routine before accelerating up to a canter. While he carried out his routine, Henry took the opportunity to ask Lauren about their Christmas plans.

'Are you still expecting a full house at Christmas, Lauren?'

'Yes, we believe so. There's a couple of my family that haven't responded yet, but I'm sure they'll join us at some point.'

'OK. I was thinking there's a possibility that Juan Marco may be staying on into the new year. He's enjoying himself, I think, and you're happy with his work commitment? My God, he's good on that horse, isn't he? Well, he wouldn't have anywhere to stay over Christmas, so I was thinking of seeing if I could get him a room in the hall in the domestic quarters. If it works out then he'd probably stay there after Christmas is all over and done with, if he remains here, so you'd be back to having your privacy again. Wouldn't that be nice?'

Lauren was alarmed and couldn't hide her reaction as well as she'd like. She didn't want to be the one to tell Robert that some of his control would be disappearing, as she'd be the one to feel his displeasure. There was also a tinge of regret that her handsome house guest might be moving out.

'Erm… if you think that's best. Have you mentioned this to Robert? I wasn't aware that there was a possibility of his work placement being extended. In fact, I thought he was headed back to Spain shortly.'

'No, I haven't, but I'm mentioning it to you now. That's OK, isn't it? I don't want to cause any concern. Oh, I see, are you concerned about money, you know the expense of having him around? I'm sure I can sort something out in the short term, if you'd like? Perhaps Robert needs to balance the books, and if it's a question of having to make provision for some wages…?'

Lauren was still hesitant. 'I don't know about that, that's Robert's area. I don't think he'd have any objection to keeping him on,' she said, trying to regain some composure. 'His work has been really good, and if he was to stay on then I think we'd both be happy if he came back to the farmhouse,' she said with a smile.

'Well, I don't think there'd be any problem with him up at the hall,' replied Henry offhandedly. 'Besides, I meant what I said about giving you both your privacy back. Not that I'm ungrateful for what you've done, quite the contrary. In fact, please stress that to Robert when you tell him.' Henry now felt slightly nervous about his private arrangement with Robert, and how the latter might react if he was suddenly dropped like a stone. 'Look, I tell you what, why don't you mention it in passing to Robert and see how he feels, and then perhaps let me know what he says?'

Lauren was about to suggest that Henry should come to the farmhouse later to talk to Robert directly, when they were interrupted by the sound of a car approaching from the direction of the hall. As they looked up, Lord Belvedere stopped the Range Rover and climbed out. After greeting both of them, he asked Lauren: 'Who's that young man riding Anna's mare? I've seen him before, I think. Splendid rider, great balance and confidence.'

Lauren looked at Henry waiting for him to take the lead. To her surprise, he stepped in smartly. 'Well, that's very coincidental, Father! I was looking at a way of introducing you to him and now seems like the perfect moment! His name is Juan Marco and he comes from Spain. I got to know him and his mother a little, and it was clear to me that they could do with a helping hand, so I offered him an opportunity for work experience on an

English farm, to try to give them both a brighter future. I checked with Lauren and Robert that they could make use of him, as well as teaching him, and it's all working out rather well, isn't it, Lauren?'

Lauren was transfixed to the spot, suddenly feeling she and Robert had got themselves into deep water. 'He's a good worker,' she said meekly.

'He's not on the payroll so the estate is benefitting,' continued Henry brazenly.

'I see,' replied Lord Belvedere, wondering why Henry hadn't told the family about this. 'So he's doing other things then besides the horses?'

'Of course!' laughed Henry. This is just exercising the horses as Robert's away today, isn't that so, Lauren?'

'Oh yes, he gets stuck into everything on the farm rota,' Lauren said, recovering her composure. 'This morning, he's been delivering produce, mucking out the stables, checking the sheep in the field, and then there's a fence repair later. Robert's been working him extremely hard, but he's stood up to everything. Exercising the horses is a bit of a treat for both him and the mares. He really is very accomplished,' she finished, as they all turned their heads towards the rider in the paddock. They watched him in silence for a minute, executing turns and changes to pace, and then Henry called out to him: 'Juan Marco, there's someone here I'd like you to meet!'

Juan Marco broke his concentration and turned the horse towards the gate. He dismounted and looked at the well-dressed older man, guessing he was someone important on the estate.

'Juan Marco, this is my father, Lord Belvedere. He owns the family estate. I've told him about your training programme and he was admiring your horsemanship!'

'Thank you, sir,' Juan Marco replied politely, looking at Lord Belvedere with a half-smile. You have a beautiful home here and a wonderful estate. I have learnt many things since coming here and I hope I have worked hard enough to please everyone. It's a great opportunity for me and I hope I am repaying the trust given to me.'

Henry smirked at his politeness, this couldn't have gone any better. Lord Belvedere nodded and replied in a more relaxed tone: 'I have seen you here before with the horses but didn't know you were working here as well. I hope your training is going well and you're being well looked after? Do you know much about horses? You ride beautifully.'

'Thank you, I used to ride in Spain but have fallen out of the habit, but an occasional ride here gives me great pleasure. They're beautiful mares.'

'Yes, Robert does a fine job with them. The one you've been riding is my daughter Anna's. She's not here at the moment.'

Juan Marco nodded. 'Yes, Lauren explained.'

'Well, Henry, you must invite Juan Marco up to the hall for dinner. Where are you staying now?'

'He's staying with us at the farmhouse,' Lauren quickly responded. 'I think we've made him very comfortable.' As she spoke Henry flashed her a look of annoyance, but before he could say anything, Lord Belvedere continued.

'Well I'm glad it's all working smoothly. I should like to hear about your life in Spain, Juan Marco, and my wife and I look forward to seeing you for dinner. Henry, you'll make the arrangements with your mother?'

'Of course, Father, very soon.'

Henry started on his way back to the house, and his initial annoyance at what he saw as Lauren's attempt at control, was soon replaced with a sense of walking on air. Could it have gone any better? A chance meeting with his Father; Juan Marco's exemplary manners; an invitation to dinner which would inevitably lead to Juan Marco's charm weaving its effect. Surely the arrangement of a room in the hall would be a breeze, and the icing on the cake was that no other family members could interfere!

He resolved to speak to his mother quickly to make the dinner arrangements.

Back at the estate office, Lauren was fretting over the conversation she would have to have with Robert. He would fume when he discovered he was being distanced from whatever was going on between Henry and Juan Marco, and would react aggressively towards both of them. But she was more concerned that his temper would be aimed at her initially. The longer she left it, the worse it would be. She couldn't say anything at the farmhouse with Juan Marco there, so her best hope was that Robert would come to the office after his meeting, rather than going straight home. She was therefore partially relieved when he appeared.

'Did the meeting go well? Did they feed you?'

'Yes and yes. All washed down with a couple of glasses of Malbec. Anything that's happened here that I need to know?'

Lauren inhaled quietly and prepared to give her best performance. 'Well, we had two surprise visits from the family, one from Henry and one from Lord Belvedere. Henry was just checking up on Juan Marco who was exercising Arabella. And then his father was just going out in his car and saw Juan Marco riding, and stopped to find out who he was.'

'Oh, and how did that go?' asked Robert interestedly. 'Did Henry squirm?'

'I can't say that he did. He seemed rather pleased with the opportunity, actually, and stuck to the benevolent benefactor script to a tee. His father seemed to swallow it.'

'I see, that's a pity. Anything else?'

'Well, I think Lord Belvedere must be going soft because he invited him to dinner!'

'What, the boy? You're joking! A general dinner you mean for the key staff – we must be there, I mean it's us who are doing all the bloody work and babysitting him!'

'No I don't think so,' replied Lauren as disinterestedly as she dare. 'I think it's just with them and Henry.'

'Oh, I don't think so!' Robert was becoming heated now. 'I'm not being shut out now after I've kept that shitty bastard's dirty secret. What does he take me for? And what were you doing while all this was unfolding? Standing there like a lamp post?'

'No I wasn't!' responded Lauren. 'I said how much time you were putting into his work experience and how comfortable we'd made him.'

'But you didn't think about getting a dinner invitation!'

'No. I couldn't very well suggest it when Lord Belvedere was talking directly to Juan Marco and Henry was there too! It was his baby, not mine!'

'For fuck's sake!' countered Robert.

'Well if you're going to be like that, you might as well know that I think Henry's planning on getting him a room at the hall for Christmas! There's no 'room at the inn' after all, if you'll excuse the pun.'

'Ah for Christ's sake, if you'll excuse the pun! Sometimes I wonder what you're good for! So on that point, you'd better do something about finding out what goes on at that meal. Use your womanly charms on your Spanish toyboy! Flash him some smiles and skin and be extra nice to him! I won't be left out and taken for a bloody fool by that waste of space!'

When Henry spoke to his mother about the dinner, like her husband she was surprised that Henry hadn't mentioned Juan Marco's presence before. 'I'm pleased that you're doing something for someone else, I mean it's a

183

good thing you're doing for a young man with limited prospects, but you could have told us. We wouldn't have been critical, especially as your father says he is well-mannered.'

'I just wanted to be sure it would work out. He had a placement in the UK before which I arranged and that went OK, but his mother came with him and had a health scare which ended the placement, so I wasn't sure how long he would stay here, or what his commitment level would be like.'

'Oh, how is his mother now? Is she still here?'

'Yes, I believe so. Although I'm not directly in touch with her, but I'm sure Juan Marco is. He told me she's recuperating with an old friend she has in England.'

The dinner was arranged for that Friday evening, and Henry was light-headed beforehand, partly because of his sense of euphoria at how his plans were coming together, and partly because he'd helped himself to a couple of gin and tonics. He had no doubt that Juan Marco would remain civil and polite throughout, and that his natural manners would charm his parents once he was over his nerves.

Henry had sent him a text asking him to dress smartly, and said he would come and fetch him in one of the estate cars. On the short journey back to the house, he explained the etiquette of a formal dinner, and told him to relax and enjoy himself, before adding: 'By the way, what are you doing about Christmas? Have you any plans where you're going to stay?'

'Yes, I will be seeing my mother.' Juan Marco was careful not to say he would be staying with her.

'Oh right, is she well? She's still in London?'

'Close to it, yes.'

'And her recovery?'

'Yes, she's getting better,' he replied economically.

'OK, well I'd had a thought about where you might stay if you hadn't other plans. You know Robert and Lauren are full up for a few days, so I thought you might be able to stay up at the hall. If tonight goes well, which I'm sure it will, then I think my parents would be quite happy for you to have one of the spare rooms. After Christmas, if your stay can be extended... well we'll see how it goes, but maybe you could remain there if you were happy. You wouldn't be intruding on Robert and Lauren's privacy so much.'

Juan Marco gave an indifferent expression before replying: 'I'm fairly certain I want to be close to my mother.'

Henry was silent for a few seconds. 'OK, we'll take it one step at a time.'

The dinner turned out well for Juan Marco. Lord and Lady Belvedere asked lots of questions about his upbringing, his work and what he hoped to achieve in the future. He spoke politely and simply in answering the questions, and said all the right things about what he was learning at Hillingstone from Robert and Lauren, and how he appreciated their time. He spoke of returning to Spain to start a smallholding that could grow over time, and calmly avoided any pitfalls to do with his first work experience at George and Mary's farm, and anything to do with his mother or father. By the end of the meal, he had turned the conversation towards the history of the estate and the modern challenges of running such a large operation, and was then able to relax, as both Lord and Lady Belvedere were glad of having such an interested young listener to talk at.

When the meal ended they all saw him off at the door and, as the car pulled away, Lord Belvedere turned to his son. 'What a thoroughly pleasant young man, wouldn't you agree, Caroline? Interested in everything and seemed to know quite a bit about the estate already. Well done, Henry, on giving him such a good briefing. I expect Robert fed him all the farming information, but the family history knowledge he displayed must be down to you.'

Henry hesitated, accepting the compliment although his mind was asking the same question. But he assumed it must have come from Robert and Lauren, and there was no harm in taking the praise anyway.

'I'm glad you both liked him, I think he deserves a foot-up in life. Actually, while we're talking about him, I'd like to mention that he may be short of somewhere to stay over Christmas. The farmhouse will be full as usual, and it had occurred to me that we would have room here if he really found himself out of luck. It may not be necessary but could we accommodate him if he absolutely needed it?'

'Well of course I see no problem with it. Caroline, what do you think?'

'Of course, Henry, it would be a pleasure if he needs it. He's very interesting company.'

In Mrs Tanner's cottage, Maria was still continuing her efforts to recover her strength. She now felt embarrassed about their continued absence from the bar in Spain, and had sent some money electronically to their landlord to keep the flat rent up to date. Her mind was set on having Juan Marco with her at Christmas and returning to Spain as quickly as possible in January, if not before. She had been trying hard to persuade Mrs Tanner that Henry shouldn't reappear, but as a minimum urged her to message him a reminder about not visiting unannounced. This caused a little tension between them, and she had to desist in case her own position became difficult.

Juan Marco spent the next few days on estate and farm duties, and tried to act as normal as possible, despite Lauren's subtle but persistent teasing about him now being too good for their little abode. She seemed freer with him, especially when Robert wasn't around, and he noticed a combination of her dressing up and dressing down in equal measure, almost as if she was testing him, or at least trying to get his attention. His mind was split over where to stay at Christmas. He knew his loyalty should be to his mother but they were on different paths for now – she wanted to get him back under her control; he wanted her to understand that things wouldn't go back to how they were before, and that going back home was something he wasn't contemplating for now. He wanted as much for himself from Hillingstone as he could get in terms of knowledge, and felt even possible employment in the short term might be an option, rather than living off cash handouts from Robert (as nothing had materialised from Henry). In short, he wanted to stay for longer, so that when he returned home he'd have many of the skills to think of the future as a farmer.

The subject of where to stay was therefore thorny, but the rising tension between Lauren and Robert made the farmhouse an uncomfortable choice for much longer. If he secured a room at the hall and proved himself to be a decent house guest over Christmas, but spent part of his days with his mother, then it might hold him in good stead for extending his stay. The only problem he could see was the inevitable reappearance of George and Mary, who must surely visit at some point. He would have to keep well out of the way and deal with one problem at a time.

By the end of November, Juan Marco's help was needed in preparing the hall for Christmas, which included the traditional invitational carol concert for village residents, and a children's party. The entrance hall and second sitting room would accommodate the Christmas tree and nativity play performance space respectively. The local primary school children would give two shows to their families, and carol singing would take place

186

around the tree. Outside the hall, local farmers would bring in a few sheep and a couple of cows for a small temporary enclosure, and a villager who kept a couple of donkeys would add to the nativity theme. This was another opportunity for Lauren to shine, and she enjoyed bringing it together with Lady Belvedere, without Robert being heavily involved.

Once the tree had been delivered, Juan Marco and one other farm worker were tasked with scaling the temporary scaffolding to decorate the tree. He enjoyed the job and couldn't help but notice how Lauren's eyes shone with pleasure as it came to life. It also meant that he spoke more with Lady Belvedere, leading him to decide that she had a natural warmth which would make her an easy person to like.

After the weekend, he decided to speak cautiously with Henry about the possibility of moving to the hall. With Christmas fast approaching, he decided this was the best time to drop the bombshell of his mother's presence just a few hundred metres away. He asked Henry to meet him in one of the grazing fields, while he was checking the feet of two sheep that had picked up a limp.

'I've been thinking about where to stay over Christmas,' he started. 'I liked your parents, and perhaps being on the estate means I can help out with any emergency work that's needed.'

Henry raised his eyebrows with pleasure. 'Well, I'm pleased to hear that's how you feel. I've already raised it with them as a precaution and they're only too willing to help you if you'd like, so I'll let them know. What will you do about visiting your mother?'

Juan Marco twisted his mouth and gently bit his bottom lip. 'I've discovered she's not been honest with me about where she's staying. I dragged it out of her and I've seen her. When I found out she was staying with Mrs Tanner, I made sure they both understood how angry I was.'

'Mrs Tanner!' Henry said incredulously. 'But she can't be. She wouldn't be underhand with me, especially after I specifically asked her...'

'I had my suspicions after our visit there, the feeling there was somebody else in the house,' Juan Marco said, cutting in. 'I know that you respect her a lot, but I left both of them in no doubt that their deceit was hurtful to us both. I believe Mrs Tanner is racked with guilt now and wants to apologise, but doesn't know how.'

'I'll say she should bloody apologise!' fumed Henry. 'I've trusted her with so many things I've never told anyone else, and this is how she repays me! I'm off to bloody well see her now!'

'No, please don't go off in a rush!' pleaded Juan Marco. 'I think I've already been rude to her and she's embarrassed. Please, wait until you're calmer, maybe we can go see them together? Instead, why don't I come to the hall and speak to your parents about taking up the offer of the room? I'd really like to be there when you tell them and I can thank them personally. I'll be finished up here in half an hour and then I can come straight to the hall. Besides, there's something else I need to speak to you about – Robert and Lauren, especially Robert. There's tension between them at the moment, and he seems irritated about the offer of moving to the hall. I may need you to speak to him.'

'Robert,' snorted Henry. 'Speaking to Robert is the last thing on my mind. I've already spoken to his fucking wife and that should be enough. He can whistle!'

'OK, see you in about forty-five minutes then at the hall,' Juan Marco quickly responded, eager to deflect Henry away from Mrs Tanner's cottage. 'I really think it's important they know they've got another guest at Christmas,' he emphasised.

Henry rolled his eyes and looked to the sky, before letting out a huge huff and stomping off in the direction of the hall, muttering as he went: 'What is wrong with these people? It's normally the family that treat me like an imbecile, now a member of the staff, no, not even a current member...'

Chapter 20

Party Time

Juan Marco couldn't risk Henry demanding his pound of flesh from Mrs Tanner. Firstly, it felt wrong that he had known from the start that his mother was on the estate and he was party to Henry being in the dark, and secondly, he didn't want another battle of words between his mother and father. He had his own needs to think of and they wouldn't be served by all-out war. He, therefore, decided to go to the cottage and talk to both women in advance of Henry's inevitable visit.

'Come in, Juan Marco, your mother's in the sitting room. I'll give you some time alone together.'

'Um… it's OK actually, I need to talk to both of you.'

Mrs Tanner ushered him in, and after some small talk about Maria's health, he began.

'Of course I'd like to spend Christmas Day with you, Mother. In Spain, Mrs Tanner, the 25th December isn't such a big day, although it's becoming more widely celebrated. For us, the 6th January is the big day, celebrating when the Three Kings brought their gifts to baby Jesus. But we're in England now and, besides, we've always recognised Christmas Day because Mother remembers it from her working times here. I hope that's OK with you?'

Mrs Tanner nodded her head and smiled. 'Of course, I want you to be with your mother as much as you want to be, and the offer to stay here for a few days still stands.'

'Yes, I was going to talk to you about that. I'm feeling it's time we stopped having secrets between us.' He turned to his mother. 'Henry has suspicions that Mrs Tanner has a guest staying that she's trying to hide. I don't know where from, but perhaps my attempts at being sneaky, when we came here together before, weren't as successful as I thought. He's definitely going to return here, and he's asking me questions about where

189

you're living, how I'm going to get to you at Christmas, that sort of thing.'

Maria's face coloured as she drew in her breath. 'It's got nothing to do with him! He should mind his own business!'

'I know, but it could be difficult for Mrs Tanner, too. Mrs Tanner, Henry told me he used to tell you secrets that he wouldn't tell anyone else. Has he ever told you about my mother or asked you for any help?'

Mrs Tanner went white and stammered but Maria cut in: 'He's not going threaten her! Everything she's done has been from the goodness of her heart!'

'Oh my!' cried Mrs Tanner. 'What have I done? Oh, Maria I so wanted to help you when Henry told me about your plight, but I've been disloyal to the very family that employed me all those years, and still house me now!'

'What? Henry told you about me? But I thought you found out from Mary who was talking to Juan Marco?'

'Oh, I've made such a mess!' said a tearful Mrs Tanner. 'I didn't want you thinking that I was acting on his request because I knew how you felt about him. I told him I wouldn't help because I thought it was underhand, but as soon as I had time to reflect, I realised I wanted to help you without him knowing about it. This was personal for me, a chance to help you when I felt I let you down all those years ago!'

Maria sat stunned while Juan Marco waited for the right moment to say something.

'Well, all this secrecy has got to stop,' continued Mrs Tanner determinedly, as she looked at Juan Marco. 'You think Henry has suspicions, maybe more?' He nodded. 'In that case, we need to deal with this now. I will apologise to him and remind him of the difficult circumstances when you left the estate, Maria, and hope for the best. I have no regrets about trying to help you and I'll tell him that. Can you please get him to come, Juan Marco?'

'Of course. I'm a little relieved by your decision,' he said with a half-smile. 'I'll do everything I can to make him see why you acted this way.'

'I don't want to see him!' interrupted Maria, struggling with the idea that Henry had helped her in a roundabout way.

'I'm afraid I think you should,' replied Mrs Tanner as kindly as she could. 'No more secrets.'

Juan Marco realised that it was best for him to be direct with Robert about moving to the hall for Christmas, even though Lauren had already told him the news. Since then, Robert had been cool towards him and had mostly left him alone, sometimes leaving Lauren with his routine for the day. But as they breakfasted together in the second week of December, Lauren was animatedly explaining what was going to happen at the staff Christmas party, which was taking place on the coming Saturday. As even Robert managed a smirk or two, Juan Marco decided to clear the air when Lauren had finished.

'When do your Christmas guests arrive?'

'After next weekend,' came Robert's reply, looking up to Lauren as he spoke coolly.

'Yes, that's right,' she added. 'The 23rd.'

'OK, well I'll move my things out the previous day to give you a chance to prepare,' Juan Marco said, as he turned his head from Lauren to Robert. 'I'm moving to the hall for Christmas, I think you're aware? I knew you didn't have space but there's a room available in the staff area, which will work out well if there's any emergency estate work that I need to help with.'

'If there is any emergency, it won't be anything I can't handle,' replied Robert tetchily. 'I thought you were going to stay with your mother?'

'The room is a bit short there, but I will still be seeing a lot of her.'

'I suppose Henry's sorting out transport for you, is he? I hope you don't think I'm going to be running you about, because I'll be having a skin-full most of the time and won't be going anywhere.'

'Robert, please, show some manners,' Lauren said, cutting in with a chiding voice. 'We said we didn't have any room and Juan Marco's made other arrangements as he should, and it's all worked out.'

Robert glared at his wife before saying: 'Yes, he's certainly been taken care of.'

'I want you both to know how grateful I am for making me welcome and taking me into your home. I will be giving you a Christmas present, it's the least I can do. I also want to ask you about the possibility of staying on after Christmas. I don't know if it's possible and I haven't spoken to Henry yet, but I've learnt so much and feel there is more I can do. Do you think you would find me useful if I stayed for longer?'

Robert's interest was piqued. 'I thought you were going back to Spain with your mother?'

'I'm not sure she's ready, but if she is, it can only be because she is fit enough to look after herself. I'm not planning to stay here long term but, I don't know, maybe a few more weeks is possible. I'll know more about her recovery when I see her at Christmas. Do you think you can make use of me around the estate if I stay, and continue with my training too? It will be a big plus if I can tell Henry that you need me... or at least that I'm useful.'

Robert sucked in his cheeks and thought for a few seconds. It annoyed him that he still didn't understand the relationship between Juan Marco and Henry, but had figured the game was over. Now there was a possibility that he might still have some leverage.

'Would you plan to come back here after Christmas, to stay?'

'I would hope so,' came the reply. 'After all, it would make the most sense from a work point of view.'

'Well, OK, let's see. Why don't you mention it to Henry and then tell him he needs to discuss it with me. Tell him that he *personally* needs to agree it with me. I'm sure he'll understand.'

By Friday evening, Juan Marco was feeling the collective excitement of his estate colleagues for tomorrow's party, enhanced by comments made by the contract farmers he bumped into, and some of the estate's customers. He got a lift into Maidstone with one of the labourers on Saturday morning, and joined him in buying a new shirt and a casual jacket. The weather wasn't great as they set off in the early evening for the party in Robert's pick-up truck. He explained they usually drove down to the hall anyway and left the cars there overnight, staggering back to the farmhouse as a tradition at the end of the night. Juan Marco picked up on the smirk Robert and Lauren exchanged, when Robert mentioned an occasional detour.

They arrived at the hall before the first guests, and walked through to the ballroom to check on all the preparations. As usual, it looked fabulous with all the decorations, a beautiful eight foot tree, lighting complemented by the rays thrown out by the two chandeliers, and tables and chairs arranged in groups of eight, all decorated festively. In the centre of the tables was the buffet, already half-filled with savoury dishes, and the outside caterers were laying the rest out. At nine p.m., they would clear away what was left and depart, and then the housekeeper and two kitchen staff would bring out the desserts, which by tradition were always baked at the hall. Within a few minutes, the caterers finished laying out, and by half past seven the room was filling with guests and the disco had started up.

Robert's instructions to Juan Marco were quite simple – eat, mix, get drunk and make a fool of yourself. He grinned at the last part, yearning that the young man would particularly take it on board.

As Robert turned away to meet more guests, Lauren and Juan Marco looked interestedly at each other for a few seconds. Her hair was freshly waved and tied back either side; her sexy, curvy body was clad in a slinky, ruby-red, knee-length dress, which also exposed a little cleavage, and her eyes sparkled with self-confidence. She knew she looked hot, even without his eyes boring into her. She looked him up and down approvingly, checking out his chest muscles pushing against his shirt and jacket, and the way his chinos moulded to his legs and slender waist. As she gave him one last flash of her eyes before turning back to join Robert, she whispered to herself: 'Oh you would, wouldn't you…'

Juan Marco gritted his teeth and turned away. He would have to be careful tonight, not too much to drink, and make sure he ate plenty. He had no intention of making a fool of himself, whatever Robert wished for.

The party officially started with a short welcome from Robert, which ended with pretty much the same comments as he'd made to Juan Marco. The newcomer mixed well and easily with his natural charm, and he only occasionally gave Lauren a glance to remind himself how beautiful she looked. Once or twice he took some satisfaction in catching her eyes briefly on him. He avoided her on the dance floor, despite her waving at him once to join her, loudly encouraged by an increasingly drunk Robert. No, he sensed the trap, even if Lauren was innocent in its laying.

By half past ten the food was finished and it was time for the karaoke to start. Robert started with a drunken rendition of 'Something Stupid', which he tried to get Lauren to join him in, but the star of the show was having none of it, and he dragged up the drunk daughter of one of the contract farmers instead, whose toneless lyrics were a match for Robert's drawl. After three guests had had a go, Robert started a tasteless chant of 'we want Lauren!' and the lady of the moment quickly took to the stage to shut him up, having already picked her song from the disco master earlier.

The opening bars to Cathy Dennis's 'Too Many Walls' began, and Lauren's smiling face searched the room for the man she was going to impress. Her voice was pitch-perfect, and she licked the first few lines, before finally spotting Juan Marco in the crowd towards the back. He was staring at her but half-hiding behind another guest, but she now had her target. She teased her way through the dreamy lyrics, singing them as provocatively as she dared. Her performance was mesmerising and the whole room swayed, except one half-hidden figure who just stared. The star of the show took her bow and walked off the stage taking the plaudits, gushing at Juan Marco's inevitable congratulations to come, but he wasn't there in the immediate circle, and she had to settle herself among the admirers still talking at her.

'Well,' whispered the female voice in his ear. 'This is a surprise, Juan Marco.' He turned to see Mary close up to him as she put her arm through his. 'Enjoying the songstress? She's good, isn't she? But you may need to be careful that you're not seen to be enjoying it too much. It may not be just me that notices you've taken a shine to her, being a married woman and all.'

Juan Marco stood stunned before stuttering: 'Mary, I didn't expect to see you here... I mean, they said someone from the family might come by but...'

'I think it might be a good idea if we escaped for a few minutes, don't you? Come on, before anyone notices.' Mary whisked him out of the door and into the library, which she knew was too close to the ballroom for the family to be using it.

'So Henry managed to get you here then? I didn't think he had it in him. You look well, and the fact that you're at an estate party and clearly familiar with Lauren means presumably, you're on the staff here?'

He nodded slowly, determined to give up as little as possible in answer to her questions.

'Right, OK, not much to work with there,' she replied smartly. 'Look, I understand me being here must be a shock to you, but remember I like you and have a lot of respect for you. So please, if you can be open with me then do so. Help me to help you. OK?' He said nothing so she started again.

'Right, well maybe if I ask you some questions it will be easiest if you just reply to those, without having to give me a story. So is it just you here or your mother too?'

'She's here as well, but she's not staying with me. It's complicated.'

'Really? You surprise me. So how did Henry persuade her to come? You, I can understand because you were clearly prepared to listen to him, but her? I don't think so.'

'He didn't get her to come, she made her own way.' As Mary stared

194

open-mouthed he added: 'I told you it's complicated. She's staying somewhere else on the estate.' Mary's jaw was still open and her eyes ever-wider, so Juan Marco knew he had to explain. 'She's staying with Mrs Tanner at her cottage.'

'Mrs Tanner? Does Henry know?'

'He does now, although he's only just discovered it.'

Again Mary's jaw hung apart.

'What was his reaction to that?' she asked incredulously.

'It's OK I think, at least it is now. He's made his peace with her, at least I haven't heard that they haven't sorted it out. I arranged for him to go up to the cottage this morning and I hoped they would talk it over. She's a very nice person, Mrs Tanner, and I think she and Henry share a lot of history. I like her.'

'Whoa!' puffed out Mary. 'And what about your mother? Is she on speaking terms with him?'

'Not really, but I think Mrs Tanner is acting as referee and she figures my mother needs to calm down. I think she has influence over her.'

Mary's face was still an expression of surprise. 'How is your mother now?'

'She's slowly getting better. I think she wants to return to Spain next month.'

'And you, where are you staying? You're not at the hall surely?' she said looking around the room.

'No, I'm staying with Robert and Lauren,' he replied economically, not willing to offer up news of his impending move. 'It fits with me working here, learning and helping out.'

'Do Robert and Lauren know who you are, I mean your connection to the family? And do they know about your mother?' He shook his head.

'Well, I can see why it's complicated! So they don't know she's here?'

'Not as far as I know. Well, I'm sure they don't. Robert would be using it, if he knew.'

Mary chuckled quietly. 'Well, you've worked him out, so well done for that. He's sly and smarmy and not to be trusted. As for Lauren, she's a good-time girl, do you understand? She'll chew you up and spit you out. Whatever you do, keep your guard up and don't fall for her. I know what happens from history, and you'd probably end up giving Robert ammunition.'

He nodded, expressionless, at her, determined to say nothing more. He wasn't going to share his attraction with anyone.

'So you're working on the estate? Is it going well? Have you been… erm… introduced to any of the family?' she asked cautiously.

'I've met Lord and Lady Belvedere. Henry introduced me as a young man from Spain that he's trying to help, nothing more.'

She bit her lip. 'Is there anything more going on, Juan Marco? What are your plans?'

'I want to stay a little longer on the estate. I'm learning so much, and I think after a few more weeks into next year I'll feel confident enough to return to Spain, and try and get a job on a farm, maybe even go to college to get some qualifications. In the future, I'd like to have my own land and start a farm.'

'Good for you. Henry's not… I mean, he's not putting you under any kind of pressure to stay longer, or mix with the family?'

Juan Marco looked blankly back at her to give nothing away. 'No, not at all,' then he thought better of it. If he would be staying at the hall soon and Mary and George were already here for Christmas, then how likely was it that he could keep out of sight all the time? Besides, Lord or Lady Belvedere could throw his name out in conversation. Suddenly, he felt nervous; he needed a friend.

'Look, can you keep a secret? I think I might need you to be discreet. I knew the family were bound to arrive for Christmas but I didn't expect you so soon. I am staying at the hall over Christmas for a few days, as there's no room at the farmhouse. Henry's arranged it with his parents, they seem fine with it. Obviously, I intend to keep out of everyone's way as I'll be up in the staff area, and I will be spending some time with my mother at the cottage. But can you warn me if there's any time I absolutely have to hide, or not be there?'

Mary looked crestfallen. 'Oh, Juan Marco,' she wailed. 'Oh, this is going to go horribly wrong! It's Henry, manipulating you and everyone else! I told you a long time ago not to trust him, not to ever trust him! He only cares about himself and he's using you to score points against his family! Can't you stay somewhere else?'

'I don't really have much choice, and I thought if I had a couple of days start on the family arriving, I could work out the layout of the house, how to avoid people, etc. I could stay with Mrs Tanner and my mother, I suppose,' he added gloomily. 'It's just, well, I don't really want to live with her at the moment, even for a few days. She hurt me, you know, with all her lies and bitterness. Even now, she wouldn't tell me the truth if I asked her to. Besides, when I'm with her now I feel like she's sharpening her claws, waiting to dig them into me, to grip and hold me, thinking that she can make me love her the way I did before. She must understand, things will not go back to the way they were before. I am no longer a boy, I'm a man and I want her to understand that!' he said angrily with tears in his eyes.

Mary felt pity for him and reached out to touch his face. 'Couldn't you just go back for a few days?'

'Fine, I'll find somewhere else to stay!' he snapped, turning towards the door. 'I'm not staying with her!' he added, as he stalked out of the room and back to the party.

Once he was back in the ballroom, he immediately looked for Lauren. Paying her a compliment on her performance would now be easy with his temper up, but he also knew just the sight of her would have an instant calming effect. She was now in a semi-circle grouped around the temporary stage, watching someone else's performance, so he made for the bar and got another glass of wine, waiting for her to become free. After a couple of minutes, two girls came over to him and introduced themselves. They were Emma and Tess from a supermarket in town that stocked estate produce, and they recognised him from his delivery runs to the store. They were both twenty-ish, pretty and drunk already, and he found the giggly schoolgirl routine easy to cope with, even in his darkened mood. He found Tess the more attractive of the two, and after five minutes of flirtatious chat, began to think about finding somewhere private where they could go for sex, something he had a sudden urge for.

Lauren had seen him although he didn't look up. She felt a streak of annoyance that he hadn't yet complimented her, but tinged with a little jealousy too. She arched her back and turned away, reminding herself that the queen of the evening shouldn't be distracted by an estate labourer.

Mary, too, had come back into the party and started to mingle again, while keeping her eyes on Juan Marco in case he did something stupid. She saw the look Lauren gave him, and realised that was where the danger lay, not with the two young girls whose company he was enjoying. Half of her was torn towards protecting him, and the other towards avoiding the family explosion that Henry would probably find amusing. Her own intake of wine was clouding her judgement, but her priority had to be to repair his temper and maybe put some distance between him and Lauren, so nothing spilled over at the end of the night. Perhaps she'd been harsh with him earlier – she couldn't have known the situation with his mother had deteriorated so badly, and maybe right now he needed some support – a friend, like he said.

She took a circuitous route towards him, and then walked the last few paces directly in his line of sight.

'There you are, my young Spanish friend. I'm sure we hadn't finished discussing your work on the estate. Hello girls, I'm Mary from the Belvedere family, hope you're both enjoying the evening. We love providing this opportunity for all the estate working team to get into the Christmas spirit. Do you mind if I take him away from you for a couple of minutes? There's just something I need to discuss with him.'

'Now hold on just a minute,' interrupted Juan Marco.

Mary lightly touched his arm. 'It won't take long. He'll catch up with you girls.' As they walked away disappointedly, she continued: 'Calm down, you win. I won't interfere with your plans to move to the hall but we're going to have to be really careful, do you understand? I mean *really* careful! Look, I want to be your friend, but you must understand I can see both sides of the situation and I don't trust Henry. We'll find a way to work together to avoid any conflicts, I promise. Please, calm yourself and don't let your emotions get the better of you, especially tonight. I hadn't realised that your relations with your mother had got so bad. I guess there's a lot I've missed out on, not just that, but how you came to be here, how your mother came too, what you've been doing, etc. How about we find a quiet spot again and you can bring me up to date?'

He hesitated, so she added: 'Look, I think I need to be brought up to speed, for both our sakes. Afterwards, if you want, you can come back to the party and pick up where you left off with those girls.' He half-smiled so she went on: 'I think you preferred the brunette, didn't you? Not as shapely as the blonde, but her mouth was prettier,' she giggled. His face collapsed in a grin.

Mary left the room first, after telling him to follow her to the library in a couple of minutes. Once inside, she led him to a bookcase and said, 'Watch this.' She pushed a recessed button and lent on the case, and with a gentle click the shelves started to turn, revealing a small reading room with no window. She flicked on the light. 'Better to not risk being disturbed.'

They sat on the sofa, and Mary asked him to fill in the gaps after their last conversation in Lincolnshire. He started with the implausible offer from Henry, and Mrs Tanner's appearance, then Henry's serious suggestion, and then the deceit that had being going on until recently. He was sure Robert and Lauren knew nothing of his mother's presence, and admitted he doubted Henry was just happy with getting him work experience, but he couldn't see how the situation could possibly develop in Henry's favour. In his own mind, he was here to increase his farming knowledge and would take as much learning as was on offer, before heading back to Spain with the intention of starting some new beginnings. He would go as soon as he could, but on his terms.

Mary sat and listened to the calm, determined young man who seemed to have morphed from boy to man in a matter of weeks. It was when he started to talk about his relationship with his mother that she saw the cause of the hard edge. It was her unwillingness to admit anything from her time in England, including the circumstances of Juan Marco's conception, that caused him real anger, especially when she continued to shut him out by planning her convalescence with Mrs Tanner. What hurt even more was that he had Henry's version of events, and ordinarily would have severely doubted them, yet they seemed believable in the light of Maria's final admission that they had a consensual relationship. At that point, when she could have finally opened up, she slammed the door shut again, pointedly reminding him that he was a child and had no right to know anything more.

Mary reached out and put her hand on his leg as she looked into his eyes. 'You've put up with a lot. Now I understand why you don't want to stay with her. I still see her side of the story but, after all this time, she should have moved on, especially as she had the gall to come back here. You still feel she thinks things can go back to before?'

He nodded glumly. 'Yes, she expects it. I don't want to fight her, but I'm absolutely going to show her she won't win this battle. Enough is enough. She has to accept that I will make my own decisions from now on, and the sooner she sees it, the sooner she can get back to having a close relationship with her son.'

'My God,' said Mary, taking his hand. 'You really are growing a mane now.' He looked slightly annoyed as if she was making a childish joke, but she reassured him: 'I'm not being funny,' she continued as she squeezed his hand, 'I see the heart in you and all of your signals are right. You're doing the right thing, feeling the right things, you're becoming a man, following your instincts. I don't think you need me to tell you how to feel, but... you're one hundred per cent on track.' She leant forward and kissed him on the cheek as a final apology.

'You know, bloody families are a pain in the arse,' she continued as she sat back again, letting go of his hand. 'This house, this estate, do you realise that the family have it within their grasp to sort all the mess out? They're stuck in the dark ages. Hardly any acceptance of eco-friendly farming. No pushing the local produce angle, other than supply to some places that they've supplied for years. No effort to bring in new crops, and no business sense at all. They refuse to let the public in, other than at strictly controlled times, despite the demand. Won't sell any land so they can invest in what's left, including refurbishing this place, that needs some serious maintenance. Anna, Henry's sister, she's the brains of this family, make no mistake. With her business acumen, and George's real belief in sustainable farming, they could drag this place kicking and screaming into the 21st century. But will they? Will they hell! Instead, they're focused on the line of succession, and instead of ignoring Henry and going around him, which is what they should do, they dig their heels in and sulk like children! It makes me so angry!'

Juan Marco looked quietly at her but said nothing, sensing she wasn't done.

'I'm sorry to speak so ill of your father, but he needs to be ignored if things want doing. He just, I mean, I think he has some good intentions, but it all turns to dust really. You've spent quite a bit of time with him I imagine. How do you find him?'

Juan Marco shrugged. 'Like you say, I think he has some good intentions, but he ducks out of situations he'd rather not face, and I think he has a good side and a dark side. I've seen him in Spain and England, and he just takes himself off sometimes when he can't face the outside world, and loses himself in drink. I think he's dependent.'

'I'm sure you're right,' Mary replied. 'You know you're walking into a bear pit staying in this house, don't you? I'll do everything I can to protect you, but you need to be wary what Henry might be up to in terms of revealing who you are. I wouldn't put it past him, if he thinks he can get one over on the family.'

Juan Marco nodded. 'I'm learning to take care of myself.'

'I believe you are. You couldn't lend some of that grit to George, could you?' She laughed before her face turned serious. 'He drives me insane sometimes. He's got a genuine interest in managing the land, as well as farming in harness with the environment. He understands about better quality produce and, therefore, better yields and prices, and he's willing to get his hands dirty. He should still be here on the estate, lending his knowledge and experience and driving change, but he's so proud and detests Henry, and the fact that the title doesn't go with responsibility in his case. He can be a bit over-emotional sometimes and, oh, that bloody woman! Have I told you about George and Lauren? I know you like her but she dangled him on a piece of string, and left him humiliated when she started seeing Robert. I know he took the whole thing too seriously, but he's never seemed to get over it.' Mary's voice was rising in pitch and despair, and this time it was Juan Marco who put his hand on her shoulder in support.

'It sounds exhausting and it can't be easy knowing that you can advise and support him, yet can't quite seem to get through. He's a good man, I've seen it myself in Lincolnshire.' Their eyes met and Mary raised her hand to place on top of his.

'You relax me, Juan Marco,' she said, slipping into a giggle. 'Or maybe that's the drink talking. I don't know. All I know is that you're incredibly easy to talk to. You're a good listener but you seem to understand communication better than most men.' They were still looking at each other and she leant forward to kiss him, but instinctively he withdrew.

'Oh sorry,' she gushed. 'I didn't mean to…'

'It's OK,' he smiled, 'we know where that led last time.'

Still they looked at each other, feeling the temptation grow, breaths shortening, mouths drying, tension and desire sneaking into their bodies. 'I want it!' she gasped, throwing her mouth on his and clasping his hands against her breasts, as she fell on top of him. He responded with his mouth, and then her hands were on his belt yanking it free and pulling down his flies as he groaned. He unzipped her dress and put his hands up the hem and pulled her knickers down. As she lowered herself on to him, they both moaned and she started her rhythmic motion, whispering, 'I want it hard, hard!' After thirty seconds he rolled her on to her back, pulled down his trousers and pants and entered her firmly, and as he started powerful thrusts she had to stop herself saying 'imagine I'm Lauren, imagine I'm Lauren…'

Five minutes later, she was laying in his strong arms without a care in the world. She was relaxed, satisfied, protected. His muscular chest was all the pillow she needed. Neither of them said anything for several minutes before she recovered her thoughts.

'Where are you staying tonight?'

'Back at the farmhouse,' he replied drily. 'I guess I'll need to reappear at the party, otherwise questions will be asked. Apparently, it's tradition they walk back together afterwards, but it should pass off easily enough.' He smiled down at her as their eyes met again, and she laughed. 'Well, that's one potential situation I've handled already then.'

Over the next few minutes they dressed and he made his way back to the party, ignoring the two girls he'd been chatting to earlier. Instead, he made for a group of men who were laughing noisily, and joined their circle, thinking there was safety in numbers. He checked his watch. It was midnight now and just an hour to go, which would pass quickly enough.

Guests started to disappear from midnight onwards, and by half past twelve, when Juan Marco started to look around who was left, he realised that while Lauren was still there, Robert was nowhere to be seen. He asked one of the men in his group if they'd seen him, and was told he'd been given a room in the hall for the night, as he was completely wasted and unable to stand. He asked whether that also applied to Lauren, but was answered with: 'Don't ask me, mate, I'm not her keeper! Maybe it'll be your lucky night!' which led to uproarious laughter.

Juan Marco left the group and was courteously attending to a few of the guests that were leaving, when Lauren walked up.

'Well, you've been absent for a while, haven't you? I was looking for you to make sure you were having a good time, but I couldn't see you.'

'Oh, I've been having a good time for sure,' he replied calmly. 'Just mixing and getting to know a few more people, it's been fun. Your performance was amazing by the way.'

She fixed him with a 'it's too late for that' look. 'I'm not sure if I'm coming back to the farmhouse or not; I've been offered a room here. You've got your keys?'

He nodded. 'Do we have to help to clear up?'

'No, the house staff will see to it tomorrow.'

'OK, well I'll leave in ten minutes, so if you want me to escort you home, then that's the plan.'

Still looking at him, she replied: 'I have certain responsibilities here, Juan Marco. I'm on my own without Robert, so I can't just walk out when there are still guests here.'

'Yes, I see, sorry for being slow. You might be here a while I guess…
so I think I'll go. I'm feeling very tired. Well done tonight, you promised
me a night to remember, and it certainly was.' He turned to leave, as a cool
breeze blew between them.

Chapter 21

Christmas – A Time for Families…

There was tension at the farmhouse the following week, and Juan Marco couldn't wait to move his stuff out on Friday. Lauren was offhand with Robert because of his behaviour at the party, but she was cool with Juan Marco too, something Robert picked up on. When he was out wall-repairing with Juan Marco, he asked him directly if there was anything he should know. Juan Marco shrugged and said he'd enjoyed himself at the party and got immersed with a couple of girls, and maybe Lauren was frustrated that she'd been left to deal with the party organisation and guests on her own.

Three days before he moved out he decided to message Henry to see if he could move earlier, which would also give him more time to find out if his father had any family-related games planned. He met Henry in the formal garden at the back of the hall.

'Is it possible I can have the room on Thursday instead of Friday? Lauren's starting to worry about cleaning up the house for her guests and I feel I'm in the way.'

'Yes, I'm sure that will be OK. I'll let the housekeeper know.'

'I'll only have my rucksack and maybe a couple of bags of other stuff to bring, as it's mainly what I brought from Spain. I can come round this way to get access to the hall? I don't want to disturb anyone, just keep it low-key, especially as the family must be arriving soon?'

Henry turned his head sharply and his eyes narrowed. 'The family. Ah, yes they've started arriving already, as a matter of fact. George and Mary are already here and will stay until the day after New Year – you know them, of course, but I think it would be good to delay a renewal of your acquaintance, do you agree? Let's let things slide for a couple of days. There's also my sister, Anna, and her husband, Alexander, arriving, but they don't get here until Christmas Eve, but I think they'll stay until early January. You've not met them. I'm not proposing to thrust you into the limelight, don't worry, but I'm sure my parents will want to see you again and invite you for a get-together, and I hope you'll politely accept,' he said with a look that said it was mandatory. 'Mrs Bassett will look after you if you need anything, and you just need to tell her if you'd like evening dinner each day. Of course, Christmas is a time for families and you'll want to be with your mother for much of the time.'

Juan Marco tried hard not to wince, and while he was happy to hear he would be under the radar to start with, could not help feeling that Henry had plans for something bigger. He tried a change of tack.

'How did it go with Mrs Tanner?'

'Well enough, after she crawled her way through an apology,' replied Henry with intent, then he softened. 'I find it hard to put her in her place when she is retired and no longer on our payroll. She's good-natured and generous, although on this occasion perhaps a little over-generous. I think we understand each other, but I have no such hopes with your mother! Talk about cold!'

'What did you say to her?'

'Nothing contentious!' replied Henry indignantly. 'She looks better, but I'd have thought a smile wouldn't go amiss. It's turned out very well for her and Mrs Tanner is clearly fond, so I think she ought to be more capable of looking forward. I'm still the evil one in her eyes.' Juan Marco said nothing.

'She's talking of returning to Spain in January,' continued Henry. 'How do you feel about that? She seems to think your mind is made up too.'

Juan Marco checked himself before replying. 'I, of course, want my mother to be back home again where she is happiest and to be able to get back to normal life. I never thought I would stay here for long, but... I've enjoyed the work here, and the thought had crossed my mind that I might be useful on the estate for a little longer.'

Henry picked up on the short break in his reply, and though he tried to disguise it, his smile was smarmy. 'Well I'm pleased to hear it, my boy, it seems you and I think along similar lines.'

'I've already asked Robert what he thought about the possibility, but he said he'd need to discuss it with you.'

'Did he now? I think Robert may well be informed at some point, but I think any discussion may well be at a much higher level than him. Leave it with me. Let's not let it get in the way of Christmas. New Year is the time to tackle these sorts of ventures.' With that, Henry walked back into the hall.

Tomorrow night would be Juan Marco's last night at the farmhouse, and he resolved to leave on good terms. He had presents to buy, and Robert had already told him to finish at lunchtime and not return to estate work until 2nd January, unless he was needed urgently. Dinner the following night was pleasant enough, Lauren and Robert's tensions seeming to be eased by a couple of extra days and the effect of their attention switching towards Christmas proper. Lauren seemed playful again, and wanted to know all the things he'd enjoyed since coming to the estate, and repeatedly teased him about staying a little longer. As the wine flowed, Robert mellowed and made similar noises that he'd see what he could do. He'd really been useful and keen and perhaps they could put up with him a little longer!

The next morning, he packed his things and messaged Mary to tell her that he was moving to the hall that day, blushing when he realised that was the first contact he'd had with her since the party. He told her what Henry had said, and she replied that it sounded like they had a few days' grace, whatever Henry was planning. To make himself scarce and take advantage of the weather which had turned cold but dry, he decided to walk on the public footpaths around the estate, taking food and drink with him. They took him out to the neighbouring villages and well away from the hall. He had one dinner with the staff on Saturday night to get to know them a little, and then left to see his mother and Mrs Tanner at the cottage on the Sunday afternoon, which was two days prior to Christmas, planning to stay four nights.

Mary, meanwhile, couldn't wait for Anna to arrive at the hall; at least then she'd have an ally and confidante, and Anna's strong mind would help when it came to telling George that Juan Marco was at the hall. After their arrival at four o'clock, the family had drinks in the drawing room and then Anna left to shower, giving Mary her opportunity for a one-to-one chat. She gave her twenty minutes head start and then made her excuses, and knocked quietly on Anna's door.

'Mary, you're so lucky to have been here for a few days! Honestly, the flight was delayed, the traffic was awful and that drink, boy I needed that! Come in, it's nice to have a chat without the others.' Mary sat on the bed while Anna continued. 'How's the farm? Have you got temporary help, because you're away quite a while this time, aren't you?'

Mary quietly updated her, but Anna noticed she wasn't bright and breezy like she normally was. 'Is there anything wrong, you seem subdued. You're not unwell, are you?'

'No, it's nothing like that,' smiled Mary.

'Oh my God, you're not pregnant, are you? Oh, that's fabulous news!'

'No, I'm not. Hold on there just a minute! With all the work on the farm, we hardly have time to... you know!' They both laughed. 'No, it's not that, but I do have news. You'd better sit down.'

Resolving to venture no more guesses in case there really was something wrong, Anna sat down on the bed.

'Juan Marco's here. Henry's found a way to bring him here, taking advantage of the fact that there's been a breakdown of communications between him and his mother. But as it turns out, she's here as well, by a separate, but not unconnected, route.'

Anna's jaw dropped, then moved as if she wanted to say something but no words came out. Then she gagged: 'What?... Why?... How?...'

'I know, it's unbelievable, isn't it? He's working on the estate under Robert who hasn't a clue who he is, but he's moved to the hall to stay, as their farmhouse is full up over Christmas. He's on the top floor in the staff quarters, but he's not here at the moment, thank God. He's staying with his mother at Mrs Tanner's cottage for a few days, which at least gives us some breathing space.'

'Mrs Tanner? What, you mean Henry conned her into putting her up? The devious—'

'No,' Mary cut her off. 'She's here because... oh God, it's complicated... Henry tried to rope Mrs Tanner into helping Juan Marco's mother, but she said no. Then privately, behind his back, out of some sort of loyalty to her from when she left the estate, she offered to house her while she recovered from a bad fall. Juan Marco found out pretty much straightaway, and was angry that his mother didn't tell him where she was going. She used some weasel words without actually saying that she was coming here, but at the same time Henry was trying to get them both here, and when he discovered Maria was out of the picture, well, it was much easier to get Juan Marco here on his own.'

'What the fuck?' replied Anna, shocked. 'Henry must have gone nuts when he found out.'

'I should think so, but Juan Marco seems to have calmed it all down.

Don't ask me how. He seems to have grown up a lot in the past few weeks, he's more mature, more confident about making decisions.'

'Oh, is he now? So, he's going to make trouble, is he? Well if he wants a fight then bring it on!'

'No, not like that, Anna. Look, I think he's worked out that he can use Henry to extend his time here, to gain more knowledge of farming and land management and then, in a few weeks, he'll go back to Spain, and he's planning eventually to get some land and start his own farm. He doesn't want anything from us other than that. On his mother's side, well I think he's working out how to handle her too. She's kept too many secrets from him and it's backfired, big time. He's becoming adept at managing the two of them.'

'You still sound like his fan,' Anna replied suspiciously.

'I just think he's straight, that's all. The one we've got to worry about is Henry. I think he's planning something, and if we're not careful we'll all get caught up in it, including Juan Marco.'

'How do you mean? Like he's still planning the "I've got a son" speech?'

'Exactly. He's already introduced Juan Marco to your parents as a Spanish charity case that he's helping out from the goodness of his heart, and, of course, they don't know any different. The question is will he leave it there, because we can't trust him. We might be all right over Christmas because Juan Marco is staying with his mother, but that might give Henry an opportunity to launch his news without putting him on the spot. But, he could wait until the new year because Juan Marco will be back by then.'

'Sneaky bastard! I knew he could try something like this but I didn't think he could plan it, but he's had help along the way. We need to agree how we're going to deal with him, so we can cut his balls off before he tries anything, or, steal his thunder and get his news out there with our spin on it, before he does!'

'Yes, I agree,' replied Mary. 'But first, I need your help with George. He'll listen more if you're there. He doesn't know that Juan Marco's here yet. I've been waiting for you to arrive so you can use the big sister stick if it's needed, otherwise he'll just throw his toys out of the pram.'

'OK, but it's Christmas Eve, we can't do it tonight or tomorrow. Let's get him on his own on Boxing Day. We normally go out for a family walk, let's do it then.'

Mary left Anna to dress for dinner, both of them anxious that Henry could literally spoil the party at any time of his choosing.

Christmas Day at the hall passed off without event, as it happened. Lord and Lady Belvedere were happy to have their closest family around them, and Henry appeared relaxed and a little smug, although that may have been the result of his usual alcohol intake. Mary took to trying polite conversation with him and, as it went OK, Anna tried a little of the same, which eased the atmosphere.

At the cottage, Juan Marco probably felt more tense at first than they did, as his mother repeatedly tried to talk to him on Christmas Eve about returning to Spain. In the end, he had to tell her that he'd make his own decision, and if she wouldn't drop it then he'd spend Christmas Day on his own at the hall. A gentle rebuke from Mrs Tanner didn't do any harm either.

The weather on Boxing Day was damp in the morning, but dried up enough by lunchtime for an afternoon family stroll. Fortunately, Henry was sleeping off a hangover, which gave Anna and Mary the opportunity to extend their walk, and tell both George and Alexander about Juan Marco's presence. George was predictably furious, but bowed down to Anna's firm instruction that she and Mary would deal with Henry. Juan Marco returned to the hall on the 27th December and kept a low profile, but this was the day that Anna and Mary had decided to tackle a still grumpy Henry. They caught up with him having a snooze in the library.

'Henry, sorry to disturb,' started Anna. 'I know you need your beauty sleep. Now then, we'd just like to know what your plans are about Juan Marco. Please, don't say anything to deny it, we both know he's here and staying on the estate, and at the present time he could even be about sixty feet above our heads.'

'You're guessing,' he replied grouchily.

'My eyesight's pretty good,' responded Mary, leading to a glare from Henry.

'You? Humph. I should have known you'd stick your oar in.'

'I'm not the one who's up to something. You haven't answered the question yet.'

'And what's it got to do with you?'

'It's got to do with all this family Henry, including our parents who you're playing a game with,' said Anna, jumping in. 'They're old and Father's health isn't as good as it was and, if you think you're going to launch your own fireworks at New Year, then forget it.'

'Please, Anna, don't be a drama queen! How is a little bit of honesty going to hurt them?'

'Well, that rather depends on whether you've started off with a little bit of dishonesty. I tell you what, why don't we both go and tell them now who he is? Come on, they're only resting in the drawing room, we can go and have a fireside chat. Come on, snap to it, no time like the present, it can't hurt after all. You've got a bastard son you want them to know about, so what's the problem? It's no big deal.'

'Don't talk like that!' he snapped. 'He's a good young man and you'll respect him!'

'Right!' said Anna, as she walked four steps to the fireplace and removed a poker hanging at the side, pushing it into Henry's chest, even causing a gasp from Mary. 'There's only one person around here who doesn't get my respect and that is you,' she said with two jabs of the poker. 'He's your bastard son from a filthy, disgusting relationship that you always denied, and were happy to see his mother get sacked from her job while you went around playing the innocent! So, let's have it all out now, the whole shebang! And as his mother's here on the estate, let's bring her in on it too, see what she's got to say to Mother and Father about how she was treated, and what a shit you are! Mary, get one of the estate cars and drive up to Mrs Tanner's cottage.'

'Why don't you just fu...' he started before checking himself. 'What do you want, Anna? And take that fucking thing out of my chest.' He coughed.

'I want the truth, the whole truth and nothing but the truth, as we say in my profession! Alternatively, you keep your gob shut, let him finish his work experience and training, arrange his polite goodbyes, and then he's gone and finished with as far as this family is concerned!'

'You can't just pretend he doesn't exist! He's my son!'

'Correct, he's *your* son, illegitimate, distanced, never been a part of your life and of no consequence to this family! If you've got a problem with this then, Mary, get the car and we'll do this once and for all!' howled Anna, waving the poker about.

'Shit, you're mad,' said Henry, leaping up. 'Just mad. And you can leave that bloody woman out of it, she's even worse than you. The sooner I'm out of here the better!' With that, he fled out of the room, only stopping

210

to dive into the dining room, where he pinched a half-open bottle of port, and ran upstairs with it.

Mary blew her cheeks out and breathed for what seemed like the first time in ages. 'Christ, Anna, I thought you were going to impale him! I hope you know what you're doing.'

'It's the only way, Mary. He's always been a scaredy-cat, and if you put the fear of God into him, he'll cave every time. You have to be brutal with him. Now he'll run away with his drink for company and sink into a hole. Then he'll be gone again, and forget all about us for months on end.'

Henry woke the following morning feeling awful, and desirous of avoiding Anna at all costs. He knew he only had one card up his sleeve, and that was to introduce Juan Marco's identity on his terms. If he could somehow get some time with his parents alone then that would have to do, but with eagle-eyed Anna and Mary around, it might be difficult to achieve. Besides, he preferred his original plan of the triumphant fireworks in front of everyone, even more so now.

Early afternoon he went down to the kitchen to get some toast and jam, but used it as an opportunity to discover when his mother would be going down to the kitchen to check on the menu for tonight. She was expected later that afternoon, so he slid down there a few minutes early and drank tea with some of the staff, offering up a sleepless night as an excuse for his rough appearance. His mother was surprised to see him there, but he asked for a quick word after she'd finished with the cook, and they went into the small parlour together fifteen minutes later.

'Sorry you missed dinner last night, Henry. Anna said you were unwell?'

'Humph... I should say so. Fortunately, my powers of recovery are iron-clad,' he muttered. 'There's something I've been meaning to ask you about New Year's Eve. You know we normally have the family meal, and then invite the staff in for a party? Well, I was wondering if my young protégé, Juan Marco, could join us. He's spent quite a bit of Christmas on his own and I thought it would be nice if he could join us.'

'Of course he can, Henry, he's one of the staff really so he has an open invitation to the party.'

'No, I meant, er... the meal actually as well. It's just I feel it would be a nice gesture to him, being away from his home for the first time at Christmas and all. I think he might be a little homesick.'

'Oh, Henry you should have said! I feel so awful now thinking of him on his own at Christmas. Why on earth didn't you say? I thought he must have plans elsewhere, otherwise we would have helped.'

'No, it's OK, he did spend Christmas and Boxing Day with friends, but after that, he was at a bit of a loose end. He even asked me if there was any work he could do on the estate,' he added for effect.

'Of course, in that case, he must join us for the meal! Tell him he can be our special guest.'

'I will, Mother, and thank you,' Henry replied with a duplicitous look.

He went immediately to Juan Marco's room but there was no reply to his knock, so sent him a text message asking him to be in his room at ten the following morning, as he wanted to update him on a couple of things.

The next day, a sleepy Juan Marco ambled down the corridor a few minutes after ten, to find an impatient Henry standing outside his room.

'Where have you been?' he started. 'You look as if you haven't slept all night.'

'I was out with some people from the estate team and we went into town. They met some friends and I ended up sleeping on someone's floor. Can we make this quick as I need to get to bed?'

'Now look, Juan Marco, I know you're young and all, but please remember where you are. Did anyone see you come into the hall?'

'No, I don't think so. I came in the staff entrance and up the back stairs. There wasn't anybody about other than the noise I heard from the kitchen.'

'You need to be really careful, OK? The less people see you the better, especially as the family are still here. You also need to be on your best behaviour from now on, because you've been invited to the family New Year's Eve dinner. This is a big deal, right? Not only will you see my parents again, and it was they who invited you, not me, but if you make the right impression then that will help with the conversation I need to have about extending your stay here, understood? If my parents agree, and I told you this is going above Robert's head now, then it should make staying on at the hall easier too.'

'But hold on,' replied an irritated and tired Juan Marco, 'what's going on? Your parents are one thing but what about the rest of your family? What are you planning? I'm not some sort of a toy to be thrown around in public. If you're planning to use me—'

'Button it, Juan Marco, it's in your interest! You want to stay here,

212

don't you? Well, you'll learn a lot more about farming and managing the land if you have more than one teacher, and I and my father, we know a lot of history about this place, and my father's wealth of knowledge isn't to be sniffed at. If he shows the right level of interest in you, then he'll take you under his wing. All you've got to do is what you did the last time – ask lots of questions, show genuine enthusiasm and I'm sure you'll learn a lot. As for the family, don't worry about them. I'm going to sort it all out beforehand and they'll be as quiet as mice, I promise you.'

'But what about Robert and Lauren?'

'They'll still be involved, if they know what's good for them. Look, you'll still spend time with them, it's just that it will be more official, more formal. I expect you'll get paid a wage. You'd like that, wouldn't you?' Juan Marco half-nodded almost unwillingly. 'Well then, new year, new programme, accelerated learning, all so you can achieve what you came for! What's not to like? Now, remember, keep a low profile, stick to the staff areas, and nice smart dress for Monday night! It's a great time, new year – new beginnings!'

Henry avoided too much involvement with Anna and Mary over the next two days, seeing them only at mealtimes. He gave the excuse that he was painting in his bedroom and walking the estate, looking for potential scene-scapes. His mind was full of his plans for his party piece, the essential part of which was arranging pre-dinner drinks for him and Juan Marco, with his parents. Give them the opportunity to renew their acquaintance with the young man privately, and get them looking cosy and comfortable, prior to the other family members joining them. Then wait and see just how much courage Anna and Mary really had in front of his parents.

Juan Marco was now between a rock and a hard place. Did he believe Henry's statement that he'd take care of the family politics, or did he let Mary know what was going on? Life was getting uncomfortable, but if he told Mary then there was little chance of him staying on the estate, and a few more weeks with the possibility of being paid was the best outcome for him. Should he back Henry, with all his flaky control, or side with the solid Mary who had always supported him? In the end, it came down to two things – firstly, he didn't want to return to Spain at the same time as his mother, and secondly, he didn't owe this family anything. He didn't care if he never saw any of them again after his work experience and training was over. He could return to Spain and build a new life and forget all about

213

them. So, when Mary messaged him for an update on his plans, he replied he was going back to his mother for New Year, and gave her his best wishes.

Henry's plan was therefore set in motion. At half past six on New Year's Eve, he and Juan Marco went down to his parents' private sitting room for pre-dinner drinks. Again, his parents were charmed by Juan Marco's questions about Christmas traditions at the hall, how the changing seasons impacted the land management, the priorities for the new year, employment criteria on the estate, etc. Henry, of course, gave a glowing account of his performance, including an entirely concocted summary from Robert, and their discussions ended up at horse breed characteristics, on which Juan Marco could contribute. A couple of minutes into this theme, they were interrupted by the sound of the dinner gong.

'Now, Mother and Father, as I asked you to keep Juan Marco's invitation private until tonight, I think it would be ideal if you personally introduced him to the rest of the family. And if he's sitting by you, Father, you can continue your conversation on horses.'

'Absolutely,' said his father enthusiastically, gin and tonic just coming to an end. As he led the way into the dining room, he and Lady Belvedere greeted their family and then announced: 'Now I, or rather we have a little surprise for you all! Henry's been doing something wonderful quietly over the past few weeks, and it's our pleasure to welcome a young man as our guest tonight. Juan Marco comes from Spain and, under Henry's guidance and sponsorship he's been working here at the estate as he tries to build a new life for himself. Your mother and I have met him twice, and find him thoroughly good company and a very pleasant young man, and I hope you'll all make him very welcome!'

As Juan Marco walked cautiously into the room, he caught Mary's disbelieving eyes, George's look of horror and Anna's dagger eyes, but knew that he needed to move swiftly to Lord Belvedere's side and take control with his first words. 'I hope this isn't too much of a shock to you, and, don't think it rude to join your family meal, but it would have been impolite to turn down Lord and Lady Belvedere's invitation. May I first wish all of you a very happy New Year.'

'Well said!' jumped in Lord Belvedere. 'In fact, let's all raise our glasses in a toast. Happy New Year, everyone!' One by one, the others all raised their glasses still stony-faced, mumbling 'Happy New Year'.

'Right, you're sitting here, young man,' beamed Lord Belvedere. 'Now then everyone, I'm sure you'll all have plenty of questions for our guest, but let's eat and be merry tonight and think only of positive thoughts for the new year!'

As soon as they were seated, Lord Belvedere started again about what Juan Marco had seen of Arabian horses. Then the soup arrived within sixty seconds, with the staff filling all the glasses with white or red wine. During this bustle of activity, Henry looked warmly at his father and son's rapport, mainly driven by his father's unwillingness to give ground and let anyone else into the conversation. As he turned his head towards Anna and her husband, he let the warm smile continue for maximum effect, but by the time his eyes met Mary's, his expression was cool. He finished by turning to George, to whom he couldn't but help relaunch his smile, which was met with a thunderous look.

While all this was unfolding, Lady Belvedere scanned the faces of her children and their spouses, and couldn't decide if they'd all been overcome with a sudden attack of mean-spiritedness, or something really wasn't right at all. Erring towards the first, she decided to lead by example, and engaged all of them in conversation and did her best to encourage Juan Marco to open up, when she could get a word in ahead of her husband.

Henry was thoroughly enjoying himself trying to prise open the mouths of his sister and brother, with all sorts of generic questions about what they had planned for the new year, the farm's priorities, travel destinations, etc. By the time they had finished one glass of wine, he had downed two, and his merriment was obvious.

Mary whispered to George: 'I don't believe this shit, I'm going to get plastered,' and downed the rest of her second glass in one. George thought for a second and then did likewise.

It didn't take Alexander long to adopt the same approach, although he hesitated when Anna glared at him, before shrugging his shoulders. 'In for a penny, in for a pound.'

Juan Marco did his best to avoid George and Mary's looks, but tried to engage with Alexander, after Henry brought up the topic of classic cars, which he did with some success. His sense of not belonging was really saved by Lord Belvedere's persistent waffle, which seemingly had no end. One question about his ancestors could lead to a whole hour's recounting tales from the first or second viscount's time. By the end of pudding, and on the second glass of port, it seemed tiredness was setting in and Juan Marco made his excuses to go to the bathroom. As soon as he was gone, Anna banged her dessert spoon on the table.

'Right, I've got something to say!' As the guests turned towards her Henry stood.

'Now come on, Anna, as eldest son, it falls to me to say something. It's tradition!'

'On this occasion, I think we'll give tradition a miss!'

'Anna, I really think you might have had too much to drink!' chided her mother softly. 'You know it's Henry who should start things off and besides, Juan Marco is out of the room. Let's be polite and wait until he returns.'

'Actually, Mother, I think it's rather good that he's stepped away for the moment,' replied Henry with a happy slur. 'He might be embarrassed by me thanking you all for making the latest member of this family so welcome. To be precise, your first grandson! That's right. Juan Marco's my son, and long may he be made welcome in this house!'

Lady Belvedere stared at her son and then looked at her husband. Before either could find any words, Anna retorted: 'Oh, he's absolutely right, Mother. He's been planning this little surprise for ages!'

'Yes, I have,' laughed Henry, 'and they've all known about him for some time, but I'm sure you'll agree they've kept the secret marvellously well! I wanted to reserve this moment for such a happy occasion as this and as you have discovered, Mother and Father, he really is a very fine fellow!'

Lady Belvedere glared at Anna and then George, the latter rising from his chair in anger at the notion that he and his sister had any responsibility for what had occurred. There have probably been a few punches thrown at Hillingstone Hall over the centuries, but George's right-cross on Henry would rank highly among them, leaving Henry sprawled on the floor.

Henry groaned then chuckled. 'Oh my, George, I didn't think you had it in you!'

As George went to launch a kick, the dining room door opened and Juan Marco walked back in, coming to a rapid halt, still holding the door handle. George glared at him and took two paces towards the door.

'George!' shrieked his mother. 'That's enough! Juan Marco, I suggest you retire to bed! Henry! Take yourself away too! What kind of a circus is this?' she added, glaring around the room.

Juan Marco sped back to his room, ignoring Henry's calls to hold up for a minute, and that everything would be all right. In the dining room, the atmosphere could be cut with a knife. Lady Belvedere glared at first Anna then George.

'Mother, you must believe that Henry's been manipulating the whole situation and us. His sordid behaviour has been used against us, and George and Mary in particular, for... a long while,' said Anna, trailing off as she tried to avoid using the word "months". 'We've repeatedly told him how disgusting his behaviour was and that we wanted nothing to do with it and I thought... well, we thought, we'd persuaded him to come to his senses. We knew nothing about Juan Marco being here until we got here. This is as much a shock to us as it is to you.'

'I doubt that,' responded her mother quietly.

'We've been conned, used incredibly badly,' chipped in George. 'Henry got us to take in Juan Marco for work experience for several weeks, under false pretences. We had no idea who he was until Mary worked it out.'

'So, you've had him working for you before, for several weeks? And you, Mary, you'd got it all worked out?'

Mary's eyes widened and she swallowed before replying weakly: 'I smelt something was wrong and challenged Henry, and he categorically denied it. It was only when Juan Marco's mother fell ill that Henry finally admitted it.'

'I see. I can see we've been taken for a ride. And what are we to make of Juan Marco? Who's going to give us the truth about him, his culpability?' Lady Belvedere added, looking around.

'I thought him such a pleasant young man, but now are we to see him as some sort of leech?' said her husband.

'Personally, I think that's exactly what he is!' George replied severely. 'I wouldn't trust him as far as I could throw him, although I think Mary has a warmer opinion of him,' he sneered.

She turned to look at him. 'What's that supposed to mean? I offered him kindness and advice when I saw he was distressed, what's wrong with that? I was just as taken in by Henry's deception as anyone else!'

'You saw yourself as his much-needed replacement mother, you slipped right into the role and enjoyed every minute of it... slimy little turd...'

As Mary's mouth opened in anger Lord Belvedere shouted: 'That's enough! This night has turned into a disaster and I will not have open warfare in my house... in our house! I've never known anything like it! Lies, deceit, excuses, blame, violence, bad language... I'm not having it! To bed everyone, now! Some New Year's Eve this has been!'

217

Chapter 22

Fall Out

Juan Marco was up at half past six the next morning and dressed and packed by seven. He left the hall quietly, aiming for Mrs Tanner's cottage initially, before ducking into a woodland walk where he shed a few tears. The relief was short and quickly turned to anger as he recommenced his journey. He knew he'd have to offer some explanation for his arrival, but if he drove it home that he wanted to return to Spain as quickly as possible, then he expected his mother would soon be immersed in booking the flights and making plans, which would prevent her asking too many questions.

He muttered 'Happy New Year' on arrival and tried to keep his words as few as possible. He'd realised over this Christmas that family was more important than anything else and he didn't belong with the Belvederes. His mother was initially suspicious, but then delighted at her son's change of heart. She was all for returning to Spain straightaway until Mrs Tanner reminded her of her GP check-up, and suggested she didn't book the flights until after the appointment in the middle of the following week. Maria huffed and puffed for a while and said she'd be edgy until it was done, but reluctantly accepted the common sense of the advice.

Mrs Tanner was less convinced by his arguments and that evening, when Maria was taking a shower, she poured them both a glass of sherry. 'Now you can tell me to mind my own business if you like, but neither of us expected to see you here with your bags packed, at least not so soon. You're obviously upset by something. If you want to talk then I'll listen but if not, then that's fine.'

He looked at her sullenly, unsure whether to say anything, then let out a groan. 'Oh, it's all gone crazy, I should have known it would! I went out of the room for a pee and when I got back, I heard a crash from outside the door. When I opened it, George had just punched Henry and I was shouted at to go to bed! All evening I tried to be polite and not cause aggravation, but I could feel the tension and just hoped that Henry wouldn't say anything. He was relaxed and merry when I left the room, and then 'boom' as soon as I was out.'

'That sounds like Henry, I'm sorry for you. I've never thought of him as a bad person but he has this emotional streak in him that just has to explode at some point. If I'm honest, I think it was inevitable; his bringing you here was half well-intentioned and half vanity. But try to find some positives – think of what you've learnt since you've been here and use that when you return home. For all the way it's ended, I think you've grown up a lot and your future looks different now. Can you see that?'

Juan Marco's sullen look was unchanged. 'Do you think she will accept me as a changed person, a new man?' he replied, jerking his head upwards towards the ceiling.

'I don't think it will be easy but if you stick to your guns then I think you'll persuade her eventually. I know it seems like a massive defeat at the moment but really, it's just a temporary setback. You're a very resourceful young man and I think you've come a long way in a very short time. You should believe in yourself – I think you've a very bright future.'

He shrugged without conviction. 'I hardly slept last night. I think I'll go to bed.'

'Good decision. Switch your mind off, let the soft pillow carry you away. Tomorrow morning, why don't you go for a good long walk before either of us are up? Have a quick bite of toast, take some drink with you and stomp the estate for a couple of hours, or longer. You'll find the open air is marvellous for clearing the mind and generating new plans for starting afresh! Oh, and one other thing – now that the new year is over, I expect the hall will clear of the extra family members very quickly, it usually does. So you probably don't need to worry about bumping into any of them.'

The following morning Juan Marco took her advice and was out of the cottage just before eight. He decided to walk towards the main entrance to the estate, keeping to the wooded bits out of sight of the road. He would have to cross it at one point, but he'd check the coast was clear beforehand and then continue to loop around the grounds, passing within a few hundred feet of the estate office and stables, and finally ending up in the woods behind the hall that he could follow back to the cottage. The going was tougher in places than he expected, the cold weather having followed a period of rain, and by quarter to ten he'd only reached the view of the office and stables.

He hesitated, looking longingly at the paddocks. What he wouldn't give right now for some time alone with those beauties! Temptation got the better of him and he edged towards the enclosures, unsure of whether anyone would be working in the office. The sunlight was bright and he couldn't see whether a light was on in the back office but, on balance, he thought not. As he edged around the building, he could see the two mares grazing and his heart lifted. There were no sounds coming from the yard immediately in front and there was no car parked. Brilliant! Robert must have come to let the horses out and then gone off somewhere. The offices looked quiet, so he took his chance and crept up to the rails and began talking to the mares, who both came to him straightaway with mouths full of straw before turning back to their feed. He stood and watched them peacefully and gracefully gorging themselves, as a smile spread across his face in the silent, cold morning. He must have been there for ten minutes or more when the sound of the office door opening caused him to freeze. He knew he couldn't pretend he hadn't heard it and started to turn around slowly.

'Good morning, Juan Marco,' came Lauren's teacher-like voice. 'Or would you prefer me to call you something else now? Mr Juan Marco? *Señor*? Or perhaps sir?'

He started walking away at a fast pace and she allowed him a start, before her conscience got the better of her.

'I'm sorry that was crass! Please stop! I didn't mean to offend you.' He stopped and turned but had no words. She looked him up and down. 'Well it looks like you've been out a while, your jeans are filthy. Truce. Come in for a coffee. There's only me, we won't be disturbed until lunchtime... or if you're more comfortable, I'll bring the coffee out here and you can stay with them,' she said nodding at the mares. 'You probably like their company more.'

She brought the coffees out and they stood in silence for a couple of minutes. She knew he wouldn't be starting a conversation about what had happened so it was down to her, but how to start? She was racking her brains for something weighty and meaningful when she noticed he was slouching against the rails.

'How long have you been out? You look tired and it's not that warm just standing here. Why don't you come inside for a sit down?'

He looked at her gratefully and they went inside. That seemed to break the ice.

'When you live in a place like this, news travels fast, it's just the way

221

it is. Robert knows the staff up at the hall, so do I, we all talk and share information, it's natural. I don't know the full details of what happened at the dinner, just that there was a major blow-up and Henry was heard shouting at you, and there was some kind of rumpus at the meal. Words were said when Anna and George left yesterday, unexpectedly early. Also, of course, you've not been seen since… whispers, conversations overheard, you can imagine. Don't think you're being crucified behind your back because all the talk is about the family, er… I mean Henry, really. You've been spoken of well, I understand, and people have wondered how you managed to keep silent.' He said nothing so she went on. 'I guess you must just want to get out of here now. Is your mother far away?'

Juan Marco sniffed and raised his head. 'No, she's very close, really close. She's staying with Mrs Tanner.'

'What? With Mrs Tanner? We knew she had an old friend staying there but she's your mother? How on earth did Henry persuade her to take your mother in?'

Juan Marco looked at her with sullen eyes. 'Don't tell me you don't know about my father's infamous affair with a Spanish maid at the hall. I thought everyone knew about it!'

'But we didn't know she got pregnant! So that's how Henry got her here. I suppose Mrs Tanner was the housekeeper at the time so she would have known her. Maria isn't it?'

Juan Marco nodded. 'But he didn't really get her here. He sort of told Mrs Tanner what was going on and she acted on her own. He only discovered she was here a couple of weeks ago.'

'Oh my, what a tangled web! And your mother and you are close I take it?'

'We were,' he nodded. 'Now I'm not so sure. She kept so many things from me and, while I know it's sometimes done with good intent, there comes a point when lying directly to a son who's now an adult is too hurtful, especially when he's shown natural interest in being told the truth.'

'But you'll get through that right, now everything's in the open? Are you flying back home?'

'My mother wants to go at the end of next week.' He said nothing more so she decided to push.

'You're OK with it?'

'Life won't go back to how it was before. I'm not going to carry on at the bar. I want to buy some land and become a farmer, but first I think I want to go to college to study agriculture.'

'That sounds like a plan and you've got the work ethic. We've been really impressed with you around here. You've turned your hand to anything, been prepared to watch and learn, asked good questions and you've never shirked anything – getting down into boggy ditches and the like, you've never refused anything. I think you'll make a really good farmer one day. Even Robert... I mean he can be a bit rough sometimes, but he really appreciated all your help. You've a lot to offer.'

'It would be nice if my mother could see that,' he replied with a sigh.

'Have you spoken to your father... I mean Henry... since the new year?'

He shook his head. 'I've nothing to say to him. I've been naïve, I came here to get training and work experience and even though I didn't trust him, I figured I could stay out of his way and any trouble. Instead, I just walked straight into his trap! If only I could have avoided it just for a few more weeks. I just thought a few more weeks of working here and my experience would have been enough for a new start back home!'

'I think you should speak to him, even if it's only to tell him what you think of him. Sometimes it just makes you feel a whole lot better. He owes you some sort of explanation, at least. Hurt him if that's the way you feel, but get it out of your system. After all, if you don't think you'll ever see him again then what harm can it do?' As she finished, she put her hand on his knee, but he looked uncomfortable so she withdrew it.

'I must be going,' he said standing up. She looked at him and felt she'd not been able to do enough to comfort him, then she remembered something.

'Remember when we first met, we had a little joke about the Spanish greeting of a kiss on both cheeks?' He nodded and smiled. 'Well as this is goodbye, let's do it now,' and with that she leant forward and kissed him twice, then let her hand stay on his neck. They looked into each other's eyes for several seconds and though neither said anything, they both felt this was the end of something.

Juan Marco completed his tour of the estate and arrived back in time for a late lunch. He was ravenous and agreed that the long walk had cleared his mind a little. He nodded and smiled whenever his mother mentioned their return to Spain, but he was keen to get Mrs Tanner on her own so he could ask what she thought about speaking to Henry, knowing there was no point in seeking his mother's advice. When his mother went into the garden to walk, he took his chance.

'Do you know what you want to say to him?'

He shook his head. 'Not specifically, but I want him to know how awful he's made this. I've used him as well as the other way around, but it's him that's made me have enemies that I never sought. I feel bad for his parents, they seem like really nice people.'

'Yes, they are,' she agreed. 'I don't think they'll blame you in the end, especially when they know the full story of how poorly your mother was treated, and how Henry really wasn't the innocent party. I know your mother was the adult and a lot older, but she was quite naïve about the politics in a country house, and I've always bitterly regretted that I didn't spot what was going on between them and intervene. By now I expect Lord and Lady Belvedere know that she left here pregnant with you, and they'll feel something for sure.'

'So, what do you think… about speaking to him?'

'Do you want to get things off your chest? If you do then speak to him, otherwise… you'll end up like your mother, and I don't think you're quite the same personality.'

'That's what Lauren said.'

'Oh, you've spoken to her? Well she's… got a mind of her own and she's good with people, so maybe two voices are better than one.'

Juan Marco texted Henry that afternoon to ask if they could meet tomorrow to talk, away from the estate. He suggested a local park in Maidstone. 'Can you drive?' texted Henry back.

'Yes, but I can't ask for one of the vans now,' replied his son.

'Best find somewhere quiet on the estate then – I can't drive!' replied Henry.

The next day, they sat inside the greenhouse at the bottom of the formal garden, hidden behind foliage and a brick wall. Juan Marco had his approach worked out but Henry jumped in first.

'I'm sorry if you feel dumped on, but I've been itching to drop some doo-doo on my snotty sister and brother for a while. They're both so bloody high and mighty and think they're the future of this family, so a shot across the bows was long overdue. Don't feel bad, in fact you've not come out of it too badly. I've explained how you came to be, you know with your mother

224

and all that, and I've held my hands up to being a bit of a shit at the time. Obviously, my parents aren't exactly rolling in the aisles but I've seen worse looks on their faces.' Juan Marco looked at him blankly. 'You don't understand? Oh I see, rolling in the aisles! Well I mean they weren't overly pleased.' Juan Marco gave him an ironic look. 'Look, focus on the headlines, Juan Marco. They genuinely liked you and I've come out of it with the dagger between my shoulder blades, not you!'

Juan Marco was stunned by Henry's almost jovial attitude, but now he could turn the conversation his way.

'How did it go with your sister and brother's departures? How do they feel now?'

'That's not really your concern, is it? I mean they banged on about it, being Henry this and Henry that and what a devious shit I am, but they couldn't escape they had some responsibility in all this. I mean, George and Mary put you up for several weeks so they knew all about you, and Anna had knowledge of you too. But the fact is they kept quiet because they really thought I was an incompetent twit who couldn't organise a piss up in a brewery! Now they're found out, they're scampering around trying to defend themselves and George and Mary are turning on each other. I mean it's all very ugly!'

'I feel responsible, especially towards Mary. She really tried to be a friend to me and I let her believe that I'd update her, and then shut her out at the last moment!' said Juan Marco raising his voice.

Henry laughed. 'Yes, she spoke up for you. You know I think you've got a bit of a fan there! Mind you, with George as a husband it's hardly surprising.'

'I don't find it funny!' snapped Juan Marco. 'I'm grateful to them for what they did for me and now they're my enemies! Your sister was frosty but it's not surprising given the circumstances! On top of that, I deserve to take what I came here for, which was education and training, and just when I felt a few extra weeks was going to be offered you snap it back like a mousetrap! I've got to go back to Spain and have endless rows with my mother about the future being different, and I actually don't want to be there with her at the moment! You used me like you use everybody and I'm bloody angry! This was supposed to be some sort of recompense for the way you treated my mother all those years ago, but instead it's just a game to you, isn't it? I hate you! I'm glad George punched you, you deserve it!'

With that, he got up to leave.

'Juan Marco, wait, just wait a moment! If you don't want to go back, I can work it for you, let me try! I told you my parents don't blame you, I'm pretty sure I can persuade them that you have something to offer and I'll stay out of it. You can deal directly with them. Don't worry about Robert, he'll fall in line with whatever my father says, he's got no choice. But you don't need him, you really don't. Let me fix you up with my father and you'll fly, you really will. Come on, give me a chance. You can still get your extension here and can learn about *owning* an estate, I mean owning land, not just farming it! Come on, seize the day and all that!'

Juan Marco turned to walk away again and shouted back: 'It's all just a game to you! I'm going back to Spain and don't follow us!'

Henry now felt a pang of responsibility to someone else for maybe the first time in his life. He didn't much care for most people, but even he was affected by the position he'd left Juan Marco in. He'd given him what he initially intended to, but a few more weeks didn't seem much to ask, and besides, the thought of him shooting back to Spain now right after the big announcement, well that wasn't part of the plan was it? There was more mileage in this situation, surely. He realised he'd have to speak to his parents, preferably alone with his father who was less judgemental and more attached to Juan Marco, so he decided to eat lunch with them, appear contrite, drink only a little, and see if that would earn him an audience later in the afternoon.

Henry knocked on his father's study door at half past four, and was met with a look of disappointment. 'I'm sorry to interrupt, Father, but I wanted to apologise personally to you about the way things have ended up. Could I talk to you for a few moments?'

Lord Belvedere's instant reaction was to send him away, but when he looked down at the statements, accounts and invoices sprawled out on his desk he bit his lip. 'I don't suppose anything you're going to say to me will make any more sense than this mess...' He looked up again, and Henry took this as his cue to sit down.

'Looks complicated. I'm afraid financial matters were never really my strong point, but er, managing people, I mean relationships, isn't too high up on the list either. Look, I just wanted to say how sorry I am for the debacle at New Year. I realise now how badly I've handled things, and what could have been presented in a much less harmful way has now resulted in

226

a lot of bad feeling in the family,' he said rubbing his jaw where George had hit him. 'However, I think, I know Juan Marco is a decent, polite young man and he carries my blood in his veins, he carries yours too…'

'If you think that you're going to play the guilt card then you've miscalculated, Henry.'

'No, sorry, I didn't mean that the way it came out! What I meant was I owe him, I mean I owe all of you, but however, er, sordid, the way he was conceived, I behaved badly at the time and in this muddled sort of way, I've been trying to balance things out.'

'And you think we can't see that you intended to cause maximum impact to your sister and brother with this revelation? Come on Henry, there's a nasty streak in you that can't resist sticking the knife in.'

Henry's face dropped at the realisation that even his father had seen through him. 'Yes, I've played them and now… I must live in my own mess. The person that I've most hurt though is Juan Marco. He's my son…' Henry started to sob.

After several seconds of silence, his father replied: 'I don't think you should get too carried away with all of this. The way he was conceived wasn't really out of a loving relationship, and you've never been a part of his life until now. I will give you the benefit of the doubt that somewhere in you there's a bit of feeling towards him, but I imagine the way he's turned out is down to his mother. I think it extremely regretful that he's been used in this way, when he appears to be such a pleasant, decent, keen young man. Perhaps he does deserve a foot-up in this world, whether it comes from you or anybody else.'

Henry looked up, wide-eyed, before his father continued. 'Now don't start thinking I'm suggesting something from our side. You have given him something over the past few weeks, and I think it is better now that we draw a line under it. What you do, well that's up to you.'

Henry could see his chance slipping away. 'Father, I do feel a need to do something extra for him, well it's not really extra it's more fulfilling a promise that I made to him before Christmas. I must do the right thing, the decent thing now, before he goes back to Spain. This outburst at new year, it just happened, I wasn't thinking clearly, the drink got the better of me… but before Christmas he told me how much he was enjoying working here, free of charge really, although obviously we were putting in training time, but also I knew he was unhappy with his mother. She's not innocent, not at all. He's changing into a man now and she's making his life uncomfortable, trying to keep him down, stopping him from pursuing his dreams. He's already told me he didn't want to go back with her until he'd completed the few extra weeks I'd promised him, so that when they return home, he can make the changes that are necessary to give him, both of them, a better life!'

Lord Belvedere stared at him. He had little sympathy with Henry but the words 'keeping him down' grated against his instinct for fairness. 'She just wants him to return to Spain with her, that's all.'

'Father, I wish I could say that's all it is, but he's taken what we've been able to give him so far and is planning a different future based on what he's learnt. All she thinks he's good for is bar work. He's got a lot more to offer and with the extra few weeks, we could give him a launchpad to reach his potential and improve both their lives. I really don't want his time here on the estate to have been wasted!'

His father's resolve was weakening. 'What are you suggesting then? More of the same?'

'Yes, partly. I can see no reason why Robert won't appreciate the continued help, although I think we might have to help his budget a little. I had meant to contribute something, but Robert's been paying him some expense money, which perhaps isn't entirely fair on Juan Marco. It would be nice if we could give him something extra to replace his lost wages in Spain. But also this sort of stuff' – he pointed at the scattering of invoices and accounts papers on the desk – 'he's young and bright and maybe he can help you with reconciling things. I know you're very reliant on Robert and sometimes he's not the easiest person to ask about things. Maybe if you explain that Juan Marco's going to get involved in that side of things too, you know, from a business oversight perspective sort of thing, so he'll be helping you out and learning about the finance side of an agricultural business.'

'I'm not sure Robert would appreciate another link in the chain,' responded his father.

'But he's helping you, that's the point, Father. He's not interfering, he's privately helping you run your office, improve admin, etc. If Robert says no, well maybe he's got something to hide. But you're the boss, it might be an opportunity to remind him of that.'

'That's quite enough, Henry. I don't need to be reminded who's in charge around here. I'll talk to your mother and then give it another thought, but I don't want to discuss it further now.'

That night, Lord Belvedere raised the subject with Caroline. He didn't shy away from the fact that this was another problem created by Henry, but if there were issues between Juan Marco and his mother over his future life direction, and, there was a danger of his time on the estate having been wasted, then he thought that was a crying shame. Caroline agreed but wouldn't accept any offer being made until they themselves had spoken to Juan Marco, without Henry being there – he'd lost his place in the chain and they couldn't trust him. She also insisted that any deal must be kept secret from Anna and George, which her husband readily agreed to. They discussed who should make the call to Juan Marco and agreed it would come better from her, in case he thought a man calling spelt more trouble. She made Henry give her his phone and rang from his room while he was there, to make sure he didn't try to influence events.

When his phone rang, Juan Marco saw his father's name flash up and ignored it. Then he saw a message had been left and was surprised to hear: 'Juan Marco, it's Caroline Belvedere. I hope you're well. I know that you're preparing to return to Spain but we'd like to have a talk with you before you go back. If you could come up to the hall tomorrow we'll have tea in the garden room. We hope to see you at three. Goodbye.'

He was bemused by the invitation and embarrassed, as he didn't want to go, especially as Henry must be involved. He decided to sleep on it, and the following morning could only decide on one thing – he didn't know what to do. If he asked his mother she'd say no, if he asked Mrs Tanner she'd say yes, so that wasn't helpful. In the end, it came down to manners – did he feel he could be rude to Lady Belvedere by not turning up? Finally, he decided to go, but if Henry was there orchestrating things he'd make his excuses and come back. When he arrived at the hall, he was shown to the garden room, and only Lord and Lady Belvedere were present. They sensed he was expecting his father.

'Don't worry, Henry won't be joining us,' Lady Belvedere reassured him. 'This is a private chat between the three of us.'

'Juan Marco, notwithstanding the somewhat clandestine way you were introduced to the work on a country estate, have you learnt things that have interested you?' ventured Lord Belvedere. He received just a nod. 'May we ask what your plans are when you return to Spain?'

'I intend to get a place at college to study agriculture, perhaps combined with environmental studies. I'll need to continue with my bar work to help with funding, but I want to own a piece of land in the future and farm it. I think I'd like to be self-sufficient, but also to grow it into a business.'

'I see. There's a lot to learn but we've good reports of your willingness to learn, and a formal qualification is a good starting point. I need to ask you a direct question now and we'd like you to be honest. We just need to understand what may have been said to you. Did Henry speak to you about extending your time here before things all got a little heated?'

'I… can't remember, it was vague.'

'OK, so you don't have any interest in staying on a little longer?'

'I wouldn't put it that way. I feel that other things have taken over.'

'Quite, understood. Have you been happy here, in your work?' Another nod. 'And you're happy to go back to Spain now with your mother?'

Juan Marco looked down uncomfortably before replying: 'I think it's the right thing to do.'

'In the end, that's the only thing that matters. OK, we just wanted to satisfy ourselves you hadn't been promised something that should be delivered. We've had various conversations with Henry over the past few days and he's explained his conduct all those years ago, and let's say that some of it was less than responsible. In his attempts to make some sort of amends to you as his son, it's important to us that we make sure his obligations are met. I say 'we' because Caroline and I feel he's let himself down, and it's our wish that you leave here with the most optimism for your future. Making good on any promises made is part of that.'

'We'd also like to add that you're our grandson, Juan Marco,' added Lady Belvedere kindly. 'Whatever the circumstances, you're a part of us and we'd like to help in giving you the new start we understand you're seeking.'

Juan Marco was taken aback by their thoughtfulness and unexpected kindness, and it turned his mind to what might be on offer.

'I did discuss with Henry the possibility of staying on and I thought at the time that I'd like to.'

'Well, all we want you to understand is if it's what you want, and you're OK with staying here, then it's fine by us for another six or eight weeks. You can continue with helping Robert, which I'm sure he'd appreciate, and there's also the financial aspects of running a farm which you might be interested in looking into. Obviously, this is a large business and off the scale for your future plans, but the basics are the same – investment, budgets, income, expenditure, reserves, etc., it all has to be learnt. You could help with restoring some order here in our office and perhaps liaising with Robert, as well as him showing you how he accounts for things. How does that sound?' offered Lord Belvedere.

'Can I think about it until tomorrow? Where would I stay?'

'It would make sense for you to continue here, wouldn't you agree, John?' Her husband nodded. 'Oh and we almost forgot, we'll make sure you're paid for these weeks too at the rate of a junior farmhand, just so you've got something to go home with.'

'OK, thank you very much. How do I let you know my decision?'

Caroline handed him a personal contact card with her number and they said goodbye.

Juan Marco thought that evening about his answer, and the longer he did so, the more appealing the offer was. No more game-playing by Henry, continuation of the work experience, gaining some knowledge of finances, and some wages!

The following morning, he rang Lady Belvedere and accepted the offer. Now came the more difficult conversation with his mother. As expected, she was furious at the offer and his acceptance, and tried every parental emotion to change his mind – hurt, anger, reward, punishment, guilt. He held firm, which led to insults and abuse, so he took himself out of the cottage and headed for the stables and estate office in search of the company of the horses, but also to ask Robert if any work needed doing. He managed to avoid seeing Lauren, but Robert drove up forty-five minutes later, staring hard at Juan Marco as he skidded the van on the shingle.

'Well, Juan Marco, it appears we have the benefit of your company for a while longer! But our humble abode isn't up to the mark. It's the big house for you with the grandparents!'

Juan Marco couldn't tell whether Robert was teasing or being sarcastic.

'I always thought there was more to your relationship with *him* than just generosity. That's not his style at all, but you must have impressed their lordships, especially as they've released the purse strings. I just hope you won't feel used when all this is over. They'll be polite enough to your face, but once you're gone, I wouldn't bank on being invited back any time.'

Juan Marco swallowed. 'I want to be useful and learn more, that's all.'

'Hah!' sniffed Robert. 'And I understand you want to know about budgets and accounts and credits, accruals and forward planning and all that guff! Well, it's as dull as ditch water, so don't expect me to spend hours on that stuff. You concentrate on sorting out his lordship's paper pile, and speak to me when you need to. I don't have time for going through that rubbish!'

As he headed for the office door he turned around. 'Looking for something to do? The pigs need more straw and a water check. After that, you can muck those two out,' he said nodding at the horses.

Juan Marco wasted no time in packing his clothes and belongings that night and, after another heated discussion with his mother, left for the hall the next morning. He did his best to be positive about her improving health, her lack of need of him, and the benefits to them both of extending his stay, but it still ended in tears and claims of selfishness.

For the next few days, Juan Marco reverted to his previous duties assisting Robert, whose attitude was a strained mix of formality and casualness, depending on how much supervision was required. He also spent some time with Lord Belvedere compiling a list of estimates against invoices, and payments against debts, but by far the most interesting aspect for him was learning the history of the estate management, from times of aristocratic landlords and teams of servants through to the present day, with farming shared between the estate and contract farmers. He also discovered how much hall renovation work put a strain on the estate's finances.

Maria had attended her GP check-up by this time, and as there were no reasons to prevent her from returning home, she wanted to get on with booking the flights. She wanted one more go at preventing her son from staying on at the hall but listened to Mrs Tanner's advice. 'Be gentle with him, go softly and try to convince him rather than push him. He's growing up and isn't afraid of making decisions, and believes he has a different future ahead. Try to make him see you're on his side.'

Maria invited him to dinner with a tempting paella on offer. The evening started off well, but she found it hard to appeal to her son when she was used to complete obedience from him.

'You don't need me back at the bar straightaway. Luis can employ someone else to help you and, besides, I need to apply for my place at college, maybe attend an interview, and then I can help out, but only until the end of summer.'

'But I will need you in the apartment to help me like you always have!

232

My fitness isn't good enough to be on my own.'

'You're moving fine and getting better all the time. My staying here is going to benefit both of us. It's not long ago you wanted me to go to college, now you're against it.'

'I'm not against it, I just don't think this place is useful to you. It's totally different here. Come home with me now.'

The mood darkened and neither would give ground. Mrs Tanner tried her best at peace-making, but Maria turned to tears as her final tactic which led to Juan Marco leaving, frustrated at what he saw as attempts to hold him back.

Maria went to bed annoyed, tense and upset. She fell asleep and was still in bed at eight the following morning, which was unusual for her, so Mrs Tanner went to check on her. When she went in, she found Maria still in bed with a frightened look in her eyes, her mouth lower on one side, and unable to speak properly. She rang for an ambulance straightaway and then called Juan Marco.

'I'm so sorry, Juan Marco, I think your mother's had a stroke! I found her in bed this morning. She's having difficulty speaking and one side of her body is affected. They'll take her to Maidstone General Hospital and I'll go with her. Can you get someone to bring you?'

One of the gardeners drove him, and he waited with Mrs Tanner for news. The doctor came and saw them after an hour and said Maria was lucky, she'd had what they call a mini-stroke and the blood supply had only been cut off temporarily. She had received blood-thinning drugs and pills to lower her blood pressure, which was abnormally high. While it was early days, it looked as if they'd been able to begin the treatments in time to avoid lasting damage. Only time would tell.

They both spent much of the day at the hospital before returning in a taxi to the estate. Juan Marco was given as much time off as he needed, but on the third day the news from the hospital was good – Maria could speak with more ease. Her left side was weak but the strength was showing signs of coming back, and the drugs appeared to have done their job. They were happy for her to go home in two days if the signs were all still positive, but she needed quiet rest and recuperation, especially as her blood pressure was still higher than it should be and probably was the cause of her stroke.

Juan Marco was able to return to work, but had been shaken by his mother's sudden illness, feeling guilt that the arguments between them had contributed to her deterioration in health. It was plain that her blood pressure had to be kept down, and so it was obvious that there could be no more disagreements now as she recovered. He was glad of distractions at work, which was made easier by a huge downpour which made one of the brooks overflow, causing flooding in one of the fields which was contract-farmed. The farmer was less than happy that the crops were underwater, and complained to Robert that previous requests for drainage ditch clearance had been ignored, which exacerbated the impact of heavy rain. Robert told Juan Marco that hiring diggers to widen and deepen the channels wasn't in the budget, and wasn't possible to do in this weather anyway, but he had no objection to him manually trying to clear a wider path on the next side of the field, which might help drain some of the excess water. Even though it was heavy labour and didn't achieve a great deal, Juan Marco was glad of the physical workout for four hours, which left him shattered.

Two days later Maria returned to the cottage to recuperate, and he felt lucky that Mrs Tanner was still willing to help nurse her back to health. He made calls to their landlord and employer to keep them up to date. With the weather not improving, he returned to the hall where he sifted through piles of invoices and estimates, trying to match them up. His heart really wasn't in it, but he did repeatedly notice that on machinery and vehicle invoices, there was no consistency in allowances given against the value of old assets being traded in. Some referred to a discount while others didn't, and this made no sense to him. Robert had told him that all redundant plant had a value, so he couldn't understand why some of the estimates showed a deduction which wasn't then carried over to the invoices. He decided to take a walk to the estate offices to speak to him. When he arrived Robert was out, but Lauren met him sympathetically.

'I'm so sorry about your mother, Juan Marco. How is she?'

'I think she'll be OK, it's just a matter of time hopefully. She's lucky to have such a good friend as Mrs Tanner. She needs plenty of rest and no stress, so that means no more rows about going home!'

'I'm sure you'll find it easy to avoid that,' she said smiling.

'It's really important for her to realise this could happen again unless she stops getting so emotional. I think I can handle my side of things,' he replied quietly.

Lauren nodded at him. 'So what brings you here today? Is there anything I can help with? Robert does most of the financial work but I might

234

know something.'

He showed her the estimates and invoices he'd brought with him and pointed out the differences.

'Well I'm not sure I can help with this,' she said shaking her head. This is a bit above my head. I mainly deal with staff payroll, expenses, bits and bobs, that sort of thing. This is not something I get involved with really, but I'm sure Robert will have it all figured out. Maybe the price of the new equipment gets netted down or something. I'll tell him you dropped by and if you message him, he'll tell you when he's got time to go through it.'

Juan Marco had been hoping for an easy answer and showed his disappointment.

'I'm sure it's all OK,' she reassured him. 'Look, why don't you come to dinner one night, not to discuss this, but so we can have a catch-up, just the three of us, or two of us if Robert is busy?' He stumbled and looked confused. 'Oh, I wasn't thinking, you probably don't want to be away from your mother. Dim of me,' she continued. 'Don't worry about me being dizzy. I'm sure we can have dinner when she's well and truly on the mend.'

Two days later he managed to pin down a reluctant Robert, who said he didn't want to see any of the documents, but he'd talk to him when they were on a break from coppicing in the wood.

'The thing you've got to remember, Juan Marco, is that all assets depreciate over time, and the way that things get accounted for is different to giving everything a cash value. The usefulness of a particular item gets written off over a number of years so it has a nil book value, but it may be worth something second-hand or it may not, it depends on how the new item supplier feels when it comes to the transaction. Sometimes, he'll see something as saleable, other times scrap, other times it'll be worth nothing. An estimate might indicate their original thoughts, but by the time of the purchase they no longer have a buyer lined up, or perhaps they haven't seen the exchange item and wrongly guessed its condition, or perhaps their sales figures are down for the month and they can't afford to give anything back when the money changes hands. You'll never be able to see a consistent pattern so don't worry about it.'

'You get rid of most of the rubbish though, I suppose? I mean I don't see much lying around.'

'I keep a clean and tidy ship, but there'll be stuff lying about that's useless, for sure. You just haven't found those places yet.'

'OK, it's just once you told me everything has a value, so that made me think there must be other invoices I've not seen yet.'

'Maybe, but I wouldn't worry about it. Just look at the final goods invoice, that's all you need to worry about.'

'Can I ask about the old JCB you said was broken when we were talking about improving the field drainage? You said someone would pay to take it off your hands.'

'Don't worry about it, Juan Marco, it's being looked at now. Let's crack on.'

When Juan Marco returned to the hall that evening, Henry came and found him. 'How's it going, Juan Marco? Still managing to get along with Robert OK? Oh, bugger me, how insensitive! What I meant to say first was how's your mother? Is she stable, improving?'

'She's doing OK, her speech is getting better and she's getting more movement in her left side,' he replied factually but without enthusiasm.

'OK well, erm, give her my best. Just well......erm.... wish her a speedy recovery. It can't be easy being bedridden and having limited contact with other people, but I hope you're able to spend some decent time with her.' Juan Marco nodded blankly. 'Right, well, I'll away then.'

Henry was bored, in truth, and the idea of returning to Spain was on his mind. He'd been the centre of attention over Christmas and New Year, but now the family group was back to just his parents and suddenly he was afforded civility, and pretty much nothing else. He wasn't in the loop anymore; his mother and father had shut him out of Juan Marco's duties, and even getting drunk every night was becoming a bore. He'd had the idea of painting a portrait of Juan Marco, but when he'd carelessly thrown it into conversation with his father, the icy stare back made him retreat rapidly.

But before going back to Spain, he had the seed of a plot in his mind that needed germinating, the possibility of one more mischief-making enterprise that quickened his pulse. A trip to Mrs Tanner's cottage was required.

Chapter 23

Future Planning

'Good morning, Mrs Tanner. How are you?' Henry said sprightly, standing at the cottage door the next day. 'I was wondering if Maria was up to receiving visitors? I know that sounds strange coming from me, but I was hoping for a few words with her about Juan Marco, if that's OK? Is she well enough to be able to talk a little, or even just listen and understand? I know it sounds unwelcome, but I don't mean any harm at all. It's just that I'm going away again soon and wanted to speak to her about him before leaving, and ensure we part on at least civil terms.'

'I don't think that's a good idea, Henry. You're not her favourite person, as I'm sure you know, and she's very tired and upset by her condition. She can speak a little now, but she mustn't be upset as she recovers. This isn't a good idea, I'm afraid.'

'I understand perfectly, but I'm sure she'd like some news of her son. He's modest about his achievements and before I go, I'd just like to bring her up to date on his progress. It's all positive stuff and I won't stray into anything controversial. What he's learning here will really benefit both of them when they return home.'

'That's likely to upset her, Henry. Thinking of returning home isn't going to make her feel better now.'

'On the contrary, I think it may do her some good. The future's always just around the corner and she needs to look forward to something. Just a few minutes with her if she's feeling up to it, please. Juan Marco said she can speak a little easier now and I promise I'll keep it short. As the father of her son, I really feel we should talk one final time. I know this may sound odd, but we share a common bond because of our son, and I really am running out of time to make efforts to be on civil speaking terms with her. Unless she really is too unwell to receive any visitors, please just give me a few minutes with her. Juan Marco shares things with me you know, things that he won't say directly to her, but I can help bridge the gap I think,' he said with an expectant look, deciding that a period of silence was now more persuasive.

'Oh Henry, you put me in such a difficult position! Just don't upset her, that's all, not after all she's been through.'

'Thank you, I won't,' he said, heading upstairs.

He knocked gently at the door, and hearing no reply, put his head around. 'Maria, it's me, Henry. Just wanted to check on you. Juan Marco's busy, so I said I'd pop in and see for myself how you're doing.'

She turned her head towards him and tried to say something, but it sounded inaudible, so he continued.

'It's OK, don't trouble yourself. I understand speaking's difficult, so let me talk for the two of us. Now firstly, don't worry about Juan Marco, he's doing just fine,' he added, assuming that was at least part of the reason for her concerned look. 'In fact, he's doing really well. We're all pleased with him up at the hall and I think he's managed to charm my parents. He really does handle himself very maturely and you should be proud of him... I'm sure you are.'

Again, her eyes showed fear, and she mumbled 'my son' before trailing off.

'Now you need to remember that sometimes one stroke can be a precursor to another, so don't look so tense,' he chided. Her face sank and a more resigned look took over her eyes. 'That's better. It makes you think, doesn't it? About our mortality, I mean. God knows how many times I've thought about how long I've got. I'm not trying to scare you, but it comes to us all and I feel it too. Sometimes, I think if I go I'll leave nothing of any consequence behind. No one will really miss me or even care that I've gone.' He shrugged his shoulders. 'But maybe that's my own fault. Anyway, I must admit that Juan Marco's existence has changed that for me, to some degree.'

Maria tried to force herself upright and stuttered: 'He's my son, not yours.'

'Well, that's not really true, is it? He's *our* son,' teased Henry. 'What do you think your legacy will be to him, you know if the worst happens? I mean obviously his personality, his manners, all that sort of thing is great, but what of his future life? You'd leave him a little bit, I'm sure, but you'd want more for him than bar work, wouldn't you?'

238

Maria summoned her strength and concentration. Her words were slower than normal, but her eyes burned. 'He's nothing to you and your family! He doesn't need you, even if you think he does!'

'It's not a case of whether he needs us, it's a question of what he wants. I think you'll find there's far more for him here than you imagine. Education, work, money, opportunity, women... they're all here for him in abundance. He's a bright, intelligent lad with charm. Doors can open up here. You're not as close to him as you once were, you know... he tells me things... I think your days of controlling him are over. Well, on that positive note, I'll leave you to ponder your own legacy to him, and maybe when you've thought some, we'll speak again! No, please don't get up, I'll see myself out. And remember what the doctors said about taking it easy and avoiding stress.'

As Maria's head sank back on the pillow and tears wet her cheeks, Henry made his way downstairs. 'I'd give her a while, Mrs Tanner. We've had an interesting chat, and she spoke a little, but I think she's tired now and needs to sleep. I'll be off. Take care now!'

As Henry made his way back to the hall, the battle between good and evil swayed back and forth in his mind: 'Cruel man, harsh uncaring man!' 'That sorted the old witch out! You just told her the truth. Her days are numbered!' 'Are you actually trying to finish her off, murder her?' 'She's got no future with him, whether she recovers or not. She's his past, you're his future!'

In her bedroom, Maria gently cried herself to sleep, her mind full of resentment and anger towards Henry, but tinged with fear over her own future. Was this really a warning that her life might be coming to an end? More importantly, Henry's words stung that she might be losing her bond with her son, maybe already had lost it, and he might have more interest in staying in England than returning to Spain with her.

In Lord Belvedere's study the following day, Juan Marco was attempting to read the estate accounts for the past two years. He kept seeing depreciation mentioned in relation to plant and equipment, but no allowance for any actual residual cash value anywhere. It troubled him that this didn't tally with things Robert had said, but he didn't feel confident enough to mention it to Lord Belvedere. His phone buzzed, and he saw his mother's name pop up with a short message: *Come to the cottage tonight, I want to see you.* He instantly thought the worst and asked if he should come right away, but she said tonight was OK, after dinner.

He ate with the house staff and one of them drove him to Mrs Tanner's. He went straight up to her room. Maria smiled at him with more warmth than he could remember for a while, and then spoke slowly and deliberately, but clearly enough.

'Are you enjoying your extra time here?'

Juan Marco was puzzled by this unexpected question. 'It's different with the finances and I see a different perspective at the hall, but the other work's the same, it's fine.'

'OK, well, good. I'm not angry with you, the opposite. I want you to be happy, and if you want to stay here, then that's OK.' She'd controlled her feelings well to this point, but now the tears fell. 'I know I've been unpleasant and unkind to you recently... I know I shouldn't have said those things, but you're my son and I love you unconditionally... you must never doubt it. You are my world, and if I've been selfish it's only because I was afraid of losing you! I know you want to change your life to achieve what you're capable of, and I know you're doing it for me, too. I want you to be happy and to do whatever you need to make that happen, and I'm sorry if...'

'Mother, what's happened? Please tell me, you're frightening me,' he replied with tears running down his cheeks now as well. They sobbed in each other's arms for a minute, before Maria recovered herself.

'Nothing's happened. I've just realised how proud I am of you, and that I need to look at what you're achieving and be happy for you, not put my own selfish needs first. I'm going to be fine. I just want you to know that you must do whatever you want to make your life your own... whether that is here or back home. If you need more time here then you have it with my blessing, that's all.'

Juan Marco wasn't convinced by his mother's apparent change of heart, but he left her to rest, feeling utterly confused. Her words were such a shock after so many arguments, and should have lifted his spirits beyond belief, but Mrs Tanner seemed as bemused as him at the change, or if she knew more, she wasn't saying. She offered endless shakes of her head, reiterating she didn't know of anything the doctors had said that would make Maria feel she didn't have a good chance of recovery. As he left, he asked her to let him know immediately if his mother's health changed, no matter what time of day.

The following morning, he rang Mrs Tanner before starting work to check on his mother's health, and was calmed that she was no worse, if a little tired. That lifted his spirits as he headed to the stables for a day mucking out and cleaning up the harnesses, bridles, reins, and other equipment that had deteriorated over the winter months. He was also going to enjoy two hours out with Anna's mare, as her stable door footplate needed replacing and some vertical timbers, which would give him time for a mixed ride around the estate. He enjoyed some light-hearted banter with Lauren as he exited the yard, and felt that today was a good day! He was on his way back down the main drive at three when he met Henry walking towards him.

'You look fine and dandy up there! You look happy!'

'Yes, it's been a busy day but I've enjoyed it.'

'How's your mother? Have you seen her in the last couple of days?'

Juan Marco nodded cautiously. 'She's tired... very tired... but I'm hopeful she'll be OK. We had a good talk last night.'

'Oh? Did she manage it OK, the words I mean?'

Juan Marco nodded and couldn't help showing a weak smile. 'She said some things that were very reassuring.'

'In what way?'

'Just that she supports me in whatever I want to do, that's all.'

Henry tried to read his son's face for more meaning but didn't want to press, but his instinct was it couldn't have been a bad conversation, otherwise Juan Marco wouldn't look so relaxed. 'OK, that sounds good. I'm pleased she's improving. Enjoy the rest of your ride.' Henry headed over to the edge of the woods to give Juan Marco some time to get ahead, before he started his walk back to the hall. His mind was alive again with possibilities. Could it be that Maria had undergone a change of heart since their conversation? After weeks of arguing for a return to their home, what else could have made her tell her son she was now happy for him to choose his own path? Henry had reminded her of her mortality and maybe that had done the trick! If that was true, then it was time for the last throw of the dice before he went back to Spain.

The following morning, he returned to the cottage after swallowing two brandies to pluck up courage. He initially made small talk with Mrs Tanner on the pretext that the visit was to her, waiting for the conversation to turn naturally towards Maria.

'She seems… different in the last day or so. I'm not sure why. She's smiling more, still very tired, but she seems calmer for some reason. It's like she's at peace, which should fill me with optimism, and I think her speech is getting better too. But it's like she's had an epiphany. She had a talk with Juan Marco last night and I think it got emotional. I'm guessing it did some good. She's more relaxed, which is good, but it's like she doesn't care so much any more. I'm worrying too much, maybe.'

'I had a good few minutes with her the previous night and, you know, I think she might be getting the message that we should work together, not use Juan Marco as the excuse for our differences. Whatever the circumstances, we're united by a common interest in him. I really think she's beginning to see it's not all about her life. I'll pop up and see her. It might help to reassure you.'

Henry knocked on the bedroom door and waited for the 'come in'. As soon as Maria saw him, she hissed: 'Get out of here! There's nothing I want to hear from you. You spread poison!' She turned to her bedside cabinet, looking for anything she could throw at him.

'Now, now, I came here to congratulate you! I spoke with Juan Marco and he told me you'd decided to support his decision to remain with us, and I just wanted you to know what a great thing it is you've done! I mean it. He really looked happy and relaxed yesterday for the first time in ages. You've realised that you've got to let him grow in his own way and that's marvellous.'

'I don't need any compliments from you! My relationship with my son has nothing to do with you!'

'It's our son, and that's what I wanted to speak to you about. Together we can help him in so many more ways, if we just stop fighting and work together.'

'Leave me alone and go! He doesn't need you.'

'Ah, well, I think I can be of real support to him and let me just remind you of what the doctor said about your blood pressure. Steady there!'

Her eyes flared at him and she was about to launch another attack when she started coughing, and reluctantly had to accept the glass of water offered by Henry. 'Now calm yourself,' he continued. 'You see, if we can work together, there's no need for this war. Now, I hope you've had a chance to think about what we discussed the other day. Your legacy, you remember? Now it appears to me that Juan Marco can have the best of both worlds. He can continue his education in Spain and supplement it with visits back to the UK whenever he likes, always having a place to stay and practice what he's learnt. A marvellous position for him to be in if he chooses it. That's the point really, Maria. You're now accepting he has the right to make his own choices?'

'His choice will always be to be with me! You're dreaming if you think it otherwise!'

'I think that it's him that has the right to dream, and perhaps *we* can offer him far more security than you ever could. It comes back to your legacy again. Now, what if we were to help him together, give him a choice of futures, the ability to combine the best of both worlds? A mere slip of paper, a formal agreement between us, and your son, our son, is guaranteed a secure future with different lives in different countries if he chooses it.'

'What are you talking about, dividing him up as if he's a piece of land?'

'Ah, but that's the point. It's us giving him the right to make his choices, not imposing them on him.'

'This is you and your twisted mind trying to tie him to you as if he was your possession!'

'It doesn't sound as if you're really willing to look out for his interests after all. I think I'd better enlighten him about this conversation to let him know nothing's changed. I have to say, I'm surprised, particularly bearing in mind your health. You're not looking well, Maria, you've just had a warning, and here you are, raising your blood pressure again. Take a look in the mirror, in all senses, and think what your son would do if you were no longer around,' Henry said, staring at her.

A combination of slow speech and fright came over Maria as she stuttered. 'Don't think you can crush me... even in this state. How do you make a contract for someone's life?'

'It's easily done. It's called a marriage contract. That's right, nice and easy, and he doesn't need to know anything about it. A quick civil service that nobody else needs to know about, bar a couple of witnesses, and everything's set in place in case something happens to you or even me!'

'What? You're crazy! Why would I ever marry you? You don't even like women!'

'It's not a contract of love, it's a contract to guarantee your son a future. It's entirely for him. Don't you understand anything that doesn't give you a personal benefit?'

'And you think that marrying you is a way of protecting my son?'

'Well said. There you are in a nutshell. You see, I told you if you saw it from his perspective it would start to make sense. I'll leave you to dwell on it for a few days. The more you think about it the more it'll make sense. Bye then.'

Maria was left dumbfounded as he strolled down the stairs and made his farewells to Mrs Tanner. Either way, he'd fired his final shot in this battle and Spain was calling. He'd make one final visit and if she accepted his offer, he'd depart as soon as possible after the wedding. If she turned his offer down, then he was done with his family for now.

Maria's state of mind was now unsettled, and Mrs Tanner was forced to call the doctor out for a home visit two days later, as she was showing signs of confusion and tension. The doctor was concerned enough to call for an ambulance, and Maria was readmitted to Maidstone General Hospital for observation. This time, Mrs Tanner was under no illusion that Henry's visit had upset her, and was bemused by Maria's confused mumblings about marriage and a father for her son. When Juan Marco came to visit, she reluctantly kept Henry's last visit from him, but knew that things would have to be different from now on.

After two days in hospital and numerous tests, the doctors gave consent for Maria to return to the cottage at the end of the week. She had returned to lucidity and her blood pressure was back under control, but they advised her they had discovered a faint heart murmur which wasn't serious, but she should be aware of it. They advised complete rest with a minimum of visitors.

Maria's first week of recuperating was quiet and uninterrupted by outsiders, but Mrs Tanner noticed a more serious mood had descended over her. She had no real interest in getting out of bed, and was less positive in her conversation, even on the topic of returning home. Juan Marco also commented that her mood seemed darker, so Mrs Tanner decided to risk pressing her a little one morning.

'You know you're supposed to get out of bed and move around a little to avoid the risk of blood clots, just like the doctors said?'

'Humph… they didn't have any good news for me, did they? Perhaps moving around will worsen my heart murmur.'

'No, come on, they said that was abnormal, but nothing to worry about. You were doing so well with your little trips into the garden. It's not as cold as it was, so maybe's now the time to resume your exercise.'

'One step forward and one step back! So, I go home with more health conditions than I came with, and no son! What's the point?'

'Maria, nothing's going to happen to you. The stroke was only minor and the doctors are confident you can make a full recovery. Your confusion has gone and your speech is better. You're expecting too much of yourself. Just try to relax and stimulate your body with a bit of exercise to help ease your thoughts. Your mind is working overtime.'

'That's hardly surprising, is it? Other people put thoughts into my mind, it's their fault not mine.'

'Who's been talking to you to make you worry? Your last visitor before your confusion was Henry. Did he say anything to upset you?' An angry look flashed across Maria's face.

'Only that he thinks I should marry him to give Juan Marco a future in England, if he wants one!'

Mrs Tanner was speechless and her jaw moved up and down several times before she could actually say anything. 'I can't believe it! How could he? His parents would never support it. I mean the family wouldn't support it! It wouldn't be right... for him, for them, for you! What did you say to him?'

'What do you think? It's madness, but he thinks I should do it for Juan Marco's sake, in case I'm... not around any more.'

'Oh, no wonder you've been in a state! How could he suggest something so devious and cruel in your condition? I can't believe that even Henry would stoop so low, but this really is the darkest thing! I shall be giving him a piece of my mind when I see him next, but it won't be in this house, not ever! He won't come through that door again.'

Chapter 24

Lies, Damned Lies and Statistics

Juan Marco wasn't enjoying his time at Hillingstone any more. His mother was ill and irritable with it, and he was concerned for both her health and her prospects for returning to Spain. He was still learning practical skills when Robert found the time to teach him, but there was a distance between them that hadn't been there before. He sensed this was due to the interest he'd shown in understanding the estate finances, but it was frustrating to be encouraged into a task by Lord Belvedere, only to find that all roads led to a dead end. Robert glossed over everything, Lord Belvedere seemed more concerned with the tidiness of things rather than whether the numbers added up, and Lauren wasn't able to help either. Invoices with VAT on, invoices with no VAT, estimates the same, accruals, cash books, staged payments, invoices for house repairs that seemed to leave a trail of confusion, rather than clarity... it was a mess with no one helping to understand what was going on.

One morning, he remembered something Lauren had said and decided to raise it with Lord Belvedere. 'I was wondering if it would be good for me to talk to Andrew, your brother, about the accounts? Lauren mentioned that he checked them on behalf of the family before they went to the auditors each year? Might he be a good person to ask about the way the accounts are prepared?'

Lord Belvedere thought for a moment. 'Hmm... he does provide oversight after Robert shows him the figures. I think I'd need to be present though. Let me call him now and see if he'll come over.'

After speaking with Andrew he turned to Juan Marco. 'Right, well, he didn't want to commit to a time without speaking to Robert to check how up to date things are. You heard me explain that I wanted just an overview of some of the general procedures, and I referred to having an assistant who's helping me in the office. But he'll check with Robert first, so I guess

246

we'll have to wait. I won't let him keep us hanging for long.'

As soon as Andrew had received the call he phoned Robert, but it went straight to voicemail. 'Robert, it's Andrew. Hope you're well. Look, I've just had a call from my brother, he wants a meeting to discuss the accounts. He was talking in general terms and he's obviously got this illegitimate grandson involved, because he alluded to an "office helper". Obviously, I didn't agree to anything right away, but I'm going to have to go and see him. Can you let me know the state of play for the current year? The year-end is up in a couple of months so I'm assuming it's all tickety-boo, but can you give me a heads-up if there's anything I should know? Oh, by the way, the land deal's no further forward, but I guess you figured that as I hadn't been in touch. Talk later.'

Robert returned his call two hours later. 'Andrew, Robert. It's that bastard grandson all right, stirring things up. He keeps asking me questions about invoices and allowances, and I feel like telling him to mind his own fucking business and stick to putting in fence posts. Avoid the meeting if you can and if you can't, keep it bland and talk only to your brother. Don't engage with superboy at all, he'll just ask more questions. There's nothing to worry about on this year's figures. I'm a bit behind but I'll get Lauren to sort it out and dress it up over the next month, then we'll have provisional numbers for the year.'

'I'll have to go,' replied Andrew, 'and I'll try to blind him with capital investment, reserving and all that stuff, so he won't know the wood from the trees.'

'One thing that'll amuse you,' Robert laughed. 'The Spanish bull can see the attraction of selling some of the farmland! He even said building housing on it sounds a good idea to maximise value, so perhaps you can bring it up and see what impact it has!'

Andrew laughed and then rang off, feeling more optimistic about seeing his brother again.

They met two days later, and after Andrew's tack of enquiring if the meeting was to be in private had failed, he, his brother and Juan Marco sat down. Andrew started off trying to set the historical scene for past management of the estate, but Lord Belvedere cut him off and said he'd already explained the history, and suggested that Juan Marco start his list of questions. Andrew listened uncomfortably to the first two, which required detailed knowledge to answer which he simply hadn't got. So he deftly switched to treatment of capital investment for tax purposes, linking that loosely to budgets, drawdowns and accruals between tax years. Thus, he concluded, separate accounts were really required to manage budgets, cash flow and investment, and it was really the auditors that made sense of it all at year-end. A figure might appear in a budget, but the same item could also be included in the other worksheets, but with a different value, because of the different treatment of it depending on allowances, deferrals, etc.

To ask him to comment on individual invoices and estimates was really too granular for him, and he suggested they work with Robert and Lauren to sort out any minor queries like these.

Lord Belvedere sat embarrassed that he really didn't understand a lot of the terminology, and Juan Marco's face was a picture of frustration when he answered that Robert really didn't have the time to help him, and Lauren had said she didn't do much except manage payroll.

'Well, I think she's being a little modest there,' smiled Andrew. 'I've always found her extremely helpful and I think she knows more than she's letting on. I don't think Robert would disagree if I recommended you push her a little harder. She's a clever woman, so make it clear you won't be fobbed off and I think you'll make some progress. Now, John, I know we've not spoken about it for some time, but have you thought any more about the merits of the land disposal plan?'

'Er... that's not something I want to discuss right now. I'll decide in time how I think it should be handled, but that's not relevant to today's meeting.'

'Ah, OK that's fine, I understand if you want more time. I believe young Juan Marco here expressed his approval of the idea when he discussed it with Robert.'

Juan Marco flushed as Lord Belvedere gave him a sharp look. 'As you're aware, I make the decisions in consultation with the family, and I'd appreciate it if the fors and againsts of any such major proposal were discussed in the appropriate forum.'

'Quite,' replied Andrew smoothly. 'Well I think that concludes our business. I hope it was useful to you Juan Marco, and perhaps we'll see each other again one day. My regards to Caroline, John.'

Juan Marco felt the tension in the air as Andrew left, and was relieved when Lord Belvedere said he felt tired and needed a lie down, so could he come back to the office tomorrow? As he glumly walked to the estate office,

Juan Marco was in no mood to be charmed by Lauren.

As soon as Andrew was in his car, he phoned Robert. 'Pretty good, I'd say,' he replied to Robert's greeting. 'I think I gave enough high-level stuff to bamboozle them both, and boy did it go down like a lead balloon when I mentioned the land sell-off! Thanks for the tip. You should have seen John's face when he heard Juan Marco approved of the idea! Priceless! There's just one thing you should know. I sort of set Lauren up as someone who knows more than she lets on, and perhaps would respond to a bit of squeezing. The look on the boy's face indicated he's probably going to pay her another visit. Is that a problem?'

'No, far from it. Good idea. He likes her, so I'll tell her to keep him sweet and be nice to him. If he pushes too hard, I'll tell her to think creatively how to manage him! She's got all the tools, well at least she used to have!' he laughed.

Juan Marco waited at the office while Lauren finished a call, moving outside to stroke the horses, which always worked its own magic on his mood. When she came out he had calmed down a little. 'About that dinner invitation, is it still open?'

'Yes, of course!' she replied pleasantly.

'Perhaps we can mix it with a little business, you know, finances and accounts. Mr Andrew Belvedere told me you're a little modest about your talents, and he suggests you're a good person to help with day-to-day things.'

'As I've said to you before, Juan Marco, I manage the payroll and sure, Robert gets me to help out with supplier payments and banking receipts sometimes too, but I'm not the best person to address specific queries to. That's Robert... I can make sure he'll be around on our chosen night?'

'Yes, sure, if you're both there that will be much better.'

'OK, well we're busy tomorrow and Saturday, so we're in to next week. How about Wednesday? That's a good day, middle of the week and all that, and you can see how everything's shaping up for the end of the week.'

'Perfect, see you both then.'

At dinner that night Lauren told Robert about the planned evening with Juan Marco. 'Next Wednesday? No, sorry I've got a social night out with the boys but you can handle it. You don't need me.'

'But you know he's going to ask about money things. I think he's going to bring along some papers and invoices to check. I need you there to deal with it! You know I don't get involved in your dealings with suppliers and contractors. OK, sometimes I see some of the paperwork but not often all of it. I'm not involved enough if he starts asking detailed questions. You've got to be there, otherwise he'll be disappointed and I don't want him getting shirty with me.'

'Oh right, that's what it's all about is it? You don't want him to be disappointed in you? Worried your vanity will be hurt?'

'Don't be so childish! He came over today as a bit ruffled, as if he'd got irritated by something, and I got the impression it was this stuff, the finances. Who's it helping if he goes back pissed off?'

Robert grinned at her. 'Well make sure he doesn't. Charm him. You know the routine – nice dress, stylish jewellery, wide smile, anything you like. Look, he's only here for a few more weeks and then his tiresome questions will stop, so let's not get too excited about it. Just deal with him anyway you choose; I've every confidence in you.'

'No, that's not how it's going to work! I'll tell him we need to rearrange for another night.'

'You'll do no such thing. I mean it,' Robert said, lowering his voice to a growl. 'Take care of him. Since he's discovered his half-blood inheritance, he's started interfering in stuff that's not his place to poke around in. The sooner Belvedere realises he needs me and should rely on me, and not use his half-whelp to do his dirty work, the better!'

'He might be here longer!' protested Lauren. 'With his mother's health, maybe he won't be going back to Spain as quickly you'd like! You can't rely on it, you need to keep him onside!'

'Incorrect. *You* need to keep him onside and I expect you to do it. I don't care what you do and I mean anything, even if it involves taking your clothes off! Relax him and everything goes away!'

'What do you think I am?' Lauren shouted. 'A whore?'

Robert glared at her. 'You're my whore and on that subject…' He moved around the table and grabbed her by her arm, pulling her up off her seat, whilst his other hand roughly grabbed her right breast.

As she struggled and swore at him he pulled her towards the door and stairs, releasing her breast and gripping her neck in his large hand, while forcing her arm up her back.

Chapter 25

Slipping the Knot

Juan Marco visited his mother on Friday evening and could still feel the lowness in her mood. She came down for dinner but ate little, and contributed the same to the conversation. When they had finished she asked him to come and see her upstairs before he left, giving him some time alone with Mrs Tanner.

'You know she's not been the same since your father… Henry… came to see her? I don't know what he said but she's sunk into a kind of depression since then, and I'm sure it's not just the after-effects of the stroke. She keeps going on about the heart murmur but the doctors said it was only slight. I'm trying to encourage her to get out of bed and move around a bit, even take a few steps in the garden, but she's resisting it. I don't know what more I can do. But I've decided that I'm not having Henry in here again until your mother's returned home. I'm not having him upset her and raise her blood pressure!'

Juan Marco said he'd hardly seen Henry in the past few days and had no knowledge of the conversation, but he'd ask his mother shortly what it was about. If he'd been creating trouble then he'd have it out with him, as he was in the mood for a fight. He then proceeded to recount his frustrations at understanding the finances of the estate, and the walls that were being put in place wherever he turned. He hoped the dinner with Robert and Lauren would finally lead to some progress.

When he went upstairs to see his mother, she asked him to close the door. 'Sit down. There's something I want you to do for me. Tell Henry that I want to see him, but I'll text you with the time and day. I need it to be private.'

'What's going on, Mother? Mrs Tanner said he's been here and upset you and I'm not having it! You need to recover and avoid stress.'

'Now listen to me, Juan Marco! Mrs Tanner is a good friend but she doesn't know everything, and I wouldn't want her to! There's some things that are private and I can't tell her, and I'm sorry if she doesn't understand but it can't be helped. There are some things I want to clear up with him, things from the past... maybe I have misremembered them or misunderstood them. But these are things I can only ask him. I will feel a lot better afterwards knowing the truth.'

'You can't trust him to tell you the truth! He uses people, including us!'

'Juan Marco, I need you to respect my wishes. These aren't things to do with you either... I mean getting pregnant and what happened after. These are things from before, personal, things I need to have peace of mind over. I know I'm miserable at the moment, but with these things sorted my spirits will rise.'

'How do you know? You might get the wrong answers!'

'No, you don't understand. I said you wouldn't. What I need is just to ask him about things face-to-face, to cleanse my mind. I know where I must go from here and to move on, I want my mind settled. Please, do it. I will text you a date and time when I know Mrs Tanner is going out, then get him to come here. It won't take long.'

'But Mrs Tanner doesn't want him in the cottage, she said so just now!'

'Exactly, so I have to be careful, but I don't want her to be here, do you understand? These conversations are private.'

Juan Marco groaned. 'I like Mrs Tanner, I respect her, I don't want to go behind her back!'

'And I need you to respect me on this very, very private matter. She won't know, it won't take long and he will be gone way before she comes back, I promise. My son, you won't get into any trouble, I guarantee it. Now, will you help bring me peace of mind or not?' He groaned again. 'Just tell him and pass the message on when the time comes, that's all.'

He stood to leave and she held his hand. 'You're a good boy, do this for me, your mother.' He nodded glumly as he left the room.

Juan Marco hadn't seen Henry for a few days and had no interest in doing so, so he sent a text message saying that his mother wanted to see him soon when she had worked out a date and time, but he didn't know anything more. Henry replied sounding keen to catch up with him, but the voice message he left was drowned out by the noise coming from whatever pub he was in.

It was on Monday that Maria messaged her son to tell him that Mrs Tanner would be out on Wednesday between eleven and three, and could he get Henry to come then, not too close to the end of the window. Henry confirmed he'd be at the cottage for midday.

Henry's eyes were gleaming and his hands sweating as he rang the doorbell. Either he'd won her over, or he was back on a plane to Spain – either way, he was in the driving seat again. Maria opened the door and motioned for him to come in. She was fully dressed but moved awkwardly towards the sofa, and Henry sat down opposite in an armchair. He was about to launch into one of his bullshit-laden greetings when she held her hand up.

'Don't say anything. You're to listen and answer my questions. I don't want any of your speeches or waffle, just listen. Let me say that your… proposal isn't the right word… offer, disgusts me, and if it was for me alone I'd throw you out. But my son comes first and he deserves every chance in life, especially when it comes to *your* family. So if it can be done quickly and quietly with no one else knowing, I will agree to it as long as you agree to my conditions. Juan Marco must know nothing about it unless something happens to me; your family must know nothing about it; it must be done away from here in secret and as soon as possible. I want no religion, as this is not a marriage contract made from anything other than practicality. How quickly can it happen?'

Henry couldn't conceal his satisfaction at her response. 'Let me say I'm so pleased you've come to this decision Maria, it's—'

She cut him off with a look and a swift chop of her hand. 'I don't want to hear any of your rubbish! Just answer the question.'

'OK, well you'll be pleased to hear I've given some thought to it already. The logistics are that we need to register an intent to marry at the local register office, then the ceremony can't be any earlier than a month after. I had thought about where, and I think Deal is far enough away on the east Kent coast. You'll like it there if you haven't been before, it's a pleasant…'

Another look from Maria stopped him in his tracks.

'Well, as I say, it's far enough away, it's got a register office and we can easily be there and back in a day. Taxi ride to the station, train to Deal, taxi ride at the other end, quick twenty-minute service, couple of drinks if you like' – another glare – 'and then back on a train. All done in a day. A couple of strangers will do as witnesses. Have you got all your documents with you – proof of address, driving licence, that sort of thing?'

Maria nodded. 'Can't it be done any quicker?'

'Afraid not. I don't think it's a special licence situation, unless you're er... expecting a sudden deterioration in your health?'

Maria sat upright and glared at him. 'No I am not!'

'OK, that's it then. We'll need to go together to register the intent as soon as possible, and I'll contact the Deal register office to see when they've got a slot. Presumably you don't care about which day of the week, so that should help our situation?'

Maria nodded before adding: 'And you agree to total secrecy?'

'Oh, yes, I think we can both agree that nobody else needs to know, until such time as something unfortunate happens to one of us. Of course, if it's me then you'll have the fun and games of introducing the new heir to the family, so you might want to think about that at some point. But of course, you have absolute discretion as to how you proceed, or indeed if you proceed at all when the time comes.' He looked at her with as little mischief as he could manage.

Maria pursed her lips and said: 'Our business is done. Let me know about the appointments and dates. You have my mobile number, as I will need to make my excuses for when I have to be out, medical appointments or something. Wednesday is often a good day as Mrs Tanner usually goes off to town to meet a friend and do some shopping.'

Henry nodded and made for the door, turning to watch Maria rise uncomfortably from the sofa, raising his eyebrows as his farewell.

Today was also a big day for Juan Marco, as he hoped the finances of the estate would become clearer at tonight's dinner. He had a card folder with several invoices and estimates in it, a copy of the last estate accounts, and some notes he'd made so he could remember to ask the right questions. He arrived at the farmhouse carrying a bottle of wine that the housekeeper had given him, after he'd told her about his difficulties with understanding the accounts. He hoped the gift would have the effect of getting the evening off to a good start. Lauren answered the door, and he noticed her nervous expression and fragile smile as she welcomed him in. She looked beautiful in a shimmering gold-coloured dress, with large 'V' cut-out front and back, but her dress and long, shiny hair with front fringe and tie-back to one side, didn't seem to fit with her nervousness.

The strangely formal atmosphere continued as she thanked him for the wine, and asked if he wanted a glass straight away or something else. He said he'd have a beer first and sensed there was something she wanted to say. As she gave him the glass and bottle she plucked up the courage.

'OK, so I just need to tell you that Robert's not here tonight. He's at an

254

urgent meeting away from the estate that cropped up suddenly, and he's had to go. I'm so sorry because I know you wanted us both here tonight, and this is going to be a terrible disappointment to you. I will try my best to help you though – I've been going through some papers to see if I can glean more information and I really will help you all I can, but I understand if you don't feel there's any point in staying. I really feel I've let you down.'

Juan Marco looked at her with a mixture of confusion and emotional flatness, but his sense of disappointment was blunted somewhat by Lauren's discomfort. He'd always seen her looking confident and in control but this was a first for him – she appeared sheepish, serious and subdued. His manners came to his rescue. 'What you're cooking smells fantastic and my stomach is rumbling already, so I don't want to miss out on that. Will Robert be back later to join us? Surely he won't want to miss out either?'

'No I don't expect him back. In fact, I think he may stay the night. He's had a call from his father. I think his mother and he have had words and it's all blown up, and Robert's gone to be peacemaker. He took an overnight bag with him so I doubt he'll be back.'

'Oh, I'm sorry. Look, if this is difficult for you and you'd rather be with your husband then I'll go. Families are important.'

'No, it's fine, I don't need to be there. It's best left to him to resolve it, he knows them best. I just don't want to disappoint you... even if the food smells good,' she replied with a half-smile.

'Mr Andrew Belvedere seemed to think you have more of a grip of the detail than you say. He thinks you're being modest.'

Lauren shuddered. 'I think he's flattering me,' she replied coolly.

'OK, I know Robert's not here, but I'd still like to try and make some progress. So we have two options, I think. We either look at the financial papers before dinner or after. Which would you prefer? Or do we not have time before dinner – the food's smelling like it's ready.'

Lauren smiled back at him. 'The ham has about another thirty-five minutes, and I'll put the potatoes on in ten minutes. I was going to serve salad with it, if that's OK? That's already prepared so we have a little time now, if you want, or we can leave it until later, it's up to you.'

Both of them felt awkward about making a decision for different reasons. There was an uneasy silence for a few seconds, and then Juan Marco said slowly: 'OK, well, why don't I show you what I've brought with me and see if the invoices and estimates look familiar? That might be a good place to start, and if you recognise them we can get into it, and if you don't, then you have some thinking time while you're finishing preparing dinner.'

Lauren was relieved by the offer of more time and accepted his suggestion, and they sat down at the kitchen table. He showed her invoices for works done at the hall as well as on the farm, quotations for replacement of agricultural machinery, and pro forma for vehicle replacements, all of which he had questions on. Lauren immediately responded that she knew nothing about expenditure on the hall, other than she recognised the names of the contractors and that Robert had dealt with them for a long time, and she knew they were reputable. She was able to suggest that sometimes they had building supplies left over after completion of a job, and it could be that another job had used, in part, some of those materials, which could have led to a lower final invoice. Alternatively, they'd received a credit for materials not used after completion of the works, and the credit note was missing from his papers. At least that seemed a credible partial explanation to Juan Marco, and gave him something to check up on.

They took a break while Lauren saw to the potatoes, then resumed while finishing their first drinks. Some of the machinery and vehicle invoices she thought could be related to reducing VAT liability. She remembered changing vehicles herself in the past where the provisional invoice differed from the final one, because the dealer inflated the value of the part-exchange on the final invoice, to reduce the overall VAT amount. Again she suggested that perhaps he was missing some of the paperwork, which seemed plausible.

She felt she was making good progress in dealing with his questions despite her nervousness, which was lessening because of the glass of wine that now sat empty. But her ease wasn't improved when Juan Marco asked about the missing JCB. She had also asked Robert about it, and now regretted not pressing him further when he told her it was being "taken care of".

That left them on a flat note when the cooker timer sounded but gave her the opportunity to serve up the food, and Juan Marco opened the wine that had come from the hall after putting his papers back in the folder.

Over dinner, he asked her about her connections to the area, and her mood brightened as she recalled her childhood in the local village, and the fun she had both at home and at school. Her face grew in animation as she talked about the social nature of her school life, giving the appearance that her education was of secondary importance. She'd left school with decent but unexceptional grades, and worked in an estate agents for a while in Maidstone. But the hours had interrupted her social life too much, and she'd returned to the village and got a job in the local grocery store, where she was able to reconnect with many of her old friends. It was there that she'd become more friendly with Robert, although she already knew George Belvedere from the Hillingstone family before then.

Juan Marco's ears pricked up when he heard George's name, as Mary had alluded to a relationship between them. Lauren instantly regretted mentioning his name when Juan Marco asked her about him.

'Oh, well, it was a long time ago and I suppose I got a bit carried away really. He was awfully sweet, I guess, and I was flattered by his attention, you know, son of the local lord and all that. But it was an opportunity for me to see another side of life which I didn't know a lot about, and it seemed like fun. I let it go to my head a bit, I suppose, but I was young and he was quite a bit older and I just got swept up in it all. It wasn't really serious from my perspective, and I moved on and became involved with Robert not long after.'

'Someone on the estate said George took it badly,' he probed.

'I'm not sure about that,' Lauren replied defensively. 'He was always the sensitive type and resented the attention that Henry got from being the elder son, despite the fact that George worked much harder. I think it was a series of things that led to him leaving the estate, but I imagine you've heard his side of things, having worked on their farm?' Juan Marco nodded but said nothing. 'Mary's very practical and good for him anyway, a far better match than I would have been.'

Juan Marco smiled and replied: 'Yes, I like Mary. She's practical and down to earth, and I agree they're good for each other.'

'You know she was at the staff Christmas party, don't you? Did you see her? It must have been odd for you both, you already knowing her, and she must have got the shock of her life seeing you when she knew nothing of you being at Hillingstone!'

This time it was Juan Marco on the defensive and he blushed. 'Yes, I did see her but she handled it really well. Like I said, she's very practical and didn't want to make a drama. We went off for a while and had a talk, and agreed to deal with things away from anybody else.'

'Ah, is that why I didn't see you for a while when I was searching for you to make sure you were enjoying yourself?'

He blushed again and Lauren picked up on it, trying to read his eyes.

257

There was a glint there, but not enough to work with. 'Yes that's it,' he replied economically.

'Gosh, I remember that night, it was a great party other than Robert's... antics,' she glowered. 'I know I show off sometimes but there were responsibilities on both of us that night, and he just left me to it!'

Juan Marco felt the shift in mood and saw the brightness dimming in her eyes, so he complimented her on the food and poured another two glasses of red, while she fetched the dessert. They both realised without anything being said, that the financial chat was over, and this had just become a pleasant dinner with two possibilities. The first was that their light-hearted jousting would continue until it fizzled out. The other was that they could recognise that the purpose of the evening had fundamentally failed, and not to let their heads run away on the alcohol.

Juan Marco decided to take the bull by the horns, and started talking about his mother's health and mood, which led to the subject of a return to Spain. When he referenced his failure to understand the estate finances, and linked it to going home, Lauren realised that he hadn't forgotten the real purpose of the evening, and her relief from the pain of the past few days was interrupted.

They finished the wine with small talk, and he politely kissed her on the cheeks at the front door as he thanked her for the wonderful meal and company. She gazed into his eyes trying to read his disappointment in the outcome of the evening, and his lack of warmth gave her no comfort. She felt a tear in her eye and lowered her head, causing him to tilt his head to one side and look at her.

'I don't blame you for Robert not being here, and I meant what I said about the meal and the company,' he said gently, as he saw the tear roll down her cheek. She raised her eyes and he was alarmed by how emotional she looked. 'Are you OK, I mean are you unwell?'

Lauren lifted her hand to his face and moved her lips involuntarily towards his, her mouth opening.

'No, no!' he said, 'I must go.' As he turned and walked away, he muttered: 'No! Not now, not here and not with you!'

Chapter 26

A Day at the Seaside

Within four days of seeing Maria, Henry had found a slot for a civil marriage ceremony at Deal registry office on a Wednesday, in five weeks' time. He was able to book an appointment at Maidstone to register their intention to marry in two days' time, and texted the details to Maria. Between them, they concocted a plan to have Mrs Tanner drop Maria at the medical centre for a supposed GP appointment, and then go into town for a coffee, and wait for Maria to call her to be picked up. Henry's taxi would pick her up outside the medical centre and drive them both to the registry office, and then return Maria to the medical centre, where she'd ring Mrs Tanner for the ride home.

Henry tried to talk to Maria in the taxi about her reasons for accepting his proposal, to see if he could weed out any vulnerability, but she coolly dismissed him. Dissatisfied, he made a joke that at least they didn't have to consummate the marriage, but a look of pure fire from her put paid to any further attempts.

Henry so wanted to enjoy himself in front of the clerk when talking about their future together, but knew if he play-acted, Maria would walk out. So he was forced to limit himself to the odd patronising look and hand-squeeze, much to Maria's distaste. Nevertheless, the day was set, and all of the organising of the actual ceremony could be done by email, as choices of vows were as plain as possible, no flowers and the registrar just had to supply two office staff as witnesses. Other than booking the taxis to get them to the station and the train tickets, it was all done.

Maria was determined to reveal to no one how she actually felt about her health. While it was common knowledge multiple sclerosis shortens life spans, she hadn't felt well in England from about two weeks after her arrival at Mrs Tanner's. At first, she put it down to the cooler temperatures and wetter climate, then the effect of mixed memories about her previous time at Hillingstone, and then finally down to the worsening relations with her son. But there was something more to it and it wasn't even eased by the prospect of a return to Spain. She felt old before her time, tired of fighting and the recent stroke worried her. It was a foreboding, and the heart murmur didn't help her frame of mind, even if it was minor. It just added to her sense that something wasn't right, and that led her to take the course of action that she'd taken – protect the one thing that mattered to her, and that was her son's future. She would give him whatever helping hand she could, even if that meant getting into bed with the devil in the form of Henry.

A return to Spain shortly could in theory be possible as her speech had recovered well, but she'd decided to not raise the subject again until Juan Marco was the one pushing for it. While he thought there was a reason to stay in England she would rather be close to him, and if that meant taking a bit of advantage of Mrs Tanner, then so be it.

Juan Marco was trapped in the same position as her, but she didn't fully realise it. His sense of frustration at Hillingstone had grown further since his dinner with Lauren, fuelled by his inability to find further invoice trails within Lord Belvedere's office, which inevitably led him back to a request to Robert, who placed his queries and reminders to the bottom of the pile. Going through Lauren seemed like a waste of time because she hadn't been able to give him anything concrete at the dinner. Besides, her strange emotional state made him want to keep his distance. He couldn't help wondering if she knew more than she said and was protecting Robert, perhaps under pressure, but that wasn't his problem. Her looks and charm had their attraction, but her loyalty was to her husband and that meant they were cast together.

What trapped him now was his mother's health, which seemed inconclusive. Her recovery from the stroke seemed genuine, and yet her mood and physical weakness made him worry about how long it would take for her to recover sufficiently to return to Spain. She had stopped bringing the subject up, seemed willing to accept being almost bedridden, and no amount of encouragement would get her to exercise again. He decided to visit her to persuade her that it was time to return home. When he joined her and Mrs Tanner for dinner at the cottage, he was relieved she was eating a little better. Her mood wasn't happy but it seemed more level than before, so he brought the subject up.

'Mother, I've almost done all I came here to do. The work's getting repetitive and the finances are confusing. So how about we book the return flights home?'

'I thought you mentioned about sowing spring crops, and that Robert had said he'd take you to meet some of the contract farmers?'

'Yes he did, but he doesn't have so much time for me any more, and I feel I've learnt enough to be confident about being useful. Plus, the sooner we go home, the sooner I can enrol on the agricultural college course.'

'But that won't start until September so you still have plenty of time. There's no rush, you can apply later or maybe you can do it online? Wouldn't that be simpler?'

'Yes, but I thought you wanted to go back home? You're looking and sounding better.'

'I still feel weak and sore sometimes and I'm so tired. I don't think I can face waiting at the airport and then the flight and journey back home. I need a few more weeks of rest Juan Marco, that's if my good friend will put up with me any longer?' she said, smiling at Mrs Tanner.

'You know staying here's no problem, but I think Juan Marco's right, you do need to be thinking of the future and getting on with your life again. I tell you what, why don't you book your flights now for a month away, you can cancel them if you need to at probably very little cost. You can probably just swap them if the date doesn't work out. By the time you arrive home, the Spanish spring will be well under way and you'll have so much to look forward to!'

Both Juan Marco and Maria smiled and then profusely thanked her for giving them a solution that pleased both of them. After dinner they checked the availability of flights to Jerez, Seville, Gibraltar and Malaga and, after a minor disagreement, settled on a date six weeks hence, which would be in early April, just before Easter.

Juan Marco felt like a weight had been removed from his shoulders. The end was now in sight and so the estate finances no longer mattered. He'd do what he could in Lord Belvedere's office, but he'd limit his activities to ordering and filing. The physical estate work now seemed more important, and he threw himself into tree lopping and pruning, mucking out, repairing the pigsty and other animal enclosures, and joining in with loading the hoppers for sowing the spring crops, including taking his turn ploughing and scattering. His lighter mood was noticed by everyone, including Lord and Lady Belvedere who, bereft of company other than Henry's, started including him in dinner invitations twice a week. With both Juan Marco and Henry feeling their futures were about to change, these dinners passed off surprisingly amicably, and what started with forced civility between them often turned into light-heartedness, which provided some pleasure to Henry's parents.

It was over dinner one night that Lord Belvedere informed them both that Lauren had suggested putting on a small scale Easter event this year, perhaps on the Friday and Monday bank holidays. This would be a new departure for the estate, but Lauren was apparently looking for a project and so they had agreed. While the estate only had sixty sheep, they had a yearly crop of new-borns and they would attract visitors, especially if some of the contract farmers brought in some of their lambs, or opened up their pens too. This was likely to attract significant numbers of families over the two days, and two local pubs had agreed to provide food and drink facilities and small snack sheds, on the estate and farm areas. Lauren was proposing to use one of the hall rooms as a drawing studio for children, with the best sheep pictures winning a large soft toy sheep, and a smaller version being given to all other participants. The cost of entry would exceed the expense of any prizes and materials, so the estate would turn a small profit too.

Juan Marco thought of the enjoyment Lauren had shown at Christmas time, and reflected that this type of event was her forte. She had the creativity and personality to make things like this work, and be a commercial success. The estate was the better for it and she could probably do a lot more, but was the problem her own lack of ambition, or that Robert kept her wings clipped? He felt in two minds about her, not for the first time. He found it impossible not to feel attracted to her, but her apparent confidence seemed more shaky recently, which emphasised that he didn't know her well enough to understand who she really was. But it didn't matter in the end – his return to Spain would clear his mind and he would be troubled no longer.

The date of Henry and Maria's wedding soon arrived, and Maria relied on another medical excuse to keep Mrs Tanner in the dark. The former housekeeper drove her to the outpatient clinic at the local hospital, and as soon as she had departed, Henry's taxi appeared to carry them both to the station. Henry wore a smart suit with a carnation in his buttonhole which infuriated Maria, and he only removed it on the first leg of their train journey under threat of her returning home. However, sometime after

Ashford, he popped it back in when she was snoozing, and laughed off any suggestion to take it out again. They had time for a light snack in Deal, close to one of the defensive forts that used to protect the coastline. Henry waxed lyrical about day trips to the coast with his family, before hinting that this was also the location of some of his first romantic encounters, at which point he was silenced by a look from Maria.

He was desperate to ask her whether she looked back on their affair with any fondness. Maria had been an education to him, and he hadn't been with more than two women since – and that was during a brief period when he wondered whether he might be bisexual rather than gay. The result of his experiment confirmed he wasn't, but the passion he and Maria had shown for each other had always left erotic memories in him, and he longed to know if she felt the same, but pushing her before the ceremony was too risky. When they were on the second leg of the train journey home, Henry's child-like impatience couldn't be held back any longer.

'How do you look back on our romance all those years ago? I think that's the right word, for me anyway. I know things are different now and we've gone our separate paths, but at the time... what a ride!'

Maria's jaw dropped and she fixed him with a glare. 'Have you learnt nothing from all these years? Are you so stupid to ask me that question? I lost everything I had as a result of my foolish behaviour, and ended up pregnant with a child that I didn't want, no job, and I had to go back to Spain and face my family and all their questions! You... you just had your pleasure and dumped on me when your own comfort was threatened!'

Henry sat back in his seat, surprised that she still couldn't or wouldn't accept that they'd had fun.

'But when you look back on it, I mean like everyone looks back on their youth, don't you think about the passion and get a tingle?' he jabbered.

Again Maria's jaw dropped. 'You are such a stupid, useless fucker! I can't believe I've just gone ahead with this, even to give my son a future! I wasn't a child when I worked at Hillingstone, I was thirty-two! Thirty-two! I was a grown woman who should've known better and was stupid enough to think that it was more than... Oh, what's the point? You're too stupid to even contemplate somebody else's feelings, just as you were then!'

Henry looked baffled as his mind came round to what she was saying. 'You mean, erm, you thought that we could... Oh my God! I was just a child. I thought you were giving me lessons in love that fulfilled your own desires as well. I never thought you felt anything!'

'I want a divorce! The shortest marriage in history! How could I be such an idiot? Again! I can get this marriage annulled as soon as I get back! Juan Marco can manage without you even if anything happens to me, he's so much more capable than you could ever be! I'm moving to a different seat – don't follow me!' she hissed, conscious of them being overheard in the carriage.

Henry sat stunned in his seat, powerless as his scheming unfolded. They changed trains at Ashford and he followed Maria into the same carriage, despite her turning to glare at him. It was now or never as Maidstone wasn't far away, so he sat diagonally opposite her and stretched his legs under the table to block her escape.

'Right, I shall say this only once, so listen up. If you annul this marriage it's for your own selfish reasons, as always. It's in the best interest of Juan Marco, *our* son, and don't forget that. Now, I'm returning to Spain as fast as I can, this week probably, and you'll be here with him for a few more days I imagine. I'm coming back to the town, our town, but I'll keep my side of the bargain and avoid your bar, and both you and him, as agreed, if you keep to your side. I'll be contacted via the hall if there's any attempt to annul the marriage, and I'll fight tooth and nail to resist it! But more than that, I'll tell every person that I meet in the town that I'm the father of your son! And don't think I won't! You'll be the talk of the town and I'll drink in every bar until nowhere is safe. I'll tell them your full history from England! So, you make your mind up what you're going to do, and if you do the wrong thing then you'll never be rid of me, either of you! Now, I'm going to another seat and when we get to Maidstone you get your own taxi, and let's hope we never see each other again!'

As soon as Henry was back at the hall, he booked the first flight he could to Seville – Friday – and then went to see his parents to tell them he'd made the arrangements, reminding them of their conversation a couple of weeks before. They weren't really disappointed as they had both been wondering just what he was doing with himself. He informed them Juan Marco would be departing soon with his mother as well. It seemed to them that this episode in all their lives was coming to an end. Furthermore, with Easter just around the corner, George and Anna would return for a couple of days at least, which would freshen their circle anyway.

Juan Marco and Maria's flight was booked for six days after Henry's, but both her son and Mrs Tanner were concerned about her mood again ahead of the trip. She shrugged off their enquiries about her out-patient appointment by saying nothing had changed, she had been given a supply of blood-thinning tablets and was advised to see her own doctor immediately on return. Due to the recent stroke, she told them she had been advised to move around in the aircraft occasionally, but a two-and-a-half-hour flight shouldn't present any issues. All of this she had gleaned from a GP appointment she'd had a week before the supposed clinic visit.

Juan Marco was excused any further work from the Friday, and had a final dinner with Lord and Lady Belvedere that day to which they invited his mother, something Maria had barely been able to decline without spitting the word out. They wished him well for the future and gave him some extra money on top of his wages, but didn't enjoy his company as much this time as he seemed more distant than previously, something they put down to concern about his mother.

Mrs Tanner said goodbye to Maria on their final morning with mixed emotions. She had done all she could to make up for what she saw as her shortcomings from nineteen years before, but couldn't feel any relief in Maria's downbeat mood and coolness. She had really hoped her return to Hillingstone would lay to rest some of the ghosts of the past, and it would be a different Maria after all this time, someone whose love for her son had won through. Perhaps she was reading too much into things – Maria's health must have caused her great worry, in which case a return to Spain in early April might be just what she needed. There were tears from both of them on the doorstep, and real warmth in the hug she shared with Juan Marco, as she needlessly whispered 'take care of your mother' in his ear.

Chapter 27

Return to Spain

As soon as they arrived back in their town, Maria went to bed to recover from the exertions of the journey. Juan Marco went into his own room and drew up the shutter and threw open the windows. It was still light, the sun glistening off the rooftops below him, and the open window letting in the quiet buzz of the plaza two streets below.

He could hear the clink of glasses as people met with friends and family for an early evening catch-up, and the footsteps in the street below as they passed over the cobbled surface. There were faint traces of music in the background and the excited chatter of children playing in the plaza. He took a long breath and slowly exhaled, before repeating the same again twice more. This was the air that he wanted to breathe – fresh, dry, vibrant.

He went to the bar at seven to take a drink and speak to the owner about getting their jobs back. He'd hired replacement help while they'd been away, but each person worked shorter shifts and he was glad of the return of the commitment shown by Maria and her son, even if he had to accept that Juan Marco would be travelling to college from September and wouldn't be around so much.

He returned to the apartment later to see if his mother wanted some food, but as she was still sleeping, he went back to the bar and ordered some tapas. He had an anxious moment when he recalled the times Henry had come into the bar, which reminded him that he too was back in the town. All he could do was hope Henry would keep to his promise to stay away.

Upon returning to the apartment later that night to check on his mother and finding she was still asleep, he decided to have an early night himself. He slept well, waking at eight, but still there was no sound from her room which was unusual, as she never normally slept in beyond half past seven. But, he reasoned, the trip to England had probably taken it out of her when combined with her health and the flight home, so decided to give her another couple of hours.

At ten, he knocked on her door, and receiving no response he went in. The blind hadn't been lowered last night so there was some daylight in the room, and he spoke gently to her as he reached to touch her arm, but as he looked at her face he was horrified to see her lifeless eyes staring at the ceiling. He rocked her gently and called out to her, then touched her face, but it was stone cold. He cried out as he pulled his mobile phone from his pocket and half-called, half-cried for an ambulance. It was there within ten minutes but the paramedic shook his head after examining her, and told him he was sorry but his mother had died several hours ago. He asked whether she'd been ill recently, and when Juan Marco said she'd had a minor stroke, the paramedic gave a sympathetic smile and told him given his mother's slightly twisted face, she may have had another larger stroke, but the post-mortem would confirm it.

The next four days passed in the blink of an eye for Juan Marco, informing their relatives, arranging her funeral, notifying her friends and their landlord and bank. By Monday, he stood inside the chapel with a small group of others, waiting for her funeral service to begin. An hour later, the hearse drove her coffin down through the pretty cemetery gardens to a concrete burial block housing ninety-six plinths, where her coffin was gently slotted into her chosen resting place, and the opening covered with a temporary headstone, where he and several others laid flowers.

Watching from a respectful distance and partially hidden behind the next row of plinths, Henry Belvedere looked on at the proceedings, shocked but not surprised by what was unfolding, but feeling tenderness towards his son. He'd never been able to reconcile Maria's anger towards him, and even when faced with her own mortality after the first stroke, she'd still had the same fire in her spirit, despite the obvious risk to her health. Did he feel partly responsible for what had now happened? Yes, a little. He knew he'd wound her up a great deal, but he'd also detected what he thought was a fatalistic streak in her over the past few weeks, and wondered if she'd known more about her deteriorating health than she'd been willing to let on. As these thoughts went through him again, he shrugged his shoulders. *Que sera.*

When he'd known her at Hillingstone, she'd been passionate but serious, always serious. The intensity of their love-making had shocked him and excited him equally, and there, just one hundred metres away, was the product of their passion. He stood for a few more seconds looking at the crouching, weeping young man and frowned again, before turning away and walking back to his taxi. He knew his next steps but he'd take them gently.

A week later, Juan Marco received an envelope unstamped and written in pen. Inside was a copy of his mother's marriage certificate, and on a separate slip of paper were the words: *I am so sorry for the loss of your mother, but there are things that she wanted to do for you. Call me when you feel up to it.*

He stared incredulously at the document, going over again and again the fields in which typed details were shown, and checking and rechecking the dates. What was this evil paper? Torture to add to his sense of pain? This was fake, had to be, but the cruelty of it enraged him. In moments when he stared at it again, the date kept coming back to haunt him. It was the date when his mother had said she had an appointment at the hospital and was gone all day, and afterwards seemed vague and offhand about what had happened. His anger was only directed at one person.

He sent a text message to Henry. 'Tell me where you are you bastard! I'm going to kill you!' When there was no reply he sent another: 'I'm coming for you, I'll search every bar in this town and when I find you I'm going to kill you!' Still there was no response.

As good as his word, he paced the streets of the town for the next three evenings, trying every bar he could think of, and paying particular attention to any that were off the beaten track or dingy and dark, tuning in to where he thought Henry might hang out. Still nothing.

Four nights later, Henry sent him a reply. 'It's been a lot to take in I imagine, and you're angry and confused. I can tell you why she did it and why I suggested it, but beating me to a pulp isn't going to solve anything. When your mind wants answers then we can meet, but it's up to you. It's a fact and you will need to accept it at some point.'

Juan Marco sent him a two-word expletive response and vowed never to contact his father again, but the doubts wouldn't leave him and by the following week he sent another message: 'This trick of yours isn't going to work. My mother would never marry you, even if she thought it was for my benefit! But it's obvious you knew she was dying and kept it from me, and I'm going to get my revenge. Tell me the place.'

Henry chose the remains of the old castle on the top of the hill, and arranged to meet at half past ten the following morning, banking on his son being in a calmer frame of mind when he didn't have a full day to work up his anger. The castle ruins were open to the public but weren't busy so they should have some privacy, but the presence of a few other visitors might offer some protection. When Juan Marco found him they stood looking at each other in the open air twenty feet away, among the remains of a Napoleonic-era barrack room. Henry tried to blunt the glare coming the other way by offering a neutral smile.

'I'm sorry again about your mother, really I am. You must have so many emotions running through you.'

Juan Marco took two strides towards his father who held his ground, but then stepped back over the low wall and onto a wooden bridge that covered the gap in the old walls a few feet below.

'I thought you came here to talk, Juan Marco? I can escape for a while but you'll catch up with me no doubt and then let it all out, but you won't find out any more by beating me up. I know you were close to her but you need to know that I shared some private conversations with your mother which you don't know about, and things will become clearer and calmer, I promise.'

'All I want is to smash you for not telling me she was dying!' said his son, leaping towards him.

'Oh for Christ's sake!' yelped Henry as he started towards the end of the short bridge, but then stopped and turned. 'We were married! It's true. Don't you want to know why?'

The two men stood facing each other, one poised for attack and the other half-heartedly resigned to being chased and caught. Henry broke the short silence. 'I didn't know your mother was going to die! But I think I found a weak point in her when I suggested we get married. I didn't know she was that unwell, but I thought we should both consider what legacy we should leave to you if anything happened to either of us. I didn't think anything would, not for a long time, but looking back on it I think your mother maybe had a vision that something was wrong, and the first stroke was a warning of something to come. I swear to you that I didn't know anything! I was just trying to persuade her that we both owed you something for your future if you needed it. Really, I didn't expect it to come to this!'

'You don't owe me anything,' Juan Marco snarled, 'neither of you! My mother gave me everything I needed, and what I did with it was my choice, nobody else's! My life will be just fine because of me, not you!' he added, taking two lunges towards Henry who backed up one pace but then stood still, thinking words were his best defence.

'Look, I mean it, I had no idea that she was so unwell! The marriage was sort of an insurance policy for you, so if you ever needed something to fall back on, a place to go, a place to practice what you'd learnt, well you'd have it. You could think on a big scale, have a foot in both countries, access to money if you needed it…'

The last words riled his son who leapt forwards, drawing his fist back to punch Henry who was cowering, but then turning his head towards footsteps coming from behind. Two tourists were stopped in their tracks looking at the two men, making Juan Marco halt his swing.

'We're just practicing for a fight scene in an historical play!' blurted Henry in English, before realising how stupid that sounded, especially in English. The two tourists looked at each other and edged backwards, before turning around and heading off, muttering 'English'.

The momentary lull in Juan Marco's attack now became a pause and both men caught their breath.

'Why do you think I would ever want to return to England? This is my home and this is where my future is! All you've brought into my life is deception, dishonesty and misery!'

'That's not how your mother saw it, I promise you,' Henry said boldly, leading to a growl and lurch forward by his son. 'There's no point in hitting me, it's the truth!' he shouted, cowering again. 'She saw how much you were learning and how you enjoyed it, being practical, being taught things that were useful. It was building on what you'd learnt at George's and she saw you getting something that she couldn't give you. I'm not saying she wanted you to become the future Lord Belvedere one day, but she wanted to protect you, to give you something that you were never, ever going to have as an option here if things became desperate!'

The words about his mother gaining pleasure from seeing him learn stopped Juan Marco from throwing another punch. They flew into his heart like a knife, causing him to gasp out loud and lean over the bridge rail, groaning. Finally, he sobbed: 'I don't want to be connected to you ever. Oh how that would go down with your family! The future Lord Belvedere!' Suddenly he stood upright and turned to Henry. 'Of course, this marriage is hidden from them all isn't it? It's a farce, just an opportunity for you to stick a knife into your family again!'

'It's gone way, way beyond that, Juan Marco. My family… they're at each other's throats silently already. My parents' disappointment in me, George and Anna's contempt for me and unbending determination not to help the estate out, despite the fact that it's theirs too, and the pain that causes our parents. An estate manager who runs rings around my father and relentlessly pursues his own agenda. God knows what he's up to! You think that you're the battering ram here? Think again, my boy, it's me that takes the blows, every time.'

'You expect me to feel sorry for you?' sniffed Juan Marco.

'No, I don't. But you're different… different to all of us. You see it all from a distance and don't let anyone pull you around. You've changed since being in England. You've grown into a smart, perceptive young man, adept at understanding what's going on and never allowing yourself to get drawn into the politics. You handle yourself with the kind of maturity I can only dream of, and if there's a part of my vanity that's proud of you, well so be it. I told you your mother didn't want to see you left with nothing and that's why she agreed to the marriage. For my part, well, I see the future in you, and I'm sorry if that upsets you. Bear in mind that I'm here and despite my best efforts to drink myself to death, I'm not going anywhere soon. So there's time for you to grow, in whatever ways you want, and I'm sorry if this sounds overly emotional but should you ever decide to go back to Hillingstone, then I will fight for your rights with all the arguments I can muster, and I am very sure that my family will end up being eternally grateful to you! That's it. I've nothing more to say. I just wanted you to know your mother had your best interests at heart, I didn't know she was going to go so soon, although I now see that might be part of her reasoning for the marriage, and to assure you that you have a place in England if you should ever want it.'

As Henry turned and walked off the other side of the wooden platform, Juan Marco's head hung low as his sobbing resumed. As his tears died away the anger returned, but tinged with conscience that at least part of what Henry had said made sense. It was possible that Henry hadn't known how ill his mother was whether he liked it or not, and he couldn't seriously believe that his mother had been bullied into the marriage – she would never have agreed to it unless she had seen a benefit to her son. There was simply no other reason why she would have gone through with it. Yet could she have envisaged that he would return to England, even encouraged him to return? Was she so poor that she felt it was the only option, despite knowing how the Belvedere family would fight against any attempt to make him a legitimate part of the family succession? No, it didn't seem credible and she knew he had energy and wit enough to forge his own path. Whatever her intentions, his future lay here, and his plan to go to agricultural school was the right one.

Over the next few days, he continued to sort out his mother's affairs and it's true there was very little to her estate. He picked up a few shifts in the bar but despite the owner's sympathy, he had engaged other reliable staff, and Juan Marco was soon dipping into both his wages from England, and his mother's small funds. He could extend the rent on the apartment until the end of August, which would tie in with the start of the academic term, at which point he would move to student accommodation in Jerez. He decided to make enquiries about enrolling on the course, but his plans were thrown into chaos when his application was rejected as the course was already full. They would hold his application for the following year, but this year was out of the question. He tried arguing for special consideration based on his circumstances, but it was to no avail and his temper didn't help his pleading. Enraged after his third attempt was rejected, he hit the bars in the town with his friend from the large finca with the stables, determined to seduce his way through the best-looking girls available, but ending with them being evicted from a bar by the *policia* for being rowdy pests.

He went back to his friend's house to sleep, and worked his hangover off the following morning drinking huge glasses of water while mucking out the stables. After he'd finished, he groomed one of the horses and then the two friends went out on a trail ride. When he dismounted at a small stream and fussed over the stallion, his mind drifted to the times at the Hillingstone stables. To his surprise, they were happy memories. The horses were strong and well-cared for, just like these, and he'd enjoyed exercising them around the estate. When he remembered the times he'd sparred with Lauren at the stables, his face coloured infuriatingly! The first time he'd seen her she was just so beautiful, and he cringed as he recalled his weak attempt to cover up his obvious attraction. He'd never expected to think about it so soon, and after all that he was dealing with now!

His mind wandered away from her and on to Robert. He'd never been able to make him out, but his lasting impression was of unease. There was something about his avoidance of clarity on the estate finances that made him feel uncomfortable, a nagging feeling that despite him hiding in plain sight, he was cheating the estate, and they weren't knowledgeable or brave enough to challenge him.

As he remembered Henry's comment after the funeral, he bit his lip. Even his father, who really couldn't bring himself to lift a finger in the running of the estate, knew there was something going on. Juan Marco shrugged his shoulders. Maybe Henry was right. All wasn't well at Hillingstone and someone would have to sort it out, otherwise they'd be a storm coming, but it wasn't his problem. As they continued their ride he realised that on some level, theoretically, it was his problem, if he was a future Viscount Belvedere! The notion made him laugh out loud and it felt good, even if he had to lie to his friend about the reason for his outburst.

Juan Marco spent the next few days impatiently trying to find regular work to tide him over for at least fifteen months. He could pick up bitty jobs, but nothing that would be full-time. The summer season was slowly starting up and shifts were available at some bars and restaurants, especially in Cadiz, and the towns running down the south side of the Bay of Cadiz. But realistically he'd have to move there because he hadn't got a car or motorcycle, nor the funds to run one. That would mean giving up the apartment and breaking his links to the town, which was emotionally hard at the moment. With his mind not liking any of the available options, he found his thoughts drifting subconsciously back to England. Was Robert really hiding something or was Henry just trying to provoke his conscience with wild accusations? Had he actually witnessed the behaviour of someone who was stealing from his employer and the whole family? How much did Lauren know? Was she blocking out her suspicions, too stupid to see what was going on, or right to support her husband, believing him to be honest? She still intrigued him, especially the change in her the last couple of times they'd spent together. When they first met she was calm, elegant, sexy and self-confident. The last couple of times she seemed brittle, nervous, desperate even. The dynamic between her and Robert had changed and while he hadn't cared at the time, because she wasn't helping him with his questions, now that he was feeling unsettled, thinking about someone else's problems was almost a welcome distraction. Then there were the questions over Henry's motives in marrying his mother. Did he really think that Juan Marco could be the saviour of his family, making up for his own shortcomings? Did he really think that he would be desperate enough to return to England at some point in the future, and have a life on the estate? At what point did Henry plan to reveal that his own son was now part of the family line? How big would the war be that followed his disclosure? Did he seriously think that one day his son would be accepted as a part of the family?

All these thoughts rattled around his head with no conclusions. One day, while doing some shopping, he saw Henry sitting at a café drinking coffee. His father acknowledged him with a smile, and Juan Marco steeled himself against the expected invitation to join him and inevitable interrogation about how he was feeling, but no offer was forthcoming. Instead, Henry put his head back into his paper and let him pass. He was relieved at first, but then frustrated that his own father was here in his home town! He couldn't get away from that family even here.

More days passed, and it looked like he'd have to give up the apartment and move to Chiclana or Conil. A year would pass where he wouldn't be using his hands on the earth, unless he wanted to work eighteen hours a day and have two jobs. His opportunities to learn would be delayed by over a year; it shouldn't be a problem at his age but patience wasn't his strength.

Two days later, he was working in a bar on the edge of the town when in walked Henry, who didn't notice him initially. He was served by a colleague and Juan Marco was able to escape to the outside terrace, only to get involved in a dispute with a customer who said he always had the second refill free. Juan Marco insisted he stay put while he went and got the owner, and voices were raised which caught everyone's attention, including Henry's. As he stalked back into the bar with the owner telling him to go home early, as his attitude wasn't right, Henry stood up.

'Juan Marco, is everything all right? Do you want to go somewhere else?' As the owner started to protest as the young man glowered at another customer, Henry held his hand up and said: '*Es vale, le conoco*,' (I know him). Before Juan Marco could react, Henry led him out into the street before releasing his arm. 'Come on, let's go and have a proper drink, away from here.'

There was a moment's hesitation by Juan Marco, and then an angry huff as he said 'fuck it!' and followed his father. They ordered at a bar off the next small plaza before sitting down, and Henry jumped right in.

'It looks like you should have given me that beating after all! You look

274

like you need to punch someone. Come on, what's frustrating you? I know you're going through a difficult time but maybe sharing will help.'

'Of course, you're such a useful person when someone is in trouble,' snapped his son.

'Ouch! Fair enough – if someone deserve both barrels then I'm probably due. Go on then, get it off your chest. Use me as your punchbag, go on, I mean it. You can't go around swinging at customers. Better me in the firing line.'

Juan Marco didn't need any further encouragement. 'Well as you insist, every way I turn is shitty! I'm grieving for my mother, trying to sort out her estate, can't get full-time work unless I move to the coast and leave my home town, and can't get into agricultural college for at least a year! So everything's going really well. And if you try to tell me there's a job waiting back for me in England, then I *will* punch you!'

Henry asked about the delay in attending college and listened to his son's expletive-laden answer, and then sat quiet for a few moments. He signalled to the waiter for another beer for Juan Marco, hoping that lining them up would sugar-coat what he was going to say. When the beer arrived and his son had almost drained the first, he settled himself into his most 'wise man say' posture.

'Well, of course I would say that there's a job in England if you wanted it. And I'd say a year would cover it, maybe less, a very specific job.' As his son rose from his seat, he held his hand up. 'Yes, I know it's predictable, but I'm thinking of a one-off task, something you can go and do and get paid for, achieve something, be part of the estate and stay in that environment. Then when the job's done, and I'd say it would take a few months at most, you can clear out and come back here and start your new life. I see it that simply. Just one focused job.'

'And what might that be?' sneered Juan Marco.

'Well, come on, you know Robert's cheating my father and the estate, don't you? I mean you're a bright lad, I don't need to spell it out for you. He's always thought that his father, who was estate manager before him, got a rough deal from the family, and that contributed to his early death. The truth is, that's rubbish. His father had heart disease and was never going to live a long time, especially as he continued to smoke even after his diagnosis. But Robert... oh no, he wasn't having any of it, and he confuses my father and ties him up in knots and is stealing right from under his nose,

I'm sure of it. Plus, he's plotting behind his back with my uncle to engineer a land sale that would benefit both of them enormously. He thinks I don't know about it but I've heard my father muttering, and if Robert can present the estate finances as negatively as possible, then he's hoping to push him into the sale for his own reasons. He'll get a cut of what my uncle earns from the deal, I'm sure of it, and then he'll be off, leaving all manner of shit behind!'

'Why don't you intervene then?' came the gruff response.

'Because I'm no good at that sort of thing. Money, finances, details, arguments, family politics… I don't have the head for it, you must realise that. Plus, my father doesn't respect me really. He tries to be kind but he doesn't understand my artistic mind and personality, he's just polite really and that's about it. No, what's needed is someone to go in there as a sort of consultant. Someone who he trusts, as he doesn't like outsiders and money-men, dealing directly with Robert with my father's authority. All estimates to be approved by that person in consultation with my father. All invoices to be paid directly by the same two people. All contracts to go through the same channel. Just really clip Robert's wings and make him dance to the piper's tune!'

Henry was getting into it now and stopped as he worried his archaic language was too much for his son. 'Do you follow? It would be a trial period, that's the way it would be sold to Robert. A pilot scheme to last a few months to overhaul the estate finances, and maybe dangle the carrot of it being a necessary process before any land deal can be considered. That little morsel might force him to at least start going along with it.'

'But why would your father agree to it? He made it clear in front of me that he's against any land sale. Anyway, why on earth would he give me all that authority at my age? What do I know?'

Henry slapped his empty wine glass on the table. 'Your authority would come naturally because you're his grandson and an heir to the estate! *Camarero, otra copa por favor*! I wouldn't let you go in there empty-handed… no, my job would be to take you there and spell it out. You are part of the family and here's the document that proves it. A legitimate son who stands to inherit, the future of the estate!'

Juan Marco stared at the increasingly wide-eyed figure opposite him. 'You're mad, completely mad! You are the showman working the puppets, getting caught up in the story and believing that somehow this children's story is coming to life! I'm gone!'

'More drinks are on the way. Sit and enjoy! You need to relax and stop saying no. You have shitty options in front of you, you said it yourself. Now, I offer you stable full-time work, a salary, working in the environment you crave, a distraction from your grief, a worthwhile task with no long-term commitment, no interruption to your future plans. And you say I'm mad? What have you got to lose? Don't tell me you like Robert, I don't believe it! His wife might be a different matter but you can handle her, can't you?'

Juan Marco felt the challenge and with his second beer almost gone, couldn't help rising up to it. 'She's not important, she can be brushed aside.'

'That's the spirit! Look, you're in the right place at the right time. You know the place, the people, with your right to be involved and I assure you the marriage will really resonate with my father, you can clear out the mess, learn some more, earn decent money and be back here in less than a year to start that college course!' Henry sensed his flow was making waves and Juan Marco's objections were being silenced. Time for the kill. 'You know, Juan Marco, if this goes well, as it should, if you help me and this family to get things straight, I think I might find the courage to finally take my place and run things as they should be run! I never thought I'd say those words, but how could I fail to support the work done by my own son! What sort of a man would I be if I just walked away after that? Come on, let's work together on this, you for your short-term reasons which I fully respect, and me for mine. Ah, the refill, and you, another beer?'

Juan Marco stared back at his father, his muddled mind incapable of seeing if there was anything actually remotely serious about what Henry was saying. He had no words, just a continuing stare. Then he stood up, drained his bottle, and walked off without saying anything.

The following morning, he went back to visit Alejandro, his Spanish friend with the stables. They fed and mucked out the horses together but there was little conversation, and Alejandro could see his friend was thinking about something else. When they stopped for a drink, he asked him if he was OK, but the answer was dismissive. They hadn't planned a ride, but he offered one on the basis that Juan Marco was never more relaxed than when he was on horseback, so they set off on the same trail as the other day. They reached the stream as before and washed their faces while the horses drank. Suddenly Juan Marco laughed out loud.

'Oh my God, there's something I have to tell you! It's crazy and you won't believe it but it's true. I have an English family and my father is the son of an English lord! He wants me to go back to England and sort his family out for him!'

Alejandro assumed he was joking, but between laughing and crying his friend told him he had to listen to this fantastical story that he'd kept secret for so long. He recounted a potted version of the main events, going back to his work experience in England the previous year. When he was done Alejandro stared in wonderment.

'So you have to give him an answer, or does he know already that you won't go back?' Juan Marco looked at him but said nothing. 'What, you mean you're thinking of doing it?' Again, no words, but a laugh and a moan were the response. 'I guess you're at a loose end for at least a few months. The money would be nice and it's your family, I guess you have a right to get involved. I mean if it was me, I think I'd want to think about it, especially as your mother is gone now. Maybe you should. You've had a lot of disappointments lately and a change of scenery would do you good. It's not as if you're losing anything. Your college place next year is safe and waiting for you when you come back.'

Juan Marco looked at his friend with pleading eyes and then sank his head back to his chest. 'I need someone to tell me what to do,' he sobbed. 'How am I supposed to live like this, on my own? I know we all have to grow up but this is madness; I have nothing, nothing.'

His friend rested his arm on his shoulder.

'That's not true. The way you've handled all this on your own is magnificent. A trip to England under false pretences and yet you admit you've learnt so much and even enjoyed some of it. Discovering the father you never had, even if he isn't the man you hoped for. Managing the difficult relationship between your mother and father. Mixing with your father's family including his parents. Working full-time in an environment that you want your future to be in. Coping with all the family dramas that you witnessed. Come on, Juan Marco, you've become a man. I am very, very proud of how you have handled this. I say this not because I want to influence you, but you have a right to know the life of your family in England, and if you do want to go back and set your mind to this task, just for a few months, then I am one hundred per cent sure you will pull it off. I'm not saying you belong over there, but you are entitled to be there if you want to learn more things, and then when you come back here it will all add

278

to your future. Think of it as a horse ride, like today. Some parts are harder than others, but if you stay in the saddle until the end, look at what you can achieve. You are a big man now, my friend, a big man.'

There were more tears, and then they rode back to the house at a leisurely pace, Juan Marco rising up in the saddle the more the ride continued. When he said goodbye to his friend, his mind felt clearer than it had for a while. The short-term options in Spain didn't look appetising, so maybe a return to England for a specific period was the best option. What had he got to lose, after all? It would be on his terms and if Henry didn't agree to them then it was time to dismiss England from his thoughts, once and for all.

He messaged Henry later and they met up at noon the following day, before the latter had had a chance to start drinking. Juan Marco's confidence from the previous evening started to evaporate as soon as they sat down at a café, and he was nervous about how to start.

'I've been thinking about what my plans are for the next year, no further than that. I want to stay here but if things don't improve quickly, then I may have to consider other options.' Henry smiled knowingly. 'Don't look at me like that or I'll get up and walk away!'

'OK, OK, I understand. Take it easy. You just want to investigate the possibilities, that's all. So do you want to know how I think things can happen?' His son nodded. 'OK, well, like you I've considered the possibilities. We agree that it would be necessary to fully reveal your position, your status in the family? My parents would need to understand that you are a full, legitimate member of the family.' Another nod. 'OK, so I think that's best done face-to-face, document in hand, with both my parents. But before that, to introduce the idea of us both going back with a real sense of purpose, we need to be brutally frank with them. We need to tell them that we think Robert is stealing from them, fiddling the books, whatever you want to call it. They must understand that we have serious concerns that he's damaging the estate, defrauding it, that it needs investigating and possible police involvement. It's that serious. It's vital they believe we're both of the same view.' Another nod, slower this time. 'Look, if you're not happy, Juan Marco, then just say so. Accusing someone of stealing is a big thing. If you don't want to do it then we can't take this forwards. There's Lauren to think about too, she may also be involved, although I'm not sure to what extent, but they need to be aware.'

Juan Marco looked down and bit his lip while Henry waited, before responding: 'I think he's hiding something, for sure. I would prefer we sell it to them that way, rather than just outright accusing him of stealing. I know what he thinks about the land sale and I think he's greedy for himself. My instinct is that he's not being honest, certainly with invoices, and that he's diverting money probably for his own benefit. I can't be one hundred per cent sure though. Lauren, I don't know either, but she's intelligent. If she's not involved, she should be asking more questions.'

Henry nodded in agreement. 'OK, so we have a joint approach which is essential. So, anything else you want to know about?'

'Yes, obviously,' replied his son. 'Where am I going to stay? How much will I earn? I mean would I earn?' he said tripping himself up.

Henry smiled again. 'Some things we're just going to have to sort out while we're there, I hope you can see that. You'll be staying in the hall, but it will be in one of the guest bedrooms, not in the staff area. When I say guest bedroom, I mean an ordinary bedroom, where family and others stay,' he fluffed. 'You'll be there as a family member, not as a worker. Money, well let's see on that. You'll be paid a lot more than a labourer, I guarantee you. I'll try and get you twenty thousand, how does that sound?'

Juan Marco gave a blank response while he was calculating how much more that was than he'd earn in Spain, which Henry took as a sign of disapproval.

'Obviously, if you need more then I'll ask for it. Maybe I can suggest a bonus based on savings made by the estate, if we reduce costs by cutting out some of Robert's deals?'

Juan Marco maintained a deadpan expression and just nodded, feeling mightily pleased with the twenty thousand figure.

'OK, how long do you want to think about it? I think it's best if I speak to my father sooner and get moving on this.'

Juan Marco continued with his poker face before saying: 'There's someone else I need to consult, so I need to try and speak to him today. I'll message you tomorrow.'

Henry eyed him suspiciously, half-wanting to ask who this mysterious person was, although he assumed it must be a potential local employer. He left his response at a simple 'OK' and after finishing his drink, Juan Marco left with his mind occupied. In reality, he wasn't sure he had much choice because twenty thousand pounds would go a long way to helping him finance his studies in a year's time, but he wasn't going to give Henry an easy time of it, especially as he always had doubts about his father's ability to match words with actions. He dismissed the idea of calling Alejandro for his advice – the decision and the consequences had to be his alone. Accusing Robert – and maybe Lauren too – of stealing was no small matter. There would be no going back for him and Henry if they were wrong, and undoubtedly there would be reprisals and counter-claims from Robert and Lauren. In the end, the easy money and the greater draw of working around a farming estate were uppermost in his mind, but it might all come to nothing if Henry couldn't deliver, so really it was out of his hands.

He messaged his father the following morning to say he agreed to the offer and would await further details. He was surprised by a text from Henry just before five, which said simply: 'It's on! Meet me tonight at the Plaza de Andalucia.' When Juan Marco found him, he could tell by the body language that the call must have gone well. Henry's chest was pushed out as if he'd just made a few million on a shares deal.

'Drinks are on me! It worked like clockwork! I have to say my father's initial reluctance to proceed was markedly reduced by having you on side! When I said you had independently come to the same conclusions as me, without any interference, that Robert was being far from straight on the estate finances, it really hit home. He's discussed it with my mother and they want chapter and verse on our suspicions when we get there. I'm not going to lie to you – he's not going to lift the dagger himself, it'll be up to us. But he has an appetite for this – he really can't stand Robert and only tolerates Lauren. How much detail can you remember?'

'I'm pretty sure I've laid it all out for him before. I'm not sure there's much I can add. He... I'm not sure he really listened.'

'Good, then he's not likely to remember what you've said before. It'll all come back to you when you get back to his office.' Juan Marco nodded cautiously. 'Good. Oh, the money, a room in the hall, no problem, all sorted, and I've told them about your mother.'

Juan Marco glared at him before replying. 'I guess you had to use that to get their sympathy! Makes it easier to get twenty thousand out of them!'

Henry opened his mouth in mock astonishment. 'Juan Marco, would you think I would stoop that low? How much information do you want them to take on board at once? "Your main employee is stealing from you, maybe his wife too; I'm coming back with your grandson to challenge them; by the way, he's your full grandson now because I married his mother, but I'm sorry to have to tell you she's just passed away".' Henry raised his eyebrows. 'There are some things it's better to deal with face-to-face, and I thought it would make it more manageable if I broke it up a little.'

Juan Marco's face fell as he realised his flash of temper was an avoidable loss of control, and mumbled 'sorry'. He would have to take greater care with his emotions once he was back in England, but reflected that it hadn't been a problem in the past. Maybe going back was what he needed after all – he felt less heat within him when he was watching others lead events.

Henry suggested they make plans to travel as quickly as possible, and they agreed on a flight on Monday of the following week, to give Juan Marco time to sort out his loose ends in the town.

PART THREE

Chapter 28

Return of the Prodigals

Henry and Juan Marco were greeted at Hillingstone with a degree of nervousness towards the former, and concerned sympathy towards the latter. As they took tea on that early May afternoon, Lord and Lady Belvedere offered their condolences to their grandson, and asked him to fill in as much detail as he felt comfortable with about his mother's death. Henry listened awkwardly while trying to hide his impatience to tell them the far bigger news. When his father finished by saying they'd discuss more of the business in hand that evening at dinner, Henry seized his chance.

'Actually, Father and Mother, before we go to our rooms to freshen up, there's something else I'd like to tell you which does have a bearing on tonight's dinner. Before Maria sadly passed away, she and I were married, here in England. Now I know that's going to come as a shock to you, but we both felt that to provide some long-term stability and security for our son, it was the best thing to do, although neither of us envisaged circumstances such as these occurring. We had no intentions of forcing Juan Marco to become anything he didn't want to be, nor of causing any further family conflict, but if anything did happen to either of us then we wanted him to be in the best position to make the most of his life.'

Lord and Lady Belvedere sat open-mouthed, staring from Henry to Juan Marco and back again.

'Now you're shocked as we both expected, but I hope you will see this was best told to you face-to-face. I have a copy of the marriage certificate here so you can be sure of what I'm telling you.'

Juan Marco shifted uncomfortably as Lady Belvedere looked at him. 'I didn't know anything about it,' he said meekly, 'until Henry contacted me after my mother had died. I couldn't believe it either. She never said anything to me.'

'Absolutely,' said Henry cutting in. 'Sorry I should have made it clear.

Our marriage was private and he knew nothing about it, we told no one. The witnesses were strangers. It was important to us both that we kept the information to ourselves, until such time as we felt firstly Juan Marco, and then of course you, should know. We didn't think that time would come anything like this quickly.'

Lord Belvedere's jaw moved up and down but to no avail, and he and his wife could do little more than look at each other bemusedly.

'I'll leave a copy of the marriage certificate on this table so you can take all the details in, and we can talk more at dinner. I know how surprised you will both be feeling, but when it comes to the other plans to be discussed tonight, I think you'll see eventually that this significantly strengthens our hand.'

With that, he gestured to his son that it was time to leave and they made their way up the main staircase. 'I think it's best we avoid going out tonight, Juan Marco, so no walking around the estate, just stick to the formal gardens. The more surprise we have over Robert and Lauren the better. I'll nip down to the hall office in a minute and ask the housekeeper to avoid gossip spreading up to the farmhouse for as long as possible. A couple of days should do it. Go and get changed and showered or relax, whatever. Dinner will be at half past seven so we've got plenty of time. Do you play snooker? There's a great table in the room at the far end of the ground floor. We can have a game if you like? Meet me in the dining room and we'll have a knockabout.'

Back in the garden sitting room, Lord and Lady Belvedere pored over the marriage certificate, checking and rechecking the names and dates. It seemed outrageous, even by Henry's standards, that he would do this, with a woman they understood loathed him! But however much they doubted his motives, they couldn't fathom her's, unless she genuinely thought her son needed some security. But the idea of her death so soon afterwards was numbing; did she know something? Was that her reason for marriage? Henry needed to be grilled for more information before dinner, so Lady Belvedere sent Henry a message asking him to meet them in the small reading room off the library, at six.

Henry was half-expecting the message and left Juan Marco in the snooker room to practice his game. He held his hands up as he sat down. 'OK, I expected you would want more information so fire away. I'm all yours.'

'This isn't a lightweight matter, Henry,' opened his father, 'quite the opposite. You appear to have married Maria, legitimising Juan Marco as your heir, without remotely considering the impact on us or, indeed, the rest of the family! Aside from our position, how do you think we're going to explain this to your brother and sister?'

'I understand, Father. This is a complete shock. Let me fill you in on the background and my reasoning for keeping you both in the dark. Look, you know that while I have my good points, diligence in matters of duty is not one of them. I have a creative mind and formal responsibility… well, it troubles me. But I have a conscience and I've felt some time now, going back to the Autumn Fair last year, that all is not well with Robert and Lauren. There's something too slick about the pair of them, and I had my suspicions they were getting more than their fair share of reward from the estate. As it happens, Juan Marco has the same thoughts, only he has had access to the financial details by working with you—'

'Henry,' interrupted his mother, 'can we get to the point about the marriage? Business matters can be discussed over dinner.'

'If it gets that far,' muttered Lord Belvedere.

Henry looked anxiously at them both before continuing.

'OK, well, I was aware that I'm not much of an heir and George and Anna have their own lives. I know you believe that both of them will charge to the rescue if needed, but I feel a sense of responsibility not to deflect things their way. I have long thought Juan Marco is a fine young man. Frankly, I'm proud of him, and the way he behaves and fights for the things he believes in is an example to all of us. It wasn't lost on me that with him in the estate succession, should he wish – and I stress that point – in the future to play a part in the running of the estate, then I think we would all benefit. He really is so capable and won't be pushed around.'

His parents stared at him which he took as a positive as they didn't interrupt.

'So for my part, I was thinking about the future, planning way ahead. I saw no reason for him to be involved any time soon. On Maria's part, she was concerned that her very able son was being held back by her lack of ability to fund any part of his continuing education. Furthermore, she felt that his loyalty to her was so strong, and that was also holding him back from taking his own steps in the world. Combined with her belief that she wouldn't be able to leave him much if, and it was a big if, anything happened to her, she also had long-term reasons for wanting to help secure his future. I suggested she might consider marriage, but as I've said, neither of us had any inkling that she was frail or that the worse scenario might materialise. I know how this looks but please believe me, there was no underhand behaviour here, no advance knowledge of failing health. I was just thinking of protection for the estate and I genuinely believe that Maria never thought she would die so soon. Indeed, when she left England she seemed to be on the up, but she had another stroke, maybe the flight didn't help, although it wasn't a long one. But then the car journey home as well, perhaps she went straight to bed. I don't know, they might all have contributed. Who knows?'

His parents looked at each other but didn't seem to have the words to respond, until Lady Belvedere spoke: 'I'd be very surprised if she didn't have any intuition, some people do in these circumstances, but it would be hard for you to foresee if she didn't open up,' she sighed. 'And Juan Marco, he really had no idea of his mother's health? He was the closest to her.'

'No, not at all. He thought she was on the mend and that it was the right time for both of them to return home. He had plans to go to agricultural college there.'

'What's happened to those?' interrupted Lord Belvedere. 'Surely he still has a place there? Granted he's just lost his mother and is probably feeling upset, but his future is mapped out there, isn't it? Has he had his head turned by the news you've given him?'

'It's not like that. Yes, he's been knocked back by her passing, but the course he applied for was full so he's had to accept a deferment for a year, which leaves him at a loose end. And when I say loose end, I mean it. Temporary bar work, leaving his home town, not being involved in agricultural matters for a year, moving from job to job with no security over the winter months – it's not that attractive really. So, I took the opportunity to tell him about what his mother and I had worked out. I saw an opportunity to find him some regular work in an environment that he wants to be in, secure, fixed-term, with a real opportunity to achieve something, in contact with his family, and helping them and the estate get on a better footing for the future. I hope you don't think I was being mercenary, but when I discovered he'd got the same concerns about what Robert and Lauren are up to, well it all just seemed to come together.'

'We don't know what they're up to, if anything,' replied his mother.

'This is all a bit gung-ho for me.'

Henry didn't reply, but looked at his father to see if he would switch the conversation to business. His father stared at him for several seconds before turning to his wife: 'How do you feel about the marriage side of things? It's not satisfactory but can you accept it, can we?'

Lady Belvedere sighed again before replying: 'It's not satisfactory at all, but... I don't think we have any grounds not to accept it. It's written there in black and white and it sounds like they both knew what they were doing.'

Henry nodded solemnly.

'Shall we hear them out over dinner on the plan to review the finances?' Again, another sigh from Lady Belvedere as she shrugged her shoulders in affirmation. 'We'll leave it there then, Henry, until dinner.'

Once they were into the first course, Henry introduced the subject of the estate finances, keeping it as over-arching as he could, knowing that the detail all lay with Juan Marco. On the flight over he'd listened to what his son had recollected, and all his notes would still be on the household laptop computer he'd been using. From his perspective, there was more than enough confusion to present a compelling case to his parents. When it came to Juan Marco's turn, he was careful not to make accusations, but it was easy enough to recount the unanswered queries on invoices, payments, estimates and allowances, and all roads seemed to lead to Robert. He couldn't make out exactly what Lauren knew, but he was disappointed with what little she had been able to tell him which concerned him, especially after Lord Belvedere's brother had given her a glowing reference.

Lord Belvedere winced at the mention of his brother which was noticed by his wife, who started to ask uncomfortable questions about why he'd not been able to set matters right, being family after all. After he'd tried his best to gloss over the subject, he asked Henry to spell out how he thought they should proceed.

'We need to call Robert in and surprise him, that's the starting point. You, Juan Marco and I need to tell him we're doing a full internal audit on the costs of running the estate, and he needs to work with us. Day-to-day requests will come through Juan Marco, and he'll have to be told that he speaks with the full authority of the family as an heir.'

Lord Belvedere winced again and his wife's face showed a concerned frown.

'Is there no way we can avoid this, Henry?' she asked. 'Robert can be unhelpful at times and we don't want to antagonise him. Is it fair to deflect all his heat onto Juan Marco?'

Her son nodded before replying: 'It's time for the family to be brave. I believe the very existence of the estate is at risk and Juan Marco knows what's required. He's being engaged to help us on this specific task and we're paying him to follow through with it, as a sign of our commitment. It's vital that Robert knows whom he's dealing with,' he finished, looking at Juan Marco to add some gravitas of this own. His son gritted his teeth before choosing his quiet words.

'If I'm to be of use here, then Henry's right. I'd rather go back to Spain otherwise. If you need me to be involved, both of you, then I have to stand upright. Robert will avoid providing answers otherwise. I'll soon tell you if I think we're wrong in our suspicions, and then I can leave if you prefer. Can you not request that he keeps the news about the marriage private?'

'It's not that simple,' replied Lady Belvedere. 'Robert and Anna were in a relationship when they were younger and they are still on good terms. It's inconceivable that he wouldn't tell her what he knew, and even if he swore her to secrecy, she'd still raise merry hell with us. If we took action against Robert for breaking his word, we'd end up losing our daughter. That's not a risk we will take.'

'We'll have to tell her ourselves, and George,' added her husband thoughtfully, turning to his wife who nodded.

'It's a big thing that's coming,' Henry said assertively, trying to lift the gloom. 'But the future of the estate is at hand. I've long had my suspicions about Robert and Lauren, certainly since last year, but it's Juan Marco's shared concerns, and surely your's too, Father, that bring us to this point. You know something's not right, don't you?'

'You don't drop the bone, do you?' his father replied puffing out his cheeks. 'Juan Marco, it's all coming down to you, I'm afraid. You're very young to be placed in this position and I'm not sure you know what you're getting into. I… have allowed my personal distrust of Robert, and perhaps Lauren too, to get in the way of my thoughts for too long. I had such a good relationship with his father, such a loyal man. I cannot face the responsibility of dealing with my own indecisiveness,' he cried out.

Lady Belvedere reached out and placed her hand on top of his. 'I had no idea this weighed so heavily on you! Why on earth didn't you share your feelings with me? I've always been here to support you and we share everything, don't we?'

Her husband's chest heaved as his head fell forward towards it. After a few seconds of anguished groans like a wounded animal, he raised his pain-laden face.

'Juan Marco, I mean what I say, if you have the strength of an ox then maybe this is the task for you. I will speak for you and with you, but if you really have suspicions, I mean really that the estate is being defrauded, then we should tackle this, but it's on your shoulders to see it through. I will rely on your action and your advice, but I cannot face the consequences of a botched investigation!'

Juan Marco sat still, silent, taking in the outburst of emotions he'd just witnessed, far and beyond anything he'd expected. He looked to both his grandparents as he realised they were going to depend on him, they needed him. He felt a confused mixture of thoughts towards them, but their tone was warm, protective and connected. He had always thought them likeable, especially Lady Belvedere, but he could feel a sense of family growing in him as he looked at them, a bizarre experience when he felt nothing of the sort for his father who was not in his thoughts at all right now.

'I think we should agree now to move forward with this,' he said with a kind smile. 'We all have our concerns, Robert needs to be challenged, and if you introduce the plan with firmness, I will carry it through. I will need your support, but I am not afraid of hard work or of dealing with him strongly.' On hearing some movement outside the door, he broke off. 'I think the next course is ready, I hear the staff outside the room. Shall we carry on with the meal?'

Lady Belvedere was the first to react and the staff came in with the dishes carrying the main course. Juan Marco's words produced a quiet calm for two or three minutes before Henry, feeling he was being overshadowed, spoke again.

'Juan Marco and I have spoken about tactics. My feeling is that we should speak plainly to Robert but have a reserve plan in case he needs convincing. It may not be needed but he can be bumptious, as we all agree. The idea of the land sale is close to his heart. It may not be needed and I know how you feel about the subject, Father, but if it's needed to grease the wheel…'

'What are you talking about, Henry? There's no question of a land sale!'

'No, but if he puts up resistance—'

'No, absolutely not! There will be no mention of it!'

An uncomfortable silence descended before Juan Marco spoke calmly again. 'As Henry says, it's probably not needed, but it's all about putting Robert on the back foot, only if necessary. The more pressure we put on him, the more he's likely to protest, hide and complicate things. Whether there is any merit in a land sale isn't the issue. It's whether it changes his mind to be cooperative because he thinks it's on the table. It's just a tactic that we have in our pocket. A pot of honey to attract the fly?'

'A fly trap,' interrupted Lady Belvedere with a half-smile, anxious to reduce the tension. 'You're thinking that we always have the upper hand when we deal with him, and we simply use this weapon from our arsenal if we need it? I like the plan,' she added, nodding encouragingly at her husband, whose face was covered in a scowl. 'John's never been keen on selling off any part of the estate, have you darling? Personally, I think we should consider it on a small scale when the time is right. It's not lost on me how much this place costs to maintain,' she added, raising her eyes to the ceiling. 'However, this isn't the time or place, but if needs be, and your suspicions about Robert are right,' she said looking from Juan Marco to Henry and back again, 'then it might help focus his mind.' She finished with an innocent smile at her husband, who looked dumbfounded at his wife's apparent admission of possible merit in losing part of the estate.

Lady Belvedere then decided on a change of subject and expressed her sympathy again on the loss of Maria, and asked Juan Marco about his memories of her, both past and recent. He stumbled at first but gradually spoke more fluently, starting with her death and then more about his memories. Their conversation lasted for most of the rest of the meal and added a different perspective to the fireworks from earlier. As they finished with a glass of port, Lord Belvedere reminded his wife they had better speak to their other son and daughter in the morning and give them the bare bones of the situation, including that their nephew was now part of the family line, and had a big part to play in their financial investigations. They would then speak to Robert in the afternoon. The timely reminder that a good night's sleep was required was felt by them all, Henry helping himself to the opened bottle of port as he left the room, explaining that he always slept better when he was properly relaxed.

The following morning's conversations went predictably badly. Firstly, Lady Belvedere called Anna and told her they weren't sure all was well with the estate finances. It was possible there were irregularities, errors in payments, etc. and they'd decided to introduce a new system for approval

293

of all future payments, as well as reviewing all purchases and disposals going back two years. Anna expressed surprise this was necessary given Robert's longstanding position, and the oversight provided by her Uncle Andrew. Surely some meetings with them both would clear things up? Anna's voice turned cooler when her mother told her that Robert might be part of the issue, and that he hadn't been as forthcoming as they would have hoped.

'Right, I see, well you need to have a direct conversation with him. I'm sure it will all be OK if you handle it properly. The estate is under your and Father's stewardship. I'm not going to get involved…'

'No, no, nothing like that Anna, we're not expecting you to intervene. This is something we must handle. We've been less diligent than we should have been and perhaps that's part of the problem.'

'Humph. I really hope this is not going to go pear-shaped! Father can get muddled a bit sometimes and it leads to him getting the wrong end of the stick. Don't let him, you know, start throwing mud around. It could get awfully messy,' said Anna trying to hide her frustration. Her suspicions were aroused when her mother ignored her last comment and moved on.

'We've got Henry here to help, and also Juan Marco. There's—'

Anna cut her off.

'What? What's he doing there? And Henry? When's he ever been useful at paperwork? What's going on? Is this some kind of witch-hunt led by the ambitious and the clueless?'

'Anna, he's really very sensible, and he's had his own suspicions about Robert for some time.'

'I don't believe it! You've lost your senses! You're relying on the words of an outsider with his own agenda, who knows and cares nothing about this family! He and Henry put you up to this and they'll make complete fools of you! Robert's been there years, and if you've become too dependent on him then whose fault is that? Father could never accept that he wasn't like old Mr Pritchard, and that's been his problem – moving with the times! How can you even consider listening to your bastard grandson?'

'Anna, that's enough!' shouted back her mother. 'I told you he's a good young man who's taken a real interest in helping your father with the estate finances and the paperwork. And for your information, he's your full nephew now. There have been some changes. His mother passed away but before she died, Henry did the decent thing and, well, he's part of the family, your family now. He shows more interest in helping the estate than… well, you know what I mean!'

'What?' screeched Anna. 'You're accusing me of failing in my responsibilities? When that useless shit of a brother is …my God, I'm going to scream, I'm going to explode—' With that, the line went dead.

When Lord Belvedere phoned his other son, George couldn't help but smugly reply that he'd always known Robert was a barrow-boy out of his depth, and would await further news of his comeuppance in due course. The mention of Juan Marco's name produced anger and bad language enough, even without Henry's involvement also being spelt out, but his father's statement that they all had to accept that Juan Marco also had a place in the family as Henry's legitimate heir, sparked an outburst that shocked his father into silence. George's final words referred to 'a shit, the son of a shit, the estate's going to shit,' and then he too cut the line.

Lord and Lady Belvedere were bruised and upset by their encounters, and called Henry and Juan Marco down to tell them they'd changed their minds about the whole plan. Whatever Robert was up to, it wasn't worth losing the rest of their children over. Henry had anticipated what would happen, and told them he'd already asked Robert to attend the hall that afternoon for a business meeting involving most of the immediate family. His father burst out that he had no right to do that, that his actions were seriously endangering the welfare of the family, and to call Robert back and cancel the appointment. Henry looked at his parents then Juan Marco and back again.

'I won't do that,' he replied quietly. 'There's more than just the welfare of this family being endangered. It's the very existence of this estate, something you're sworn to protect. The rot stops here,' he finished, rising up to his full six-foot two frame. As his father's eyes widened and mouth began to open, he added: 'Juan Marco and I will see you in the small dining room just before half past two. It's time to find out what's been going on.'

Chapter 29

To Business

Robert had an inkling of what was going on as he strode over to the hall that afternoon, his contacts having already told him that 'Batman and Robin' had returned. It had to do with estate finances certainly, which caused him some tension, but the fact that he was meeting Lord and Lady Belvedere and Henry and Juan Marco, meant something else was going on. Either trouble was afoot and they would put him under serious pressure, or perhaps Lord Belvedere's health had changed for the worse.

He'd phoned Anna earlier to see if she knew what was going on. She was between meetings and hadn't been able to give him much, but said it was about money, before dropping the bombshell that Juan Marco was now in line, after Henry, for the estate. Her language made it quite clear to Robert where she stood, and she'd said she was done with the family and the estate for now and that he should come out swinging, whatever their approach.

He gritted his teeth as the hall came into view from the gravel path. He wasn't afraid of any of them, but Juan Marco was becoming more than a fly in the ointment, and was willing to get into the detail of things which the others weren't. That meant he potentially had the bullets to hurt him, and if the worst came to the worst then he might need to make a quick escape. As things stood, he'd siphoned off one hundred and seventeen thousand pounds over the past four years which was sitting in a private account, plus there was the Land Rover Discovery hidden in one of the barns, which was worth another twenty thousand. Not as much as he would have liked, but enough to get him well away from here if there was any fuss, and he was banking on the family not wanting to risk bad publicity by involving the police, something he was pretty sure they'd shy away from. Of course, this would mean the end of any serious money being made from a land sale, which was damned frustrating, and he bit his lip as he took his last few strides towards the front door. But if the time for self-preservation came, then that was his first priority.

As he entered the room, he glanced coolly at Henry and Juan Marco and then started his act, breaking into a smile. 'Well, it's a surprise to see you both again so soon. Juan Marco, I'm sorry to hear of your mother's passing. If there's anything I can do please let me know. Lauren and I would be only too happy to help.'

The father and son looked at each other incredulously that the grapevine worked so quickly, but then it registered with Henry that he'd probably spoken to Anna, and he recovered himself. He was about to reply when Robert added: 'Is it just the three of us? I thought your parents were joining us?'

He was answered by a quiet knock on the door as Lord and Lady Belvedere entered, apologising for being late, and quietly taking their seats. Henry looked at his father to see if there was a hint as to whether he was going to start off, but the non-committal look he got back made him swallow. 'Right OK,' he started slowly. 'Thank you for coming over Robert. The family wanted to talk to you as we'd like to conduct a review of the estate finances, and to introduce some new procedures going forwards.'

Robert sat upright and put on an indignant look.

'Am I to take it that you're dissatisfied with my work? You're mob-handed so I assume this is something formal, in which case why wasn't I informed so the proper procedures could be followed?'

Henry stared blankly back before responding weakly: 'It's not formal, just a friendly chat that's all. We'd like to clear up a few—'

'Well, it looks pretty formal to me. Sir,' he said turning to Lord Belvedere. 'As you're my actual employer don't you think this would be better coming from you?'

Lord Belvedere started to open his mouth, trying to find some words to placate his estate manager, but Juan Marco cut in: 'There's a list of queries we'd like you to respond to. There's nothing on there that you haven't seen before, but it's typical of the type of thing we'd like to avoid in the future.' He reached down to an envelope that was leaning against his chair leg, and pulled out a spreadsheet containing columns and lines of text and figures, which he pushed across the table. 'There's more to follow as well, but when I was trying to help Lord Belvedere before we didn't really get to the bottom of reconciling the accounts. You'll remember I brought the subject up with you several times, but you couldn't find the time to respond, and Lauren wasn't able to help either. Lord and Lady Belvedere have decided it's time to get the papers in order and control things more closely in future, at least until the estate office paperwork is back to where it needs to be.'

Robert stared angrily at him, before switching his attack to an easier target. 'Your brother and I have managed things quite satisfactorily over the past five years, and you've never spoken to me about any problems before,' he said sharply to Lord Belvedere.

'Robert, please don't take this as criticism of you or your work. I am willing to admit I've allowed things to get messier than they should have been, and I take full responsibility for that. The family business meetings have taken a back seat and it's been difficult to get everyone in one place, and I've allowed things to slide. Entirely my fault, but this reflects a desire to make things easier to manage in future.'

'What about all this lot?' Robert said as he waved the page of queries. 'If you want to improve things in the future then I can help you with that, you only needed to ask! But I'm extremely busy and I don't have time to pour over every detail, but I trust my suppliers, the estate workers, your brother. We all play our part and none of us are infallible, but if we work together then we can avoid… misunderstandings and challenges like this,' he hissed, swiping the piece of paper to the floor.

Lord Belvedere hesitated and his wife decided to step in, but again they were interrupted by Juan Marco. 'How long do you think it would take you to respond to those queries?' he asked, reaching down and extracting a copy from his envelope and placing it back carefully on the table in front of Robert, whose head turned back towards him with eyes blazing and nostrils flaring. Henry sat completely still, wondering who would throw the bigger punch as he contemplated the inevitable fisticuffs, half-thinking he should protect his son while also wishing to avoid getting hit.

'You don't understand, boy, you don't understand!' As soon as he uttered the words in anger, Robert knew they'd band together, and uniformly Lord and Lady Belvedere called out.

'I won't accept that way of talking to a member of our family,' Lord Belvedere said sternly. 'Whatever his background, whatever his introduction, whomever his mother is, I won't accept it!'

His wife was absolutely sure that Robert had already spoken with Anna, and decided on a more direct approach.

'Juan Marco is our grandson and stands in line to take over this estate one day. Therefore, he has as much interest as anyone in understanding how it all works. We cannot answer his queries and the way he's laid them out for us seems perfectly reasonable, and it doesn't appear to us too difficult for you to respond to them. If it's a question of time, then you'll have to make the time. If you need help with other tasks around the estate then please ask us. Juan Marco made himself useful before, perhaps while you're attending to these matters, he can manage the other issues.'

Robert's face turned to stone as she finished her sentence, and Henry saw an opportunity to join in, taking courage from the team's solidarity.

'When all of that is sorted, there will be some new auditing procedures put in place,' he said confidently. 'We don't want these queries coming up again for all our sakes, so with immediate effect, we'd like to instigate bi-weekly financial meetings, where expenditure and disposals can be discussed and authority obtained from the family to proceed on all items. Of course, these can be relaxed as quickly as possible so we're not messing about with petty amounts of money, but let's get things working smoothly as a start.' He was beginning to enjoy himself now.

Robert's head moved mechanically around to face him as he spoke, his eyes locking on to his target as if they were heat-seeking missile launchers. To avoid his father being intimidated Juan Marco once again cut in.

'That's right father. Are you OK with us involving the actual auditors now, Robert? The accounts must be being prepared now, so this would be a good time to meet with them?'

Robert's mouth opened and closed again, twice, before he responded slowly. 'I've been very patient here, having provided many years of loyal service to this estate and, through my father, many more. My family has been tied to this estate for decades and this is the thanks we get for all we've given. I sense a witch-hunt, a seeking of a whipping boy. Well you've picked the wrong man. You've completely broken the trust in this employer-employee relationship, and that's fundamental. This isn't the end of this, oh no, mark my words!' he ended, throwing back his chair and stalking out of the room.

Robert walked hurriedly back to the farmhouse enraged, and with fists clenched. All of his carefully manipulated work was in danger of crashing down around him, and to think that he'd only got this far! This was just the starter; the main course was supposed to be his share of the land sale, and that stage hadn't got beyond the architect's plan yet! He'd been prepared to bide his time, thinking that the longer Lord Belvedere muddled along, the more the estate's financial position would worsen and while he was awaiting the inevitable crisis, he could continue to fiddle the books and keep topping up his gains, as and when the opportunity arose. But now that all lay in tatters. He yelled as he recalled their faces in the meeting, a mixture of concern and smugness! God, he'd like to take an axe to them one by one! The biggest bunch of pathetic losers he could imagine ganging up on him, and thinking they could dangle him on the end of a string, jerking him this way and that. Individually they would never have had the courage except, perhaps, the misguided fool of a boy, who was laughingly now part of the family line, courtesy of his father having shagged a cleaner whom he'd then somehow tricked into marriage! You couldn't have written it if you'd tried, it was pure pantomime! He fantasised about taking Juan Marco shooting in the woods, gradually slipping back behind him, and then opening up the back of his head with one cartridge. How satisfying that would feel right at this moment!

The farmhouse coming into view around the edge of the trees brought him back to reality. It was fight or flight time. His instinct said the former, but his head said the game was up. He couldn't fudge the transaction trails any more and 'Robin' wasn't going to let it go, and the others would now listen to him. It was time to get away before they realised the full extent of what he'd been up to, far enough that they wouldn't find it easy to track him, and also banking that they'd want to hush things up and put it all behind them as quickly as they could. Scotland would do, maybe Wales or northern England. He'd got enough funds to tide him over and start again. As he reached the farmhouse door he thought of Lauren for the first time. Fuck her. She wasn't part of his plans any more. Maybe she hadn't been for some time.

He entered the farmhouse expecting to find her there, thinking that he'd calmly pack while she stood there flustered and questioning, telling her just how unimportant she was. Then it clicked that she'd still be at the office, which was annoying because if she hadn't returned by the time he'd packed his things, he'd have to make a detour to deliver his message which would be a waste of time. He swore under his breath, and went straight upstairs to find two suitcases and started filling them, before heading into the study and extracting his personal financial records and statements, plus the keys for the Land Rover Discovery hidden in a spectacles case. After half an hour he was about done, when he heard the keys in the front door.

'You're home early!' she shouted as she came through the door. 'What happened?'

'Up here,' he grunted, waiting for her to come up the stairs. As she entered the bedroom, she found him standing at the side of the bed looking directly at her, the two suitcases zipped up on the bed.

'Oh, we're going somewhere, are we? What, they want us to take a holiday? My God, they're actually showing you some appreciation, are they?' she said in forced light-heartedness.

'You're not going anywhere,' he replied dourly. 'It seems that my time here has unexpectedly come to an end rather sooner than planned. Of course, I could stick around and fight it out, but I don't think that's a good use of my time.'

'What, they've sacked you? They wouldn't do that on the spot, they aren't those sort of people. There are procedures, warnings, etc. that have to be given! What's happened? Let's go downstairs and discuss it over some tea.'

'The time for drinking tea and friendly chats has gone,' he muttered scornfully. 'I'm getting out of this shit-hole before they find out what they should have known for ages, if they'd had any brain cells. But they're too stupid and vacant, the lot of them, and now's the time to get out and leave them to clean up their own mess. They're so weak they're listening to that bastard twat of a grandson as if he's the Messiah! I really think they believe that "boy wonder" can save them! Some people! Of course, all this could have been avoided if a certain person had done what they were told to do, something really not that difficult, but their own stupidity got in the way. You, you fucking stupid cow, all you had to do was manage him. I mean, how difficult could it be? He was eating out of your hand right from the start but you let him slip away, even when I told you exactly what you had to do – manage him with your charms – something you used to do so easily just, what, three years ago? No, less than that! And what are you now? Someone with scruples, someone with morals, someone who suddenly gives a shit about how other people see her? You make me sick, you fucking whore.'

Lauren stood still, mouth agape. 'This is nothing to do with me. If you've been up to things you shouldn't and they've caught you... I warned you, didn't I? I told you not to screw things up!'

He took a pace towards her and she flinched, at which he stopped and laughed. 'Oh you're brave aren't you! Fire some bullets and then duck! Pathetic.' With that, he grabbed the suitcases and stood in front of her. 'Well, are you coming or not? Here's yours,' he said, swinging one of the heavy bags at her legs which caught her knee, and led her to yelp as she fell back on the bed.

'Oww. No. I'm not coming with you, why the hell would I do that?' she gasped as she sat upright and tried to stand. 'I told you, this is your mess!' Looking down as she rose, she couldn't see the back of Robert's right hand lashing upwards towards her right cheek, the loud crack sounding like a snapping twig as the force lifted her up, throwing her over the corner of the bed and onto the floor behind.

As she cried out he growled, 'Don't worry, the invitation wasn't real,' before grabbing the two cases and heading downstairs and out to the waiting pick-up truck.

He drove to one of the storage barns and stopped the truck by a corner, where a hedge one metre away offered some protection from the elements, and some security. There was a padlocked pedestrian door which looked like it was never used. Robert unlocked it and went inside to a small storage area lined with racks, which led to another door. This, too, was padlocked, and once through it he was faced by a short wall of bales of straw, three high. Using an old pallet, he climbed on top of one and moved to the next across. He heaved at the first one until it toppled onto the pallet below. Stepping down, he was able to jump to the floor, where a tarpaulin covered a large rectangular object. He removed the tarpaulin and then two sheets, revealing the gleaming grey Land Rover Discovery, which caused a grin to appear on his face. He moved the straw bales from around the back of the vehicle and unlocked the sliding metal outer door of the barn, before reversing his pride and joy onto the earth outside, and loading his luggage from the pick-up truck. He then drove into the woods and reached a disused gate to the estate that was also padlocked. As he drove through and out onto the country lane, he grinned again and said out loud: 'The Scottish Lowlands, I think!'

In the farmhouse, Lauren had lain on the floor for a couple of minutes crying, and trying to work out if the blow had broken any bones. She then staggered into the en suite bathroom and looked at her face in the mirror, her tears renewing when she saw the swelling around her right eye, which was already restricting her vision, and the huge blotches lower down on her cheek. She washed and walked carefully downstairs before pouring a brandy to calm her nerves.

As she sipped her drink with an ice pack on her eye, she began to think of what was going to happen now. If Robert had gone, and it looked like he'd done a runner, then what would be the impact on her? Presumably the family would come looking for him and when she couldn't give them answers, would they leave her alone, or was she likely to be kicked out too? The latter seemed probable; they just wouldn't believe that she didn't know what he'd been up to, whatever it was.

That led her to worry about exactly *what* he'd been up to – stealing presumably? Were they going to involve the police? Her face crashed into tears again as she realised her time at the estate, her life in and around the area, was all about to end through no fault of her own. She'd done her best but had she been too trusting of Robert, allowed him to go unchallenged for too long? That's how it would look to the family and the police!

That evening and night she drank more, ate only snacks and waited for the knock at the door. She contacted no one until eleven when she tried calling Robert's number, which went straight to an 'unavailable' message. By that time, she knew no one would come that night so she went to bed; drunk, sore, partially sighted and emotionally wrecked.

The farmhouse phone started ringing just after ten in the morning, raising her from her fitful slumber, but not sufficiently to stop her groaning and burying her head under the covers. Then her mobile rang a couple of times. She couldn't face answering it, but after half an hour decided to check if there were any messages. Her voicemail opened up, and it was Juan Marco saying he couldn't find Robert at the estate office and he wasn't answering his mobile. Did she know where he was? The sound of his voice made her crumble again. Of all the people to chase her, discover her like this, kick her out of the house, why did it have to be him?

Her thoughts turned to the police. If they came, did she want to greet them like this? What would she say about her face? Would she press charges, or would they be more interested in the probable misappropriation of funds and her supposed role in it? She couldn't face the world in her clothes from the night before looking like shit, so she dragged herself into the bathroom and as she showered, gulped down some of the warm water as a lazy way of taking in some fluids.

After dressing and making some coffee, she ate two biscuits, knowing that she needed to force something down herself to help with digesting the alcohol, even though each nibble aroused a sense of nausea. Just after midday she heard voices from the front of the farmhouse, expecting it to be the police, but all she could recognise were Henry and Juan Marco conversing with each other. She ducked down beneath window height and sneaked out of the kitchen and upstairs to the main bedroom at the front, which would enable her to hear more clearly. They were asking each other about where they could be. She heard something about the office being locked but her car was here, so even if Robert wasn't around, she should be here. More discussions followed about keys, and then she heard Henry say loudly that they must have duplicate keys back at the hall, so they'd have to come back. Both of them called out her and Robert's names loudly and she thought she heard the kitchen door being tried, but breathed a sigh of relief when she remembered it wouldn't have been unlocked from the day before. Their voices ceased and she heard the footsteps on the gravel drive as they left after about twenty minutes.

She realised now she had a window of opportunity to get herself organised. After making a couple of slices of toast and forcing herself to down two glasses of water before pouring another coffee, she went upstairs and started packing some things. Whatever happened she had to prepare to leave this place in case things went badly, and needed to make sure she took everything essential in case they didn't give her much time. If there were no more visitors before the afternoon, she'd head down to the estate office and try and get on with some work. If she behaved normally, that was her best chance of convincing the family that she wasn't tied up in whatever Robert had done.

She heard her phone ring in the kitchen a couple of times but ignored it, then the message chimes started, prompting her to go down and check who was trying to contact her. There was nothing from Robert, but two messages from Juan Marco, and a couple from estate workers asking when Robert was going to decide on what materials to purchase for maintenance jobs. Another popped up while she was looking, from a supplier chasing an unpaid bill. She shivered, realising this was just the start of the storm, and that going to the office would open up the possibility of more than visits from just the family, so perhaps waiting at the farmhouse quietly was the best option. By half past two she'd finished packing her things. Her phone rang again – it was Juan Marco – and she hesitated, before deciding it was time to bite the bullet.

'Hello, Juan Marco.'

'Lauren, we've been trying to reach you and Robert. You're not at the office and Robert's phone is switched off. Where is he?'

'I'm sorry, I'm not well today. I haven't been down to the office and have only just started picking up messages. Robert left first thing. I'm not sure where he is but I guess he could be driving. He's probably got an appointment somewhere but, like I said, I've not signed in today yet so I haven't checked the electronic diary.'

'OK, I'm sorry you're not feeling well, but I'd like to know when Robert's back. Can you check where he is and call me?'

'Absolutely, give me a few minutes,' she said, ending the call.

She immediately rang Robert but his phone was switched off still, and she already knew there was no reason for him to be away from the estate on a Friday afternoon, something he always avoided. Did she continue the dialogue with Juan Marco or go silent? She left it fifteen minutes before calling him back.

'I'm sorry but the diary says there are no appointments, perhaps he's had something come up last minute. Like I said, he was gone first thing before I awoke.'

There was a huff from the other end of the phone. 'OK. Did he take one of the estate vehicles do you know, or did he get a taxi?'

'I'm sorry, Juan Marco, I really don't know,' she replied as innocently as she could. 'I was out for the count… I mean, sleeping.'

'OK, so when will he be back, what time? You are expecting him back today?'

She made the fatal error of hesitating before responding which he picked up on.

'Er… I expect so, there's no reason why he wouldn't be back—'

Suddenly she heard a gruff 'give me the phone!' in the background.

'Lauren, it's Henry. We want to talk to Robert and to you, too. We'll be round at the farmhouse in twenty minutes. Make sure you're there.'

The phone went dead and Lauren's stomach rumbled with the tension. She was frozen to the spot for two minutes, before inching her way into the lounge, where she looked at each wall in turn, taking in her surroundings and wondering if these would be her last memories of this place. She sat down to try to compose herself, before deciding on one final act of normality, returning to the kitchen to put on a fresh pot of coffee, and taking some biscuits out as an attempt at providing a proper welcome. Then she returned to the lounge and switched on the television.

She heard their footsteps before their voices and was already heading to the hall when the doorbell rang. There was no greeting from Henry as he pushed passed her saying, 'Let's go into the lounge.' Her partially closed eye and huge red mark only received a cursory glance. Juan Marco stood on the doorstep waiting to be invited inside, but when he saw the bruising, he took a small step back, unable to avert his gaze. Lauren quickly turned sideways to show the left side of her face instead, and muttered 'come in' to him.

As she entered the lounge, her mouth opened to offer them coffee. Henry jumped in. 'Where's Robert, Lauren?'

Her jaw rose and fell as she tried to change her words to answer the question, so just air and an ugly jabbing sound came out.

'Your face, I suppose that tells us all really, doesn't it? Has he legged it?'

'What he means is have you called the police?' added Juan Marco, receiving a double-take from Henry who was wondering if that referred to the theft, the assault or both.

She shook her head. 'I don't know where he is, so what's the point, and even if I did—'

Henry jumped in again. 'You're still loyal to him anyway.' There was a slight gasp from his son who was now the one doing the double-taking. 'What, you think she'll dish the dirt on him? Help bury him? You're being naïve!'

'We're here for Robert,' snapped his son. 'We should show some respect, especially as she's obviously not well!'

Henry was about to lay into his son about being too weak when Lauren's sobs stopped him.

'Please, don't fight over me. I don't know what Robert's done or where he's gone, but he came back from the meeting yesterday in an angry mood and stormed off, having...' She raised her hand towards her face. 'I really don't know what he's been up to but it must be bad, that's all I know. I'm his wife and I should have had suspicions, maybe I did, but I chose not to ask the right questions, or if I did, I didn't ask them strongly enough, and that's my fault. I have to take the blame for that so I don't want anyone feeling sorry for me. Please, just tell me, what's he done?'

Henry let out a loud snort. 'Well we were hoping you could tell us that! Oh, you're tied up in this all right—'

306

'We don't know exactly!' Juan Marco interrupted angrily, glaring at Henry. 'But we suspect he's been stealing from the estate, falsifying accounts, selling equipment off privately, obtaining discounts from suppliers but keeping them for himself, that sort of thing. We don't know anything one hundred per cent for sure, but he was given an initial list of transactions yesterday to report back to us on, and he knew there would be others as we went back further over the past two years. Plus we were bringing the auditors in.'

'Oh!' sobbed Lauren. 'I assumed it must be something like that. I didn't really understand, he kept me away from capital expenditure items...' Her voice trailed off as her tears increased, leading to an aggressive grunt from Henry and another fiery look his way from his son.

'So, what do you want from me?' she said through her tears.

'To be gone from here, if you seriously can't help unravel what he's been up to,' Henry responded chidingly. This time the stern look from his son was met equally; it was time to bring the blade down on the Pritchards' reign of thieving.

'OK,' sobbed Lauren. 'Will you allow me to pack some things and make some arrangements? I suppose the police will want to talk to me?'

'We'll involve them when we know what we're dealing with,' replied Henry. 'First, we need to know how much money is involved.'

'But you'll want me to stay in the area, or do you just need a forwarding address?'

Henry looked into her sad eyes, losing patience with the saintly "I haven't done anything wrong but am prepared to admit my guilt in turning a blind eye" performance. 'I don't have any interest in this shit,' he said offhandedly as he rose. 'Talk to him.'

Juan Marco's eyes burned into the back of his father's head as he disappeared from sight, then his eyes softened as he looked back to Lauren.

'Are you going to call the police yourself? That looks bad,' he said nodding towards her right eye. 'Have you been to hospital?'

'No, it's not that bad. It was a slap that's all, nothing's broken. It'll soon heal. I don't want any fuss, and besides, I've no idea where he is, they'll probably not be able to find him for weeks. He was angry, worse than before, but if he's not coming back then I've nothing to worry about.'

He bowed his head. 'Is Robert's laptop here? We'll be able to access the office computers if you give me the log-ins, but the laptop will have other stuff on it.' As he raised his face, she lowered her's.

'No, it's gone.'

He sighed before adding: 'I'm sorry it's come to this, but the family will expect you to go. We have a lot of work to do to investigate our suspicions, and it will be easier if you leave and take what personal possessions you need. But anything to do with the estate, you know you must leave it. Don't go into the office but give me the log-ins now. Do you have somewhere you can go?'

She started sobbing again. 'Yes, don't worry I've got friends, but my parents moved to Derbyshire two years ago and I think that's where I need to go. Maybe just a night or two with friends first to let this heal a bit,' she said jerking her finger in the direction of her face. 'I don't want too many questions asked,' she added.

He nodded. 'I still think you should see the hospital or a doctor before you go. I'll take you if there's no one else.'

'No, no,' she replied waving her hand. 'Forget it.'

He stood to go and she went to the table to write down the computer log-ins and to give him her parents' address.

'I have a job to do here,' he said slowly. 'Lord and Lady Belvedere, my grandparents, I feel sorry for them. They're good people and don't deserve this. I know I'm only filling in time, but they're paying me to help get this mess sorted and I will do the best I can for them.' She nodded back at him. 'How long do you need to pack? You'll need to leave tonight.'

'Just a couple of hours. The furniture well... I'll take some soft furnishings but the rest of it, I guess it's your's really. I mean it might help to go towards anything that Robert's taken.' Suddenly her face froze and then broke into tears as she gasped: 'Oh, the car. It belongs to the estate, too. How am I going to get my things to my friends?'

'Take it,' Juan Marco said firmly. 'Are you staying locally tonight?' She nodded. 'Right, well write the address down where you'll be staying. I'll come and collect it tomorrow afternoon. That'll give you some time to unload it. I'll be back at seven tonight to make sure you've gone. One of the labourers will change the locks, I'm sorry but...'

'It's OK,' she sobbed, 'it's not your fault, I understand.' She added the address to the piece of paper which she gave to him without looking up, as he turned and walked out of the house.

Chapter 30

Stretching the Family Bonds

'Robert's done a bunk and Lauren's been given her marching orders!' Henry announced smartly to his parents when he found them. 'She claims she knows nothing about what he was up to, but basically admitted she had suspicions, she just didn't want to follow up on them! In other words, her loyalty was to him and not to us, so she'll be gone by tonight. Juan Marco's just getting her to write down the details of where she's fleeing to, so we can track her down if needs be. She claims to know nothing of where Robert's gone; he left early this morning apparently and has taken his clothes and personal possessions, so it looks like he's legged it. His phone is switched off.'

'Has he taken one of the vehicles?' asked Lord Belvedere. 'Unless we really have to, I don't want to involve the police. But if he's stolen one of the vehicles…'

'Surely he'd dump it?' replied his wife. 'He wouldn't seriously take off in one of our vehicles knowing that he could be traced?'

'I'll get Juan Marco to check around the estate and find out who's got each vehicle. You must have a fleet list somewhere, Father?'

'Uhh, yes, somewhere. Perhaps Juan Marco will know better than I about the vans.' Henry looked hard at his father, before making a mental note to add this to Juan Marco's task list.

'So we need to have a staff meeting, I think,' continued his father, changing the subject. 'The team at the hall as well as on the estate need to know. I also need to get Andrew back here and bring him up to speed. Other than that, will you speak to the auditors, Henry, if I give you their number? They're going to have to investigate a lot of the potentially faulty transactions, speaking to suppliers especially to see what they say.'

He gave Henry the number for the auditors, while he rang his brother and told him he needed to come over tonight for a "bit of a chat" as there was a "problem".

Henry didn't really feel very confident about phoning the auditors, but reluctantly went to the end of the room and got through to the secretary of the partner whose name was on the business card. The secretary was reluctant to engage with Henry as she didn't have any proof of his identity, and said the first call should come through their nominated client contacts, who were Andrew Belvedere or Robert. Henry gasped at the mention of the latter and said they wouldn't be hearing from him again, before telling them that Andrew would ring later on the partner's mobile, and asking her to pass a message on that the matter was urgent.

Juan Marco reappeared at this point and just as Henry was jumping in to start issuing orders, his mother said: 'Well, Juan Marco, what do you think of all this? Sit down and have a drink. How do you feel about your suspicions now – more justified?'

'Mother, he isn't a fool, I told you that before! We've both suspected for some time, haven't we, that all wasn't smelling right?' Henry interrupted, making sure he wasn't sidelined.

'Henry, I'm asking because it appears the size of the task just got bigger, and I'm very aware of just how much work is going to be coming his way. He will be taking a significant share, won't he?' chided Lady Belvedere much to Henry's annoyance, who flared his nostrils and glared at what he took as a snide remark about his own abilities.

'Yes, he definitely will!'

She turned back to Juan Marco.

'I think his departure tells its own story,' Juan Marco said, 'and he knows we were going to uncover his stealing. If I had any doubt then the way he's treated Lauren convinces me.'

'Oh, what do you mean?'

'I think she worked out something was wrong before he left, or maybe challenged him, and he took it out on her physically. I think she should see a doctor but she won't go.'

'Oh, what's he done? You're concerning me!'

'Oh please!' interrupted Henry again. 'Let's not get the violins out for her! She admitted to having her own suspicions for a long time but wanted to protect him!'

Both Juan Marco and Lady Belvedere looked at him confusedly before turning back to each other, her eyes demanding an answer.

'He hit her hard, across the face. Her eye's almost closed up, it's a real mess.' Lady Belvedere gasped and Henry groaned before muttering: 'She had it coming...' When they both glared at him, he continued, 'I need a bloody drink. Where's that bottle of sweet sherry in the library? Let me know when the staff meeting is,' before skulking out of the room.

'I don't think she knew anything specific,' Juan Marco continued. 'I think she had some suspicions. Whenever I talked to her about details she tried her best, but admitted Robert kept her out of anything big. I don't think it's reasonable to assume she helped him. I'm quite sure she didn't and she's ashamed, both of him, and herself for not being enquiring enough. But I don't think this is the first time he's used violence against her. Before I left for Spain she was quiet, even weak with me, over dinner, and I thought that something was wrong between them.'

'Well there's nothing to be done,' commented Lord Belvedere. 'I hope she reports the brute to the police and eventually they'll catch up with him. I'm not trying to be insensitive but we have our own problems to resolve, and quickly.' The others looked at him and silently agreed.

That evening, Andrew Belvedere came to the hall under some apprehension, as he'd been trying to get hold of Robert for two hours with no success, and Lauren wasn't answering his calls either. Something didn't add up. He met his brother and sister-in-law in the large sitting room with Juan Marco there too, Henry having cried off with a headache, announced with a slur through the closed bedroom door.

He was shocked to hear of their suspicions and couldn't entertain the idea that it was as bad as all that, even if it worried him greatly that Robert had fled. He called the partner at the auditors and they agreed to come to the hall at eleven the next day. Once their business was concluded, the estate staff would be briefed at four p.m.

The meeting went ahead and a joint plan of action was drawn up. Juan Marco was to focus on visiting some of the suppliers and trying to find out the full details of the individual transactions he'd already researched. The auditors agreed to make official requests for assistance from all suppliers, including those on Juan Marco's list. They'd collate their answers and the auditors would calculate any shortfalls discovered.

Before the staff meeting, Juan Marco toured the estate to make sure all the vehicles were accounted for, knowing who normally had custody of each. He found the pick-up truck left by Robert at the storage barn. He gulped when he entered the unit and found the empty space where the bales had previously been, guessing Robert had hidden something behind there all along. Afterwards, he cycled into the village, to avoid taking someone else on the journey to collect the old Toyota Rav 4 that Lauren had used. His ring on the doorbell was answered by an unsmiling female who simply handed him the keys. They nodded at each other and he took the car back to the estate.

The auditors stayed for the staff briefing to add gravitas to the request for people to come forward in confidence, if they knew anything about possible financial mismanagement. By this time Henry had emerged from his room, and sat sullen-eyed on the edge of the group, studying their faces to see if he could spot any signs of embarrassment or fear that might indicate complicity. The two groundsmen for the hall sat po-faced, and Henry decided they looked far too innocent for their own good. As he listened to his father pleading for any information that would help them, and promising no retribution for anyone who stepped forward, he imagined his own brand of justice being dished out to anyone implicated, which would involve one of the English Civil War pikes in the dining room, and their stomach.

When questions came about the management of the estate going forwards, Lord Belvedere announced he would work with Juan Marco to supervise and authorise all continuing and additional tasks. Staff should continue as normal, referring to either one of them. The auditors would supply payroll services on a temporary basis. There were some uncomfortable looks and seat-shifting when Juan Marco's name was mentioned, something Henry couldn't help smirking at – their own fault for leaving his name out of it. Then his father, picking up on the sentiments, added that of course Henry was also available, something which caused more movement and murmurs, which struck at Henry's pride. Right, he thought, if that's how you bastards feel, then don't come to me with your tales of 'this information might be useful, sir' and expect to get away with it! Swift justice would rain down like an avenger!

After the meeting, Juan Marco decided to speak to his grandparents about whether George could fill the gap left by Robert. Not only did he have a stronger family connection, but he had proper farming experience, and Juan Marco had always admired his dedication to organic and environmentally-friendly farming, something that he had wondered why Hillingstone hadn't developed. But before he could ask them, they said they would be calling their other children to update them, so he decided to see how those conversations went first.

After the previous calls had ended badly, each parent decided to speak to the other child. Lady Belvedere rang George that evening and dealt her cards plainly. It appeared that Robert had been up to no good although the extent wasn't yet quantified. He'd left in a hurry and Lauren, although probably not involved, had left too, as they couldn't be one hundred per cent sure. They needed to investigate how much money had been lost and consider their options. The whole family needed to work together to get through this crisis.

'Well, of course I told you before he wasn't trustworthy. Always felt there was something smug and sneaky about him, it goes back a long time. When the police catch up with him you'll be able to pin him up, and I don't expect he's the sort to have squandered the money. He's a grand schemer, so it will have been squirreled away somewhere.'

'We're not going to involve the police, if we can help it,' his mother said cautiously. 'The estate doesn't need that sort of publicity and nor do the family. Your father feels his responsibility very keenly and you know he has his cancer to think about. This is our mess, and it won't help us to get back on our feet by involving the police. We have to manage the estate better.'

'Not involve the police?' George exploded. 'What the hell do you think you're playing at? You're seriously going to let him get away with it? It could be hundreds of thousands of pounds, maybe more! How many years has he been duping you?'

'George, please be calm. We have to think about the future now, not the past, and there's your father to think of!'

'Well, he's the one who got you into this mess!'

'That's cruel George, he needs your support, not your blame! Help us to pull this together, please. The estate workers respect you and if you could spare us some time, just a little, show some support by visiting, it would go a long way towards making the employees realise we are determined to get through this and build a brighter future!'

'What a crazy notion! Steal from us and get away with it! That would look great in the job description! Anyway, what do you need me for? You've still got the great Henry and his bastard, no, sorry, his now legitimate son to help you out! Maybe he can ride in on his charger with a Moorish battle cry and send the peasants running!'

'Oh, George!' cried his mother. 'How can you be so vicious and hateful? At this time, when the family needs you most!' The phone line went dead.

Lord Belvedere rang Anna early the following morning from his study. She didn't pick up from the estate phone number and he guessed she might be ignoring it, so tried again on his mobile. She hesitantly answered after three rings. He spoke quietly and economically, fearing this call more than his wife's the previous day, because while Anna was far away and had little experience in the farming side of the estate, her business acumen and drive to achieve things was exactly what the estate needed at the moment. Yet she was compromised by her personal friendship with Robert. If she could come home to assist, he felt very certain that any disruption to life on the estate would last the minimum time possible, but how would she take the news that Robert appeared to have been a deceiver?

'I can't believe it, no I won't believe it!' she said passionately. 'His father served the estate for all those years and he's followed in his footsteps! It's ridiculous to suggest that he's been stealing from the family that gave him security for years! How can you believe that? I bet it was handled poorly! I told mother not to accuse anyone of anything, but I can imagine that's exactly how it went and he probably went off in a huff, quite-rightly, deeply hurt. And now he's playing hard-to-get for a few days to teach you a lesson! When he gets back in touch, you'll all have some apologising to do, and all because of your blind trust in a Spanish schoolboy who can't add up, probably!'

'Anna, you're ignoring the facts. He's gone, fled the estate, taken his clothes, made off in a vehicle which was hidden on the estate and we assume bought with estate funds. And given his wife a beating into the bargain! If he's innocent, he's not behaving like an innocent man. His phone's switched off, has been since he left.'

'Rubbish, he's just ignoring you,' she retorted. 'Let's sort this out right now while I ring him, and show you he's just blocked you. I'll dial him on the apartment line, hold on. You'll end up feeling so silly and when I've done this, I don't want to hear about this again. Do I make myself clear? Ridiculous nonsense. I'm not getting involved in this when I return to the estate... What? What do you mean this number is unavailable? Bullshit, it must be the wrong number. Hang on, Father, I'm just re-dialling. Shit, it

314

must be off. Well, he's probably annoyed with us all, so I expect he'll make contact in a few days on a new phone! He'll make you pay for this you know! The boot will be on the other foot then!'

'Anna, darling, we just gave him a list of transactions and asked him to provide the evidence of gross price and net amounts, so accounting for the differences. The way he reacted, as if he'd been ambushed, is a classic defence tactic. He reacted as if he was being bullied, sacked even. But why did he return home, swat his wife, pack his clothes and make off in a vehicle that had been hidden behind some bales in a barn? It doesn't add up, surely you can see that? If he was going to fight, he'd have stayed put, got a lawyer on to us, not fled.'

'Robert isn't the sort to run from a fight, I know him! He's worked his socks off for the estate and he wouldn't let it go lightly, but he'd be furious with you all ganging up on him, especially involving that boy that he's been training. And throwing Henry in as well!'

'Anna, you're blinded. I thought you would be, but hoped your fantastic brain would help you realise that this is for real. The auditors agree that things look shady…'

'Oh, well that's another thing that falls on the estate that presumably you're blaming him for – mismanagement, lack of instructions – to the auditors! You reap what you sow father. I'm so angry right now that I'm putting the phone down! Why is it that whenever something goes wrong on the estate, it's always "call Anna, she can sort it out, she's got the right head on her shoulders", despite the fact that the affairs of the estate have nothing, repeat nothing to do with me, just being a poor little inadequate female who counts for absolutely nothing in the history of this family. Just like they all do!'

Chapter 31

Digging In

The next few weeks flew by for all the family on the estate, checking inventories of machinery and plant, vehicles, food produce stocks and production figures, livestock movements and rent receipts. Then they compared them to anything that resembled an invoice, which in some cases looked decidedly unofficial.

Bank statements were trawled through by Lord Belvedere and the auditors, checking all payments and receipts. They discovered multiple transactions where money disappeared out of the account to a personal account, and then reappeared some days later, indicating that Robert had been borrowing money, presumably to speculate with, and keeping the profits. It was clear that two of the contract farmers had signed contracts for higher rent than the estate was actually charging, and the difference had been paid into the same personal account. They found performance bonuses paid to suppliers which didn't tally with invoices, and machinery that had disappeared without anyone having a clue how or where it had been disposed of. Some of the machinery suppliers said part exchanges had been taken out of the deal at the last minute, even when they had plans to re-condition it and sell it on.

For Lord Belvedere this was deeply troubling, and the energy for tracking things down largely came from Juan Marco and the auditors. To his grandson this was a job, and he felt uncomfortable that some of the fraudulent activity had gone on while he was working under Robert's supervision. He knew he carried no blame for any of it, but it made him more determined to work as hard as he could to sort the mess out – it was his obligation to his grandparents, even if he had the added incentive of being paid.

After three weeks of work covering the last year, just under sixty-three thousand pounds was estimated missing – not a fortune but it was just one year, and they had further to go back. Fortunately Robert had only had the estate manager's job for four years, and they were hopeful that his thieving had taken some time to get going.

Andrew Belvedere offered his profuse apologies on many occasions, and offered his own services and those of his children in investigating the trail of fraud, but his brother and sister-in-law coolly declined. Not being able to trust an employee was one thing, but to feel let down by someone close in your family was another.

Henry initially accompanied Juan Marco on some of the trips to suppliers and customers, but found the structured presentation of queries and responses stifling. It felt like a boring office job after a while, and he increasingly left the talking to his son. After the first week, he made his excuses and said he wanted to walk around the estate to see if he could find any other clues, checking outbuildings and sheds. That lasted a day and a half before he went into Maidstone for lunch and got drunk, spending the latter part of the afternoon sleeping in a friend's car in a car park.

At first, he always came to breakfast, anxious to appear as if he was part of the driving force in discussing the day's agenda. But again that quickly subsided, as he had no real interest in doing any of the work. Staying out of the way became his daily habit, finding a use in informing the housekeeper of every empty or low drinks decanter that he 'came across' in one of the hall rooms.

By the middle of June, they'd gone back two years, and estimated a further forty-seven thousand pounds was missing from the estate. What they could never track was what had happened to much of the disposed machinery, including the old JCB. There was no trace of any of it on the estate, and none of the suppliers could or would offer any evidence of what had happened to it. If it had been sold to breakers yards that would have provided another route, but after two calls from the auditors, they came back with nothing. What they hoped was that based on their discoveries, Robert had increased his stealing in the past year, and so there would be diminishing returns from going back any further than two years. The lost machinery values would be estimated at anywhere between thirty thousand and fifty thousand pounds, so their best guess was that Robert had defrauded the estate of between one hundred and fifty and two hundred thousand pounds.

This wasn't an insignificant sum, but the family's shock was reduced by the realisation that if this had gone on for just a couple more years, they would be in a far more disastrous position.

By late June, the auditors were starting to suggest the estate should diversify to increase its income. The word immediately spooked Lord Belvedere, and went right over Henry's head, leaving Juan Marco and his grandmother as the only ones keen to look to the future. For Juan Marco however, it gave him a sense of release, as he'd already had ideas, and a third party voicing the same views gave him some confidence he wasn't on his own. The issue of selling off low-value agricultural land wasn't far away in his mind, and then there were other suggestions – eco-friendly farming practices; working with the contract farmers to follow similar ideas, and then guaranteeing to buy their produce at a higher price than they would get at market, then sell that produce at a higher rate again from their own farm shop. They could open a café on the estate offering locally produced foodstuffs. It wasn't too different to a bodega in Spain growing their own vines, picking the fruit, fermenting it and then selling drink and food directly, opening their doors for guided tours into the package. The estate had no public footpaths running through it, although from its grounds you could connect to other footpaths. Opening up one or two tracks could be done to increase visitor numbers, maybe with an honesty box at a point of entry, to cover the costs of additional forestry, fencing or way markers. Perhaps a children's nature trail could be started, visits to the animal pens, even tours of the house? There were many things that had to be worth a try, and he had to do more than just find evidence of missing money – it was up to him to do a proper job and help get the estate onto a better footing for the future. Then he could return home knowing he'd done all he could. The notion of even returning at some point in the future to check on progress, and maybe even help out, entered his head. How surreal would that be?

He realised there was way too much work here for just himself, plus he had to recognise the limits of his own abilities. His grandmother would pull her weight, he knew that, but she needed someone to drive alongside her, someone with energy, ideas and ambition. His facial expression turned sour when he thought of who would be best placed to make things happen – Lauren for her ideas and drive and commercial common sense, working with Mary and George. The two women would clean up as a team, and with Mary working with her husband as well on the farming side, it was the strongest possible strategy. That would leave him to talk to his grandfather

318

on the land sale issue, which was the easiest way to secure a capital injection into the estate. He sighed as he dwelt on the loss of Lauren from the estate, but as he couldn't fix it, it had to be time to contact Mary and see if she would see it as an opportunity, and be willing to use her influence with George. But first, he had to speak with Lord Belvedere about the land position.

The following day they met in the private study.

'Overall I suppose we have to count our blessings, the situation could have been a lot worse,' Lord Belvedere said as he reviewed the latest email from the auditors.

His grandson nodded. 'But the estate needs to restore its finances and grow them in the future. I have ideas on that and we need to discuss them with everyone, but I just wondered if we could talk about estate land privately. I'm sure you realise how the estate would benefit from a one-off cash input now.'

Lord Belvedere huffed. 'I knew you would bring this up, the auditors raised the same thing quietly. I can't express how much I detest the notion. And people wandering around the estate, turning us into a sort of tourist attraction. There's got to be another way, surely? I know that's what they're hinting at.'

'I think this estate is an agricultural business, and adding different elements to that business doesn't change its nature,' replied Juan Marco.

'Management-speak.'

'There's so much to discuss, but if these things are going to happen, even slowly and not all of them, you will need to invest some money to start them off. Where is that going to come from?'

His grandfather gave a huge sigh before replying: 'Oh God, go on then. Tell me your thoughts.'

'Well, that land at the bottom of the field that borders the contract land, it's obviously liable to flood, so one of the contract farmers suggested turning it into a fishing lake, a nature reserve, woodland or something. It was just an idea that he had. He hadn't done any research or anything, but he thought that grants might be available for that sort of thing – government subsidies, environmental grants maybe. Or he also suggested a boating lake with a café that you can earn money from. I asked him about access because it would involve a route across the land he rents, but he said that wasn't a problem – he would change the terms of the contract if needed, and when I talked to him some more he wasn't that bothered about keeping the contract going anyway. He said he'd only taken that field on because Robert had pressured him into taking it with the one that he wanted. Maybe you could authorise a feasibility study to see what options there are and how much they would cost, and earn the estate in return?'

His grandfather could only manage a grimace in reply.

'I know your brother thought you should sell the land for housing, but I think there are other areas on the estate where you could easily do that, and not lose any privacy. At the edge of the woods there's a clearing which leads to a country road, you know it? That would be a better place for housing, just a few, say six, shielded from the estate by the trees, It wouldn't interfere with the estate at all, but I saw some figures in a filing cabinet in the estate office and maybe you could raise a lot of money, maybe a million pounds, from just a few houses. It would give a cash injection that is needed.'

'Juan Marco, you're new to all this. I don't think you should suddenly assume you're an expert. If the land was any good then why didn't Andrew look at it?'

'Maybe because it wasn't big enough?' Juan Marco shrugged. 'He and Robert saw a bigger plan to make more money?'

His grandfather grunted before answering: 'Probably not enough money for them! I don't know about all this, I really don't. You want to spend money as a gamble on it making money?'

'Look, I only want the estate to explore all options, that's what I see as my job. I still plan to return to Spain next year. I'd like to know I've tried my best, that's all.'

Lord Belvedere looked at him sullenly and pursed his lips. 'So it will be just us to manage it then, as normal.'

'I think if the options are explored now and a real plan made, then hopefully, the family will see things differently. I still think George and Mary have so many of the skills to help, and I have hope that I can influence Mary, and maybe she can work on George.'

'Oh, Juan Marco, I admire your industriousness and optimism but really, I think some bridges have been burned.' Juan Marco looked at him, wondering exactly what those words meant, but understanding the gist of them.

However, he had a plan and was going to stick to it, and messaged

Mary that afternoon to start things off. She didn't reply until six, saying they were both well and busy, and asking him how things were going. He wasted no time in telling her they were on the point of starting investigations into using some of the land for other purposes, starting feasibility studies into a farm shop, restaurant, leisure areas, public access areas and a small-scale housing development – it was now or never for the estate to look to the future. He also mentioned interest in moving to organic farming, hoping that would attract a response from her.

Mary was in two minds about how to reply. Did she exchange bland messages with him and keep her distance, or speak to him when George wasn't around? In the end, she decided on the latter, because at the moment they were completely out of the loop and there seemed no prospects of restoring communications with George's parents soon, something that made her feel uncomfortable. They spoke on the phone the following morning while George was out in the fields.

'So they're definitely not going after Robert?'

'No, they don't want a fight. They just want to focus on turning things around and managing things better in the future.'

'So who's leading this, Juan Marco?' she asked tentatively. 'Lord Belvedere is getting on a bit. Is he keen, or just embarrassed by what has gone before?'

'The auditors have been really helpful and have suggested a couple of farming consultancies who can help us plan a future,' he replied economically. 'I think he knows what some of the options are anyway – it's not the first time some of them have been suggested. They need to diversify and modernise. I can see some of the benefits and I want to help as much as I can. I still intend to return to Spain next year, so I think it is my job to supply as much energy as I can to the ideas now.'

Mary pursed her lips, guessing exactly who was carrying the load.

'I also don't understand why the estate hasn't tried organic farming methods, like you and George practice in Lincolnshire.'

Subtle, very subtle, thought Mary, while she considered how to reply. 'This is our land to do with as we please, but it's fairly small scale. George wouldn't try to influence his parents' approach, especially while Robert was there.'

'And now, now that he's gone?'

She couldn't help but admire his way of finding a way through the swamp. She ought to be able to tell him he didn't know anything, yet she respected him too much to crush his youthful optimism.

'I can see where you're going with this, Juan Marco, and I don't want to rain on your parade, but there's been so much water under the bridge. There's blockages everywhere. Lord Belvedere, Henry, Robert and Lauren, there's—'

'Me,' he interrupted. She didn't correct him.

'Let's just say that you're right to have hope for the future, the whole family needs it, but to expect things to just turn around, I mean that's not going to happen. Sorry. What's your father, Henry, up to in all this?'

Juan Marco puffed his cheeks out and blew into the phone. 'Not much. He gets excited at the start of the project and then when the actual work starts, he's nowhere to be seen. He attends the odd meeting looking like he's hardly slept the night before, drinks all evening, doesn't rise until midday, and then disappears off the estate not telling anyone where he's going. At the end of last week, he disappeared for three days. I just don't understand him. He shows the right instincts, gets things started and then just as quickly loses interest. When things get down to detail level, he just closes his eyes and falls into a deep sleep.'

'He's never been any different, I told you that before. He has ideas but very few of them are grounded in reality, and he's just never happy. I'd like to think he'd step up with the mess the estate's in, but sadly I wouldn't expect it.'

'We need you here,' he replied, 'both of you. Not just because I believe in trialling organic farming, but because you understand the economics of it, who buys the produce, how much extra profit you can make. I think you would understand the commercial aspects of it, Mary, the farm shop, the café, using ecology in a way that brings people onto the estate, holding events here… you know how to carry things off.'

'Oh, Juan Marco, you say the sweetest things and you're a hard man to say no to, but there are some things that can't be made to happen just because you use the right words,' she sighed.

'But you know I'm right. You have the abilities and you have influence over George. I admire you both greatly…'

'That's enough, please, Juan Marco. You over-estimate my influence! George is his own man – very proud and stubborn and he'll only do what he wants to do.'

'OK, but can you try, just test the water? The estate needs you, I need you. I admit a lot of the energy is coming from me but I won't be around forever. My father isn't the answer for the future. The family needs drive from within and when I head back to Spain, anything I try to do will be wasted if someone doesn't carry it on. My grandfather will accept change, I know he will. Maybe he is stubborn too, but my grandmother is very sharp, she understands a lot, but she can't do it all.'

Mary sighed again before replying: 'Yes, she's very capable, I respect her a lot. But don't push Juan Marco, please. I'll think about it, that's all. I'll think what, if anything, I can do, but don't get your hopes up.'

'That's fine,' he replied. 'I want us to stay in touch, share things, so you know what's going on. That's OK isn't it?'

'Yes. I must go, the vegetables won't water themselves.'

As Lord Belvedere and Juan Marco continued to deal with the daily management of the estate, he realised the sooner the family came to terms with the future development of the estate, the better. Consultants needed to be engaged, contacts with the National Farmers' Union made, and relationships started with other country house owners who'd been in similar circumstances. But he needed the family to engage in the process, so he asked his grandparents and his father for a time when they could sit together and agree their next actions. They met in early July, Lady Belvedere anxious to be positive, her husband just anxious, and Henry looking bored and sullen from the start.

'You must have contacts with other property owners and farmers that can help in the process. You need to speak to these people and find out about their own experiences, then agree the terms of reference for the consultants,' he started.

'Yes we'll do that, won't we, John?' responded Lady Belvedere. 'We're on good terms with the owners of Goodwinds Hall and Thornberry Manor. They've both opened up to the public and they've found a balance between preserving their privacy and increasing their income. Can you draft out the ideas you've already had Juan Marco, and John or I will call the consultants to set up meetings. Henry – do you have any thoughts we can work on?'

Henry looked up and stared at his mother. 'What do you need from me? I've pointed out the problem, but it's no good looking at me to resolve it. I've brought you to the face of the mountain but it's got to be you that climbs it. Juan Marco's here to supply the labour and energy, and he'll keep me up to date with what's happening, won't you?'

'Henry, we're all involved in this!' retorted his mother. 'The family should pull together and that includes you. You can't just throw your hands up and say it's not your problem! It's all our problem!'

'Mother, look, I'm just a fixer, a connector, a man who brings the horse to water. I'm not into details and consultants and plans and projects. Nothing's changed – I don't have that skill set. But what I have brought you is Juan Marco, and I'm sure you'll make a great team.'

'We need all of us!' shouted his mother.

'Does that include George and Anna?' he replied sarcastically.

Lady Belvedere was about to return fire when Juan Marco butted in.

'I am working on something for that. I think if we use the right approach we can encourage them to show interest. It may take a little time but I'm optimistic.'

Everyone turned their heads towards him, but Henry was the first to react. 'Well there you are then. Fucking yankee-doodle-dee. You get George and Anna on board and then Bob's your uncle... too many cooks and all that, you won't need an extra pair of hands! Right, I need a drink, catch you all later!'

As he stood to leave, his mother cried: 'Sit down where you are! You will participate in this family and you will play your part in this estate's future! It isn't for you just to dump it on your son!'

Henry looked at his father who gazed in bewilderment, then back to his mother. 'So much anger... so much displeasure... so much disgust. What was it that Lady Catherine de Bourgh said? Something about being seriously displeased? Yeh, that just about sums you up... in a permanent state of disappointment. You just don't accept it do you?' he finished, stalking towards the door.

'Henry!' shouted his mother and father in unison, but he took the two paces to the sideboard adjacent to the door, picked up a drinks decanter, and hurled it at the table, the glass shattering as they recoiled in their seats. Henry stalked out of the room and Lord Belvedere got up to follow him, brushing the glass from his clothes as he moved, but Juan Marco jumped in that he'd go after him, and reached the door first.

'Father, what's wrong with you? Why can't you accept you're part of the family? They're only asking you to help out, not do it all yourself!'

Henry was a third of the way up the staircase as he stopped and turned.

'You don't understand, you could never understand,' he snarled. 'You've had it easy, but I've had nothing but expectation placed on me since I was a boy! I wasn't allowed to grow up. I had to be groomed for the future, their future! Well I'm fucking sick of it! What do they want from me, even now? I bring them you, someone who can be what they need you to be, and still I owe them? Fuck it! I'm going upstairs to get drunk *again*! Don't follow me! I'm sick of this place. I'm getting my things together and disappearing – Spain, London – I don't give a shit. Good luck with it!'

'I'm not yours to give!' flared up Juan Marco. 'I make my own decisions and do what I think is right! You don't tell me what to do! You deceived me persuading me to come back here, but I won't abandon your parents as you are! I care about them and I've been given a job, and I'll do it the best I can!'

'Superman, aren't you? Mr Perfect,' growled Henry as he climbed the stairs.

Chapter 32

Forward Planning

'He's gone,' replied Juan Marco, when Lady Belvedere asked where Henry was as they sat down to dinner that night. 'I saw a taxi arrive and he got in and left with his cases. He's not in a good place, I think. Maybe some time elsewhere will help him find peace.'

She bit her lip before replying: 'I hope that you're right, but I don't think he's ever been able to find peace, especially not here. Maybe you're right, some time away will do him good,' she said quietly.

'He's worse than before, more destructive, I... we... can't have that behaviour. When he comes back we must sit down with him and talk this through,' added her husband. Nobody said anything further while the main course was eaten.

'John, you mustn't forget about the Autumn Fair,' reminded Lady Belvedere a few minutes later. 'It's only two months to go and you're normally at detailed planning stage by now.'

'Oh, I don't think we'll bother with that this year. There's far too much other stuff going on. I've had enquiries from some of the stallholders and caterers already, and I've just parked them for now. I'll have to tell them at some point soon that it's cancelled.'

'I don't think you should,' she replied. 'We should be showing our best face, that we're not in distress. It should be business as usual as far as the outside world can tell. You said yourself that you didn't want any fuss, didn't want any negative publicity over the fraud, wanted to present the same exterior to the world. Well here's the chance. We usually make a profit too, so that's another reason to go ahead with it.'

'What's the Autumn Fair?' chipped in Juan Marco.

'Oh, of course, you haven't been here for one of those, have you? It's a public event in late August where we basically celebrate the old time of harvest. We open up the grounds to the public, have a fair where there are stalls, entertainment, shopping opportunities, food and crafts, things for children to do. John organises a classic car show with Alexander. Some parts of the hall are open to the public, and there's normally themed activities in the old nursery for children to take part in – games, parties, crafts – that sort of thing. It's always a success and we're usually lucky with the weather.'

'Sounds great,' replied Juan Marco. 'It's exactly the sort of thing you should continue, Grandfather.'

Lord Belvedere raised his eyebrows, realising he'd been outvoted.

'The children's activities…that's one thing I'll have to think about,' she continued. 'It was always Lauren that came up with the ideas for that, and she had the creative streak to make it a success. She also had friends in the village that helped with supplying materials, outfits and the like. Damn it. She was always at her best then and she was great with the children. I'll have to take that on. Maybe I'll talk to Mrs Carter and see if she can come up with any ideas, maybe Mrs Tanner too. She's seen so many Autumn Fairs, she's bound to have noticed what's worked the best.'

Neither of the men said anything, but the mention of Lauren's name caused them both to let their minds drift for a few seconds, Juan Marco's for a little longer.

Lady Belvedere contacted their estate-owning friends over the next two days, and took some details of how they'd opened up to the public and added more commercial activities. One of the consultants they'd used matched to a name provided by the auditors, so she left it with her husband to set up a meeting. He was still grumbling to Juan Marco about the organisation of the fair, something that had largely been Robert and Lauren's responsibility before. So his grandson offered to get involved in talking to suppliers, activity and entertainment providers and caterers, if he would talk him through the process. Juan Marco sensed his grandfather needed to commit to the long-term changes that were needed on the estate, and didn't want to give him reasons to delay progress through this diversion.

Lady Belvedere followed up her chat with Mrs Carter by paying a visit to Mrs Tanner at the cottage. After some small talk, Mrs Tanner tentatively asked about the fall-out from the Pritchards' departure.

'Well, I think financially we've about gotten to the bottom of it. It's not good reading, but if he was planning to steal more, which we think he was as the activity level was increasing, then perhaps we've got off more lightly than we should have. John really allowed Robert too much rope, because he's always found him difficult to deal with. He blames himself and so he should, but I think some of the suppliers knew more than they let on. Whether they were in cahoots with Robert I don't know, but the trouble is Robert spoke with the authority of the estate, and when he pushed something through with his usual bravado, they all went along with it.' She sighed before adding: 'Never mind, we'll get through it and have to look to the future now. There's going to have to be some changes, but Juan Marco really is a bundle of energy and ideas, and what we'd do without him, I don't know.'

'Yes, he's a good person I think, strong values. What about Lauren? Is she implicated in any of the dealings?'

'I don't think so,' replied Lady Belvedere, sighing again. 'I think she didn't know what was going on, really, and if she's to blame, it's for not questioning Robert when she had suspicions, rather than any direct involvement. There's no evidence she participated in any of the transactions and I just can't see it really. Of course, John and Henry both feel she's tarred with the same brush and she's guilty by association, but Juan Marco's judgement is rather more sound, I think, and he had some sympathy for her, especially after the assault. Nobody would have told you I expect, but they found her bruised and cut after Robert departed, quite badly I believe, judging by the shock on Juan Marco's face. It looks like he needed to lash out at someone when he saw the game was up, and she was in the firing line.'

'Oh my! That's awful. He always had a determination about him that he'd trample on anyone who got in his way, and I wouldn't have wanted to cross him. His father was so different. Is there any news of where they are?'

Lady Belvedere shook her head. 'No trace of him and we're not looking. Lauren was staying in the village temporarily, but Juan Marco said she was heading back to her parents in Derbyshire.'

'I see. I hope that works out for her,' Mrs Tanner said with concern. 'I understood her relationship with her parents, especially her father, wasn't the best.'

'Oh, don't say that! She's probably been through enough already! Let's hope she can make her own way again in the near future. Oh, isn't it ironic?' she said in exasperation. 'I could have done with her here for the fair! It's still going ahead and I need ideas for the children's activities – she was always so good with that. Can you wrack your brains and think of anything over the next few days that might work? You've seen so many fairs over the years and helped make them happen. Even if it's something that's been done before, if it worked we can use it again. You know the format – any ideas will be appreciated.'

'I'll think on it and let you know. You're right, she always used to come up with something different each time. Even if it was just a tweak, she'd sprinkle her fairy dust and it would all work fine. She was good with the children, although she told me once she didn't want any of her own, which I was surprised at. I thought she'd make a good mum, although I'd have reservations about him as a father, especially if the baby wasn't a boy!' They both laughed nervously.

A few days later in July, Lord and Lady Belvedere and Juan Marco met with the consultants, and agreed on the areas to be reviewed to enhance the estate's income – land sale; leisure facilities; organic farming; public access; special events; retailing and catering. Their report was to be delivered by mid-August. Henry had now been absent from the estate for nine days, the only contact being with his father in the form of a request for a thousand pounds, to help him with some expenses in London. He sent him five hundred reluctantly and didn't tell anyone else about the message.

Juan Marco enjoyed the dealings with the fair stallholders and facilities providers, as it gave him something to focus on besides questions on the running of the estate, a lot of which were going direct to his grandfather rather than through him anyway. He couldn't do anything further on the business plan, but as soon as they received the consultant's report he intended to email a copy to Mary, and encourage his grandmother to send one to Anna. Surely when both read it, they would realise the scale of what had happened and what was now needed? The classic car show was left entirely to Lord Belvedere, whose mood soon improved when returning to deal with such pleasant tasks, albeit he fretted over contacting Alexander to check if he would be involved with the judging again.

A few days later, as usual on a Wednesday morning, Mrs Tanner was sitting in her favourite tea shop in Maidstone, when a youngish woman walked in, her dark hair hidden under a hat, dark glasses, and wearing baggy casual clothes and trainers. She headed for a table against the wall with her back to the street. Mrs Tanner instantly thought the woman was Lauren, but the dress sense didn't seem right. There wasn't the usual sense of style. So she continued with her coffee and cake, while giving the newcomer an occasional glance.

The young lady seemed unsure of herself – she put her shopping bag and handbag on the floor, then she picked them up and put them on the other side of the table, then she moved them to the other chair. She raised her hat then left it where it was. She tried to take off her dark glasses but the hat got in the way, leading to the woman giving a huff. Finally, she gave up, and took the hat and the dark glasses off to choose something from the menu, quickly putting the glasses straight back on. The waitress came over to take her order and Mrs Tanner stole another look at her as the woman briefly glanced around, her eyes locking onto Mrs Tanner's with horror. They held each other's gaze for two seconds before the older woman gave a warm smile of reassurance, and mouthed 'hello' across the room.

Lauren was briefly stunned, but then stood and reached for her hat and shopping, looking for a quick escape, only to hear the light scrape of the chair legs on the floor as Mrs Tanner moved her seat back, and stood up. Again, there was a kind shake of the head, with a gesture to join her at her table. Lauren stood frozen, bags and hat in hand, other heads beginning to turn towards her, and then the waitress was walking towards her with the coffee. She just wanted the ground to open up. Instead, there was a gentle call from the other side of the room: 'Can you bring the drink to this table please? My friend's going to join me.'

Lauren watched as the waitress headed to the other table after giving her a quick smile, and with heads still looking at her, decided the least noticeable thing to do was to join Mrs Tanner. Her cover, if she'd ever had any, was blown.

'How are you? Are you back with us now or is it just a short visit? I understood you might be staying with your parents?'

The younger woman's face sank as she replied: 'Staying there is never a long-term thing. There's only so much opinion-giving and criticism that someone can take.'

'So are you staying locally again?'

'Just for a short while, with one of my friends in the village, before I go for a job in Canterbury. If I get it I'm going to move there. It will have to be cheap so maybe just a bedsit to start, but I'll be away from here and can attempt a new start.'

330

'I'm sorry for you with what's happened. I mean, I don't know the whole story, obviously, but Lady Belvedere let slip they couldn't attach any blame to you. That is, they don't think you were part of the missing money.'

'But I'm guilty by association and for not asking the right questions, I understand that all right,' Lauren shrugged. 'Of course I didn't steal any money, but that hardly seems to matter, does it? I'm a part of it whichever way you look at it.'

Mrs Tanner nodded slowly. 'I know it must seem bad right now but it's Robert they blame. What's the job you're going for?'

'Retail assistant in a clothes store. It's nothing special but it's a start.'

'Have you heard anything from Robert?' Mrs Tanner asked edgily. Lauren looked seriously back at her and shook her head.

'No, and I don't want to either. I don't care what happens to him, whether they find him or not makes no difference to me.'

Mrs Tanner nodded. 'Are you all right though?'

Again, there was another long look between them before Lauren answered. 'You don't have to worry about me. I'm tough and can take care of myself. It's better being that way. Let's just say I won't be making the same mistake again. I was naïve, I trusted someone without listening to my instincts, and fell flat on the floor. I guarantee that won't happen again,' she said determinedly. 'I suppose our names are mud at the hall. The whole estate and village will be talking about it, hence why I'm trying to keep a low profile – not always successfully!' She managed a half-smile before continuing. 'I've got good friends here and they'll look after me until I can get to Canterbury. They give me privacy.'

'I'm glad you've still got connections here. It was your home village and it would be nice if you can find some comfort around there. All the talk is about Robert, I assure you. I don't believe anyone's tying you to what he did, indeed I think there's a great deal of sympathy towards you...' She cut her words short as Lauren's face hardened.

'Sympathy for the stupid little girl who got herself under the thumb of the bully! Ha! People love juicy details. I bet they're making up jokes about me losing a boxing contest!' Mrs Tanner shook her head and tried to speak but Lauren continued. 'Who blabbed then? Who's been telling the jokes?'

'I can only tell you what I know. But Lady Belvedere felt very sorry for you and she was genuinely concerned, partly because Juan Marco was very sensitive to what you'd been through.' Lauren looked up at the mention of his name, and her face showed something Mrs Tanner couldn't quite work out – regret, remorse?

'He's decent enough,' Lauren replied, recovering her composure. 'He's doing what needs to be done for the sake of the family and the estate. I can't blame him for that.'

Mrs Tanner thought for a few seconds before replying. 'Yes, I think you're right. Doing the right thing seems to sit well with him. He shows maturity beyond his years and a strong sense of treating people with respect. Maybe that's his Spanish upbringing or it's just him, I don't know. You know I shouldn't say this, but Lady Belvedere mentioned you the other day in connection with the Autumn Fair. They're still doing it this year, so they send a message to the community that they're moving on and it's business as usual. She asked me for ideas for the children's activities. She said you were so good at them and she would miss you.'

'Humph. I guess I had my uses! There's not much chance of me doing anything like that for a while. I had thought of doing my training to become a teaching assistant or even a teacher next year. I'm not sure I'm cut out for clothing retailing on a permanent basis.'

'I think you'd be good at either of those. You are good with children; you know how to appeal to their sense of imagination. But don't lose all hope of other things, you never know what might come around.' Lauren shrugged her shoulders resignedly.

'I couldn't be cheeky, could I?' Mrs Tanner added. 'Lady Belvedere asked me if I had any ideas for the children's activities, even recycling something that's been done before. You wouldn't be able to think of something over a couple of days, would you? I'm sure we can come up with something, but you always had such good ideas! Sorry for asking. On second thoughts, scrub that, how could I be so insensitive? Just ignore me.'

Lauren screwed up her face and shrugged her shoulders again. 'Well, what does it matter? I can tell you what I was going to do anyway. I'd already had the idea after last year's fair. If you want to use it, use it, if you think of something better then ditch it. It's all the same to me. I was going to get children from the primary school to give a guided tour of the farm harvesting processes. You know, get them dressed up in typical farm wear, with different children working on different parts of the trail, that sort of thing. Some of them can be taught to talk about what happens to grain, barley, rape, apples, all that stuff. Then the visitors go on to other bits where the children talk about livestock on the farm – the birthing cycle, how different animals affect the land, what they need for grazing. Sort of a whistle-stop tour of farming, but given by the children and aimed at children. I thought it would be fun. Then inside the nursery, I was going to suggest having different samples of the crops and getting children to touch and feel them, see if they can remember which products they end up in, maybe have a go at stripping wheat ears. They'd be a mini-tractor area with plastic tractors with buckets, where the children can drive through gates and take cereals out of one area and transport them to another. I thought that would be fun too. Maybe that bit would have to be outside, but there's enough driveway around the hall to have several children on tractors at any one time.'

Mrs Tanner looked at her thoughtfully. 'Hmm. Sounds like an idea. I'll have a ponder. Of course, if we used it I don't think I'd be able to take the credit for it, I mean that would be cheating. I'd never be able to claim it as my own idea. She'd never stop asking me to get involved in the future!'

Lauren chuckled before answering. 'Well I think you'll have to. I hardly think mentioning my name would help. Maybe you could say you spoke to someone on the estate who remembered something I'd said to them before? Also, I'd already talked to the school head about it just after the Easter break.' Mrs Tanner raised her eyebrows to indicate that was possible.

'What about all the costumes though? I know you used to make some of them yourself but you had help from the village, didn't you?'

Lauren nodded. 'Yes, some of my friends helped out. We never needed more than, say, ten uniforms. I daresay they'd help you again.'

'Really, after you not being on the estate any more?'

'Yes, that's a point, I wasn't thinking. I could have a word if you liked, obviously if you don't come up with a better idea? They all enjoyed the fair, and if I said I wanted them to continue to be a part of it they'd respect my request, I think.'

After five more minutes of chatting Lauren rose and said her goodbyes, taking the best wishes of Mrs Tanner with her, and her hope that she'd see her again soon.

Chapter 33

Homecomings

Mrs Tanner couldn't offer up Lauren's ideas directly to Lady Belvedere without being troubled by her conscience. But the more she thought about them, the more appealing they became. They combined all the best points from previous fairs, and using children to tell the farming story was a sure-fire way of appealing to a younger audience, who would inevitably attend with their families. School children would love the opportunity to perform to an audience too. She decided to send Lady Belvedere an email sketching out the details, with a comment that she'd heard it from one of her friends in the village, who'd heard it direct from Lauren after last year's fair. There was no way she couldn't give credit to the rightful person.

Lady Belvedere rang to thank her and say how much she loved the idea, but she was concerned about the lack of honour in using something from a person they'd thrown out on her ear! Mrs Tanner found herself feeling duplicitous, not for the first time in the last few months, but said if they couldn't come up with something better they should give credit in the programme notes. Then at least they were being honest and respectful, something the local community might appreciate, particularly as Lauren had many friends in the village. This placated some of Lady Belvedere's scruples.

As she thought about some of the things she'd witnessed over the past few months, Mrs Tanner's thoughts turned to Juan Marco. Since his return, she hadn't seen him except from a distance, but had sent him a handwritten note sympathising about the loss of his mother, and suggesting he come over for a chat whenever he was ready. She'd not heard back from him and it had been more than two months now, but she could only assume his memories were still too sensitive for him. Besides, recent events had rather taken over his priorities. Nevertheless, she wanted to contact him again to renew their friendship, and offer her support with everything that had been

334

going on. It was clear from Lady Belvedere's own words that he had a key part to play in shaping the estate's future.

As she had his mobile number, she sent him a text message asking if he'd like to pop in for coffee. When he received the message, his heart jumped – it jolted him into thinking about his mother. But it also reminded him that Mrs Tanner had been such a good friend to her, and he'd entirely shut her out since his return, which was neither friendly nor sensitive, considering how generous she'd been. He'd thrown a lot of his energy into estate things in the past few weeks. Perhaps that was masking his need to face up to his feelings, and those of someone else who'd cared for his mother. He replied to her that he'd come over on Tuesday afternoon.

When they met there was polite civility to start with, and he thought he was doing pretty well, but when Mrs Tanner asked about her last hours his voice broke, and she came and sat by him, the tears flowing from both of them as they comforted each other.

After he'd recovered, they spoke about plans for the estate. She assured him that whatever he told her would be kept in strictest confidence. He ended by saying he was now helping to organise the Autumn Fair and how much fun that was, especially as it was ironic they were using an idea of Lauren's for the children's activities.

'You're OK with it, though?' she asked.

'Yes, it feels like a really good idea to me, although whether we can make it happen like she would, I don't know. My grandmother has spoken to the head at the local school and they're meeting to discuss writing the scripts the children will learn. They are about to break for the school holidays, so it will have to be learnt during then. I understand you're talking to some people in the village about making some costumes?' Mrs Tanner nodded. 'That's good, I think it's really great the village is trying to get past what has happened, and that Lauren's friends feel they still want to help.' Mrs Tanner gave a wry smile before asking him a question.

'You found her after Robert left, I understand?' He nodded.

'I can't believe what he did to her, the bastard. In my country, when a man hits a woman like that both families make him pay!'

'You were kind to her, I think?'

'Of course! Whatever she did or didn't do, and I don't think she was mixed up in his plans, to take it out on her in that way was cowardly! If I'd seen him do that, I'd have punched him hard! Her face was such a mess. I

335

wanted her to go to hospital, I was concerned about her eye, but she wouldn't have it. I wish there was some way of finding out she's OK – it troubles me.'

'My suspicion is that she's probably OK, Juan Marco. She still has friends in the village that know people on the estate. If there was any lasting damage, I suspect word would have got around.'

'I hope so, she didn't deserve that. She was always kind to me and she did try to be helpful, it's just that Robert kept her in the dark. I don't blame her for the fraud – I'm sure she wasn't part of it. You know, Mrs Tanner, I think she was a good person, someone who contributed to the life of the estate and I think we will miss her, which brings me back to the fair. She's still involved in a way. Some of the other things we're looking at, she could have been a part of those too. I think she had the ability to do successful things that would also have made a profit. You think she's OK?'

'Yes, I do. Perhaps her future will be different but she'll have learnt some things about herself in all this, and I expect she'll come out stronger. You would wish her well for the future?'

'Oh yes, definitely,' he said with keenness, leaving Mrs Tanner with an odd thought.

As a matter of courtesy, Mrs Tanner messaged Lauren to let her know that the family were going to use her idea for the Autumn Fair, and would she mind speaking to her friends to gauge their willingness to help with costumes. She was pleased to advise her idea would be properly credited in the programme, and she hoped that gave her some comfort. Although she understood how difficult things appeared at the moment, she'd be very happy if Lauren wanted to be involved any more, in a background sort of way. Lauren replied saying she didn't want the credit, but she'd speak to her friends and they should be able to manage. If they couldn't then she'd help out, if they asked her to.

Progress continued over the next few days, with Juan Marco organising the construction of temporary pens for the animals that would feature in the story trail. Local farmers also helped out, and even Lord Belvedere made calls to borrow some children's tractors, in between agreeing the terms with individual stallholders and catering providers. He and Juan Marco also spent some time responding to requests for information from the consultants, who were preparing the estate business plan and feasibility study.

Nobody initially noticed Henry's return to the estate. He arrived at midnight, slipping into the hall via the domestic entrance, responding to the surprised looks from the two of the staff with just a jerk of his head in their direction. He looked tired, gaunt and sombre. He didn't leave his room the whole of the next day, and Lady Belvedere's gentle knocking on the door went unanswered. His father hadn't forgotten Henry's outburst at the last dinner, and was reluctant to make any move until his son had come to him with an apology. There was stalemate therefore, until Juan Marco saw his father sitting in the private garden, still in his dressing gown, the following afternoon. He approached him quietly from behind, speaking as he took the last couple of steps.

'Hello, Father. You've been quiet since you returned.' Juan Marco frowned as his father looked up at him, shocked at how unwell he looked.

'Don't judge me,' he replied slowly. 'I've enough trouble judging myself, though God knows what's the point. All I want is a little happiness. Is that so hard to achieve?'

'Where did you go?'

'London, with friends...' he snorted, as if the description brought back unpleasant memories.

'You need rest and food.' Henry looked up at him with a soulless expression. 'You must take a break from alcohol, too.'

'I don't think you understand its purpose, its calming effect. It's my friend, my staple, always there for me.'

'It's not there for you, it's not helping you. It's masking things, stopping you being who you want to be.'

'Bullshit. You haven't a clue who I am. Don't try amateur psychology on me, boy, there are people far more experienced than you who've failed with their wise words. Save it.'

'I'm worried about you. We all are. There's so much going on and that you're a part of. We want you to be involved, to continue the good work you started.'

'Oh please, Juan Marco! Don't pretend that I did this for me! It was a way to get you back here and help these people out, you know that! I knew you'd carry it off, drive it forwards, give them a future to believe in. I was never part of that.'

'They're your family! You are a part of it. You recognised a wrong and wanted to help right it.'

'Yeah, right, I'm a fucking saint! The hero returns! Please, save it. I haven't lifted a finger since I got back and don't intend to. I can't.'

'I want you to get better, get—'

'Treatment? For my sickness? My little fever? My little ups and downs? Yes, that's it, a little treatment and then after a few pills it's all going to be all right again. Don't believe fucking fairy stories, Juan Marco.'

'You need help. There are people who will give it to you, starting with your family. Me! I've lost one parent already, have you forgotten that?'

'Please, it's a bit much to start using responsible terms like "parent"! That implies I've done something for you – I've done fuck all. You've turned out the way you did because of nothing I've done! In fact, my absence is probably the reason why you've turned out like this!'

'Stop it, just stop talking like that! My mother saw something in you once. It didn't last, but she wouldn't have married you if she thought there was no hope for you!'

'Hope? Now that's a strange word. Hope. Hope of being happy for instance. Now we're back at the start. Do me a favour, just leave me alone. I don't want anything else.'

'I'll give you what you want for this moment, if you give me something that I want for this moment! Is that fair?'

'Depends on what it is…'

'Don't drink, for one day, today. That's it, just today. Then tomorrow, I give you something again, and you give me something back, just for one day. Little by little, *poco o poco* as we say at home.'

'Forget it. Nice try, Juan Marco. I won't drink today, but only because I feel shit and not because I don't want to. Now just go.' His downcast son didn't raise his eyes, but did as he was asked and walked back to the hall.

Henry kept out of the way of the family for the next few days, only appearing occasionally for dinner, when he drank more than he ate. His parents wanted to ask him to slow down, but his sullen mood wasn't conducive to conversation, and their gently-expressed concerns about his health and seeing a doctor were pushed away dismissively. Henry claimed he'd picked up a bug in London which made it hard to keep food down. If they asked him about his health again, he changed the subject to the estate and the consultant's report to deflect them, saying the delivery of the report would give him a big project to focus on, which he was looking forward to.

Just four days later, the consultants rang Lord Belvedere to say the

338

report was ready, and asked if they wanted a meeting to present its findings. This was declined as he wanted an opportunity to read it first. It was emailed to him and Juan Marco, and the latter dived in as quickly as he could, racing through the sections on what was, and was not recommended, and the cost-benefit analysis of each measure. He sought out his grandparents to gauge their views and was disappointed that Lady Belvedere said she hadn't had time to read it, and his grandfather had really only looked at the financials. All Juan Marco could see was opportunity for the estate – more private events, selling off small parts of the land, leisure-use possibilities, a farm shop and café – all received a positive review, and there was a strong case put forward to at least start farming some areas organically. The three of them agreed to meet with Henry at the end of the week, to allow them all an opportunity to study the proposals. In the meantime, Juan Marco told his grandmother he was going to send a copy to Mary, as part of his attempt to influence her and George's future interest. He suggested she also sent a copy to Anna. Lady Belvedere frowned, and said she'd consider it once she'd read the report herself.

By Friday, they were all ready to meet and discuss the way forwards, and had deliberately agreed an afternoon meeting to give Henry two chances to eat something beforehand. They sat in Lord Belvedere's study waiting for him to appear, but when there was no sign of him Juan Marco went to check his room. His knocks and calls went unanswered, but when he tried the handle the door was locked, so either Henry was still in bed or had gone out and locked the room behind him.

Juan Marco headed back to his grandparents to obtain a spare key and tried it in the lock, but there was obviously a key in it from the inside. He tried knocking again and shouting but with no response. By now his nerves were jangling, memories flooding back of discovering his mother in her bed. He ran back to the study, telling his grandparents in a panicked voice they needed to get into the room. Could one of the estate workers remove the lock, or could one of the gardeners use a ladder to see into the room from outside?

Lady Belvedere asked her husband to go and find one of the gardeners, while she and Juan Marco headed to the housekeeper's room to find out who was available. But as soon as her husband had disappeared she looked ashenly at him.

'The doors are heavy, but do what you have to do to break it down!

Fetch a tool, anything, but just get in there!'

Juan Marco ran to the hall garden shed and the door was already swinging open, so someone was around. He grabbed a small sledgehammer and ran back to the room, swinging it with all his strength at the lock. The door shuddered and metal parts jangled. He swung twice more and the sound pitch went higher as the door started to move. Two more swings and he felt it was giving, then two more and it was free. He threw it open, and saw his father lying on the bed on his back, pale, stiff and silent. His grandmother followed him in, and he turned to her instinctively to tell her not to look, but she shook her head at him.

'I want to see him. He's dead isn't he?'

After years of excessive drinking, Henry's liver and heart had finally given in. He was dead at the age of thirty-six. The hall was plunged into despair and sadness, Lord Belvedere struggling to contemplate his thoughts, his wife crushed by the loss of her beautiful, wayward, first-born child, and Juan Marco stunned and left parentless at the age of nineteen.

George and Anna both took the news in silence, the former pledging to leave Lincolnshire the next day, and Anna would leave Singapore within two days if flights would allow. Their parents started on the rounds informing family and friends and contacting the funeral directors. There would be three weeks before the funeral could take place, their wishes being that his body be cremated and the ashes returned to the estate, for internment in the family vault.

With the funeral scheduled for just shy of two weeks after the Autumn Fair, Lord Belvedere couldn't countenance the latter going ahead, and slowly started to contact suppliers to tell them it was cancelled. His wife went along with him, but in truth couldn't offer any opinion one way or the other. But after George and Mary and Anna and Alexander had arrived, and she'd seen how cool they were towards Juan Marco, she began to fret. Their grandson had become such a part of the future of the estate over the past few weeks, and now she could see he felt relegated and out of sorts.

He'd lost his mother and father. It was inevitable there would be further conflict between him and George over the inheritance. His temptation, perhaps even his desire, would be to take himself away and head back to Spain. These thoughts caused her huge pain, as she saw the sensitivity and straightforwardness of this young man that she'd grown to love, walking away from them. He had brought such energy and self-belief to her and her husband over the previous weeks. The thought of now losing him was too much to bear.

Just the day before Henry had died, Lady Belvedere had sent a copy of the consultant's report to Alexander, thinking it stood more chance of coming to Anna's intention if he read it first. Knowing that Juan Marco had also sent a copy to Mary, on an afternoon a few days later, she asked them both to accompany her on a walk to some of Henry's favourite childhood parts of the estate. They both were expecting what was coming, although neither had discussed the report with each other.

'Mary, what did you make of the consultant's report on the future of the estate? Did you see anything in it?'

Mary blushed and glanced at Alexander, who wore a similar expression.

'Well, it's radical, I mean compared to what's gone before, but it read OK. I mean a lot of it is modernising really, bringing the estate up to date. It's not really frightening stuff.'

'Alexander, what did you make of it?'

'Er, well, farming's not really my speciality as you know, but I glanced through it and I agree that it's not really radical. It seems to make a lot of sense.'

'Uh-huh. And have either of you shown it to your other halves?'

They both gulped silently, waiting for the other to say something. No one was forthcoming.

'Mary, have you talked to George about it?'

'I tried. I printed out a copy of the executive summary for him and told him he should read it, but…'

'He refused, no doubt?' Mary nodded. 'Alexander?'

'Well I haven't brought the subject up, to be honest. Not sure how to go about it.'

'I see. Well you should both know that I believe in the plans, and John will too before much longer. When we've got through our present unhappiness, we'll have to deal with the issues which aren't going away. Mary, I want your support, is that clear? There could be a huge role for you to play in the success of this estate in the future, and I want you and George fully on board. I, we, will speak to him, but I absolutely expect you to back us up. Do you understand?' Mary nodded. 'Now Alexander, I know that farming isn't your thing and, to be honest, it isn't Anna's either, and I'm not trying to change your lives or careers – we fully respect what you've both achieved and no one's planning on dragging you back here against your will. But I want you to insist that Anna listens to the business case for what needs doing. She'll understand that I'm sure, and I want her to respect those people who will play a significant role in making sure change happens. Is that clear?'

'Absolutely, I'll try my best,' he said without conviction. 'You will talk to her also?'

'Of course. Now there's one other thing. Both of you probably don't know, but should know, how important Juan Marco is to the estate. He has some knowledge, is learning all the time, has all the communication skills that could ever be needed, and he is a doer, not a shirker. He will take charge when asked but he also gets his hands dirty. He's not above doing anything. In addition to that, your father-in-law and I have grown fond of him and, well' – she put her hand up to her mouth to catch her cry – 'to love him. He's Henry's son, and if I'm very much not mistaken he could be the best of us!'

She buried her face in her hands and Mary took her in her arms, with Alexander encircling them both as all three cried. After two minutes she managed to continue.

'We've lost Henry and I don't want to lose Juan Marco. He's here for a few months being paid to help us, but he's more than that now, he's part of the family. I know he feels like he doesn't belong. Well that's got to change. If he wants to go back to Spain and he's insistent, then we can't stand in his way. But I want him to know there's a place for him here, and it's a huge place. He can be such a big part of the estate's future too, and, Mary, he's next in line to the title and the estate, and it will be his choice if he passes up on that, not ours. Do you understand? I know you'll be loyal to George and so you should be, but Juan Marco's been here for most of the past few months and he doesn't have any of the baggage of the past. He just gets on with things, and I think he can be all the sorts of things that Henry couldn't. We want you and George here with us playing your part, but Juan Marco's Henry's son, and nothing can change that.'

Mary swallowed, hating the job she was being given as peacemaker. She nodded glumly. 'It's going to be awful coming between them. George could really help on the estate management side, but I'm not sure about his business skills, and Juan Marco is so good at communication. I'll try.'

'Good. Alexander, I want you to tell Anna that we'll be having a meeting next week about the estate's future. We can't delay because of the way things have gone recently, even with Henry's funeral. Tell her what you've seen in the report, about the ideas, and if she reacts and says she's not going to get involved, then tell her we want her positive support for making things happen. If you have to, ask her who she's going to back, or something like that. Please, find a way to get her attention. Oh and that reminds me. I'm not being nasty, but the first section of the report deals with the losses from Robert's activities – I imagine that will cause her some embarrassment as she was such a strong supporter of his. Well, there's no blame attached to her, but she needs to understand what he was actually doing. I hope if you can get her to see that, it might calm her down a little.'

Alexander nodded before replying: 'Yes it's not comfortable reading, is it? I bit my lip when I glanced at that section. She is going to have to come to terms with it.'

'OK, there's one other thing I've been thinking about. The Autumn Fair is not long before Henry's funeral, and John's already started cancelling the retailers and caterers. I'm not sure we're doing the right thing. Plans are underway. The children will be leading the public tours which will lighten the mood so much. Juan Marco's got involved with many of the commercial enterprises, and is organising the layout. As well as wanting to look forwards, it's a way of showing him that he's still needed. Don't get me wrong, I think we could all do with some brightness right now. I want to show our best face, and if we cancel I think he will get the wrong message. What do you think?'

'It seems an odd time to be doing it so close to the funeral,' said Mary. 'A bit too soon.'

'Have you spoken to John?' asked Alexander.

'No, he's just working on autopilot, I think. Right, I need to speak to him.'

When Caroline returned to the hall she found her husband in the small sitting room, going over the list of guests for Henry's funeral. He put the papers down as she entered.

'Did that do you any good?' he enquired.

'Yes it did. And no. It was good to meet them away from Anna and George. They're more neutral and in that way it's easier to talk to them. I've told them the changes we need to make to the way we run the estate have to happen, and we want their support. I know it's difficult with the funeral, but Anna and George will have to go away again before it, so we need to deal with the decisions now. Then when they come back, it will just be for Henry.'

Lord Belvedere nodded.

'John, there's something else. I'm concerned we're doing the wrong thing by cancelling the Autumn Fair. I know it seems indecent allowing it to go ahead before we've said goodbye to Henry, but God knows I think we need something to raise our spirits.'

'Oh, I can't face that!'

'Well, what about a delay? Could we try and push it back two weeks? It's always a happy event and we need to show the world that we'll get through this. If we had George and Juan Marco there, working as a team, that would engender such goodwill towards us. I'm sure we'd all find comfort in it!'

'There's as much chance of that as me running a marathon! It's too soon, Caroline. I think we have to let it go for this year.'

'What about Juan Marco? You can see his discomfort, can't you? He feels the loss too, but he's even more emotionally confused than the rest of us. I'm sure he feels like a spare part at the moment. He wants to drive on with the proposals from the report, and if we're delaying that, for good reason, then at least organising the fair gives him something to do, to keep his mind off returning to Spain. His mind must be drifting that way, you must know that!'

'But he's here helping us with the plans. He won't just abandon us.'

'Oh John, I'm not sure he feels a part of us, the family! How can he, when Anna and George are so cold towards him? We have to make him feel needed, loved! He's our grandson and Henry's son. He carries our blood in his veins. I can't face losing him too!' Her face collapsed into tears, and her husband rose to envelope her in his arms, tears forming slowly in his eyes too.

'We should talk to him gently,' he said after a minute. 'Let him know what we think of him. He has proved himself to be very much part of this family. I know we need to meet next week about the consultant's report before Anna and George go. I'm not looking forward to it in some ways. You know what I mean, but we need Juan Marco. We just want the others to work with him.'

That afternoon they met with Juan Marco in the study.

'How are you feeling, Juan Marco, with all the planning going on around you for the funeral? You must feel shocked,' Lady Belvedere started. He nodded, his eyes distant and disengaged. 'We know everything else must feel like it's on hold, but it can't be for long. That's why we must sit down with all the family early next week to talk about the development of the estate, while George and Anna are still here. They'll both have to go away again before the funeral and then return. We're behind making the changes, and I've spoken to both Mary and Alexander and told them we expect their support. You did a good thing sending her a copy of the report, and I'm glad I followed your lead and sent a copy to him before Henry passed away, otherwise we'd be starting from base with Anna. It's important the whole family pulls together, and that includes you. They will see just how important your energy and ideas are. You are still keen to help us with changing things?'

He nodded slowly. 'Everything's been knocked back but the changes still need to happen. I just worry your other children won't want to help because they resent me. Maybe it would be better if I went back to Spain for a while. You can change the family rules on who inherits, can't you? It's not important to me.'

'Things will sort themselves out naturally, Juan Marco,' replied his grandfather. 'The order of things will become clear over time as we all adapt, you don't need to worry about that. Your input and energy have helped to get us through this and we've both become very attached to you, even more so now that, well, you know what I mean. What's important now is that they both, especially George, understand how vital his role could become on the farming side, and he needs to seize that and make it his own, not get stewed up by what he thinks is unfairness in the family line. Anna has a huge part to play in seeing that common sense prevails – everybody has always listened to her and George won't want to lose her support – he'll feel he's guaranteed it. But if she uses her brain and recognises how it can all work for everyone's benefit, then we have reason to be hopeful. Mary is also a very powerful woman. You have a connection to her, don't you? She's a useful ally.' Juan Marco swallowed uncomfortably then nodded.

'Right then,' continued Lord Belvedere, 'there's something else.' He looked at his wife to take the lead.

'Yes, well, we've been thinking about the Autumn Fair. You've done

345

quite a lot of work on it already and we're having second thoughts about cancelling it. Perhaps we need to be getting on with things and trying to return to some sort of normality, even though it will be so soon after Henry's passing. He never took any great interest in the fair, but it might help everyone here deal with his loss by giving us something else to focus on. You could work quietly on it and bring it on, referring to us when you need to? I don't think we'll be much help over the next few days, so we were thinking of a postponement rather than cancellation. Would you be willing to perhaps contact some of the suppliers and see if they have availability later in September? Maybe move the dates back two weeks?'

'Are you sure you can face that?' he replied quietly, looking from one to the other. 'It's still going to be difficult for you.'

'Yes, I think we'll be OK,' she replied calmly. 'Will you make enquiries?'

Chapter 34

The War of the Bloodline

Juan Marco busied himself with contacting suppliers to the fair as agreed with his grandparents. It was heavy going, as some could only honour the original dates, some could change to the following weekend only, some could only do a fortnight later, and others were now fully booked for September. In exasperation, he went to see Mrs Tanner to see if she could offer any help.

'I'm afraid Robert and Lauren looked after the fair in previous years. Lord Belvedere picked up a few bits but it was mainly those two. They had all the contacts for generators, catering, fairground rides, fencing, etc. I'm sorry, but I don't think I'd be much help. Plus, I'm working on the children's activities and I'm really busy with that. We're coordinating the scripts with the teachers and pupils who of course are now all on summer holidays, so there's a lot of chasing about to be done. If it's delayed by a couple of weeks that will help, I suppose.'

Juan Marco looked disappointed. 'I don't want to bother my grandparents. They're still upset and are dealing with the funeral arrangements. I really wanted to be able to handle this myself.'

Mrs Tanner looked thoughtfully. 'Well, it's possible, I mean I believe, that Lauren is contactable, if you think that might be of any use?'

'What? I thought she was with her family?'

'Well, yes, but she's splitting her time I believe between them and some friends in Kent.' Juan Marco eyed her suspiciously so she continued. 'I heard from one of them she's back here looking for employment, I mean in Kent, not in the village. I could find out how to get hold of her if you wanted.'

He frowned at her, only half-believing what she was saying. 'So, you know her friends?'

'I'm not on intimate terms with them Juan Marco, if that's what you mean, but I've spent the last fifty years of my life in and around the village and Lauren grew up here. Of course I know some of the people she knows. I got a message to her that Lady Belvedere wanted to use her idea for the children's activities – I think that was only right. She offered to speak to some of her friends to see if they'd help with the children's costumes, and that was very good of her.'

'That doesn't mean she'd want to help with the rest of the fair. Why would she?'

'I'm not saying she would, but when I spoke to her, briefly, she was very remorseful about what happened and feels she was partly responsible. I think she felt that by helping to organise the costumes and providing drafts for the scripts, she was making a very small reparation.'

'You didn't tell me you'd spoken to her.'

'Juan Marco, did you expect me to reveal that? She spoke to me in confidence as someone who's known her since she was a child. She's been through a lot and she knows her time at the estate is over, and you can't expect her to rush in here and offer to help with things as if nothing's happened. She's looking to get a new job away from here and start again. But perhaps, if you contacted her personally and explained the situation, perhaps she'd help. I can't guarantee it but as you seem desperate… On second thoughts, please forget it. It was a bad idea.'

'I just don't see why she'd get so involved. She must want nothing to do with this place.'

'As I've explained,' replied Mrs Tanner with mild irritation, 'she might feel that in a small way she's helping the estate and the family after all that Robert put them through. I think that's all I can say on the matter.'

Juan Marco stood still looking bemused. 'I couldn't speak to her personally, it wouldn't be right.'

'Well it would have to be between you and her, wouldn't it? You said you wanted to handle it without involving your grandparents. Well there it is. I'm only making a suggestion. She's on the same phone number she had before. Now I must get on, if you'll excuse me.'

Juan Marco left fretting over what to do. He felt it would be inappropriate to ask for her help, but there was an annoying tingle at the prospect of speaking to her. He couldn't be the person to ask her, so decided to ditch the idea. He'd just have to ask some of the grounds staff for help.

In the meantime, Mrs Tanner let Lauren know the fair was being pushed back two weeks because of Henry's funeral.

'OK, that could be tricky,' she told Mrs Tanner. 'A lot of the suppliers will be fully booked in September and if the original dates are moved, they probably won't be able to help. It will be the same with some of the stallholders – September is a surprisingly busy month.'

Mrs Tanner huffed down the phone. 'Tell me about it. I think Juan Marco is getting stressed as he's taken up the reins, as Lord and Lady Belvedere are busy with the funeral arrangements.'

'Yes, gosh they will be. What an awful waste of a life. Henry could be difficult and yet other times he could be so polite. He was a person with a split personality, maybe more than just two parts. It affects Juan Marco too, he must be so confused. Do you think he knows his emotions?'

'I'm not sure. He feels such an obligation to his grandparents and the estate. I don't know whether he's even thought of his own grief, but it must affect him, losing both of his parents at only nineteen.'

'Tell him if needs any help with the fair, I'll do what I can. I don't know how he'd feel about speaking to me, probably embarrassed and unwilling, but the offer's there. Changing the subject, how do you think I should go about requesting a reference from Lady Belvedere for the clothes shop job? I've got through the first interview, the second one's next week, but if I get it they'll want a reference and I don't know what to say. She could easily say no, and then I'm sunk.'

'Let me know how it goes. I'll think about how you can go about it. She must be willing to give you something, even if it's a bit sketchy.'

'OK, thanks. I've got a bit of time on my hands at the moment. I was thinking about running up a couple of designs for the children's costumes. I can do some sketches and borrow a machine from a friend, but I did like my own machine I had up at the farmhouse. Damn, it was bloody expensive, but I couldn't take much when I left, and I feel guilty about using other people's, especially when I'm crashing at their house to start with, and upsetting their routines. The sooner I can get a job the sooner I can get my own place again. Thank God I had some of my own savings!'

'Surely you can go back in and get some of your personal stuff? It's of no use to them.'

'I'd feel awful about taking stuff out when you think about how much Robert's stolen from them! Besides, I think I'd crash into tears if I went inside again.'

Mrs Tanner thought for a moment before replying: 'There must be a way of getting around the complications.'

The Belvedere family meeting on the future of the estate took place the following Tuesday. The body language of the people around the table told its own story. Lord and Lady Belvedere were anxious for everything to run smoothly; Juan Marco looked nervous, as did Alexander and Mary; Anna looked serious and uncomfortable, and George bristly.

Lord Belvedere started off by summarising the estimated losses to the estate from the Pritchard's activities. Anna looked sullen and lowered her head, George triumphant. 'I say again the bastard shouldn't get away with it!'

'George, we know how you feel about this, but your father and I have made our decision. Please respect it. The purpose of today is to find out if you all support the proposals for managing the estate in the future. We are reliant on you all for that, even where we know you won't be able to offer much actual help,' his mother replied as she looked towards Anna and Alexander.

'So, are you asking for Mary and I to return to the hall to run the estate?' George asked forcefully.

'We are very certain that your interest in organic farming will be a huge help, not just for the retained land but also working with the contract farmers. Then there's the commercialisation of what comes out of that – we need as much help as we can get, and you're both ideally placed to become involved, take it on.'

'Right, but you didn't actually answer the question. You're both in charge, that's accepted. But then, and looking to the future, you will work with Mary and I to plot the course?'

'We want all of you to be onside,' she stressed.

'With us being in pole position? I don't want to labour the point, but there's the slightly annoying issue of the ownership of the estate when you're both unfortunately no longer here.'

Lord Belvedere puffed out his cheeks. 'Juan Marco is here and is part of the family. He has a strong interest in helping us turn the estate around and his energy will be needed, George.'

'But he doesn't have any intention of staying here after his work is done. He'll go off back to Spain, and surely he has no interest in the ownership of the estate?'

350

'That's a matter to be decided in the future, not here and now. The focus has to be on moving the finances forward, nothing else.'

'I'm sorry you see it as vaguely as that. For some of us this really is the root and branch of the issue,' replied George testily.

'George!' interrupted his mother. 'Please can we think of the matters at hand? Juan Marco, as part of the family, is willing to commit himself to the plans in the proposals, and that level of support is critical to us.'

George looked dismissively at his nephew, who felt it was time to say something.

'George, it's true that Spain is my home, but I want to help your parents as much as I can with their future plans. For my future, I don't know what that holds, but I won't walk away from them while they need my support, whether that's for six months, a year or maybe longer.'

'Maybe we don't need you as much as they think? Maybe you'd be better off back in Spain doing your own thing.'

'George,' interrupted his mother again, 'he's our grandson, your nephew. You need to get it into your head that he's part of this family!'

George shrugged. 'He's not part of *my* family.'

'That's not true George,' Mary said quietly. 'He has been for a while. Think of the time in Lincolnshire. We both came to respect him and take an interest in him.'

George glared at her. 'You more than me, I think? And to call that taking him into the family? I don't think so.'

'He's been here for ages, more than us. He's become close to your parents, your brother...'

'Whose side are you on?' he asked with intent. 'He's an outsider, never will be anything else—'

'George!' interrupted his mother again, but before she could say anything, Lord Belvedere cut in.

'You don't appreciate, George, just how straightforward being with him is and, like it or not, he's Henry's son. You say he's an outsider, well maybe he started off that way but he's moved closer, as all things move closer or further away over time. Time changes things, which is exactly why we're discussing what we're discussing now. Can we get back to the point please?'

'So, he's moved closer, weaselled his way in, the implication being that we've moved further away? So, he's replaced us? So, it's our fault that you're in this mess?'

'Oh, for God's sake!' huffed Anna, speaking for the first time and stunning the others into silence. 'What difference does it make? You can fight your bloodline war if that's what you want, George. Just stand up and say that's all that matters to you and you've no interest in anything else, and then you can leave! I don't have unlimited time to get into family wars, I'm only here to look at the business issues. We decide if we're willing to support the changes and then I leave. I have a life away from here!'

The room fell into silence before George spoke again. 'So basically, you don't care. Ignore the family, the history, doing the right thing, because you want to get out of here and get back to your own paperwork world.'

'You make yourself sound so committed, George, but it's just committed on your terms, isn't it? Have you actually read the report, made your mind up about which areas you can or can't support? Or is it that *you* don't care, because if you can't be involved on your terms you're going to just walk away? That just leaves Juan Marco then, doesn't it?'

'Don't speak to me like that! You'll be of no bloody use whatever happens in the future. Don't pretend you'll care when you're in Singapore!'

'Enough!' shouted Lord Belvedere. 'Everybody take a two-minute breather!'

The lull lasted for thirty seconds before Anna spoke, ignoring the raised hand from her father.

'The report makes sense to me. I'm in favour. Do what you need to do,' she said, looking at her parents. 'All of it.'

Alexander nodded his approval, then Mary quietly said, 'I agree' as George's head spun round to her in anger.

'What do you think of the land sell-off, George?' added Anna pointedly.

'Over my dead body! Totally unnecessary!' he snapped, looking towards his father, whose eyes immediately lowered, giving him a sense he'd found a winning line.

'I thought you'd say that,' his sister replied dismissively. 'Of course, without the capital investment, development of the shop, café and leisure facilities will all go by the wayside. But please, if you have a plan to raise the funds, then let us in on the secret.'

George scowled at her. 'It's not necessary. Once the higher prices for the organic crops feed through, they'll be no need for extra capital.'

'You're forgetting the money that needs to be spent on the hall too, George,' interrupted Lady Belvedere. 'Plumbing, heating, window repairs, redecoration. There are already two bedrooms we can't use as they're getting damp.'

'You've plenty of others.'

His mother shook her head and silence descended again for a few seconds.

'What do you think, Juan Marco?' Anna ventured as George curled his lip.

'The estate needs capital investment, but it doesn't need to destroy its nature or environment. The areas noted as being suitable are only for small scale development, in areas hidden from the hall in and around the woodland. They're talking about three acres maximum, out of more than two thousand. The move to organic farming will take time, and any housing development has no impact on farming activities.'

'Do you work for the consultancy by any chance, Juan Marco?' George chipped in sarcastically.

'OK, I think we've heard enough,' said Lord Belvedere. 'Your mother and I, reluctantly on my part, feel the time for change is now. We have to modernise and spread the load so the burden is shared for the future. We need support and commitment and energy. There's the land sale, farming and commercial activities to consider – what are you all in for? Anna and Alexander – we just want to know we have your full support and a willingness from you to keep our minds focused on the financial details – to make sure we see a return from what we spend.' He looked around the table at each of them in turn.

Juan Marco nodded. 'I'll help with everything.'

George sneered at him. 'Snake!'

Lady Belvedere slapped her hand on the table and glared at him.

Mary sat with her head down and a look of being lost. 'I want to help,' she said quietly, feeling the heat from George's stare.

'There's no one around this table other than us who can pull off the farming changes!'

Anna looked at Alexander and said clearly for them both: 'All of it.'

'Then we move ahead on all the proposals,' said Lord Belvedere, turning to George and adding, 'including land divesture. Now that's agreed, I know you'll all be keen to get on your way. Safe travels, and when you come back here for the funeral, I hope you'll all be able to give Henry the dignified and personal send-off he deserves.' He rose from his chair and offered his hand to his wife as their eyes locked.

Juan Marco left the meeting in shock after the savage attacks by George. Everyone else seemed to be able to grasp the issues, but George had made it clear he wasn't going to work with him. Half of him wanted to leave this all behind, but the other half couldn't but feel his support was needed to keep things on track. With George around, things would be ignored and diced up as he saw fit. None of this helped with the Autumn Fair, which was still hanging around his shoulders like a millstone. Cancelling it now seemed positively attractive, yet if he could pull it off and cope with the public interest in him and the estate, then it might help to bring George to his senses. He needed help and fast, so it was time to test the water with Lauren.

He sent her a text asking if she was OK, and saying that he'd spoken to Mrs Tanner recently. He wished her well with job hunting and asked how it was going. She replied that there was plenty to apply for, even if it didn't entirely fit her needs. She sensed he was fishing, and when he didn't immediately reply she sent him another text, asking how the fair planning was going. He breathed a sigh of relief at the easy introduction, and then told her the status and options. Her next message was to the point: *do you need a hand?* This seemed too easy, but she would surely know what was possible and what wasn't, so he laid out in numbers who could and couldn't do each date. She replied asking for an email with the up-to-date attendance plan. She'd make some calls once she had his email.

That evening, as the weight seemed lighter on his shoulders, he thought for the first time about the funeral. It was unreal that within four months of each other, he was attending both his parents' funerals. Eyes would be on him as Henry's son. It would be a sombre affair, his emotions could run away with him. He was so glad his grandmother had said he should sit next to them at the service. They could support each other in their pain. The only way through this would be with their shared love and, in turn, he owed them his support with the estate.

Chapter 35

Opening and Closing Doors

Lauren phoned Juan Marco two days later to give him an update.

'Do you have time for me to run through things? OK, well here it is. The original dates can just about be salvaged but there will be some gaps. A week later is a disaster. Two weeks later can be done but some of the suppliers will change. I can't mince words here Juan Marco. I need an immediate decision on what you want, I mean what the family want. Some people are provisional only and need an answer in twenty-four hours. They've got other events trying to book them too. It has to be quick. You've also got to bear in mind that you, or someone from the estate, will have to give official instructions for the bookings. I have used my contacts but they know I don't represent the estate anymore.'

'OK, I'll check with my grandparents. Thanks, Lauren. I don't know what I'd have done without you, really.'

'Well, there is something I want in return. I'd like access to the farmhouse. There are some small personal items I'd like to take away, but also I have a fantastic sewing machine I'd like to take away or use in situ, to run up some designs for the children's costumes. It won't take more than a couple of hours, or maybe you could help me take it to Mrs Tanner's, who's got more space for work than where I'm staying now. That's if it's OK for me to spend a small amount of time on the estate.'

'Yes, of course. I'm so grateful. When do you want the machine?'

'It's Wednesday today, how about Saturday morning?'

'OK, we'll meet at the farmhouse. Can you come through the side gate off the lane? I'll be there to let you in.'

Lord and Lady Belvedere were relieved the fair could go ahead with the delay. Even though they both knew the future was going to require significant changes, they needed some time to grieve for their son. Juan Marco messaged Lauren that a fortnight later was the chosen option, and they agreed to share confirmation of the bookings between them. Lauren also volunteered to organise the advertising as she'd always taken care of that in the past. He knew that at some point he'd have to tell his grandparents just how involved she'd become, but this wasn't the time or place.

The two of them met at the gate by the lane just before eleven on Saturday. He swung the gate open and locked it behind them and they drove separately to the farmhouse. Lauren stared at the farmhouse as she got out of her car. Until four months ago this had been her home, and the estate her working life; she'd been settled and happy, and now it was all in the past. Juan Marco saw her downcast look.

'Are you OK? Take your time. I can go and fetch the machine if you tell me where it is.'

She shook her head. 'No, there's other things I need to pick up too, I know where to look.' She exhaled loudly and walked slowly towards the door, standing aside to let him open up. As she walked into the lounge she exhaled again as he stood behind her, feeling useless. The machine was on the table against the front window and he picked it up and carried it to her car, while she stayed inside. As he went back inside, he thought about whether he should give her some space.

'Do you need me for anything else?' he called out from the hallway.

'No, I'll be fine,' she replied waveringly, so he stepped back outside and walked around the exterior to check that everything was still secure. He saw her move between the front two bedrooms, and after ten minutes she came out with a small case and a plastic bag. It was obvious she'd been crying.

'That's it,' she stuttered. 'I don't need anything else. Can you help me unload the sewing machine at the cottage, if that's still OK?'

He nodded. 'Lauren...'

'No, it's OK, we can go now.'

He nodded again and they drove to Mrs Tanner's cottage separately, where he carried the sewing machine into her dining room.

'Thanks, Juan Marco, and for letting me work from here. I'll be here tomorrow, Mrs Tanner, with the materials if that's OK?' She started to walk the few paces to her car when Juan Marco called out.

'Lauren, thanks again for your help on the fair. We'll have to stay in contact over the next few days.' She turned as she opened her car door and nodded back at him, before getting into her vehicle. He followed her to the main gate where he unlocked it and let her out. Back at the cottage Mrs Tanner stood outside as they drove away, wondering whether the fact that his eyes had hardly left Lauren meant anything other than concern for her welfare.

A few minutes later, he returned to the cottage to catch up with Mrs Tanner's progress on the children's activities for the fair. She looked a little embarrassed.

'To be honest, Juan Marco, it's going well, although I'm ashamed to admit how much Lauren's taken over. She's helping the school with the scripts and will go to two rehearsals next week. There's the costumes, she found out where the toy tractors were coming from and changed the dates, she gave me contact details for the livestock farmers, she's given me her ideas for how to set the nursery up in the hall... I mean I should really have said no at some point, but I was weak and I suppose felt that her keeping busy was a good thing because there's only so much job hunting that you can do.'

'I hope she's not taking on too much. She's given me a copy of last year's plan of the site and the various activities, and she's updated it with progress so far. I'm leaning on her too, more than I should. This was supposed to be my project.'

'Well, we'll both feel guilty together,' she replied light-heartedly. 'Perhaps she recognises you've got a difficult weekend coming up and you might not feel too enthusiastic when it's all over. If you want to drop in sometime this week, to talk about anything, please do. Don't bottle things up if there's no one to talk to.'

'OK, thank you. I must go to the hall now as I'm going with my grandfather to a tailor's for a suit-fitting. Perhaps I'll see you this week.'

Lauren arrived at the cottage on the Sunday morning as planned and set about running up her designs. They made small talk, with Lauren being tight-lipped about anything other than the fair, except for disclosing that the second interview for the clothes job was this week. Mrs Tanner tried to engage her in conversation about Juan Marco but she still didn't get much back. 'He's coping very well I imagine, he has good instincts. It must be awful for him so I'll help him all I can. It's not much really, only updating what we did last year and it's all on computer.'

In the end she asked a direct question, which inadvertently or otherwise knocked Lauren off-balance.

'Will you go to the fair if you're asked?'

Lauren looked shocked before replying: 'Why on earth would they ask me? Everyone round here knows what Robert did and some people think I'm tied up with it. My friends back me and that's all that matters to me, but the family… people would be incredulous if they asked me!'

'But you're helping the family, most particularly Juan Marco, and he's going to be an important person to that family from now on, I suspect. He knows how much help you're providing and he might think it appropriate.'

'Well he'd be wrong! How could I possibly accept? I'd be talked about the whole time. I hope he shows more consideration than that! It's bad enough about the programme reference. I saw a mock-up of this year's and phoned the printers and told them to take it out. They told me they could only change it with authority from Lady Belvedere! Absolute rubbish! I'm doing what I'm doing because of what my husband did to them, so the notion that I should be credited is absurd!'

Mrs Tanner smiled weakly. 'I just meant that you'll be talking to each other a lot over the next three weeks and he is polite and respectful, and it wouldn't surprise me if he felt it right to reward your effort.' Lauren flashed her an agitated stare, so Mrs Tanner left for the kitchen to make them a drink.

In truth, Lauren had nothing specific to do this week other than the second interview, so keeping herself busy with the fair planning was a useful time-killer, as well as being something she felt she needed to do before she could up-root herself and make a new start somewhere else. The more she thought about it, the more teacher training appealed. For now it helped that she was dealing with Juan Marco – he was new to it, easily led and not part of the established family. There was nothing more to it than that.

***

The Belvedere family gathered at Hillingstone once more on the first Sunday in September, in advance of the funeral the following day. George and Mary had left their farm under temporary care again, and Anna and Alexander were working from their respective London offices until the end of September. Relatives would arrive later that night and first thing tomorrow for the service at the crematorium. Some of Henry's friends were coming, and many of the villagers were expected to be outside the village church en-route, to pay their respects. Juan Marco was dreading the exposure to many family members that he'd not met before, wondering if they'd judge him to be the snake that George had labelled him as. His grandparents had promised to take care of him but he expected nothing but silence from George, and that was the relationship he was most afraid of in front of so many people.

He'd spoken to Lauren many times in the week and she'd said some kind words to him over the phone, telling him he was a credit to himself and he should be proud of what he stood for, and encouraging him to remember the good things that his father had done, even if there didn't seem to be many of them. 'You'll be saying goodbye on the day so that's not the time to judge him.'

He spent most of Sunday afternoon on his own, but was touched when Anna and Alexander knocked on his door to ask how he was, saying that they'd all get through tomorrow and Tuesday would be a new day.

Mary also slipped away a few minutes before dinner, to make sure he was joining them to eat with four new family members he'd not met before. She put her arms around him and gave him a massive hug which he clung on to for as long as he could.

'Don't worry about George,' she told him. 'I've told him firmly to behave, and even he seemed surprised I felt it necessary to remind him. He'll be sullen, I'm sure, but I'll watch that he doesn't drink too much when we come back here for the wake.' It was this part of the day that most worried Juan Marco, as a post-funeral gathering was uncommon in Spain.

The evening dinner was uncomfortable for Juan Marco, meeting family cousins for the first time who talked about some of their memories of Henry as a boy. He was taken over by a strange set of emotions, starting with a sense of loss that he'd no knowledge of the person they were describing, then a sense of resentment that he'd never known his father until recently, then a sense of disappointment that his father had never achieved anything lasting. Finally, he felt determined that he'd stick at things to make sure he wasn't the same man as his father. But as he went to sleep that night, it was Lauren's face that he saw, and that gave him the comfort he needed to rest.

Juan Marco was introduced to many family and friends before the service began, some greeting him with curiosity, some wonderment and some struggling to hide their disdain. Whatever his own feelings, he said as little as possible as he wanted his grandparents to be the focus of everyone's sympathy. The service lasted thirty-five minutes and there were no words from the family, as no one wished to attempt to summarise or explain Henry's troubled mind and personality.

After the service, the mourners made their way back to Hillingstone, where a buffet had been prepared in the main dining room. Again, Juan Marco found himself isolated, people doing little more than greeting him and then turning back to speak to his grandparents. His sense of not being welcome was spotted by Mary who felt for him, and told George he needed their support. But all she received in return from her husband was an indifferent stare, so she went to keep him company.

In her mind, people needed to understand he was Henry's son and now the rightful heir to the title, irrespective of what had happened in the past or might happen in the future. Privately, she knew Juan Marco was better suited to running the estate than George. George knew farming, but his quick temper, reactive decision making and argumentative nature were not what the family needed now. Juan Marco was more open-minded, considered, and recognised others' contributions, plus his communication skills were on a different level. Mary knew that she and George could play a huge part in the successful development of the estate, and she was desperate for them to be involved, and hoped that if she and Juan Marco could work from opposite sides then the battle might be won. For the time being she contented herself with talking to as many people as she could at the wake, occasionally arm-in-arm with Juan Marco, to make it plain that he was a part of the family, at least as far as she was concerned.

Juan Marco had assumed that both Anna and George would attend the fair, but wasn't sure until his grandparents confirmed it as they said goodbye to their daughter and son on Tuesday. This gave him a sense of purpose for resuming the planning, and he messaged Lauren the following day to ask if they could meet up and see where they were up to. Lauren agreed to meet him on Thursday morning.

She didn't want to meet anywhere public, and as neither the farmhouse nor Mrs Tanner's cottage were neutral or private, asked him for a venue. In truth, she didn't want to see him and would have been happy to talk over the phone, followed up by emailing documents, but her instincts said it would be rude to keep him at arm's length just after the funeral. She just hoped he wouldn't be emotional and needy, as propping up someone else wasn't at the top of her priorities at the moment.

He messaged her later, asking her to meet him at the side entrance gate again, as he'd found somewhere on the estate they could talk without being disturbed. When she arrived he let her through, and she followed his van to an empty cottage three hundred metres from Mrs Tanner's cottage, parking to the side so they were out of sight.

'This place is empty now. The gardener who has it has moved out as it needs major plumbing repairs. The family are putting him up in the village for a month,' he said as they went inside.

'How are you feeling?' asked Lauren tentatively, hoping he would remain calm.

'Better, especially now the wider family has gone. I want to do something special for my grandparents to make the fair a real success, so that's where I want to focus my energies. Once that's over, we can move on to the development plans. And you – how was the interview?'

'It was fine, at least as good as it could have been, although I expect they'll give the job to some nineteen-year-old who'll be cheaper to employ than me,' she replied flatly.

He looked at her quizzically, then said: 'You have a lot of the skills the estate is going to need in the future.'

'Oh please, Juan Marco, I think that ship has sailed! The family would never employ me again. They'd be fools to even think of it. And don't talk about you having influence – that's pipe smoke and you know it.' He frowned at her although guessing her meaning, but it was a new expression to him. 'My time for dreaming is gone. I need concrete things in my life and a new future. I deserve it! Now let's get on with reviewing the plans.'

They worked through Lauren's spreadsheet, section by section, covering catering, children's entertainment, drinks outlets, merchandisers, produce from local farms and finally livestock pens. 'You've got the contractors in hand for the pens, anyone needing generators, etc.? Signs too?' she asked.

'Yes, I'm going to help erect some of the pens with the livestock hands and gardeners to save money. Signs will be re-used from last year as I've found them, but any others required we'll make. Tom and John will be on gate duty to take payment.'

'Just those two? You'll need more than that. We usually ask the local

361

Scouts to provide some volunteers. People need a break every now and again, plus it's only right they get to see a bit of the fair themselves. I'll phone the local Scoutmaster, I know him well. Are you going to be involved in judging the livestock or anything? We normally ask a local vet to do it and Robert assisted, sometimes Lord Belvedere too. It's important you do something public, or maybe George or Mary would do it, although I think you've learnt a lot.'

'No, I don't think I have the experience. I'll leave it to... well, I suppose my grandfather might appreciate a break, so maybe George...' he said, floundering.

She shook her head at him gently. 'I think you should volunteer. At the end of the fair Lord Belvedere normally gives a short speech, when he thanks everyone and points to the challenges for the year ahead. Is he doing it this year?'

'I don't know, I haven't asked. I didn't know about it.'

'I think you should. He might want you to say a few words – you're going to have to accept that you're next in line. That's how a lot of people will see it. They won't know about your future plans, they'll just assume you're being groomed to take the reins.'

'Well I'm not!' he flustered. 'George is better qualified!'

Lauren raised her eyebrows at him. 'Is that what you really think, in all the areas that are required?'

Juan Marco was suddenly gripped with a passion to fuck her. He stared at her as his temperature shot up, struggling for air and trying to avoid blurting out what his lust told him he wanted to do. He managed to turn away to try and get some self-control, and then through gritted teeth said: 'You're coming to the fair, of course?'

'Don't be silly, I'd hardly be welcome.'

'You're the one being silly. You've put in all this work, my grandmother insists on a programme acknowledgement, and I insist that you enjoy yourself. People are not wandering around talking about you all the time in a bad way. You've proved you care about the estate and that you give it something it needs, and it's time you held your head up!'

'Thanks for the pep talk, but save it for the current employees.'

'I'm insisting! The children's entertainment is where you belong and you know it!'

'That's my level, is it? I think we're done here,' she added, collating her papers and turning to put them and her laptop in its case.

'I was thinking of having a party after the fair, like the Christmas party, for staff and their families and any of the exhibitors or providers who have supported us with the change of date. Local farmers too,' he said hurriedly. 'You could come to that too. You can come as my guest.'

She turned to look at him and replied calmly: 'Juan Marco, I have the greatest respect for you and for how hard you've worked since you came here, but you still have a lot to learn about the world.' She turned and walked out of the room and headed for the front door.

He followed her at a slow pace, and as she was reaching her car door he called out: 'You're beautiful!'

She ignored him as she threw her things on the front passenger seat, but then decided she wasn't going to let him have the last word. So leaning on the open door, she replied coolly: 'What did you say?'

'You're beautiful,' he said more calmly.

She just shook her head and sighed as she flopped into the driver's seat and closed the door. As she switched on the engine the radio came on, and she upped the volume as she reached for the seatbelt. The chorus of Abba's 'What's the Name of the Game' belted out, and she tried to ignore the words before shouting: 'Oh for God's sake!' as she turned the radio off quickly, throwing the car into reverse and then heading for the main gate at speed, her body starting to inexplicably shake as she drove.

Chapter 36

The Fair and the Rollercoaster

Over the next few days, Lauren and Juan Marco finalised the plans for the event of the fair, but neither suggested meeting up again. She ignored him when he reminded her by text that she was invited both to the weekend, and to the party on Sunday night.

Mrs Tanner suggested to Lauren at the start of the week that she was very welcome to come over for a couple of days beforehand, on the assumption that she might have changed her mind about going to the fair, and expecting the family, through Juan Marco, to extend an invitation. It was also on her mind that Lauren must be tired of sleeping in spare rooms or on sofas in other people's houses, and might appreciate more space and privacy for a couple of days. She was a little surprised when Lauren didn't jump at the offer, but didn't question her when she rang on Wednesday to say things were a little cramped where she was staying, and if she could come over from Friday to Monday morning it would be a real bonus.

Juan Marco explained the full fair programme to his grandparents on Tuesday, and they were impressed by how he'd managed to pull it all together.

'I have, to be honest, needed a lot of help. As I discovered Lauren is back in the area temporarily, I spoke to her. She's sort of between jobs at the moment, and I think she really wanted to help to make things better for the estate. I couldn't have done it without her, it's as simple as that. She has all the contacts and planning skills and found solutions when I was struggling. Don't think she forced her way in, it's the other way around. I didn't want to trouble you and I took advantage of the fact that she'd got time on her hands. She's done a great job. It will go brilliantly I think.'

Lord Belvedere looked slightly unimpressed at this disclosure, but his wife asked how Lauren was.

'OK, I think, although a bit tense. Seeing her a few times has brought it home to me just how much she's lost. She's lost her job, her home, her marriage. She feels like the estate and the village are judging her and I can see it's damaged her self-respect. She's still determined about how she does things – you'll see the results at the weekend – but her eyes aren't the same somehow, less bright. She's been changed by her experiences.'

Lord Belvedere looked more comfortable at this thought but said nothing, but his wife replied: 'There were always things she was good at, and I can't help but feel she's probably a more impressive performer on her own than with Robert around. Perhaps she was too comfortable, or he was too domineering, I don't know. But she's better off without him I suspect.'

Juan Marco nodded before adding: 'She needs to find work soon, that I can guess. I think she's a bit lost. It's a shame because she has skills that we're going to need—'

'Now hold on there, Juan Marco,' interrupted Lord Belvedere. 'I can see you have sympathy for her but that's a bit strong.'

'John, I'm sure Juan Marco isn't implying we should employ her again. He's just recognising her abilities and I think he's right.'

Juan Marco winced at this exchange, deciding that sitting on the fence was the right thing through remaining silent. Then he added: 'I do think we should acknowledge her contribution to the fair by letting her know she's welcome to attend, if she's asked to come along by someone. I know she's got the programme acknowledgement but I'm not sure that's enough.'

'No, I draw a line there,' replied his grandfather. 'That's not going to help the family right now. In fact, it will detract from the need to put clear water between the past and the future.'

'I have to agree, Juan Marco,' said Lady Belvedere, 'but you're having this party afterwards, aren't you? We won't be attending but perhaps you can invite her to that?'

Her husband showed his disapproval, but Lady Belvedere's steely-eyed unbroken stare made him shrug his shoulders and look away.

Anna, Alexander, George and Mary all arrived on Friday night and preparations were complete for a ten a.m. start on Saturday. The weather was expected to be mild and dry which was a relief to them all.

Each day of the fair was a success, and the charm was enhanced by the children's presentations on the way up to the hall of the features of the different crops, and the details about livestock farming. When the children spoke it made everyone listen, most of all other children whose attention was normally focused on where they were going to next. Great fun was had in the nursery guessing which seeds grew into which crops, guessing which foodstuffs were the end product of each, and wearing blindfolds to distinguish one seed from another. Outside the hall there was a long queue for the tractors, children beaming with pride, or looking like the world had fallen in on them, depending on whether they'd been able to successfully move seeds from one miniature silo to another.

Juan Marco had said nothing to his grandparents about judging livestock and was relieved he wasn't called upon to do it, although Lady Belvedere did nudge him to go alongside his grandfather and uncle on the podium and show a smiling face, even if he was ignored by George. He was also happy that Lord Belvedere and Alexander handled the classic car show judging between them, but was unnerved when his grandfather asked him and George to go on to the presentation stage towards the end of the Sunday afternoon, praying that he wasn't going to be asked to say anything. Lord Belvedere gave his usual attendance thanks to both businesses and the public, and then hesitated before saying: 'Now it's customary that I say a few words about the estate's future at this point. This year has brought us many challenges, culminating in the saddest of events recently of which you'll all be aware. At moments like these you have to look to the future, and here on the platform today I have the future of this estate standing alongside me. With their help, and the support of the whole family, we will approach 2020 with a fresh agenda, and I hope you will begin to see a new look to the estate, something that we would very much like you to be a part of.' Then he turned to George and Juan Marco. 'Now, would either of you like to say anything?' They both froze on the spot. George was the first to shudder into life.

'Thank you all for coming, and we hope to see you again next year,' he managed, his father looking at him oddly as if to say 'is that all?' He turned to Juan Marco again who felt embarrassed, by both the request and George's effort, and uncertainly took his place at the microphone.

'My grandfather has reminded you of the great sadness that the family has suffered recently, and that if these things teach us anything, it's that we need family and friends around us, and we can come through these challenges if we work together. We have great plans to modernise the running of the estate, and you should all be able to see this in action over the coming months and years. You will be able to come here for relaxation

366

and leisure, and perhaps take advantage of what the hall has to offer if you have something special to celebrate.'

'This event has been my first and I hope you have all enjoyed it as much as I have. A great many people need to be thanked for their contributions, and I hope I can speak to a lot of them personally when we have a little celebration for them this evening. Thank you all again for coming, and we hope to see you much more in the future.'

As he finished, he found himself joining in the clapping that had begun. The next second he felt his grandfather's arm around his back and saw his warm smile, George awkwardly coming forward to join the two of them as Lord Belvedere tried to embrace him too. At the front of the crowd, Mary looked at Anna and smiled, her sister-in-law's expression changing from doubt to pleasant surprise, and then curiosity.

'George may be your husband but it's pretty clear where your vote goes,' Anna said in Mary's ear, who laughed. 'You've been rooting for him all along. There's more to this than I can see!'

The evening party was held in the drawing room. The kitchen staff laid on a buffet and were all invited to join in, alongside the grounds staff, partners and families, supporters and estate farmers, and also some of the staff from the firms that had been most helpful when Henry and Juan Marco had visited them to investigate Robert's trail of fraud. Juan Marco circulated as much as possible fulfilling his earlier commitment, and Mary took great pleasure in helping spread the family's appreciation too. George had declined to accompany her, although Lord and Lady Belvedere had come at the start to say a few words of thanks into the microphone that had been rigged up.

Lauren hadn't turned up to the fair on either day as far as Juan Marco had seen, and he reluctantly accepted her decision, made easier by the contrary opinions of his grandparents. But he had hope she would come to the party. He'd told Mary how much help she'd given and she nodded and said, 'OK, I understand,' when he informed her he'd invited Lauren to the party. He'd reminded Lauren by text the previous day, but she hadn't replied which frustrated him.

At Mrs Tanner's cottage, Lauren had grown tired of the slightly strained atmosphere. While Mrs Tanner hadn't laboured the point, she wanted her to come to the party at the hall and her steadfast refusal had caused tension, so Mrs Tanner had gone alone in her car. Edgy and unable to settle back at the cottage, Lauren decided to go for a walk and headed towards the estate office, not really having a plan, but her torch would help her stick to the trees later on. Without having any clear destination, and having talked to the horses for a few minutes, curiosity got the better of her, and she walked slowly towards the hall, drawn to catching a glimpse of what was going on at the party, even though she knew she'd have to be quick and stay out of sight. As she approached the building, she found a spot at the side of an outbuilding that was about fifty feet away from the drawing room, and enabled her to get a partial view of the celebration. Both sash windows were open which made it easy to get a taste of the hubble and bubble coming from inside.

There seemed to be voices calling out 'come on, come on', 'you know you want to', then someone else shouted out 'it's tradition!' She needed to get closer, so she walked quickly across to the side of one of the open windows. She could hear Juan Marco's voice with the microphone. He was hesitant and stuttering, others were laughing and applauding. Then he spoke.

'OK, I will try this once but no more. I don't know what music you all like, but as someone's kindly booked the DJ I'll have to give it a go!' There was loud calling out and cheers. 'Do you have "Let Your Soul Be Your Pilot" by Sting?'

As the soulful tune started and he worked through the burning lyrics, his clear voice seemed to change from singing from memory to reaching from somewhere deeper inside, and his voice began to falter. Perhaps it was the recent loss of his father, or were the words reminding him of his mother? But his emotions were getting the better of him. As his voice broke further and the party-goers fell into silence, a female voice joined in to accompany him, strengthening him and using her hands to encourage others to join in. Suddenly half the room was singing, lifting the atmosphere as tears rolled down Juan Marco's face. Lauren had to see what was going on and moved up to the window, pushing her face against the glass. She saw Mary standing next to Juan Marco with her arm around him and, as they finished the final verse, taking him into her arms as he sobbed into her neck. Lauren drew back from the window and gasped out loud, thrusting herself into the outside wall, then starting to choke as she made a dash for the cover of the outbuilding. Once there, her own sobs started in earnest as she gasped: 'It should have been me, it should have been me!'

She stayed there for another two minutes before deciding she needed to get away, heading back towards the estate office at a fast pace. Once there, she took shelter behind the building.

'Pull yourself together! What's the matter with you, you idiot? You're behaving insanely! What are you dreaming of? You don't even know what you want! This is over. It's been over for a long time! Why are you even still here? You just want to cause yourself more pain? Idiot! There's nothing for you here!'

Her body rocked and jerked as she tried to calm herself, but it took two minutes of deep breathing before she recovered any semblance of control. Finally she realised she needed to walk this rage off and headed into the woods, stomping noisily as she followed the path laid out by the torch. She reached the side gate alongside the lane that she'd been through a couple of times so recently and it felt familiar and calming. She leant against it and then climbed up onto it. She must have sat there for nearly an hour, her mind slowly emptying of all thoughts, and never thinking of the time. When she checked her watch – it was 10.15 p.m. – she knew instantly it was time for action. She slipped down from the gate and headed in the direction of the cottage. When she arrived it was just after 10.35 p.m., and Mrs Tanner's car was back. She headed straight upstairs to pack her limited things, her mind set on driving immediately to Derbyshire to get well away from here for the final time.

Mrs Tanner had already gone to bed but was reading, and couldn't help but hear the swift footsteps on the floorboards between the second bedroom and bathroom, and the zipping and unzipping of a case. She waited for the sounds to stop and it all went quiet after a loud huff. She stayed in bed for a further five minutes but heard nothing further, so reached for the small note block and pencil she kept on her bedside cabinet. She wrote: *please don't go without saying goodbye x.* She opened her door and listened again, and as there was still silence crept towards the other door, wincing as the timbers creaked, before bending down and shoving the folded slip of paper under the door, then creeping back to her own room.

Mrs Tanner rose the next morning, hoping that she wouldn't find the cottage empty. While she was boiling the kettle she heard footsteps on the stairs, and an unkempt and sullen Lauren appeared behind her in the kitchen.

'Good morning,' she said kindly. 'You look as though you didn't sleep well.'

'In fits,' replied Lauren. 'I'll have a shower and then I'll be off.'

'After breakfast, I hope?'

'I can't face anything big.'

'Don't worry, I'm not into that either. Some cereals and toast perhaps?'

'Just toast, thank you.'

'Where are you heading?'

'Back to Derbyshire first. It's the only place I can go where I can clear my head. I can stand a few days, and then when I'm tired of having my head pecked, I'll rent somewhere round here. Kent has always been my home and I don't fancy moving far away. Canterbury is probably where I'm thinking.'

'Did you get the job?'

'I didn't hear, so probably not. They said they'd phone by the following day but, as usual, you don't hear anything.'

'What did you do last night? You weren't here when I got back,' Mrs Tanner said knowingly.

Lauren stared back, her brown eyes locked with lifelessness, but telling Mrs Tanner her guess was right. 'It's time for me to go.' Her movement towards the door was only stopped by the sound of the toast popping up.

'There, that's the toast, come and sit down. Another few minutes won't hurt. Tea or coffee?'

Lauren slumped in a chair and put her head in her hands, then let out a sob. As Mrs Tanner went to comfort her, Lauren sat upright, saying: 'No! I'm all right, really. Everything's just got too much for me, that's all.'

'Coffee I think,' Mrs Tanner said almost to herself. She sat down with the drinks and poured some cereal for herself. 'You've coped amazingly well with everything. I imagine your emotions are difficult at the moment?' Lauren nodded. 'Is there no one who can give you some comfort?' she added, taking a huge risk.

Lauren's head jerked upwards, her mouth opening to utter, 'What do you mean?' but horrified that the guilty look in Mrs Tanner's eyes revealed she knew what she hoped was private.

'It's OK, calm yourself,' Mrs Tanner said, reaching across the table with her hand. 'You've been through so much and you must be so confused, and now a different feeling to cope with that you're not sure about. I wondered if, well you know, if there might be any feelings there. I saw it in

370

Juan Marco too.'

Lauren was biting down on her lip, unable or unwilling to reply. Then she found some strength. 'It's silly, hopeless, pointless, a waste of time. I've no idea what I feel for him, but all I know is I'm so confused and irritated. I can't split one emotion from another. All I know is being here is just... just crazy and totally unhelpful!' she sobbed, as Mrs Tanner nodded back at her.

'I understand and I think you're doing the right thing. Take yourself away and find some space and then things will become clearer,' she said smiling kindly. 'Just promise me one thing. When you're feeling better and you know your own mind again, be honest with yourself about your feelings. I... after my husband died, I didn't think I'd ever love again, but after a few years there was someone else who was interested in me and, well, I liked him but I wouldn't allow myself to admit just how much. He got tired of waiting and met someone else, and ever since then I've regretted how I behaved. You know what the biggest mistake was? I wasn't honest with myself and I've regretted it ever since. Always be true to yourself and your feelings. You don't owe anybody else anything.'

Lauren reached over and they locked hands, her tearful eyes comforted by the older woman's words. 'Thank you, but I think it was a dream too far, or maybe it's a fantasy or... a nightmare. I don't know. My mind's all over the place and I'm too fragile to know what I see in him. Maybe it's nothing.'

Mrs Tanner smiled kindly. 'I don't think it's that, but some time away will tell you how important it is. And then, never give up hope. Remember, nothing ventured is nothing gained. Anything is possible.'

They finished breakfast and Lauren took her shower, coming downstairs looking considerably brighter.

'I'm off. Thanks for everything and I mean everything,' she said as they embraced. 'I'm getting the train to Derby so I'm leaving my car in the village at a friend's for a few weeks. I fancy not having to concentrate on anything else except me for a while.'

'Good plan, Lauren, and you will stay in contact with me, won't you?' Lauren nodded and left.

Mrs Tanner returned to the kitchen to make another drink, dwelling on the lifetime of events she'd seen pass at Hillingstone. After some minutes of reflecting, she turned the radio on to listen to the news and started flicking through a magazine she'd left on the worktop. About twenty

371

minutes after Lauren had left, there was a knock on the door.

'Oh, poor girl, she must have left something behind,' she said out loud, but when she opened the door it was Juan Marco facing her.

'Sorry, Mrs Tanner, I know it's early but Lauren isn't here is she? Or do you know where she is? I imagine her sewing machine is still here so I just thought… well, she'd be local after all her efforts with the fair.'

'I know that she's heading back to Derbyshire this morning. I don't know if she's left already but she's not here.'

'God! I was hoping to see her! Was she staying in the village? Maybe at that house I picked the car up from? I can try there,' he said, turning back towards his bicycle. Mrs Tanner watched him mount up, flapping over whether to say something. Then she called out.

'Juan Marco! She's getting the train to London then she's going on to Derby. She'll leave from Maidstone station.'

'Shit! That's five miles away, I'll never make it. I'll call her instead. I didn't bother before because I thought she'd ignore me.'

Mrs Tanner put her hand to her head and uttered a sigh as she stepped out of the door. 'Wait. She's gone to drop her car off in the village, then she'll get a lift to the station. If you go direct there you might catch her.'

'Well I won't on this!' he scoffed, looking at the old bike.

'Take my car! I'll fetch the keys. I'll vouch for you if anybody stops you, but please try not to crash it!' He looked at her with surprise, wondering why she assumed he was likely to crash it. He was still frowning when she appeared with the keys. 'Oh, go on, get off with you! You should have enough time so you shouldn't need to drive like a lunatic!'

'Thanks,' he managed without conviction, before heading to the car.

Juan Marco drove quickly to the station and parked up, walking swiftly to the platforms to check the time of the next train to London. There were two, one in ten minutes and the other in twenty-five. At least he had time to check if Lauren was on the first, and if not he could wait on the platform until he saw her boarding. He bought a single ticket at a machine and climbed into the last coach, scanning the other seats to see if she was there. Suddenly, he felt exposed and nervous about what he was going to say. He'd thought how easy it would be in his mind, but now it seemed like a much harder task, potentially surrounded by other people. He sat down and kept his eye on the platform staircase for a couple of minutes to see if she appeared. There was no sign of her so he'd have to check the other seven coaches. At least one might be first-class and she'd be unlikely to be on that, so he rose and started his journey down the aisle. He passed through the other coaches until he reached the second from front. As he moved through, there was no one looking his way that could be her, but with seats in either direction he had to turn and check.

About a third of the way down he spotted a dark-haired girl with a hat who was looking down. He couldn't tell if it was her so he took a chance, lifting his jacket collar up and walking swiftly to the end of the carriage, settling into a seat two rows in, facing in her direction. Then he stood on the pretext of removing his jacket and studied her more closely, but still couldn't tell. So while her head was down looking at her phone he moved six rows closer, and glanced around the seat in front of him. It was her. He decided to stay seated until the train moved off so she couldn't just walk away.

As the train picked up speed he walked slowly towards her. She was sitting in the window seat, and he came to a halt in front of her backpack that was on the next seat.

'I really hoped you'd at least say goodbye.'

She looked up and drew a sharp breath. 'What are you doing here? I… I… need a break. Can't you leave me in peace?'

He smiled and looked directly into her eyes. 'I needed to talk to you, even if you didn't to me.'

'Don't be ridiculous, this is embarrassing! I'm on my way home and you're following me.'

Becoming concerned at how it might look, Juan Marco looked seriously at her. 'Don't make me say it here,' he whispered.

'Say what?'

'I love you,' he whispered, picking up her backpack and storing it overhead, then plonking himself into the seat and repeating it, refusing to blink.

'Get off the seat and off this train!' she hissed icily.

'Fine, if you look at me and tell me you don't care for me,' he whispered.

'No, just go!'

'You're afraid, aren't you? You can't admit it because you know it's true.'

Her face was beginning to crumble and her eyes turn wet. 'I've told

373

you already, just go!'

But he picked her hand up from her thigh and squeezed it, never taking his eyes from hers. 'I love you, Lauren, and I don't want you to go. No matter where you go, you can't escape the truth. I'll never accept you don't have feelings for me. We've been through so many things recently, but it's your face that I keep seeing in my dreams and I don't want them to end.'

'You are a fool!' she sobbed, but squeezed his hand back.

'And you're beautiful,' he replied, tilting his head and moving his mouth towards hers as she recoiled. 'Move closer, or I will.'

'Not here!' she whispered in a panicked voice and he relaxed, still gazing at her. 'You know this is foolish and won't work, don't you? I'm history with the estate, there's no prospect of me ever going back. I've got to build a new life for myself and move on. You do know that?'

'I don't know anything like that. All I know is that I want to be with you. Anything is possible.'

'Huh. That's what Mrs Tanner said!'

'She's a clever woman, I like her. You too?' Lauren nodded sullenly. 'Then let's not disappoint her.' He moved in for a kiss again. This time, Lauren held her position and let their lips meet as the tears rolled down her cheeks, her hand coming up to his face.

'You really do know this is ridiculous,' she repeated quietly.

'Then why does it feel right?' he replied, putting his arm around her as she dropped her head onto his shoulder and reached around his waist. They stayed in that position for a couple of minutes before she spoke.

'OK *señor*, what's your plan?'

His eyes suddenly lit up. 'Let's go to Deal!'

'Why Deal? It's heading in the wrong direction. I'm supposed to be headed north!'

'Where is it?'

'It's the other way, towards the coast.'

'Let's go now! We can change trains and go back the other way.'

'But why?'

'It's where my parents got married. I want to see it, see why my father chose that place!'

'Well it was probably convenient, the register office could fit them in, it was far enough away that nobody could find out what they were doing. There were loads of reasons probably! You're not going to find the meaning

374

of it there!'

'Yes I am. Come on, let's go,' he said reaching for her backpack.

'Juan Marco, this is mad!' she whispered. 'I'm going up north to find... myself.'

'That's mad. You're already here, with me,' he smiled. 'Come on.'

As he started off down the aisle with her backpack, she gasped in exasperation and followed him. They got off at the next station and bought single tickets to Deal at a machine. Then he texted Lady Belvedere to say he'd be away for the day, and Mrs Tanner, telling her where her car was parked and hoping that she had a spare set of keys.

'Don't you need to tell someone?' he asked. She shook her head.

'No, I'm a free agent these days. I was planning to ring my mother when I was about an hour-and-a-half out of Derby.'

'Good, then we have all day,' he replied, putting his arm around her.

The next couple of hours passed with them hardly noticing anyone or anything else. They talked about their attraction to each other in the early days. She admitted to dressing provocatively at times, and he admitted his thoughts had turned to lust on occasions. They spoke of his mother and how he felt when he'd made the decision to return to Spain with her, and the goodbye they'd shared on the doorstep of the farmhouse. Lauren was less open with him, particularly when he asked about the night he'd visited her for dinner when she seemed shaky.

'That wasn't a good night for me, I wasn't feeling myself,' she replied economically.

'Had you argued with Robert?'

'Something like that.'

'I didn't think you were telling me the whole story about him going off to his parents because they'd had a fight.' She shook her head but wouldn't be drawn further.

By the time they arrived in Deal they were starving, and headed to a tea shop near the seafront and the Napoleonic forts. They walked hand-in-hand smiling, laughing and often sharing kisses. Once seated inside the café, he looked around before saying: 'This is something like Hillingstone should have, I mean it will have. Warm, comforting, fresh local food. It will bring people in. It's all part of the plans.'

'You've thrown yourself into it haven't you?'

He nodded back. 'Yes and there should be a place for you too. You will work some magic on anything that can bring revenue into the estate, I know you will.'

'Juan Marco, let's not spoil today by talking about work. I know you have your dreams and I admire you for it, but it's raw for me,' she said reaching out to take his hand. 'I need something new.'

They spent the rest of the afternoon walking along the seafront, went into one of the forts and to a pub in the town.

'Who's Charles Hawtrey?' he asked when seeing a plaque with the name on it outside a house.

'No idea,' she replied, laughing.

By eight o'clock, they were both tired and hungry again. Slightly nervously, he asked her if she wanted to stay the night. She cast her eyes down.

'I'm not sure that's a good idea. Haven't you got to get back?'

He shook his head. 'Why would I? We're both entitled to a break after the fair aren't we?' She looked anxiously up at him.

'I don't want to get your hopes up. Single rooms?'

'A double, so we can be together,' he replied warmly and she nodded.

They took a room in a guesthouse one road back from the seafront, and then headed off to a pub for dinner. When they climbed into bed she wore a nightdress, he just his boxers. As they snuggled up she wondered if he'd be able to keep his control. When they kissed passionately, he rolled on top of her and she felt him harden and start pushing against her, making her gasp.

'Please, don't! It's not that I don't want to. It's just it's happening so fast, I need more time!'

He rolled off but kept his arm around her. 'I love you and that's all that matters,' he said, burying his face in her neck and hair.

'I love you too,' she whispered, kissing his head.

The following morning they awoke and both felt slightly awkward, not helped by Juan Marco trying to hide an erection as he leapt out of bed to make them drinks. As they sat talking about breakfast, neither wanted to go down dressed, so instead they asked for juice, cereals, toast and more coffee to be sent up on a tray. As they sat eating and drinking, Juan Marco found it hard not to look at Lauren's slender, curvy body, covered in the clingy nightdress. He repeated that she should come back to the village with him, but she was adamant she needed to be elsewhere and Derbyshire was the obvious place, even if only for a few days. Each time he tried to come to terms with the fact they must part, it made him want to see her naked, and the conversation went quiet.

'It won't be for long,' she said, breaking the silence. 'We'll work something out.' He glared back at her. 'What's the problem?' she asked.

'This is the problem,' he said, rising with a grimace, his erection bulging in his boxers.

Lauren looked stunned, then her face broke into a wry smile. 'You're having problems this morning, aren't you?' He nodded urgently. They stayed where they were, looking into each other's eyes, neither saying anything although both their lips were moving. Her eyes lost their brightness and gained the same look of intensity as his. Then he moved towards her and she rose to meet his arms, throwing hers around his neck as he slipped his hands down her back, feeling her and moaning as he kissed her. After a long passionate kiss they were both panting, and she nodded at him, gasping: 'Just be gentle, please, be gentle.'

Ninety minutes later they lay in each other's arms, having made love three times.

'What's the time?' she whispered.

'Who cares?'

'Silly, it will be throwing out time soon. The room will have to cleaned before the next people. Go on, check.'

He muttered as he turned to look at the clock. 'It's eleven.'

'God, I thought they said check-out was twelve! Come on, get a move on. We'll have to get showered quickly and get out. I'll go in first!'

'Or we could go in together,' he replied cheekily, lowering the sheet on his side of the bed teasingly.

'Forget it, stallion, you've had your share this morning!'

They left the guesthouse and headed back to the station and took the train towards Maidstone. As they were getting near, he said: 'I'm serious about what I said. I can't help thinking you belong on the estate. I will try and find a way to make it work.'

She shook her head. 'Let it go, if you love me.'

Chapter 37

Back to Work

During October and the first two weeks of November, the wheels started turning on the Hillingstone estate development plan. Land surveys took place on the area identified for sale and the plot was fenced off and marketing commenced; architects were engaged to produce draft drawings of the buildings that would need planning permission; meetings were carried out with environmental consultants, grant-aid bodies and private contractors and leisure specialists. The land for housing was under offer within three weeks, subject to outline planning permission being granted.

Juan Marco and Lord Belvedere held meetings with the contract farmers to discuss the possibility of changing boundaries, crops and farming methods, to see if the attractiveness of both the landscape and the yields could be increased, almost like a 'model farm' concept. Lord Belvedere shared his angst with Juan Marco after the first set of meetings in October. 'George should be in on this you know, it's his area.'

'It's Mary's too, so I'll feed back to her and you tell him. Just tell him what's going on. Be direct, Grandfather. He needs to understand – this is happening with or without him.'

By the first week of November, Mary's frustrations at not playing a bigger part were being loudly communicated to Juan Marco. Lord Belvedere said he'd noticed that his regular calls were getting a different response from George now, irritation and nonchalance being replaced by advice, given assertively sometimes. They agreed now was the time to strike, so had contracts of employment updated and drawn up for the positions of Estate Development Director and Estate Development Manager, both with salaries that would prove tempting to a couple managing a small farm with high demand on their time. They emailed them to George and Mary separately, hoping to force their hands. In response, George called his father asking for a conference call, and as Juan Marco and his grandparents sat in the study waiting for George and Mary to join, Lord Belvedere felt he had to ask the obvious question: 'Where does this leave you, my boy?'

'I'm staying.'

'But for how long?'

'I'm staying. I want to stay. There's so much work to do here, there's no argument. George and Mary can run the farming side of things. Mary can do other commercial projects too because she's got the skills. It's already in her contract. But seeing the overall picture is our job. There's also someone else I think we should bring in but we can discuss that later.'

His grandfather looked at him stunned. Lady Belvedere reached for his hand, and her face crumbled as she mouthed 'thank you.'

The video call with George and Mary started off on a bumptious note, as he made it clear where he would and wouldn't accept interference, but buoyed by Juan Marco's news, Lord Belvedere put in a confident performance.

'The word "interference" is inappropriate George. Discussion, engagement, negotiation are all appropriate words. We work as a team from now on. We will bow to your and Mary's greater experience sometimes, and other times you will need to listen to our views and take in the bigger picture. Juan Marco is the next custodian of the estate and he's planning to be around for some time, we're glad to say. This is a shared show and you have to respect his involvement.'

George's mood wasn't improved by that comment, but Mary couldn't or wouldn't hold back her enthusiasm, and no matter how many looks George gave her she wouldn't back down. In the end she said: 'We accept, both of us. We're going to search for contract farmers to take over what we've got in Lincolnshire. They'll need to respect our values and practices and it might be that we have temporary help before we can agree a lease, but we'll be ready to start at Hillingstone in the new year we think, don't we, George?'

He said nothing but nodded his acceptance.

Lauren stayed in Derbyshire for just over a week. She knew after two days where her heart and head belonged, but pushed herself to stay longer to prove she could exercise discipline. She could now see a slow and steady way forward to her relationship with Juan Marco, but that didn't deal with her need to find a job which her mind was restless for. Going back to Kent was now certain, but she could see no way, and more importantly feel no way, back onto the estate. Time and distance might lead to future opportunities, but for now she wanted a fresh start, and teacher training was high up in her mind.

When she told Juan Marco she was coming back and her immediate priority was finding somewhere to live, he already had a plan if she was up for it. He'd inherited a few thousand euros from his mother, and offered to help her with the cost of renting a flat or house in Maidstone, or further afield if she preferred. With her own home, finding a job, if it was necessary, would be easier and they could afford to put down six month's rent up-front to avoid issues with references. He had his salary from the estate to fall back on and wasn't paying anything to live at the hall. Having her own place away from the estate would also give them the chance to be together in private. She saw the attractions of the offer immediately, and started looking online that day for rental properties.

When she moved into the new flat just before the end of October, she was surprised he didn't immediately start to push working at the estate again, but he didn't raise the issue at all for two weeks, saying he supported her desire to be independent. Thereafter, he started dropping hints – they needed to obtain a licence to conduct weddings; some help would be needed in allocating and decorating a couple of rooms for the bridal suite; they'd need to think about catering – in-house or external; was there other accommodation on the estate that could be used by guests either short-term or long term, and did they subcontract its management or do it themselves; were there other events they could open the hall up for without compromising the family's privacy? Lauren tried to block her mind to his rambling, but it wasn't easy for someone like her with organisational skills, a creative mind and good knowledge of the estate. One night in mid-November it came to a head.

'You keep going on about all this stuff, presumably just to annoy me? I'm not interested in working on the estate.'

'This isn't really working on the estate, is it? This is something new, more like working with the family on using the hall as an asset. I'm open-minded, aren't you?'

'Of course I am, but this is just a re-hash of the past.'

'No, it's not. The kind of things that need doing don't involve estate purchasing, managing payroll, managing manual staff, dealing with suppliers and purchasers, finance, etc. I mean, bits of that would be involved but not much, and what there is would be specifically aimed at generating new, additional revenue for the estate. Imagine a tree – this is a new branch.'

'Juan Marco, you do talk waffle sometimes… you're beginning to speak like one of the management consultants. Do you dream of their prose when you go to sleep at night?' she teased.

'No, I dream of other things at night mostly,' he said, heading towards the sofa where she was trying to watch TV.

'No, no, I don't think so!' she said as she pulled her knees up onto the sofa and gently clenched her fists. 'This is a furnished flat and I'm responsible for cleaning any stains on the sofa.'

He hovered over her, smirking. 'You could always do something else for me,' and as her eyes flared, he added, 'No, not that! That's not what I meant! What I meant was, if you stop pretending you don't have the skills to be a hostess, wedding planner, venue manager, catering manager, accommodation manager, then I'll stop talking about it.'

'I've told you, I don't want to work on the estate!'

'Bullshit, you'd love the job.'

'But not on the estate!'

'But the job's on the estate, so if I employ someone else to do it you're happy watching them?'

'I won't care when I've got no time to watch them because I'm piled up with homework, when I'm a teacher!'

'Yes, that will be in two years' time? Maybe longer? You've got to get a teaching qualification first, and then of course you might not be able to get a job locally so—'

'Are you casting doubt on my abilities?' she shouted.

'Not at all!' he exclaimed holding his hands up. 'Just that you're planning your future which is great, but there also happens to be a great big opportunity right here, right now! All I'm saying is think about it! Lauren Pritchard – Events Manager, Hillingstone Hall.'

'You think you're so big you can just throw out jobs to whoever you like! Mr Big Cheese, *Señor Grande Queso!*' she retorted offhandedly, beginning to chuckle at her use of Spanish.

His face broke into a smile and then a laugh, and then he fell onto his knees and kissed her.

'Do whatever you want,' he said. 'I know what your abilities are but we both know how good you'd be at this job. Forget about your objections and just think of how you would do the job, give me your ideas. After, if you still don't want it, then that's OK with me.'

A few days later she talked to him properly, taking a free run at the job as she saw it, because it wasn't really an option to accept it so it was risk-free. He listened to her ideas, maintaining the same half-smile throughout. At the end she said, 'I'll even help you write the job description if you like. There, that's generous of me!'

'Very impressive. Congratulations on your interview, you've got the job!' As she stood up and walked towards him with her hand raised to give him a slap, he gasped: 'There's just one other thing! Christmas is coming and the hall needs decorating! There's also a nativity scene to plan and the party for the schoolchildren! It's all getting a bit tight! You couldn't sort that lot out could you, just on a trial basis?'

She stood over him, roles reversed this time. 'You cheeky little fucker! You utter... you incompetent little shit! I bet you're completely reliant on your grandmother and Mrs Carter. No! You've probably dragged Mrs Tanner in as well, that's your usual style isn't it? Have you actually done anything? Ordered the tree?' He nodded, still holding his hands above his head. 'Done anything else?' He shook his head.

'We're busy with all the stuff with the land sale and the drawings and negotiations with the farmers, and George and Mary. We haven't had time!' he cried.

She stood over him, fuming. 'It's always the women, isn't it? It's the same the world over! Men make the plans and women carry them out, and you expect us to bail you out every time!'

'Can I take my hands away now?'

'Yes, you're not worthy of a slap, Juan Marco!'

'It's the Honourable Juan Marco, actually.'

'What? You insolent toe rag!' she glared, before her face collapsed into a bewildered smile. 'Ohh you...' she said, falling into his lap and grinding herself into him before their mouths locked, only breaking for air after thirty seconds.

'Bedroom?' he gasped. She nodded vigorously.

***

382

Lauren had already considered applying for seasonal temporary work, but as she'd taken a few days to settle into the flat, the start of November seemed a little late. If she was being honest with herself, her head was too full of teaching dreams to commit to even short-term work, and her mind had focused on the new year as being the start of new challenges. That, therefore, left her with a void until January.

Two days after their last discussion, she asked Juan Marco calmly if they really were behind with their planning.

'Yes, my grandmother is taking charge now and it's not fair to ask Mrs Tanner again. The schoolchildren coming for their party and the nativity is a bit of a stretch this year,' he said awkwardly. 'We may cancel it. There's also the staff Christmas party. I mean this year has been such a rollercoaster. We want to say thank you to the staff and the farmers and suppliers as they've done no less than in previous years, but you and Robert organised it all – mainly you I expect – and that's not your task this year. We did have the party after the Autumn Fair and I'm really glad we did now. We took that opportunity to say thank you, and I think that's saved us this year. There'll be a staff-only meal this year, plus their families of course. Mrs Carter will contact everyone else just to say, you know, special circumstances, and back to normal hopefully next year.'

Lauren looked seriously at him.

'What, you still think we should have a party?' he asked surprised. 'You're not offering to—'

'No, nothing like that,' she replied. 'It's just… I was there, you know, at the party after the fair. I saw you singing—'

'No, you weren't! You didn't come!'

'Yes, I did. I didn't come inside, I just hung around outside, inquisitive to know what was going on. Not for long… I wasn't there all night, but when I crept up… oh God that sounds awful… when I listened to what was going on from outside, it sounded like they were trying to get you to do karaoke, and then you did it…'

He looked crestfallen. 'Why didn't you come in? I cried… I don't know why. I don't know if it was because of the funeral or my mother or… I don't know why. You should've been there.'

Lauren moved across the kitchen and put her arms around his neck. 'I felt all your emotion, all of it… It was the first time, when I saw Mary comfort you, that I admitted to myself I was in love with you.'

He raised his sad eyes to meet her's. 'Maybe it was for me too. I was thinking about you so much and your face kept appearing in my mind to give me comfort. The day before the funeral I went to sleep thinking of your face, it was the only thing to calm my nerves. And at the service, I had to tell myself to focus on my grandparents and stop wishing you were there by my side.' They held each other for a minute.

'You know, I've been thinking,' she said as they broke off, 'if your grandparents want it, and if you do too obviously, I'll help with setting the hall up for Christmas and organising things with the school. Only if they want it though. I don't want to tread on anyone's toes, and if they don't want me involved I'll understand. It's just a gesture.'

He nodded. 'I know I'd love you to, but after the Autumn Fair you're right. I'd need to clear it with them. They're going away to Edinburgh for three days at the end of this week for a pre-Christmas break, so I'll talk to her first thing tomorrow. I'll start with her because, well, I haven't told them about you and me yet, and I wasn't sure of when would be the right time and how my grandfather would react. I can deal with both things at the same time and then see what she says. Then maybe I can talk to him, or she'll... I don't know... we can see how it goes.'

The following morning, he went and saw Lady Belvedere in her small parlour where she was finishing up with Mrs Bassett on the Christmas hall food order.

'I have an idea and some news for you,' he began. 'The two are linked really. Firstly, I've had contact with Lauren and she's offered to help with the Christmas hall decorating and the children's party and the nativity etc., if we're short of time. I don't know how you'd feel about that?'

'OK, and what's the news?' said his grandmother coolly.

'Erm... I've stayed in touch with her over the past few weeks, mainly as you know to organise the Autumn Fair, but afterwards too. We've become close. That's not the reason for her offer, I think. She's back here, in Kent I mean, not in the village, and has time on her hands, and anything she starts new will be in January, so she genuinely can give it her full attention, if it's needed.'

'Is that why you've been staying away from the hall frequently? I thought you must have a girlfriend.' He nodded. 'What's the position between you?'

'It's serious,' he replied. 'I can't tell you how much she's changed, I mean not changed, learnt. She's been through her own problems and she's still rebuilding her life, but her energy, warmth, drive is all still there and she's got so much to give. If you saw her now you'd recognise something's different. She's had to fight for her life and she doesn't take anything for granted any more. She understands she has to set her own course, and she's got her head down and is getting on with it. You said before you thought she could achieve more without Robert than with him, and you were right.'

Lady Belvedere nodded slowly. 'Juan Marco, you need to tread very carefully. Not only is Lauren likely to be fragile and susceptible, but she also has a past linked to the estate. She's connected to Robert and his activities, although I accept we've found no evidence of any wrong-doing on her part, but you know she had a previous relationship with George?' He nodded. 'Well it ended badly, and was a good part of the reason why he left the estate in the first place. Now don't get me wrong – it was several years ago – but will it make your working relationships any easier if you're connected with her?'

'She's not thinking of coming back to the estate, at least at the moment. I know she would do the events manager job really well, but I know I'd need to talk to you and grandfather about that. Maybe I'm the one who's pushing, she's more wary.'

'I'm glad of that. I had a feeling when you mentioned you'd like to bring someone in that it might be her, just an inkling. Look, she's several years older than you and has more life experience. Despite what she's been through over the past few months, underneath she's tough and resilient and quite capable of climbing back on the horse, if you know what I mean? But you, you're very young and I thought your mind was focused on driving the changes needed on the estate? I don't mind if you have girlfriends, of course, it's entirely natural. But really, one who's been through so much and is so connected to the recent past of the estate?'

Juan Marco felt the rising tension and potentially the first crossed words he had had with his grandmother.

'I know I'm young but I'm not without experience,' he replied seriously. 'There's something between us that's been there for a while, it's just taken a change of circumstances to bring it forwards. I see her strength and I love her for it. She won't be defeated by events. This isn't just wild passion. I have feelings for her and she me.'

'Juan Marco, I know you're not what I would call naïve. You stand up for yourself and you speak and consider things like someone who's beyond your years, but we would both be worried about you being so involved with her. Since Henry's gone, you've become such a big part of our lives. Emotionally, it's all very mixed up. We've lost our son but gained a grandson. Not just that, but you've contributed to life on the estate, and the way you've taken an interest in its future is frankly astounding. We're feeling safer and more secure, especially your grandfather, than we have for a long time. I don't want anything to undermine that because I care about you, we care about you, do you understand? It would be so painful to see you hurt and lose your way. After all that we've been through, we want you to feel strong and be happy. I'm not just talking selfishly about the future of the estate. Do you understand how upset we'd be if we saw you unhappy?'

He nodded. 'We have a private life away from the estate and it's good for us and better for you that way. It doesn't have to change in the near future, and Lauren will do her own thing when the time comes. I won't try to push her, it wouldn't work anyway.'

Lady Belvedere sighed. 'You've got to think of George too. He still has a temper. We thought when he married Mary she'd calm him down and she did for a while, but all this stuff since—'

'I came here?'

Her face fell. 'Well, yes, it's knocked him back. Now we've successfully got them back into the fold and Mary's support is crucial. I believe the whole family can work together, so the idea of a little explosion, even a minor one, it seems so unhelpful.'

'I have a great deal of respect for Mary and she has strength, I think, to keep George on track. Besides, the farming project is huge, and if Lauren isn't around the estate then we can keep things quiet until there's no risk, if you want.'

Lady Belvedere's disillusioned expression wasn't changing, so he continued.

'Do you want me to talk to Mary, let her know what's going on, and see how she feels we should handle it? She's very practical.'

'Yes, she is, but that's just putting some people in the picture and not others, isn't it? I'm not sure that's a recipe for success,' she said huffing. They sat silently for several seconds, then Lady Belvedere started talking quietly, almost to herself.

'If Anna had inherited, things would have been so simple. I know you can't change things but she's got so much ability – beauty, brains, self-confidence – she's got it all. The estate would be in a much better place if she'd… been a man! I shouldn't say such things but it's the way the line goes in this type of family, everything through the male line. Is it the same in Spain?'

'It's more complicated than that. There are rules ,' he replied.

She sighed.

'She's changed a lot, you know, Lauren,' he said after another silence. 'If you could talk to her and see her, she's not the same person. She makes me happy. Spanish girls are different to English ones, more confident, I think. I've had a few girlfriends since I've been here, but I've not met anyone who attracts me like she does.' Lady Belvedere stared back at him. 'OK, I'll tell her we don't need her help with Christmas. She won't mind, she was just concerned we were too busy with other things to get it done, but we'll manage.'

'What's she doing now?'

'Nothing. She's talking about training to become a teacher in January, so she just has plenty of free time now, but it won't last.'

'I could see her as a primary school teacher, she'd be good at it. Anything to do with children, the fair, the Christmas nativity… oh bugger! It's all such a mess! We're off to Edinburgh on Friday. I'll think about it while we're away and talk to John perhaps, but that's the best I can do!'

***

The following Sunday, Lord and Lady Belvedere had enjoyed breakfast at their hotel in Edinburgh New Town and been for a walk, taking in East Princes Street Gardens close to the railway station, where the Christmas Market is held. They were now back at the hotel enjoying a late morning coffee in the bar while reading the newspapers.

'Good God!' he suddenly exclaimed. 'There's a man called Robert Pritchard who's been charged with an assault against his employer in the Lowlands! Pritchard is described as thirty-one years of age and was employed as a contract manager on a farm! It must be him! Do you think we should go after him for the fraud? We might recover some of the

387

money!'

'It might not be him. The name's not uncommon,' replied his wife. 'Besides, I thought we weren't going to the police about him.'

'We weren't back in the summer, partly because we didn't want to have to track him down. But this could just be a slip catch in our favour. We're in a much stronger position now, and if we could recover some of the money then that would help the estate.'

'But what about the publicity? We said we didn't want to be made to look like fools.'

'Well, as I say, we're in a different place now. The trajectory is upwards. George would be completely in favour!'

'Of course he would, and I daresay Anna would too. She was made to look stupid by her initial belief in him. I expect she'd have no problem with us taking him to the cleaners. What else does it say?'

'Not much more. He got into an altercation with his employer, allegedly there was an argument about priorities and he punched the man, knocking him to the ground. The case has been committed for trial in four months.'

'There are no other identifying details about him?'

'No. It says where he resides, at the farm, and says he's English, that's all. But there's a good chance it's him surely!'

'There's Juan Marco to consider too. Even if we know what the others would say, we should check with him. And of course there's Lauren. She was assaulted by him. She might want to press charges.'

'Well that's not really our business is it. She had her chance at the time.'

'John! That's a dreadful thing to say! We had our chance at the time too!'

'I didn't mean it nastily. I simply meant it would be two separate charges, two separate trials. Three if you include this one.'

'You need to decide if you're serious and, if so, speak to Juan Marco. Can you check with the police if it's the same Robert Pritchard to start, just so we don't go off half-cocked?'

'I can try.'

Lord Belvedere visited the local police station the following day. The desk constable took some details, and said he'd check with the arresting officers to see if the description they gave matched. He received an email later that day after their flight had landed at Gatwick, confirming it appeared it was the same individual, and providing contact details for the local CID team who would investigate a fraud case.

On Tuesday, Lord Belvedere found Juan Marco in the stables. After they talked about Edinburgh for a few minutes, he brought up their news. 'Juan Marco, while we were in Scotland it appears we've inadvertently found Robert Pritchard. He's been arrested for assault up there. Time has passed since he left in a hurry, and your grandmother and I are now more minded to report the fraud to the police to see if we can recover any of the money. I know it's an about-turn but things change, and the estate's moving forwards. George and Anna are both in favour of proceeding. How would you feel?'

'Well if it's just about the money then I think it would be OK, but what about Lauren? She's trying to put all this behind her and I'm not sure how she'd feel. He assaulted her too – you didn't see her but I thought she might lose the sight of her eye.'

'I'm only asking about the fraud really. I appreciate she has her own issues, and I understand you and her have formed some sort of alliance,' he said with annoyance, 'but that's a matter for her. Do you not see? On behalf of the estate we have to decide whether to take action, and you're part of that ownership.'

Juan Marco glared at him. 'I understand what you're saying, but can you please let me speak to her first?'

His grandfather shrugged. 'I suppose another day or two won't make any difference,' he said walking back to his Range Rover.

Juan Marco went to the flat after work. He suggested they order a takeaway and then asked her to switch the television off. 'There's something you need to know. My grandparents have found out where Robert is, by chance. He's been arrested for assault up in Scotland. They want to report him for the fraud.'

'I hoped I'd never hear his name again,' she said with disappointment.

'How do you feel about that?'

'That's up to them. I suppose I'd have to give evidence, drag it all up again. There's no way I could do the Christmas organisation if that starts. I'd never show my face on the estate again.'

'There's the assault, too. You have to decide if you're going to press charges.'

'No way, forget it. That's in the past and I'm not facing up to him in a court, never.'

'Lauren, you nearly lost an eye. Now he's assaulted someone else. You can't let him go on like this.'

'Another woman?'

'I don't know, but what difference does it make? He uses his fists when things don't go his way. Are you prepared to let him carry on until it is another woman? What happens if he causes a serious injury, something permanent?'

'No, forget it. Ours was a domestic argument that got out of hand, not an assault. We were both angry. I provoked him after things got heated.'

'You're excusing him? How can you say that? Can you remember how you looked after he hit you? I saw you, I told my grandparents, my father saw you.' His irritation grew when he realised how useless that statement was now. 'Your friends saw you, your parents saw you! This was real, and lots of people would stand up and say they saw what he did! You can't pretend it didn't happen when so many people know it did.'

'It's my decision, and if that's the way I want it then it's nobody else's business except mine. Now leave it! It's bad enough that I'll have to give evidence in the theft case! God, and now I'm tied to this area with the flat! The sooner I take up teacher training the better, and far away from here!'

'But he might do it to somebody else, worse! How do you think you'll feel if you read about him beating up another woman and he puts her in hospital, or worse? How will you live with yourself?'

'Oh it's beating up now is it, instead of assault?' she replied heatedly. 'You don't know the half of it!'

He sat back stunned. 'It's not the first time, is it? He's hit you before.'

'Leave it!' she growled.

'That night, when I came to dinner, you were shaky—'

'Leave it!' she shrieked, her face contorted.

'But I couldn't see any marks so... your body, he hit you where no one could see—'

'Fucking leave it!' she screamed, collapsing into a heap on the carpet, her body racked with spasms, and her breathing altered into gasps of air mixed with wailing.

Juan Marco fell onto his knees beside her and pulled her up onto her's, his beautiful girlfriend reduced to a wet, soggy rag doll. 'He raped you, didn't he? That's why at Deal...'

She collapsed into his arms and allowed herself to grieve for the first

390

time since that night.

Lauren cried her heart out for twenty minutes, Juan Marco unable to stop himself from drenching her head and shoulders with his own tears. When she stopped, her eyes were so watery they were almost unrecognisable, but she found the strength to speak.

'Don't ask me to report him for rape, just don't,' she said shakily. 'I know exactly how it'll go, his word against mine. No witnesses, no physical evidence, husband and wife. He'll get off due to lack of evidence, it happens ninety-five per cent of the time. I'll always have the scars but you... you've helped me love again... when we make love there's a connection that's so overwhelming. That's what I want to think of, not his kind of sex.' She sobbed again. 'So don't push it. It's my body, my mind, I make the decisions.' She hesitated before continuing. 'But I'll report him for the assault. There's physical proof of that and if you and everyone else support me, and I mean really support me, then I'll press charges. But you have to do things on my terms and have my back one hundred per cent. Do you understand? This is going to bring back some awful memories for me and I'll have to testify in court for the fraud too. Don't expect miracles from me. God, I won't be able to start teacher training with this hanging over me!'

The following morning, Juan Marco told his grandparents of the conversation he'd had with Lauren the previous evening.

'Oh my God!' gasped Lady Belvedere, almost dropping her cup of tea. 'How can we expect her to give evidence in court on the fraud when she's got that to deal with!' She turned to look at her husband in horror, who sat stony-faced.

'The brute. I can't believe it. And she didn't report it, not to anyone? Unbelievable. She's been bottling that up. Well,' he continued, affected by Juan Marco's tears, 'we must make sure she's protected as much as possible. If necessary we'll drop the fraud case and give her our full support for the assault charge. Poor girl. The strength of her... unbelievable.'

'How is she now, Juan Marco?' asked his grandmother.

'She slept surprisingly well after letting it all out. We went to bed, ate very little of the takeaway, and she slept in my arms until seven this morning. She was so pale when she awoke, but she managed a little joke about sleeping like a child and when I left her, at her insistence, she'd got some of her resolve back. She said she was going to telephone the police this morning and I asked her if she wanted me there with her, but she wouldn't have it. She said she wanted to get the bastard.'

'Good on her! Tell her she will have all our support, whatever she needs. If she needs a chat, money, moral support, anything, you send her our way! How will she keep her mind occupied while all this is going on?'

Juan Marco shrugged his shoulders.

'This probably sounds stupid, but there's a tree to decorate, a nativity scene to organise, a children's party to host… if she's looking for something to do and is up to it, tell her she can have free rein!'

Chapter 38

Christmas Is a Time for Families

Juan Marco and one of the labourers were up the tall ladders, hanging the decorations on the tree in the hall.

'Higher. Move left a bit. That's better!' said Lauren with a grin.

'Don't overstretch though!' added Lady Belvedere.

It was the 5th December and the nativity scene was planned for next week, with the schoolchildren having their Christmas party this week. Lord and Lady Belvedere had also decided to open the hall on Saturday and Sunday afternoon, for members of the public to come in and see a few rooms, the tree and enjoy mulled wine and mince pies. All the tickets were sold. Lauren had shakily suggested the idea to Juan Marco, but said on no account was he to own up to his grandparents. So to respect her wishes, he'd phoned Mary and asked her to suggest it as her own idea, which she'd done, casually mentioning that they'd need help with the serving. When Lady Belvedere asked Lauren if she'd lend a hand, she accepted reluctantly, the look from Lady Belvedere communicating a message that this was her way of showing her support, in preference to her speaking directly to her about what Juan Marco had told them. However, she did still plan to talk to her privately, but not until the week's festivities were out of the way.

The following Tuesday, she invited Lauren to the hall for morning coffee. Lauren was desperate not to go, fearing her own emotional response wouldn't be up to a confidential chat, and begged Juan Marco to make her excuses.

'No, I won't decline on your behalf for the sake of a coffee. That's all it is. She's asked you over for a coffee, probably to say thank you. I know your fears and I understand them and if you really don't want to go, then I have no objection to you telling her yourself, but you must do it. She'll understand if you tell her you're fragile... but think about it before you say no. You were fantastic last week with the events – it's not unreasonable for her to want to say thank you.'

'But she won't leave it there, she won't!' blurted Lauren, collapsing into tears. He hugged her and held her tight.

'Things will get better,' he said quietly. 'You know I've only told them what I think they needed to know, just the minimum, so they know what you've had to cope with. Talking about it will help, not the intimate things, but just having the courage to share. In the long run, it will help.' She looked at him helplessly. 'OK, what do I know? I'm just a man, I shouldn't be giving you advice. I'll shut up.'

'Will you come with me?' she squeaked.

He smiled and nodded. 'Of course, if you want me there.' She nodded tearfully.

The pleasure at being involved with the children and the open event at the hall had given her a confidence boost, but her nerves had returned by the time of Tuesday morning. Lauren felt even more foolish when she asked Juan Marco, just before they went into the sitting room, what she should say when she saw Lady Belvedere.

'Just try "hello",' he said simply.

But once inside, the warm greeting she received and the surprise of seeing Lord Belvedere there too disarmed her, and she settled better than she'd hoped for. After making her feel welcome back in Kent and asking about her flat and her teaching plans, Lady Belvedere said there was something they would like to say to her, and she looked at her husband.

'Yes, that's right. We understand that you've reported Robert to the police, and they've taken statements from Juan Marco and some of your friends, your parents too. We've also had a call from them and will be signing a statement shortly. What we wanted to say is that with all that going on, and with you having to give evidence against him, the last thing you need is to be called to give evidence in a fraud trial. While it's likely that we wouldn't need you to take the stand, unfortunately we realise it's quite likely that Robert's defence would certainly include dragging you in as a co-defendant, and that's something we feel is grossly unfair. So, having thought about it, we won't be reporting that matter to the police, and we can leave you to preserve all your strength and resource for your own case, which we're sure you'll need.'

'Thank you,' Lauren replied with feeling.

'It goes without saying that you have Juan Marco's full support, and he's a hell of an asset to have on your side. But you also have our's too, and if there's anything we can do you only need to ask, either through Juan Marco or directly, and we'll give you all we can. Now, I think I've said all I needed to say, so I shall leave you in peace and perhaps Juan Marco will come with me, and we'll let you ladies have some time.'

'Oh, thank you so much, both of you.'

As the men left the room, Lady Belvedere smiled warmly at Lauren, whose face was starting to crumble. 'Come here,' she said, standing and holding her arms open, receiving Lauren into her embrace while Lauren's tears flowed. After a minute she added: 'And it goes without saying that we hope you have a very merry Christmas with that lovely man of yours, and you're very welcome to spend Christmas Day with us, if you choose. Of course, if you'd like to be alone, just the two of you, then we'll quite understand, but you must come and see us on Christmas Eve and whenever else you like, and you can stay over too with Juan Marco. We'll be talking to Anna and Alexander and George and Mary very soon, to let them know that you and Juan Marco are together, and just to give them a little hint of what you've had to deal with. Don't worry about George. It's long in the past now and it's time we all buried the hatchet, and got on with living in the present and concentrating on the future. Mary will soon sort him out if there's any trouble, just you see!'

Juan Marco and Lauren decided to spend Christmas Eve evening and Christmas Day on their own at the flat, but they went to the hall on the 23rd and stayed over until the afternoon of the next day. The family were kind and polite, Mary leading the way with games, and they enjoyed a magnificent buffet in the evening. George seemed settled and content with their new roles starting in January, and Lord and Lady Belvedere talked enthusiastically about the changes coming in the new year, and progress with the land sale and planning applications. Juan Marco joined in after encouragement, and Anna found herself becoming increasingly impressed by his energy and work ethic, asking him questions and never feeling that he wasn't committed. When Juan Marco headed to the pantry to collect more drinks, she volunteered to help him.

'You know, I wasn't the nicest to you before. Perhaps that was nothing to do with who you are, more the way Henry introduced you to the family, I suspect. He didn't do many things that I liked, unfortunately, but if it hadn't been for you and him working together to uncover Robert's criminality, then we wouldn't be in the place that we are now. So he got that right, and I give him credit for that, and you too. The difference between the two of you is that you're an ongoing part of turning things around, and I'm not just saying that for the obvious reason that he's no longer here. You are committed, aren't you?'

'Yes, I am,' he nodded. 'There's enough work here to keep me busy for a long time, and I intend to keep learning about the farming side of things because that's important to me, and I know George and Mary are the right people to learn from.'

'Yes, he's climbed down from his hobby horse a bit, hasn't he? I think he was completely gobsmacked that I didn't support him automatically at the meeting. He's come to expect it I suppose, it was always me and him versus Henry. But it was obvious that he couldn't carry the whole estate forward, not with his attitude, even if that wasn't the same as me giving you a positive vote. But Mary... she's a useful ally and a big supporter of yours; she's done a lot to convince me you're the right man and deserve to take things on. So come on, how did you work your charm on her?' she asked teasingly.

'Er... I don't think it was charm!' he gushed, 'I'm just a good listener!'

Anna looked at him, less than satisfied with his answer, but smiled as she kissed him on the cheek. 'OK, round one to you.'

That night, Lord and Lady Belvedere were the first to head upstairs to bed, Caroline hesitating in the half-open bedroom door as she heard squealing from Lauren at the foot of the stairs. As she stood watching, Lauren appeared in Juan Marco's arms as he carried her up the flight and headed to their bedroom, swinging her around to turn the door handle, and catching sight of his grandmother in the process.

'Oh! Sorry!' he exclaimed.

'Goodnight, both of you!' she laughed. She was about to close the door when she heard George and Mary as they climbed the stairs.

'You never carry me up the stairs!' she teased.

'No, I never carried her up them either, perhaps that tells you something.'

'You don't ever still think of her, do you?'

'She's still got the looks but no, her world is a million miles away from mine. I was a different man then, hardly a man at all really. You're different, you're my partner in all senses of the word. I'd be lost without you. I doubt

I tell you enough what a special woman you are, hugely capable, and frankly gorgeous in that dress.'

They stopped and kissed three steps down from the top.

'I'm gorgeous out of this dress too... want to see?' As he looked at her lustfully, she giggled and started running towards their bedroom, George in pursuit.

Caroline waited at the door in case there were any more family scenes to enjoy, giving a 'shh' to her husband when he asked what she was doing. After twenty seconds, she heard Alexander at the foot of the stairs.

'You know, you've switched off much earlier than you normally do at Christmas time. Sometimes I don't think you unwind at all until well into the day itself!'

Anna laughed. 'Yes, you're right, unless it's the wine! But do you know what? Every time I've come back to this house there's always a feeling that someone's about to say, or would like to say, "Anna? What do you think of this? What do you think we should do? Could you just handle this for us Anna?" For the first time in ages, it feels like I've just come back to my family for Christmas, and that's all! It's a fabulous feeling being relaxed in my family home again. And on the subject of being relaxed, it makes me feel quite the party girl again!' she said, as she put her arms around Alexander's neck and pushed her mouth onto his.

Lady Belvedere quietly closed her bedroom door.

THE END